Also by Becky Masterman

Rage Against the Dying

FEAR
the
DARKNESS

FEAR

the

DARKNESS

BECKY MASTERMAN

Minotaur Books
New York

This is a work of fiction. All of the characters, organizations, and events portrayed in this novel are either products of the author's imagination or are used fictitiously.

FEAR THE DARKNESS. © 2014 by Becky Masterman. All rights reserved. Printed in the United States of America. For information, address St. Martin's Press, 175 Fifth Avenue, New York, N.Y. 10010.

www.minotaurbooks.com

Library of Congress Cataloging-in-Publication Data

Masterman, Becky.
    Fear the darkness : a thriller / Becky Masterman.
        pages ; cm.—(Brigid Quinn series ; 2)
    ISBN 978-0-312-62295-4 (hardcover)
    ISBN 978-1-4668-4223-6 (e-book)
    I. Title.
    PS3613.A81965F43 2015
    813'.6—dc23
                                                    2014032397

Minotaur books may be purchased for educational, business, or promotional use. For information on bulk purchases, please contact the Macmillan Corporate and Premium Sales Department at 1-800-221-7945, extension 5442, or write to specialmarkets@macmillan.com

First Edition: January 2015

10   9   8   7   6   5   4   3   2   1

For Rebecca and Jeremy, and Alex and Sydney,
who encourage my passions while not letting me
forget what's really important

Acknowledgments

Raising children may take a village, but it takes at least three major metropolitan areas and one moderately sized town to make a book. So thank you to Hope Dellon at St. Martin's for her stubborn sense of character and undying patience, Adrienne Kerr at Penguin Random House, Genevieve Pegg at Orion UK, and the entire teams at publishers around the world who first critique and then promote my books. I'm looking at you, Sarah Melnyk.

Thanks to the readers who sent me encouraging notes about *Rage Against the Dying* and made me think I might be able to do it again. And thanks to the readers whose frank criticism helped me learn.

Then we come to Helen Heller, advocate, plot doctor, and friend, so much more than anything you'd think an agent would be. Also, you and Cristina taught me everything I know about flirting.

Special thanks to:

Dr. Bennett Blum for giving his advice on poisoning but refusing to tell me the dosage. Details have been changed, so don't try this on Grandpa; it won't work.

Micah Wisely, mixed martial arts expert, who taught me the moves.

Thanks to friends from the forensic science and medical communities:

Dr. Jan Leestma for all things neurological, Kevin Gannon on drowning, Drs. Robert Powers and Michael Derelanko on toxicology, Dr. Ellen Moffatt on the limits of forensic pathology, Dr. Gil Brogdon on radiology, Dr. Mary Dudley on pacemaker identification, Dr. Jamie Whiting on Colorado River toads, and Dr. Jason Byrd for his information on clean sheet maggots (don't ask).

Thank you to all who critiqued the manuscript for facts and gently told me when it was putdownable:

Patrick Jones, reader in law enforcement.

Dr. Dorothy Dean, reader in forensic science.

Jenna Jonteaux McClay and Christine Salvaterra, readers in health care.

William Bell, Victoria Bergesen, Mickey Getty, and Frederick Masterman, authors who read.

But wait, there's more! Thanks to:

Neil Evangelista for information on guns.

Debbie Mangold for reminding me where I got my fondness for onomatopoeia.

Barbara Norwitz for talking out the logistics of a mass homicide in the lobby of a hotel in San Antonio.

Rachel Ohly for being my youth consultant.

Jody Wilson for providing details about a society fund-raiser.

Charles DeWitt—I can't remember quite why, but his name was on this list, so he must have said something helpful.

And as always and ever, thank you to my dear husband, who asks me if I wrote today, gives me a place of peace in which to imagine, and, though he denies it, provides solutions to plot problems by merely asking smart questions. Honey, we're even.

FEAR
the
DARKNESS

Prologue

There is near complete darkness, yes, but it's the least of my problems. I'd glimpsed the space before I got in, and knew the claustrophobic dimensions that would have kept me from moving easily even if I hadn't been shot in the leg. It was empty, too, except for the usual tools that were under the pad. Carlo was a tidy sort and kept it that way. I'm still conscious enough to think of the tools, but I have trouble keeping my mind on them in any useful way. *Use whatever you got,* Black Ops Baxter used to tell me. Images float through my head and the best I can do anymore is name them, if that. Jack. Wrench. Lug. That elastic cord thing. Nuts.

A little air comes from a crack between the compartments, so I won't suffocate.

No, my most urgent need is water, to bring my temperature down, to slow my breathing and stop those syncopated warning beats that tell me my heart is about to check out for good. If I die in here, the likely plan is to dump me at a secondary site. I have an image of my own body, picked over by coyotes who will start at the site of my wound and leave the rest mummifying in the desert. Don't think that thought.

George will write this on his autopsy report under manner of death: Accidental.

Cause of death, hyperthermia. Victim experienced elevated body temperature due to failed thermoregulation that occurs when a body produces or absorbs more heat than it dissipates. Extreme temperature elevation then becomes a medical emergency requiring immediate treatment to prevent disability or death.

Ignominious. Ignominious. A Carlo word if I ever heard one, and I'm not positive what it means, but I think it applies here. Ignominious death, maybe, but nobody is going to get away with calling it accidental. The least I can do is leave evidence behind proving that this is murder.

I'm lying on my left side, the sleeves of the shirt tied around my leg where the bullet grazed me. I've figured out why the care was taken to stop the bleeding. It's so I won't leave any behind. That means my blood is the only evidence of violence.

Though lethargic as a cold snake, I reach down and fumble at the knot until it's untied, and feel the wound. With the time passing and the heat and my being so still, the blood is clotting nicely as if I have been baked in a slow oven. I move the shirt out from under my leg. Clamping my jaws beforehand so I won't yell or bite my tongue, I dig at the ridge through my flesh on the outside of my thigh where the bullet passed. Not close enough to the artery to make a real mess (another body flashed through my head—there had been so many) but deep enough so if I work at it a bit . . . I yell through clenched teeth, but not so loudly. Man oh man, that hurts. But at least the pain keeps me from passing out in the heat.

My fingers come away slick. I hope I'm bleeding freely onto the carpet, but even carpets can be replaced, or scrubbed clean. Of course, you could see the blood with an alternative light source, but who would know to do that? No, I have to leave my mark where only someone who was looking for it would find it, and show it to the cops, and raise a suspicion of foul play.

I dab my fingers on the underside of the lid above my head, hoping that no telltale streak will get on my face where it might be noticed. I go back for more, digging again, and smearing it on the warm metal overhead.

Holding on to what's left of my brain, I reach for the shirt where

I had left it balled up. I wipe my fingers off on it, shift my hips to get it back under my leg, and, with some difficulty because my right arm has gone numb beneath me, retie it.

I put my fingers in my mouth and try to suck any sign of blood off of them, but my tongue just sits there, too dry and swollen to make the effort. I can't be sure the evidence isn't collected under my nails and around my torn cuticles. Maybe it won't be noticed. Even in my state I recognize the irony in thinking of myself as mere evidence, as I have thought of so many bodies over the years.

Mind you, the only use for what I'm doing is in the event of my death. The death of Brigid Quinn.

One

When I got the news about my sister-in-law I was heading back from the abused women's shelter situated outside the town of Marana, a thirty-minute drive west from where I live north of Tucson, Arizona. The shelter was called Desert Doves, or some bullshit name like that. When I wasn't working on an investigation, I volunteered to teach the women at the shelter they didn't have to be doves.

There were four of them that day, one with the bruises still purplish fading to green at the edges. All of them with the look of the victim stamped on their faces. In that respect, at this stage they were interchangeable, and I couldn't keep their names straight in my head. Maybe soon I would. A young man, midtwenties with two percent body fat, stood in the corner to watch. I hadn't seen him before and guessed he was security.

I stepped onto the rubber mat in the middle of the small room that contained a manual treadmill, an elliptical, and some light free weights, all of which looked donated. I had put the women through a little stretching and some cardio warm-up, but that was just to reacquaint them with their bodies. Now we were going for the basic defense move.

I pulled my white ponytail into a bun with a scrunchy and gave my most motherly smile. "Would one of you like to volunteer?"

Their eyes shifted away from me. I had the sense those eyes were used to doing that more often than not.

I said, "Look at me. Look at me. I'm going on sixty years old. Do I look like someone who can hurt you?"

The youngest of them, taller than me but with the muscle mass of a bird, stepped onto the mat.

"What's your name, honey?" I asked.

"Anna." It sounded like an apology.

"Anna, you come at me like you're going to attack me. Can you do it sort of in slow motion? That's good, just like that. It's okay, you can giggle if you want to. I'll move slowly, too, and when we've done it once that way I'll show you what it's like in real life. Now see how Anna is coming toward me with her right hand pulled back like she's going to slap me to kingdom come? That's fine, but it doesn't even matter whether her hand is out or her fist is coming up to clip me under the jaw or even whether she has a knife. Because all she's concerned with is her attack, and she doesn't realize that I'm not going to stand here and take it.

"See, I'm not backing away but going toward her . . . making my strike area smaller by holding my head low, ducking my shoulder under that arm and . . . this may startle you a little, but I promise you won't get hurt, Anna . . . grabbing you by the waist and rolling you over my hip. Women's hips are where it's at. We've got more power there and in our thighs than any man no matter what his size. See, I used Anna's forward momentum against her."

It made things a little more difficult to do this in slow motion while talking, so I stopped to take a quick deep breath and went on. "Now Anna is upside down before she knows what happened, and you can imagine what it's like if we were doing it fast. No, I'm not going to drop you on your head. See, if I put my foot out this way, Anna comes down onto her shoulder, while I simultaneously thrust my leg out under her. It may seem like the purpose is to keep from injuring her, and it actually does prevent her hitting the floor hard, but the main reason I do that is so I can drop to the floor and put my other leg over her in a choke hold. See how my body is perpendicular to hers?

"Your opponent can't move when you've got him like this. Your options are either to get up and run like hell while the guy is still wondering how he got on the floor, or to keep choking until he passes out. No permanent damage. I recommend the second option just to let him know you mean business. Thanks, Anna. See, in order to do this you don't have to be big, and you especially don't have to be male."

As Anna stood, smiling despite herself, the girl with the freshest bruises asked, "If I do that to my husband, what do you think will happen after that? What will he do?"

The others looked keenly interested in my answer. I could sugar-coat it, say that hubby would be respectful and bring them flowers even when he hadn't abused them first, and they'd live happily ever after. But the movies had already handed these women a lie about love, and it was time for the statistics.

The harsher the words, the gentler the tone. "Sweetheart, he won't say thank you."

She said, "He'll kill me."

I ignored the sensation that she said those words with a little thrill, something akin to pleasure, as if she was saying *He'll love me*. I said, "That's the funny thing about bullies. You think he'll come at you again, but he won't. Ninety-nine times out of a hundred he'll just go away. Leave you for someone else. He'll go look for someone he can control, someone he can beat up who won't fight back."

The girl crossed her arms in front of her. I could tell she didn't like that answer. She preferred the lie, and one day she would fall victim to it. I could tell she was already lost, and maybe already dead. I grieved all in an instant, and then turned away because you can't save everybody. Sometimes you have to be cruel to fight another battle.

I turned to the guy in the corner, a good head and a half taller than me, with eyes that spoke not at all. He was pretending to slouch, but the taut muscles stretching the sleeves of his T-shirt gave him away. The thousand-yard stare made me sense he had gotten his body someplace other than a gym.

"Iraq or Afghanistan?" I asked.

He nodded. "Afghanistan."

"What's your name?"

"Dennis." Even two generations removed from me, his eyes flickered a warning not to say "the Menace."

"Want to show them how it's really done?"

He stepped onto the mat.

"Come."

He came for me with both fists up. No problem. I put him down the way I did Anna, only with a faster one-two, and the women applauded. They had started enjoying themselves. But when I helped Dennis off the floor he gripped my wrist and swung me into the wall over the treadmill. I was unprepared, and it rattled me so I slid down the treadmill onto the floor. The women gasped, but softly, and did nothing. After all, they had seen this before.

I recovered and got up better prepared for his next assault. He came at me again with his fists balled. It must have been that slam on the mat with my legs clamped around his throat that awakened his kill-or-be-killed reaction. I could see that he had gone back to some village in Afghanistan where he had seen and done things he couldn't live with, and my whispering, "Dennis . . . Dennis," didn't slow him down.

I hated to shame him in front of the women, but this guy could hurt me bad. I threw two punches up high, not for the purpose of connecting but just to get his arms up so I could go for something more vulnerable. He didn't fall for it. Instead of covering his face, he whipped his right arm back and delivered a haymaker.

Nearly delivered. I slipped the punch, and before he could connect I threw him a liver shot. He dropped to the floor in a faint.

The women looked first stunned and then surprisingly enthused to see a large man down, but I made a note to self: Next time do not use a new veteran for demonstrations. I told the women Dennis would be fine and that we were just displaying more advanced maneuvers. I brought him to when the others left the room. We spoke our understanding briefly, really seeing each other for the first time. I told him I could use a sparring partner for the exercise because I was rusty. He doubted that, but agreed.

On the way out, when no one was looking, I stretched my neck and rubbed the spot where my shoulder hit the wall, but overall I felt good—hell, I felt great! But I also felt relieved that I was still fit after all those years undercover with the FBI, followed by a desk job, followed by my first marriage at the ripe age of fifty-eight to a Catholic priest turned philosophy professor. Life with Carlo DiForenza had all the serenity I craved, but recent experience had shown you never know when you'll need a body tuned for defense. I needed to make sure it stayed that way, and if I could combine mixed martial arts practice with helping Dennis over his PTSD, that would be double cool.

To reward a job moderately well done and nobody getting seriously hurt, I stopped for coffee from a caravan shop on Thornydale, headed north to Tangerine, and turned east to come back across the valley, on a straight road that undulated as softly as an infant roller coaster. When you first come out to this part of Arizona you think *Good grief, it's all fifty shades of beige*, but you're wrong. On this late afternoon in spring the rosy glow the setting sun cast on the Catalinas in the distance made me think of my friend Mallory's wisdom, "When the mountains turn pink, it's time for a drink."

I looked forward to a glass of red wine and a hot bath with some Tired Old Ass Soak after the tussle with Dennis. One of my peeves is people who kill time driving by calling other people on their cell, but I admit that while sipping at my coffee and holding the wheel steady with my knee, I phoned my husband to let him know I'd be home in about twenty minutes.

Carlo told me he'd gotten the news that my sister-in-law, Marylin Quinn, had died.

My heart dipped along with the road, like when a plane gets caught in an air pocket.

In the movies, that's when the pilot comes on the loudspeaker and says there's a bit of turbulence up ahead and everyone should stay buckled in their seats, but not to worry. The wit behind you makes a joke about Bette Davis.

Then the plane explodes, the fireball snatching the air out of the passengers' lungs before they know what hit them. Everybody dies.

I was headed toward a time like that. A time of betrayal, wasting disease, and the nature of evil. Because now was the time to keep the promise I'd made to Marylin.

Enjoy the coffee, toots.

Two

It's hard to recognize the devil when his hand is on your shoulder.

That's because a psychopath is just a person before he becomes a headline. Before he opens fire in a church or tortures and kills in more secretive ways. Psychopaths have preferences for Starbucks or Dunkin' Donuts coffee, denim or linen, Dickens or . . . well, you get the point. If they're successful in controlling their more destructive urges, often they become surgeons who tingle as they hold a scalpel over a beating heart, or investment brokers who thrill at the games played with people's life savings, or even religious ministers who smile privately at a confession of adultery. Most of the time these creatures live out their lives with only those closest to them suspecting they feel nothing for anyone but themselves, and do nothing except for their own gain.

I admit from the start it's at least embarrassing to not recognize the devil, but I can understand because I've been there. Partly it's because few people manage to be pure evil. During my time with the Bureau, I lived among killers who cheerfully attended their daughters' ballet recitals, and men who trafficked in human flesh while baby-talking their parakeets. The guy buying cuttle treats at PetSmart smiles shyly at you as if his only shame is to be caught loving a bird;

it's a stretch to picture him selling Guatemalan women to Las Vegas casinos. Even the worst of us has moments of empathy. Maybe the devil dotes on a Maltese.

Similarly, you don't expect to run into evil at, say, a charity fundraiser, or in the living room of a friend's house, or in a doctor's office. Especially not in a church, and especially not in someone in a position of trust. Especially not in yourself.

When people in my business talk about the One Percent, they're not talking about the filthy rich. They're talking about evil, well hidden. That's what makes it so hard to spot. In my career that only made the game more interesting; that is, when I could forget that innocent human lives were at stake.

I didn't always think this way. Life was simpler in a time when the most important thing was to avoid being discovered, tortured, or killed. But maybe being married to a philosopher has made me think through things a little more than I used to. That and being retired from the Bureau, which gives me more time to stare at stars.

Staring at the night sky makes you think about death, about whether there's actually some place you go. Someone else's demise makes you think about the times you could have died, too. Marylin died from multiple sclerosis at the age of fifty-one. She had been living in Florida with my little brother, Todd, aged fifty-two, their daughter, seventeen, and my parents.

I wanted to go to the funeral by myself so I wouldn't subject Carlo to my family, but he insisted. We had been married two years. About time to meet your family, he said in his softly blunt way, a way he'd become more comfortable with as we got to know each other better.

I would have done anything for Marylin because I loved her. Despite knowing how screwed up we all were, all of us except Mom in some kind of law enforcement, she married into our cop family and showed me how good we actually could be; how people could be soft with each other instead of like brittle glass that cracks whenever you get close. But we didn't have long to enjoy the lesson. Four years after she married Todd she was diagnosed with multiple sclerosis. She insisted on living till she died, though, and even on having a child though the doctors warned her the trauma of childbirth would affect her adversely. She slowly declined after the birth of Gemma-Kate, going to a wheelchair and then to a hospital bed, lasting another seventeen years before she died.

The promise I had made concerned that child. Marylin had called me at the start of the year and asked if Gemma-Kate could stay with Carlo and me for a few months if something happened to her, so she would qualify for in-state tuition at the University of Arizona.

"How's she been?" I had asked, not mentioning what I'd heard about her from Mom. Nothing serious, a little shoplifting, a little flirting with spring breakers on the beach when she was fourteen.

"Good. That business was just some early adolescent rebellion," Marylin had said, knowing that families talk.

"You realize I have no experience with children."

"You'll find her quite grown up. You'll like her."

I had agreed. And here it was less than three months later and Marylin was gone; now I had to make good on that promise.

Todd didn't cry at the funeral, but he sweated a lot, as if by keeping the tears back from his eyes they were forced to come out everywhere else. Throughout the funeral service he used the too-short jacket sleeve on either arm to swipe at the opposite side of his face. Could have partly been the Florida humidity combined with his weight. Todd always said he needed to lose fifteen pounds when what he needed to lose was thirty. And stop drinking. And stop smoking.

The funeral was crowded, mostly Marylin's family members plus a considerable contingent of officers from the Fort Lauderdale Police Department, where Todd was employed as a detective. The guys looked uncomfortable, not so much in the presence of death as in having to wear the suits. They kept their jaws so stiff they would have cracked a tooth if they were startled.

Afterwards, Todd was still wiping at his neck with a handkerchief as we sat in the living room that Marylin had decorated thirty years before, and which had kept accumulating the pictures and the knick-knacks over the years without ever getting rid of anything.

The scent of cooling lasagna and chopped chicken liver hung in the air. Marylin's family had already escaped, leaving Carlo and me trapped with the rest of the Quinns because we were staying at Todd's place. We'd started drinking vodka over ice because that was the easiest, and the initial stimulant effects that made us tell good stories about Marylin and laugh, like a proper Irish wake should, were starting to give way to depression.

We weren't bad people, as far as I knew at the time. Maybe it was all of us being in law enforcement, a little too much like empty glasses with stress cracks too fine to be seen. And at this moment we were packed a little too close together. It was anybody's guess what would happen, but just for today, for Marylin's sake if not our own, we were trying hard to be decent and not break each other.

"You had a really good turnout," I said, thinking that was what a person wanted to hear, wishing there were preprinted scripts so I didn't have to make the conversation up as I went. The men in our family were never much for conversation that wasn't yelled. Imagine someone barking their good-nights and you get the picture.

"Only guys from the force," Todd said, struggling to keep his voice low and ending up with just a bit of an edge. "Not so many of Marylin's friends. People don't hang around when a person is sick a long time." Todd wouldn't focus on all the people who were there, only on the people who weren't. His first inclination has always been to curse the darkness when somebody else would scrounge for a match.

I wanted to helpfully point this flaw out to him but managed to say instead, "Does Ariel know?" Ariel is the middle child, a sister I used to be friends with until she chose the CIA as her career. We sort of lost contact. These days I couldn't even tell you what she looks like, let alone where she is.

"I left a message on her home machine," Todd said. "She might be out of the country." He violently stubbed out a cigarette in an ashtray on the table next to his chair. Most of the ashes made it. Nobody said anything. Here and there we jiggled our melting ice and sipped from our glasses to fill the quiet. While I searched in my head for something else to say I cocked my head to the right and looked at the books on the shelf under the table. I always look at people's books. You can find out so much more than they want you to know. But on this shelf, an old *St. Joseph's Missal,* two cookbooks, and a book called *How to Raise an Emotionally Healthy Child When a Parent Is Sick* didn't tell me anything I didn't know already.

I hoisted myself out of one of those armchairs just low enough to throw off your center of gravity so you have to use your arms to stand up. I followed the chicken-liver-and-lasagna smell to the dining room. The Early American table was laden with potluck containers courtesy of the cops' wives. I spread some of a drying nut-covered cheddar cheese ball on a munchkin-sized piece of pumpernickel and ate it. We all have our own way of mourning.

Gemma-Kate had been working on a glass of tonic that may or may not have had vodka in it. I hadn't noticed her pouring, and she didn't seem tipsy. She joined me at the dining room table and started to pick at the sliced deli meats, unrolling a slice of roast beef, laying a piece of yellow cheese on it, lining three green olives in the center, and rolling it back up again. Methodical. I took another sip from my drink with the precision of an anesthesiologist, just enough to keep the pain away without slipping into whisky remorse.

"All older people," I said to Gemma-Kate, watching her slowly chew the roll she had constructed. "None of your friends, Gemma-Kate?"

My father, Fergus, heard me from across the room. He has uncanny hearing for such an old man, maybe from all those years as a beat cop, staying on alert for someone behind him. "We're not the kind of people who have friends, are we, Cupkate?" He didn't say it as criticism of either the family as a whole or Gemma-Kate individually. He sounded like it was a point of pride, the old bastard. It was true that Dad didn't make friends. He was one of those people whose main topic of conversation was recounting how he had told somebody off. As children we took him seriously and, when we were bad, feared his glare. Seeing him slumped with his frown set like a bow in his face, I wondered if anyone else ever had. He had as much power to frighten me now as a cartoon witch. But for the sake of peace I kept pretending he could.

Gemma-Kate ignored him. She took another bite of the roll and swallowed. "I pictured you taller," she said to me.

"I used to be," I said. When she didn't seem to get the joke I said,

"Plus last time I saw you, you were shorter." Sizing her up as well, I thought how appropriate the nickname Cupkate was. She was small like the rest of the Quinn family, nowhere near a whole cake.

She finished her cold-cuts-and-olive roll and wiped her fingers across the top of a nearby stack of black cocktail napkins. I spread another piece of pumpernickel, this time with what Mom would have called liver mishmash, and turned my attention back to the living room. I didn't think Todd was nervous, but the sweating made him appear so as he started to speak about his wife's final days.

"Marylin had a downturn recently, what would you say, Mom, last year or so?"

"Gemma-Kate was so good with her," Mom said. "She's a good little nurse with invalids. Marylin never had one bedsore."

Todd nodded. "I would come home from work and find GK reading to her. But Marylin was declining faster than before, and we were starting to talk about hospice care."

While he spoke Gemma-Kate looked past the group, through the jalousie windows of the living room, as if she was seeing something just on the other side of the glass that none of the rest of us could see. I couldn't tell for sure, but it looked like she had heard the drama of her mother's death so many times she'd lost the feeling for it. The word that came to mind was "controlled."

"And then she died," Todd said. "It seemed to take so long, years, and then in the final days it went fast." He swallowed.

There was a sudden silence. Filling the void, Carlo came up with some church-speak. "It's tragic for those who have to keep living, but there's an uncanny realization that comes to the dying. They understand the process. We have to let them go."

Gemma-Kate brought her steady gaze back to the room and let it rest on Carlo. "Aunt Brigid says you used to be a Catholic priest."

Carlo said, "That's right, or partly. I left the active ministry nearly thirty years ago. But technically once you're ordained you can't stop being a priest."

"But you can get married."

"Well, actually you can't."

"But you did."

"Yes. I did."

Todd may have feared Gemma-Kate was going to ask next if that meant Carlo and I were living in sin. That was probably Todd's opinion. God only knows what he would think if he knew we'd been married by a justice of the peace. He sweat a little more, and then cut short anything else Gemma-Kate might say by jumping to the topic he had in mind. "Gemma-Kate didn't want to go off to school while her mother was so sick. But Marylin was hoping Gemma-Kate could stay with you and Carlo for a few months before she starts the biochemistry program at the University of Arizona."

I'd been waiting for this, and I'm going to fess up that I wasn't happy about it. After growing up the eldest child in an alcoholic cop family, and spending my entire career as an FBI agent, I would still give my life for a child, but found I had little in common with them, never having been one myself. Plus I had finally begun to enjoy the world I had been serving and protecting. After a period of adjustment I finally felt I was getting the hang of marriage, and hesitated doing anything at all that might upset the equilibrium. When I made the promise to Marylin I hadn't expected I'd be keeping it this soon. I hesitated.

Carlo, on the other hand, didn't hesitate for a moment. "Of course," he said, smiling at me, expecting me to be pleased that he was supportive of my family. "That would be fine with us. We have a spare room."

Todd went on as if he hadn't known it would be that easy and needed to say everything he had planned. "It's been so hard on GK for so many years," he said, gesturing to the girl, who was staring passively out the window again while her life was being decided for her. "Not much of a mother around, and"—he ducked his head in a confessional manner—"not much of a father either. You know how the business goes."

"Todd, I already—" I started.

"It was Gemma-Kate's idea. Hers and her mother's," he said. "They talked about it before she . . . That it would be good to go to a school someplace, completely different. Staying with you will allow her to establish Arizona residency so she doesn't have to pay out of state."

I had ceased listening by this point, and had only begun to marvel that he managed to restrain himself from yelling for this long. But Mom finally put him out of his misery by stopping him. "They said yes," she said, with an impatient jerk of her hand, and stood up without trouble. Mom could hold her liquor better than any of us. "Brigid, come help me put some of this food away."

I did as I was told. I may have received awards and honors from presidents. I may have been in life-threatening situations so many times I stopped feeling life-threatened. I may have busted some of the most heinous villains in FBI history, but no matter how old I got, here I was just the oldest girl. So I obediently got the Tupperware tops from the kitchen and fastened them over the containers on the table.

Mom and I talked a little while we worked. She hadn't gotten the memo that we were being delicate with each other. Either that or she could only last at it so long.

"How are things in Arizona?" she asked.

"Good. Really good, Mom."

"Carlo tells us you left the Church," she said.

For all the care I was taking, rather than explain how similar the Episcopal church we were attending was to Roman Catholicism, I felt myself the first to go *crack*. "I was never in *the Church*, Mom."

Well, that was effective. She pushed trembling lips together into what I think they call a moue. It made all the old smoking lines radiate out, though she had given up the habit some decades before. "You received First Holy Communion," she said. "You had a little white veil and white Mary Janes."

I put my arms around her and gave her a hug, something I had learned not from anyone in my family but from Carlo. "I'm sorry. I'm sorry."

I felt her pliable aging skin get a little more taut over her bones, probably rejecting not me but the unfamiliar contact of another body. Out of mercy I let her go.

I could tell she forgave me by her change in tack. "Who's watching your dogs?"

"A friend."

"You have a friend?"

I didn't answer, and it only took me a moment to get back into peace-loving Brigid mode as I scrubbed the plastic tablecloth and got caught up in musings and family small talk. We all stayed safe until Todd dropped the three of us off at the Fort Lauderdale airport two days later.

This was Gemma-Kate's first plane ride ever. On the Dallas-to-Tucson leg she got sick, and there were some adolescent histrionics as she scrambled from the window seat over Carlo and me to run down the aisle to the head. But when she came back looking more subdued and pale I got her some ginger ale and a blanket, no small feat in coach, and let her fall asleep on my shoulder while I watched the New Mexico mountains plod past below us.

Too bad, she was missing her first look at mountains, too.

I softened, always a sucker for the small and weak. But also there was Marylin. Part of engaging with the world was helping your family, keeping your promises. Besides, Gemma-Kate could probably use a change. She'd practically been her mother's caregiver all those years. Couldn't be a good way for a kid to grow up. "Devastated," Mom had said about her at the funeral, a word she must have picked up from those news reports about natural disasters. But my brother said, "She's a tough one, that girl. Tough little kid." Apparently that's the highest praise one Quinn can give another. Tough.

I could do this. I was tough. I may be small and have prematurely white hair, but I'm as psychologically and physically fit as you can be at my age. And as I've explained, I can disarm a grown man before he could say . . . anything.

How can I put this?

Next to somebody like me, Chuck Norris is just a wuss. How hard could it be to be a good aunt?

Three

Cops will tell you the absolute worst sound in the world is *click*. That's the sound a gun makes when it jams. But in relationships, I learned that *click* is good. It's what happens when, in the course of an exchange of two or three sentences, you know you're going to be friends or lovers.

I clicked with Carlo DiForenza like that, during a class I took from him at the university right after I retired and just before he did. Before I married Carlo two years ago, my name was Brigid Quinn. I had devoted my whole life to the Federal Bureau of Investigation, being pimped around the country posing as a prostitute, a drug runner, a human trafficker. I did it for much longer than is considered psychologically healthy. You don't make any friends working undercover. The only people you meet are the kind of people you don't want to be friends with.

Just as I had to learn to be a wife later in life, I had to learn to be a friend. Mallory Hollinger and I met at St. Martin's in the Fields. Besides being more truthful, going to church was the only other condition that Carlo asked of me, and because I had had some bad experiences with the Catholic church, we compromised on Episcopalian. I didn't realize how close it was until our first Sunday service.

The main difference was that just before the procession down the aisle, a voice at the back of the church said, "Please silence your cell phones at this time." That was the signal for everyone to stand for a hymn—all the verses.

Another difference was that the congregation didn't rush out during the final hymn—again, all verses—to try to beat each other out of the parking lot; instead they went to what they called "coffee hour." Anything that includes coffee is a good thing. I had gone to the table where the silver urn was to get my share of the beloved brew, and when I came back to where I'd left Carlo standing alone, I noticed a woman talking to him.

She was a big woman, though I wouldn't say fat, more majestic. What made me take notice was her height, and the way she blended her laughter into Carlo's. As I got closer I noticed she had a thin scar, hardly noticeable, on her left cheek. And her upper lip was a little bigger than the lower. She was thrusting that lip at Carlo like a horse smelling a sugar cube. With a disagreeable flutter I thought what a good-looking couple they made, an advertisement for an erectile dysfunction drug.

I laughed at myself and shook off the thought.

"Here's your coffee, honey," I said, and handed it to him, then turned to the woman. "Hi. I'm Brigid," I said, smiling, pleased that I had regained my security enough to not sound like I was guarding my prom date. She stuck out her hand and shook mine with a surer grip than your average female boomer. The thing about Mallory Hollinger wasn't that she was knock-down gorgeous. Quite the contrary. She just acted like nobody had ever told her she couldn't have any man in the room.

She said, "Mallory Hollinger. Your husband and I were just talking about the similarities between the Catholic and Episcopal churches."

"Except that people are dressed better than usual, I couldn't tell the difference," I said.

"Hardly any difference, darling," Mallory said, turning toward me and lowering her voice into intimacy that excluded Carlo. "We're just Catholic Light—more money, less pope."

And then we were friends. *Click.* Never having had a friend before outside of the Bureau, I hadn't realized it happens so quickly.

Essentially, we shared the same wicked humor, a distaste for piousness, and a taste for luxuries large and small. Mallory was me, minus the occasional angst.

Mallory had kept our two dogs while we were in Florida and was at the house to greet us with Indian food, my favorite. The Pugs jumped me and I fell to the floor, indulging them with lavish rubbings and kissings, then calming one of them down from a seizure of delight that made him snock uncontrollably.

"Who's your mommy, you ugly dogs?" Mallory said to them, while kissing Carlo on both cheeks. It's the kind of thing I would have found pretentious in practically anyone but this woman, who brought off the gesture like she had been born to it.

"How's Owen?" I asked. Owen was her husband, as beloved to her as Carlo was to me, who had been paralyzed in an accident six months before I met them. That's a whole other story for later.

"So-so. Annette's with him." Never one for self-pity, she changed the subject back to the Pugs. "They've been totally abject, but you should have seen them when they heard the garage door go up. And who is this delightful child?"

I introduced Gemma-Kate to Mallory and watched to see if she responded to Mallory's flirtation the way everyone else did.

"Hello, Gemma-Kate! I'm Mallory!" Mallory said, flinging her arms wide. She caught my glance. "Overdoing it?" she asked.

Neither of us had had much experience with young people. "You could maybe pull back a little on the Auntie Mame shtick," I said.

She brought it down a notch and asked, "How was your flight?"

"It was just amazing," Gemma-Kate said, her eyes widening at the memory.

"This was actually Gemma-Kate's first plane ride," I said.

Even Mallory was momentarily struck dumb, understandable for someone who has taken a chopper ride so low over Mount Kilauea she could feel the heat. Then, "How wonderful to have a brand-new experience," she said, making it sound envious rather than condescending.

Gemma-Kate just then noticed the Pugs had turned from me to sniff her ankles. She watched them for a moment as if she wasn't sure what you were supposed to do with pugs. Then, grinning, she dropped to the floor beside me and patted them one at a time, actually went pat pat pat on top of their heads. She had never had a pet.

"They're so *cute*! What are their names?" she asked.

"They don't have names," Mallory said, rolling her eyes. "Brigid just calls them the Pugs."

Gemma-Kate looked up at the three of us watching her and pursed her rosebud lips. It made me notice how rounded everything about her was; big eyes, button nose, even her earlobes were little pillows.

"Maybe you'll name them," I said, to show that Mallory wasn't teasing her.

Gemma-Kate smiled.

The Pugs didn't care much for the pat pat pat technique, or maybe found it insincere. They abandoned Gemma-Kate, wandered to the door leading into the backyard, and sat there until Carlo opened it to let them out.

"Now relax," Mallory said, as Carlo took our bag into our room and Gemma-Kate's to the guest room. "The wine has been breathing far longer than it deserves. Gemma-Kate, are you allowed to have a glass of wine?"

Gemma-Kate and I got up off the floor and came into the kitchen area, she looking at me in case I objected, and when I did not, she nodded with a nice dash of shyness. Mallory opened the right cupboard to extract four wineglasses while I picked up the bottle.

"Brunello di Montalcino," I read. "This isn't ours." I gestured at a small rack over the refrigerator. "Did you see we had some here you could have opened?"

Mallory pulled her lips back against her teeth like someone was trying to dose her with Castor oil and took the bottle from me. "Yes, I know."

"Go to hell, Hollinger. I know what's good, I just can't afford it."

She poured and handed Gemma-Kate and me a glass. Gemma-Kate took hers into the living room, where Carlo was, while I sniffed and sipped. "Oh my God," I said. "I haven't had anything this good since—" I stopped, knowing that I couldn't tell her about the man who ran human traffic from Guatemala to Las Vegas.

"Ever?" she said.

"Ever," I agreed. "Thanks for watching the dogs and coming over like this."

"It's a nice place. You have good taste," she smiled, meaning her own. Mallory had helped me when I went through a brief redecorating phase.

We took our glasses into the living room area, where Carlo was pointing out to Gemma-Kate the mountains to the east of our property, he using words like "metamorphic" and she looking politely rapt.

I sat next to Carlo on the camelback couch that Mallory had advised me to keep. After answering just enough of Mallory's respectful questions about the funeral and the state of the survivors, we moved on and she made us laugh with stories about the Pugs' sleepover. They had curled up beside Owen on the bed, she said, and he seemed to like that even if he couldn't say so.

The Pugs had come back in the house and were nestled up against me, one glued to my thigh and one of them half-draped around my neck and half-reclining on the back of the couch, his breath hot and smelly. They reminded me of Mallory's invitation extended at least a month before the funeral. "Are we still on for that fund-raiser?" I asked.

"Which one?"

"Only you could say that. You said you bought a table for the Humane Society thing."

Mallory said, "You know, I might disinvite you. It could be awful."

"You, the hospitality queen, having an awful evening? How's that?"

"I didn't want to bring it up with your sister-in-law's death and all. Remember those people I told you about a while ago, whose son drowned and they left the church because they were pissed at everyone? Just before you joined?"

"Kind of. The woman who went a little crazy."

"That's the one. She blamed everyone. The church, the other kids in the youth group, the rector's wife. The thing is, her husband is Owen's doctor and he's really good. So I sort of want to patch things up, and I thought enough time has gone by, this will be neutral territory, and maybe she's not insane anymore. They agreed to come. But like I said, it could be awful."

"Oh, come on. Don't make me miss a chance to watch you flounder socially. It would be a first."

Mallory backed down then. "Gemma-Kate would be welcome," she said. "We can make room."

"That's really nice of you," I said, and turned to get Gemma-Kate's agreement.

She had gotten up from where she'd been sitting by Carlo and gone into the kitchen to refill her glass, which I noted with a little interest. After swigging a bit of it, she had been circling around the room for the past several minutes, like a fish that would die if it stopped swimming. At the moment I asked if she'd like to come to the fundraiser, she had finally paused, her back to the room, at one of the back windows looking out at the life-sized statue of St. Francis in the backyard. Was she actually staring out the window or was she staring at her reflection? In it I was the only one who could see she wasn't smiling now. I wondered, for her sake, not mine, whether it had been the best idea to pull her away from her father and grandparents so soon after her mother's death.

Right now Carlo and Mallory had begun watching her as closely as I was. "Gemma-Kate?" I said, to get her attention.

"I'll be okay," she said. "I like it here." She turned back to us, or rather, to Carlo, her smile reconnected. "I was just thinking. Should I call you Uncle Carlo, Father Carlo, or just Carlo?"

Somehow I could feel the three of us breathe again, and I was aware that we all had been a little on edge, watching Gemma-Kate without letting on to the others that we were doing so. We were all concerned for her, I thought.

Carlo smiled back and said, "No one has called me Father Carlo in a long, long time, Gemma-Kate. Rather than make a formal decision, why don't we just wait to see what comes up at the moment?"

"All right," she said.

Just then the Pug draped around my shoulder tried to french my nose, and I swatted him away.

"The Pugs adore Brigid," Carlo said, his attention swaying back to me. He put his hand over mine and left it there.

I'm sure I was the only one who noticed Gemma-Kate watching Carlo's hand on mine and the way she stiffened a bit.

She said, "Dad says animals don't have feelings. Dad says if Aunt Brigid died and they were locked in the house with her without any other food they'd start eating her in a couple of days. First they'd eat whatever wasn't clothed, like her hands and her face."

Now, some out there might find a statement like that inappropriate, maybe even a little perverse. But to me it was just Quinn dinner conversation over the Hamburger Helper, Dad playing Make the Kids Gag. Carlo and Mallory were both stunned momentarily, though; you don't say shit like that out of the blue in front of civilians. I felt sorry for Gemma-Kate because I'd stopped a conversation once or twice myself.

"Who wants some chicken tikka?" I said into the silence.

Four

Happily the chicken tikka was good enough to overcome any squeamishness about postmortem canine scavenging. We finished everything including the sauce, which we wiped up with the naan bread. I looked around the table and continued to marvel that I hadn't made the food, I hadn't even set the table, and yet I felt as if I had made this time for us where everyone was in sync somehow, in a family I had created. Look, after a long life lived alone except for the company of low-life criminals, I have a husband and a friend. We're doing small talk. This is what normal life is like, I thought, the kind I had fought all those years to preserve for other people. And I didn't even have to worry about arguments flaring the way they did with my family. I marveled at how good it could be, all of us laughing. I remember it so vividly because it was the last time together. Laughing, I mean.

After dinner Mallory said, "You know what would be even more fun than hanging around with a bunch of old people? Come to church. There's a cute boy your age."

"Oh, I don't want to be any trouble," Gemma-Kate said.

Gemma-Kate's words sounded smooth, as if they had been practiced. And they didn't sound like hers. *I don't want to be any trouble* was Todd's voice, something he would have told Gemma-Kate to say to us. I wondered what she would say if she finally spoke for herself.

"That would be good," I said. "It's a real small church, but I have seen a couple of kids there. It's not like you have to join a youth group or anything."

"Unless she wants to," Mallory said. Before we knew it she'd arranged to pick up Gemma-Kate the following night for a telescope party at St. Martin's.

With a my-work-is-done-here attitude, she hugged me and left in one of the few Jags I've ever seen in Tucson. Carlo stayed back to wash the plates and throw away the takeout containers while Gemma-Kate helped me give the Pugs their evening walk. We put on sweaters. In March after the sun went down a thick sweater felt good.

The winter rains had been ample, and when we stepped out the front door a chorus of frogs somewhere, crazy to mate after long hibernation, made the neighborhood sound like an amphibian singles bar.

Gemma-Kate didn't object when I made her put on an LED light with an elastic headband. The beam ensured that if we heard a rattle we'd be able to see where it came from. It also allowed us to see where the Pugs pooped so we could pick it up.

With a warning about snakes—"Keep a tight leash, GK"—we set out, a Pug apiece, the male stopping methodically to mark posts, plants, and patches of gravel.

Gemma-Kate had been subdued, almost withdrawn, during the funeral days, but now she practically skipped down the sidewalk. While I was sure she must mourn the loss of her mother, I could understand how exhilarating it might feel to be liberated from illness and the rest of our family. Plus the wine, and moving in Mallory's orbit, might have given her a double dose of perk.

She was happy to answer my questions. Yes, she was interested in moving to entirely new surroundings. Yes, she was excited about starting classes at the university. Yes, she wanted to see the Grand Canyon.

Knowing Gemma-Kate had an interest in biology, I pointed out the sparkles on the sidewalk that looked like pieces of glitter until they moved. I had discovered they were spiders, and the LED lights reflected off their eyes. Gemma-Kate counted them out loud as we walked.

I realized this was the first time we had been alone. With just the two of us, and the calm dark, it was a good time to feel her out a bit, get to know this almost stranger.

But Quinns are not known for their subtlety. "So how are you feeling?" I asked.

"How long have you known Mallory?" she asked, almost at the same time.

"About six months."

"Did you give her a key to your house?"

"No, I told her what the code was for the automatic garage door and I left the door to the garage open."

"Are you going to change the passcode?"

"No. Gemma-Kate, Mallory is a friend."

"I wouldn't let someone I didn't know that well into my house when I wasn't there."

I tore a plastic bag off the roll attached to my Pug's leash and stooped to pick up some poop. "You didn't seem to dislike Mallory," I said.

"Do you like her?"

"She's the first friend I've ever had, after your Aunt Ariel and your mom."

"I'm just, like, security conscious."

"Spoken like a true cop's daughter," I said, wiping the Pug's bottom so it wouldn't make a spot on my new beige carpet.

We walked down to the end of the block, rounded the cul-de-sac, and started back, stopping once to pick up a little more poop next to a cactus that reminded me of the sweet dotted swiss dresses Mom made for me and my sister. Childhood wasn't all bad. It seldom is.

"How are you feeling?" I tried again, trying to strike a sensitive auntly tone.

There was a long pause. "You have to adapt," she finally said, and stopped to examine another sparkle.

There was her father's voice again, coaching her on how to get along with her Aunt Brigid. I wanted to get past her father, to her.

"It's okay to mourn. Your mom was a wonderful woman, almost a saintliness about her," I said, with some tears I hadn't yet cried. "I loved her very much."

There was another pause then, long enough for Gemma-Kate to have summoned and dismissed a half-dozen responses. When I thought finally she would not respond at all, she said, "She talked about you all the time, all your adventures. Sometimes I pretended you were my mother."

That didn't make me feel good at all. "I wasn't always the woman I am now. I was always good at working undercover, and investigations, but not much else. I would have been more of a drinking mother than a playing mother."

"Mom didn't play much either. Mom was just sick." The way Gemma-Kate said the word sounded resentful.

"That wasn't her fault. Sick or well, you couldn't have had better."

It was dark, but I knew Gemma-Kate turned her head toward me because the light on her forehead flashed in my face. The flash of light hid her eyes. She said, "My dog is pooping. Do I have to pick it up?"

"No. Let me." I took out another bag, drew it over my hand, and picked up the poop.

When I had stood up again and knotted the plastic bag, Gemma-Kate said, gesturing with the handle of the leash in her hand, "Look at that one. Is that a tarantula?"

I saw what she was pointing at, a whole round clump of sparkles about as big as a quarter moving slowly across the fine gravel a little ahead of us.

"No, I've seen that kind before. It's a wolf spider. It carries its babies on its back."

"I thought spiders laid eggs."

"Not this one. Or maybe it does, but when they hatch they climb on the mother. What you're seeing is all the eyes of the babies."

"Why does it carry them?"

"Instinct, I guess, continuation of the species, something." Now, I had become accustomed to seeing the sparkles of spiders at night, and kind of liked the warning they sent out even if I hated spiders. But when Gemma-Kate handed me her Pug's leash, bent down, and let the spider crawl onto her hand, my stomach cinched up. She examined it under the light from her head lamp, let it crawl from hand to hand, the mother lumbering under the weight of dozens of perfectly formed babies. I watched Gemma-Kate's face as she did this, her focused stillness broken only by the throb of a rapid pulse under her jaw, and I thought she liked that I was watching her. Here is Gemma-Kate doing something that fascinates and perhaps even appalls tough Aunt Brigid.

Then Gemma-Kate set the spider down.

I thought about Marylin again and, as happens with someone who has seen too much dying, something bloomed inside me that wanted that grotesque spider mom to live. Gemma-Kate and I both watched the spider some more. Then she lifted her foot. Did she lift her foot or am I not remembering well, after all that happened? Did she pause, and glance in my direction to see me watching her, and only then put her foot down again, well away from the spider? Did she wonder what it would look like if all those sparkles burst over the sidewalk like tiny fireworks?

No. I was the one thinking that.

Someone has said that we don't remember events; rather, our memory creates them. Sometimes you don't know whether you're remembering a truth or a lie.

Five

The next night, Mallory dropped Gemma-Kate off at the church and brought her home as promised, pulling out of the driveway with a wave. I asked Gemma-Kate how she had enjoyed it.

"It was a church group, and there were only five of us," she said, while fixing a cup of tea in the microwave. "We played Ping-Pong because it was too cloudy for telescopes. I thought I might die." But then she admitted with a trace of reluctance, "There was one kid there who was my age. It was pretty cool because his dad is a cop, too."

"What's his name?"

"Peter something. Do you know him?"

"I don't know a lot of people at the church."

"We might hang out."

"Is that anything like hooking up? I get confused by the lingo."

"You're kidding me, right?"

"Yeah, I'm kidding."

Sure enough, a couple evenings after that, the doorbell rang about six. When I opened it I saw a boy standing on the other side of the screen door. He scratched his side without speaking, and I prepared to hear how he was selling candles for the sake of a teenage group home. I glanced down to make sure the screen door was locked.

"May I help you?" I said.

Gemma-Kate came up behind me. "Do I need a flashlight?" she asked.

"I've got two," he said.

"Excuse me," I said.

"I'm sorry, Aunt Brigid. This is Peter."

"Hey," said Peter, lifting two fingers but not his eyes from where they were fixed somewhere around my right shoulder. He was one of those people I think of as a Neither. That is to say, neither tall nor short, neither light nor dark. Neither smiling nor scowling. I imagined if I spoke to him I'd find him neither sociable nor un. Totally unnoticeable until the moment you see his mug shot. No, now I'm being cynical.

"Peter. From church?" I asked with exaggerated ignorance.

With Peter left standing on the other side of the door, Gemma-Kate said, "I should have said something. I'm sorry, Aunt Brigid, I got so used to being independent at home I didn't think to tell you in advance."

How polite she was. I unlocked the screen door and opened it, and said with what I hoped was a tone of mild curiosity, "Where you guys going?"

Peter finally spoke, more courteous and articulate than my first impression of him had allowed. "There's an evening hike in Sabino Canyon to see the night-blooming cactus and the wildlife. A park guide goes along. I told Gemma-Kate it's a good way to get to know the area. With the drive over and back we should be gone just a few hours. We'll stop at Eegee's for sandwiches."

"Sounds like fun. Can I see your license?"

Gemma-Kate squirmed, but Peter took it in stride, pulling a crummy wallet out of his back pocket, opening it, and showing me his card. That's how I could tell he really was a cop's son.

While I glanced to see he was who he said he was and his license was up to date, Carlo came up and slipped Gemma-Kate a twenty. For my part, caught by surprise, and never having had the experience of dealing with a teenager before, let alone playing something that resembled the role of a mother, I let them go, only thinking to call Mallory immediately once the door was shut.

"Gemma-Kate works fast," Mallory said.

"The kid's name is Peter. He looks like a punk, but he talks nice."

"Peter Salazar. Don't worry," she said. "I don't know much about him other than he slinks about like boys his age. But he comes from a very strict family. His father is in law enforcement."

"I know. What's this about a night hike in Sabino Canyon? I hope it's not like submarine races."

"It's legitimate. Don't hover, Brigid. They're nearly old enough for college, and you're sounding like a helicopter mom."

I hung up, somewhat reassured but still wondering if I should have been doing more. Carlo, having been celibate during his child-rearing years, was nonplussed as well.

"Do you think you should have talked to the boy?" I asked.

"I don't know what I'd say."

It occurred to me I hadn't heard Carlo use that phrase much. "Am I supposed to have the safe-sex talk with her?" I asked.

"I don't know," he said again. "She seems old enough that some-one would have done that already."

While we waited up just like parents, I did a quick background check. Peter Salazar didn't have a record yet.

Gemma-Kate came home by ten. Communication about the eve-ning was limited to the relief she felt talking not only to someone under twenty, but someone who shared the fascinating and ugly life of law enforcement offspring. The life that was spent inexplicably scared of your own father for the power he exuded, yet worried daily that he wouldn't come home. While she didn't say it quite this way, I knew it for myself. Actually, she looked as if the exercise, night air, and companionship of someone her own age had done her good.

The least Marylin could have done was provide a manual with her daughter.

Six

I nearly forgot to explain the cooking. The best thing, the most unexpected benefit of having Gemma-Kate visit, was that she knew how to cook and enjoyed it. I mean, really cook and really enjoy it. For the first couple of days she suffered in silence my Shake 'n Bake pork chops and microwaved frozen green beans. Then one day, shortly before the night hike, I woke up, put on my warm robe without resenting having to cover up because the morning temperatures were still in the low forties, and padded into the kitchen in my cheetah print slippers to find that the coffee was made.

Gemma-Kate was sitting in my recliner, reading a Southwestern cookbook I had bought and intended to use one day once I learned how to pronounce "quinoa" right without feeling affected.

"What's that smell?" I asked of an aroma that had overpowered the coffee.

"Scones," she said, with more caution than enthusiasm. "Is that okay? You didn't have any Devonshire cream to go with them, but there's something called prickly pear jelly in the refrigerator. That seems to work."

I turned my attention to a baking sheet next to the stove on which a half-dozen triangles of heaven rested. I nibbled one. It didn't need jelly. "Where did you learn this?"

"Mom started to teach me. When she got really sick, if I wanted to eat I had to cook it myself. I found out I was good at it."

I asked her what else she could cook. She was two steps ahead of me. Privately she had already gone through my kitchen and handed me a list of things to get at the grocery store the next time I went shopping.

"What's fish sauce?" I asked, scanning the list.

"It's near the soy sauce in Whole Foods. Do you have those here?"

"I've never been inside one. How about if I give you my car keys and credit card instead?"

An almost smile formed at the corners of her lips. "If you do the cooking I'll do the cleanup," I added. Then, not wanting her to feel like Cinderella, I added, "Just dinner, I mean. And maybe I can help and learn something."

Never look a gift horse in the mouth, Mom used to say.

Seven

Carlo and I were always on the go, me working private investigation cases I found interesting, him with his own passions du jour, like building an observatory so he could more easily use the eleven-inch telescope I bought him last Christmas. But Gemma-Kate kicked us up a notch with her youth and excitement about her new surroundings, coupled with anticipation of starting at the university and moving into a dormitory in the fall.

On the plane ride back from Florida before she got sick, Gemma-Kate and Carlo had made a list of all the things she needed to explore. Sedona. Mount Lemmon. Tombstone. The Grand Canyon! They talked about some places I hadn't even seen yet.

That day I was coming out of my office after reporting to a client that the woman she had seen in her husband's car was a silicone sex doll. That actually wasn't as bizarre as finding out he had had it designed to look like his wife. I couldn't advise her whether she should divorce him for infidelity with herself. It wasn't my job.

Carlo was sitting at his desk in the swivel chair facing Gemma-Kate where she sat at the end of the couch, her arms resting on a cushion. When she turned her head to say good-bye she looked like an old painting, that pose of serenity. They were going over to the Desert Museum to learn about Arizona flora and fauna while I went shopping.

Mallory was the one who preferred shopping, while I preferred hiking. But I had discovered from being married to Carlo that sometimes the most friendly things happen when you compromise. It turned out shopping was a great way to talk without the pressure of being eye to eye, something that always made me think of having to convince someone I wasn't lying. Plus I discovered that shopping and drinking often went together, especially when the item you were looking for was a bathing suit.

We met at La Encantada, a split-level upscale plaza with Coldwater Creek on the bottom but St. John's and a Tiffany's on the top. After a couple of glasses of Chardonnay at North restaurant, Mallory was prepared to enter a small boutique called Everything But Water. We both faced the racks against the wall of the shop, pushing the suits back and forth, back and forth, talking. It was this motion that I found most therapeutic, with or without the wine.

I had also found that women are fond of talking about two things: their children and their own hideous defects. Because neither Mallory nor I had had children, and were in agreement that we couldn't see the use of them, the bathing suits made us default to our bodies.

She said, "I look at these things and keep hearing a little voice in my brain saying, 'You have no waist.' You don't have that problem. You've got no belly fat at all."

While gone are the days of pert thighs and rock-hard breasts, I have to admit I'm still pretty trim. But wanting to show solidarity, I said, "I have monkey-face knees."

Mallory snarfed as if I was bringing a knife to a gunfight. She took a black one-piece with a peplum off the rack and held it up. I shook my head. "Get one with the legs cut out more."

"Are you still sure you want to go to that fund-raiser?" Mallory asked, jumping to an entirely different topic, knowing I'd keep up with the mental mountain-goating that friends do.

"Sure, why not?"

"I'm not sure it will be fun. One of the couples I invited, their son drowned just before I met you."

I held up two fingers. This was the gentle sign that we were repeating ourselves.

Mallory said, "Did I tell you it's kind of self-serving, my inviting them, that the father is Owen's doctor?"

"Yes, you did. I don't care. I've been working really hard on the aunt thing and could use a night off."

"How did the date go?"

"Okay, I guess. She seems to like Peter, but she doesn't talk a lot. When she does talk it's like she's considered every word before speaking it. She's quiet. Really polite but quiet. And then I'm really polite back. It gets to me a little."

"She's probably just trying to be what she thinks you expect." Mallory threw the suit back on the rack with ill-hidden disgust. "I should have had more wine."

"You're only going to wear it in your own pool. What do you even need a suit for?"

"Don't be gross, darling." She looked at me appraisingly.

"Well, it's not like I parade around flaunting it," I said, thinking of the time I was undercover as a stripper, flaunting it very nicely, thank you. It's hard to not grow comfortable with your own skin once you've pole-danced in public. That Mafia hit man never dreamed a Fed could writhe that way. "I'm just saying if I come out of the shower and I want something from the kitchen I don't put a robe on to go get it. Does anyone?"

"Yes," Mallory said, pulling in her upper lip. "They do."

Speaking of children, "Well, it's sort of moot with Gemma-Kate in the house. I have to be more modest."

"*Quelle horreur.*"

"It's actually not as bad as I thought it would be. She's getting on well with Carlo. And she's a really good cook. She's teaching me."

Funny how in retrospect that exchange sounded so ominous. Everything became so ominous.

Mallory said, "Does she always make inappropriate comments like the one about the Pugs eating your face?"

"Did she say my face? I don't remember. Anyway, it's an occupational hazard in a cop family. You toughen up. Not much in the way of empathy."

That, too.

Eight

At one time a thriving parish, St. Martin's sat on twelve acres of prime land on La Cholla, next to a golf course. The style was mission adobe, the church itself standing out stark white against the land that had been allowed to stay natural, dotted with creosote, prickly pear, and cholla. At most, a hundred people would attend the later service in which Father Elias Manwaring, potluck portly, delivered those rambling sermons that made you want to stand up from your pew and shout, "Shut the fuck up, already!" But overall he was a pretty good man, and I had never before had as much time to stop thinking as I did in the church.

After the service we all filed out to shake Manwaring's mushy hand and be rewarded with his receiving-line smile. For Carlo the smile was always a little more genuine, like for a comrade in arms. Manwaring leaned into Carlo, saying something I couldn't hear. Then we went with a couple dozen of the hard-core parishioners to a separate parish hall for coffee and kuchen.

Carlo looked around at the entrance until he spotted a guy with a ponytail, bald on top so it looked like his hair was sliding off at a glacial pace. "Visitor," Carlo said. "Elias wants me to connect." Carlo took my hand and pulled me to the coffee table, where the guy stood meekly in line, looking like a church wallflower. Fifty-something. Nice shirt, but it felt like a veneer over a surface that needs sanding. An earring, and a bit of military tattoo peeking out from beneath a rolled-up shirtsleeve, markings of a bad boy gone to seed, or tired out and looking for Jesus.

Carlo put out his hand and the guy took it. "Hi. Carlo DiForenza, and my wife, Brigid. Sorry for the line. The banana cake with chocolate morsels trumps greeting a guest."

The man took Carlo's hand, but his eyes and smile were all for me, and in that moment the ponytail and the earring and the tattoo became as sexy as they must have been in 1973, on the kind of guy all the girls have the hots for precisely because our parents warned us about *boys like him* without telling us why.

"No one can beat a good banana cake," he said. It might have been naughty, but you couldn't see that in his expression.

"I have to hand it to you, it's hard to walk into a group where you don't know anyone," Carlo said. "Shopping?"

The man looked blank.

"For a church," Carlo said.

He took down the blazing grin and let one corner of his mouth go up in a more self-deprecating smile. "Yeah, I guess you could say I am. Haven't done this for a long time. I just moved here."

"Where from?" I asked.

"Florida."

"Me, too. Broward County area."

"Oh, well, they say when you're south of Orlando you're in the North again. More diverse. I'm Alachua County," he said. "An actual cracker."

"That's up near Gainesville," I told Carlo.

"I had a restaurant there for years." His eyes filmed over and he blinked some sadness away, nearly. "I'm sorry, I lost my wife seven and a half months ago, and she was in charge of the manners in the family. Adrian Franklin."

Carlo's pastoral instinct switched on and he shared his own widowerhood. I already knew about that part, so I left him to it, my glance first lighting on Mallory, who lifted her eyebrows appreciatively.

I'd introduce her later if she hadn't already moved in on him, but for now I slipped what they call "the fellowshipping," cut the line for the coffee, and looked around for Gemma-Kate.

The parish hall had tall windows along one wall where you could look out onto the property. From there you saw a labyrinth made out of rocks carefully laid in circles leading to a cross in the center, and further away, to the right, part of another adobe structure, just walls without a roof. I had never gone out there.

The labyrinth was where I saw her. With the bustle and chatter behind me I stood at the window, sipping my coffee and watching Gemma-Kate walk the labyrinth. She seemed out of place out there, and alone. In a church setting, alone always seems sad.

"I sent my son out," said a voice that reminded me of a squirrel, fast and perky.

I turned to see a woman, on the short side like me, but much younger. "Hi, I'm Ruth. That's my son, Peter."

I turned back to the window and watched Peter Salazar walk out to the labyrinth.

"I met him. He took Gemma-Kate for a night hike." I felt a little smug, knowing something she didn't about the kids. Is that how parents are?

For her part, Ruth covered up her surprise by changing the subject. "We've been coming to the church about three years," she said. "They have a youth group. I thought Peter should be with more Christian children. There's the Manwaring boy, over there, Ken." I turned to look out of politeness and spotted a lumpish and sullen boy who would be the right age and same body type as Elias. Ruth hadn't taken a breath, "There aren't too many children, though. They need to bring in more youth. Nice to have a girl here. We have more boys than girls."

"I think—"

"There you go. See, he's walking the labyrinth with your daughter. I knew she must be your daughter because of the way you watch her. A late-in-life child. Those can be the best. We've had some trouble with Peter. But not too bad, considering. The things kids get into these days, I mean."

I noted that Ruth did not appear to need me to participate in a conversation, so while she chattered on about the church and Peter and herself and her husband who didn't attend and wasn't that too bad but with God's grace you never knew, I watched Gemma-Kate and Peter walk the labyrinth. Not together; the way the path was laid out had them passing close and then drawing away from each other, passing and drawing away, not looking at one another, like a meditative pas de deux. At this distance I couldn't even see them speaking.

"You religious?" Peter asked.

"No, just bored," Gemma-Kate answered. "What's this thing for?"

"It's called a labyrinth. It's stupid. There's only one way in and out. What's the good of it?"

"Maybe it doesn't want you to have to make choices. Maybe it doesn't want you to think. There, I got to the center." She pointed to a white adobe wall across the yard. "What's that?"

"I'll show you. Come on."

Mallory came up to say she had to get home to Owen, and spotted Gemma-Kate and Peter. "Isn't that cute," she said as Ruth and I turned to her. "No, don't bother to thank me. Carlo said to tell you he's ready to go, too."

Ruth fastened on to Mallory while my friend tried to disengage from her in the social form of unpeeling Saran Wrap. I helped by asking her to let Carlo know we'd be staying just a little longer. Then, in the hopes that Ruth would stop talking, I pretended to watch the kids out the window, though they had walked away from the labyrinth in the direction of the small white adobe structure and I couldn't see them anymore.

Peter said, "This is called a columbarium. See all the marble squares? There's a person under each one. Ashes, I mean."

"I went to the cemetery when they buried my mother, but she was Catholic so Dad didn't cremate her," Gemma-Kate said. "I think I'd rather be cremated. Did you know any of the people here?"

"This one over here. See, Joseph Neilsen. I was here when they put his ashes under that tile. They were in a little metal thing that looked like my dad's martini shaker."

Gemma-Kate did the math. "Fourteen years old. How did he die?"

"He drowned."

"That's a weird way to go here. You don't even have any water in the rivers."

"He had a pool."

"Did he, like, hit his head or something?"

Peter shrugged but didn't answer. "Nobody really liked him. He was sort of a jerk. We talked about it a lot at first, but it happened a while ago."

"Now I remember," Gemma-Kate said. "I heard my aunt's friend talking about it at the house."

"What did she say?"

Gemma-Kate turned at the sound of her name. Her aunt was coming up the path but hadn't reached the wall yet, was waving to her. She waved back and told Peter she had to go.

On the drive home Gemma-Kate sat in the backseat, texting. "Who you on with, GK? Peter already?"

"It's Dad."

"Tell him I said hi. I'll call him."

Nine

Early that week Carlo took Gemma-Kate for a tour of the University of Arizona, where he introduced her to the head of the Biology Department and they toured the labs. This was heady stuff for Gemma-Kate, who had only had access to what she could learn from books and the Internet. On return they walked in through the garage door singing Gilbert and Sullivan, but knowing I'm uncomfortable with music, Carlo shushed Gemma-Kate before the door closed.

Over lunch Gemma-Kate told me about the day while Carlo watched her, beaming with the delight a teacher has in discovering the one student who gets it.

"I saw a fly wing under an electron microscope. And I listened to Uncle Father talk with the Biology Department chair, Dr. Brogdon. They're going to give a series of joint lectures on science and religion. Did you know that ancient philosophy began with questions about the physical world instead of the spiritual world, Aunt Brigid? The word 'atom' was originally coined by pre-Socratic philosophers."

I nodded as if everybody knew that, more distracted by how Gemma-Kate might have ended up with "Uncle Father." It sounded vaguely like something from *South Park*.

. . .

In the late afternoon that same day, Carlo and I got dressed up and gave Gemma-Kate directions for the Pugs, which amounted to just letting them out in the backyard if they asked. She asked if Peter could come over and looked sullen when I said I wasn't comfortable with that just yet, but she didn't argue. Then we drove the relatively short distance down Oracle to the Hilton El Conquistador for Puttin' On the Dog, benefiting the Arizona Humane Society.

My impression for the first couple of years I'd lived here was that Tucson was where strip malls came to die. Mallory set me straight on that. "It's not Manhattan," she would say, "but it's not Green Acres, either."

Now, my career put me often enough in the path of the rich that I could appreciate the taste of Montrachet, the texture of Thai raw silk, the kick of superior cocaine, and the value of a de Kooning, but I don't envy rich people. I'm just glad I'm alive.

I mean that literally. When you've been shot at, gotten stabbed in the spleen with a nail file, fallen off a horse, gotten rabies vaccine after being bitten by a rabid Rottweiler, and offered yourself as bait to a sexual serial killer, that's not an idle cliché. I really am glad I'm still alive.

I paused at the entrance to the gathering, just past an arching trellis covered with fake ivy. Staying alive had always been a matter of staying aware. Aware even now, I thought about how the only wire I was wearing was an underwire, and I was not carrying. I looked around to see if I could figure out who was. It wasn't like I was expecting a bloodbath or anything. It's just that public gatherings like this make me a little tense. They're so uncontrolled, so many strangers, so many unknowns. And I was all too aware of what could happen. So I scoped out the place, did a quick threat assessment.

Among the older guests, some beaded tops, some silk, maybe a dozen tuxedos, none with bulges in either of the places a man hides something. Among the younger, a preponderance of black linen, dress shirts, no ties. I felt just right in a sleeveless navy blue maxi dress and lime green drape, which would provide a little warmth when the late afternoon sun lost its heat.

Most people stood holding champagne flutes and small plates, while the round tables covered with white cloths that puddled on the ground were largely left alone. The rule at one of these things is, if you sit down you're a loser, the opposite of musical chairs. Local restaurants had tents, and the smells of garlic, sweet and sour sauce, and curry competed for attention. A small combo played cool jazz, which is to say the kind without a tune that you couldn't hum if you tried. A waiter wearing a tux and a papier-mâché hound's head passed perilously close with a silver tray holding champagne goblets. You could tell he couldn't see very well.

"They don't even know how to be pretentious," I said to Carlo.

"Don't be a snob," he said. "You have to allow Tucson its pretensions. It doesn't have that many."

I estimated three hundred people, three fifty tops, not counting the animals, which were mostly dogs except for a miniature pink pig on a leash of the same color.

That man over there, khaki shorts and sandals at a formal affair. Is it because this is Tucson and anything goes, or does he clearly not belong? He's standing alone, looking isolated. Is he nervous?

I felt unexpected fingers around the back of my neck, a little tug. The nerve sparked, and I jumped a little, my muscles galvanized for action.

"Sorry to startle you," Carlo said, "but stop working, O'Hari."

Carlos knows me almost better than anyone ever has. Sometimes it feels like he knows things about me I don't even know, as if I've unzipped my skin. It's not a totally unpleasing sensation.

Partly because of this, and partly because I had been slowly sharing more and more about my past lately, he knew that I had been instinctively doing a threat assessment at the entryway to a fund-raiser. And him calling me O'Hari, an Irish version of Mata Hari, always stopped me from taking myself too seriously.

I spotted Mallory, who hadn't spotted us. Her sights were on the man we had met at St. Martin's, the one with the ponytail, which was now at interesting odds with his smart blazer and dress slacks.

48

She laughed at something he said, and even from a distance I could almost see her blush. Then she stumbled on the uneven ground and he gripped her arm to steady her, bringing her closer. Good tactic, I thought. Mallory was in rare form tonight. I dropped my guard.

Mallory saw me next, said something I assumed was dismissive to the man, and met Carlo and me halfway. She moved confidently in a prairie skirt, white blouse unbuttoned to there and no further, and a low-slung southwestern belt that hid her lack of waist. I marveled that an outfit like that could still look like it came from Ralph Lauren.

I nodded in the direction of Ponytail Man and said, "I take it you've met Adrian Franklin."

"Just now. He said he remembered seeing me at church," she said, with a Mae West roll of her eyes. But she had more critical things on her mind than her casual flirting. She put one arm around me and one around Carlo, kissing the cheek on either side of hers. But she didn't draw away immediately, and I thought I knew her well enough to see when she was upset and putting on a show. I didn't have to wait long for the reason.

"I'm so relieved you're here," she whispered before finishing the hug and pulling back, her voice breathy with tension. "I've made a horrid mistake, and I need you to save me from myself." She cocked her head back at the table behind her. "Don't stare, but you see the couple sitting with the Manwarings? Those are the Neilsens." Feeling like I was operating undercover again, I gave the table a quick glance.

On one side slumped Father Manwaring, looking defeated, and the woman Mallory had indicated was his wife. Lulu was in white linen, very upright yet fading into the background beside her husband, who wasn't even trying. I had seen her around the church but had not connected her to Elias.

Across the table and leaning back, which was as far away as they could get from the Manwarings without falling off their chairs, was an extremely uncomfortable-looking couple Mallory identified as the Neilsens. "I thought it would be a good thing to get us together in neutral territory, make peace," Mallory said, smiling while only her voice wrung its hands.

"How was I supposed to know she's still stark raving?" Anyone else would hear the usual low social chatter. Only I could hear her shouting. "I can't tell you everything right now because they'll know we're talking about them. Come."

"I can't wait," I said, but let Mallory take my hand, link her other arm through Carlo's, and guide us to what early indications promised to be a damn bad evening.

We were introduced around the table. *Darlings this is Carlo and Brigid DiForenza you know Father Elias but I don't know if you've met Lulu yet and Tim Neilsen, Dr. Neilsen, and Jacquie.*

While Mallory did the intros, I took a look at the Neilsens. Tim was slight but muscular with a receding hairline that didn't look so obvious because he was blond and pale, his scalp and hair blending together so you couldn't be sure which was which. I wondered if his angry mouth looked that way all the time or just when he was trapped with people he didn't like.

Jacquie told me more. The sight of her flashed me back to the abused women's shelter. Her dress drooped to reveal the top edge of her bra, something that a woman usually cares enough to avoid. Her teeth looked a little filmy as if she hadn't bothered to brush them for the evening, or maybe since the day before. Her hair was dyed blue-black. Odd that someone so uncaring about looks and personal hygiene would touch up her roots.

My heart went out to her, and then I put it back as I had with the lost woman at the shelter. I had known too many people who had lost loved ones, including myself, and I didn't think I could take any more of someone else's pain. Just not right this minute.

Mallory fled on the pretext of getting us wine, and Carlo and I were left to take seats pinning us between the quiet Manwarings and the wary Neilsens.

Carlo and I tried the usual prepackaged topics, which were met with a few murmurs before silence resumed. I was making plans to later bitch-slap Mallory for abandoning us to this group when Carlo opened with the usual How Long Have You Lived in Tucson gambit.

This worked a little better by enabling Carlo to speak to the Neilsens apart from the Manwarings without appearing rude. Tim talked about how Jacquie had grown up here but that he had moved to Tucson to join a medical practice, where he met his future bride. Here he picked up her hand and kissed it. I noticed her hand did not respond to the kiss, but she did murmur little agreeing sounds, ah and mm, that played behind his words like backup in a singing group.

Carlo mentioned we had our niece staying with us and that she might be interested in medical school. That was a lie of sorts, and I admired it. Tim said he knew some people and gave Carlo his card. I glanced and saw the "Internal Medicine" under his name. Then I remembered Mallory had said something about him being her husband's physician.

"What do you do?" Tim asked, the only other standard question that hadn't been asked.

"I'm retired from the U of A, philosophy," Carlo said. "Brigid here, she's the one with the interesting profession."

I hate when he does that. "It's only interesting to Carlo. I used to be in federal law enforcement. Copyright infringement investigations."

They would have nodded blandly and moved on, but Carlo wouldn't drop it. "Brigid is being modest. She was a special agent for the FBI. She foiled evildoers." That widened eyes around the table. "Now she does private investigations."

"Private . . ." was the first word Jacquie had uttered since we sat down. She fixed me with one of those stares, eyes all out on you while mind all inward. As if she wasn't aware of our attention to her, Jacquie picked up her evening bag from her lap, took out a pen, and wrote something on the back of Tim's business card that lay on the table between us. Tim scowled as he watched her but apparently could not object.

Then she stood up and leaned over the table, bracing herself on her hands. Her hands were flat on the table. Tim put one of his over hers but she didn't relax them, didn't invite his fingers to curl around hers. She smiled a too-wide smile. "How are your children, Lulu?" Jacquie asked, the lack of a conversational segue apparent to us all, which, if her voice hadn't been so strident and her grin so wide, would still have made her sound a little crazy.

Lulu murmured that her children were doing well, thank you. The "well" came out as whispered regret.

"Amanda still in school?" Jacquie said it with a glare, as if she was accusing Amanda of torturing small animals.

Yes.

"And Ken. Peter was something of a bully, Joey said. But I liked Ken." The words were darting pretty steadily from her mouth now that she had begun. "Is the youth group still active, Lulu? Are you still in charge?"

Yes, they were planning a kickball . . . but Lulu's words trailed off as she realized there were no right ones to speak, that anything she would say would have the sound of a slap. So she stopped trying to talk altogether and stopped trying to look anything but miserable.

I thought Lulu was going to apologize, for something, for Jacquie's grief, for her own children still being alive. Jacquie turned to me with a look that said *Do you see?* but I didn't see at all.

"I'm so . . . sorry," she said, all her anger collapsing into itself, though her apology was seemingly directed at only Carlo and me. "I . . . just . . . can't . . . do this. I . . . thought I . . . could do it."

Lulu turned her head as if she couldn't face Jacquie's ache. This was the moment that Mallory, ever positive that no situation couldn't be improved by wine, approached with a bottle in each hand. "I would have gone for the champagne but it would have given you all head . . ." she trailed off as she saw Tim and Jacquie standing while the rest of us sat.

"I'm so sorry we can't stay," Tim said. "Please give Owen my best. I'll stop by next week to see him."

"But," Mallory said.

Tim lifted a finger that appeared to press Mallory's lips closed from across the table. "I thought it would be good for her, for us, but I think we both made a mistake."

Mallory put the bottles down and started to come around to the Neilsens' side of the table, but then stopped. Tim reached out his hand and shook Carlo's politely, and Elias's as well, while Lulu kept her hands in her lap and looked stricken. Jacquie made her little murmuring sounds, an "ah-ha" and a "hmmm," but now they sounded like tiny verbal uppercuts to someone's jaw.

Without saying good-bye to Mallory or the Manwarings, Jacquie said once more, "I can't," then turned and walked across the lawn, Tim making her lean against him as she stumbled either because of unaccustomed heels or because her knees were buckling as she walked.

I picked up Tim's business card that had been left on the table and turned it over. On the back, along with a phone number, Jacquie had written *Help me.*

Ten

Still standing, Mallory watched them go off a little way, then without a word poured wine in our glasses to a level that she would usually disparage. She lifted hers, and when we lifted ours, wondering what the most appropriate Mallory toast could possibly be at a moment like this, she said with a shake of her head as well as the hand that held the glass, "Fuck."

It was rude and unfeeling, but I tell you, in that moment it felt like a perfect prayer, and it felt as if we had permission to be real. Lulu gave a mirthless laugh, took a slug of wine, and dropped her face into her free hand in the first sincere gesture I'd seen at the table. Elias raised his glass a little higher and followed suit with a sad "My heart is breaking for her."

Mallory fell back into her chair rather than simply sitting down and said, "I'm so sorry. I'm just so sorry. Why didn't I realize? I'm an utter monster."

"They accepted the invitation, Mallory," I said. "They couldn't even foresee what the effect would be. She wasn't ready."

They took turns telling me, with the Manwarings able to offer much more than Mallory could. Whether it was Christian concern or good old-fashioned gossip didn't matter to me. I watched Elias and

Lulu bat the facts back and forth as we listened and Mallory spurred them on as the need arose, apparently grateful that at least the conversation was flowing.

"Their son, Joe, died about six months ago. It was horrible."

I thought of another person I knew who'd lost his child, and I knew that six months, six years, was nothing. But except for Carlo, I still kept thoughts like that to myself rather than have to answer questions about how I knew all that, about the details.

"Accident. Drowning. Pool."

"Suicide."

"Which?" asked Mallory. "I heard both rumors, never knew what they finally decided."

"No, it was that thing they do with sex."

Lulu said, "No, that's just another rumor. If you ever talk to Jacquie again don't even hint that you heard that. At the funeral she overheard someone say he was found with his pants unzipped and she went ballistic right there in front of everyone."

"In denial," Elias said.

"But why are they upset with you?" Mallory asked. "I thought they left the church because of some crisis of faith, and I thought I could do some—"

"It's a whole other issue," Lulu started.

"Denial," Elias repeated. "Tim Neilsen is a goddamn homophobe." He held out his glass to Mallory for a refill.

Lulu seemed relieved to be able to tell the story, and I wondered how many more times it would take before she could let it go for good. "I help out by being the youth group director. The kids get comfortable with me. Joe confided that he wanted to tell his father he was gay."

"Stepfather."

"But Joe was so little when they married it's almost as if. I shouldn't have encouraged him to come out. It wasn't my business to do that."

"We have two kids, a boy and a girl, one in high school, one in college," Elias said to us. "Amanda came out two years ago. It was nothing. You already know, you know?" Cocking his head in Lulu's direction, he asked, "Why would she think the Neilsens would be any different?"

Lulu said, "Tim and Jacquie, Tim especially, they were in serious denial about Joe being gay."

"This day and age?" I said. "I could see it maybe being an issue in Prescott or Yuma, but Tucson? It's a university town, for Pete's sake. Tucson is"—I lowered my voice the way people do when they say "herpes"—"liberal."

Mallory nodded. "Seems like everyone here is either LGBT or writing a book. Aren't you writing a book, darling?" she asked Carlo.

Carlo's attention had been on a shnoodle that wandered up and sniffed his trousers, but he smiled his assent, not finding it necessary to express an opinion when there already seemed to be plenty about. That's how Carlo is.

"Doesn't matter where he lives, or whether he's Joe's biological father, Tim's a goddamn homophobe," Elias repeated. "Jackass."

"Oh, you're just upset because they withdrew their pledge," Lulu said to Elias, with a sharpness in her tone that indicated she didn't drink daily. Then to me, "Joe seemed to trust me enough to talk to me. I suggested he tell them, and he did."

I merely repeated, "This day and age?"

Lulu nodded. "The Neilsens were so conservative they switched churches."

"St. Bede's. I hope they're happy there," Elias said, but even those mild words came out sounding more like *They should eat shit and die.*

I glanced at Mallory, who was sipping thoughtfully. She had tried to be a peacemaker between the Neilsens and the Manwarings the way that Lulu had tried to help Joe and his family. Everyone but me should mind their own business, was my opinion.

"So you didn't know this?" I asked her.

Mallory shook her head. "We were friends through the church. You know how that is."

I handed the business card to Carlo, who said, "Brigid, you should call her. Maybe you can help somehow."

"Sounds to me like she needs therapy more than investigation," I said, hoping to change the subject. "You must have a therapist to refer her to?" I asked Elias.

Carlo said to me, "You would know how to explain things to Jacquie and help her find information. You know people."

Lulu thought that was a great idea. "You must call her."

Mallory, able to see my hesitation, looked amused and said blandly, "Oh yes, Brigid, you must, you absolutely must."

Elias started, "I don't know if that's—"

Whereupon Lulu snapped, "You're the one who said they threatened a lawsuit."

Ah, there you go. Not even a clergy wife's motivation is entirely pure. Unfortunately for the conversation, which was beginning to take an interesting turn, Adrian Franklin showed up at the table with a black Labrador retriever and that grin that made twenty years disappear.

"Look what I got!" he said like a boy with a new puppy.

The dog threw his fifty pounds of glee at Mallory, accidentally hooking the nails of his front paw into her blouse like a canine bodice ripper. Some other time, some other man, she might have used the moment to advantage, but right now did not appear amused.

Carlo was immobilized, Lulu was struck dumb, Elias overturned his chair jumping to help, and Adrian, rather than reaching anywhere near Mallory's bosom in what might be considered an ungentlemanly way, tried to disengage the dog with "Down, Ebony! Down!" Ebony did not respond. But Mallory's grabbing the large puppy paws and easing herself out of their clutches seemed to help more than the command.

Ebony was forced to stay, and sat twitching with not totally suppressed joy at Adrian's feet while Carlo introduced him around just in case and offered one of the chairs the Neilsens had vacated.

"I'm sorry," Adrian said. "I just came over to say hi because I recognized you and disrupted your whole conversation. I'd thought of getting a dog to keep me company and was going to ask around here. They have a bunch of rescue animals looking for homes if anyone is interested. Ebony is less than a year old. Can you believe someone didn't want her?"

I observed Ebony's pound-for-pound destruction potential but didn't comment.

"But it looks like we're going to have to have some obedience classes." He shrugged. "What else is retirement good for?"

"More wine?" Mallory asked, still looking a little distrustful of the dog.

Adrian and Ebony, though quite adorable, had unintentionally made the talk small, and I welcomed my cell phone ringing even as I wondered what it could be about. I dug through my tote bag, pushing aside a water bottle, hand lotion, lip balm, all the usual accoutrements of living in a place where the humidity hovers around six percent.

The phone stopped ringing when I found it. I opened the cover and saw the number was from home. I pressed the number to call back. Gemma-Kate picked it up in half a ring.

"Is everything all right?" I asked.

"I'm not sure," she said. "I wasn't sure I should bother you."

"What's wrong?"

"I think one of the dogs is sick."

"Sick how?"

"It's throwing up."

"What do you mean, throwing up? Sometimes they get a little sick, eat weeds, throw up."

"I know, but this is sort of green and foamy . . . Aunt Brigid . . . he's starting to breathe funny."

"We're just up the road and we're on our way."

I had pulled the phone away from my ear in preparation for closing it when I heard, "Oh my God, he's jerking around!"

Eleven

We said quick good-byes, drove the short distance home, and came into the house to see Gemma-Kate standing helplessly over one of the Pugs lying in a pool of green vomit. Before either of us could react, the dog went rigid and then jerked into a seizure.

"Oh God," she all but shrieked, "he keeps doing that thing and I don't know how to stop it!" She rocked with her arms wrapped about her as if she didn't trust that her hands could do anything useful.

I ran to the kitchen area and looked at an address we had tacked to the side of the fridge.

"La Cañada and River," I muttered to myself, while Carlo wrapped the sick, now shaking Pug into a towel and handed him to me.

"I'll drive," he said.

Gemma-Kate stood watching us, looking like the best she could do was keep from crying until we were out the door, but I couldn't stop to reassure her just now.

The female dog standing at my side, looking up at me with her buggy eyes like a terrified Elsa Lanchester meeting her new husband, was another matter. "Let her come along," I said to Carlo. The Pugs did everything together.

Carlo picked up the dog and we left, the well Pug whining in the backseat, me in the passenger seat holding the limp Pug in my lap while so much drool ran out of his mouth, through the towel and onto my dress, that it seemed he had to be vomiting it. I passed my finger over the oh-so-soft spot between his eyes and thought the words *Hurry, Carlo, he's dying,* but I didn't say those words. Maybe I said something like "It's okay, Mr. Puggly Wuggly, you'll be okay." I know, it still embarrasses me, too, when I think about it.

The ride took forever and it seemed as if each mile was marked by a further slowing of the dog's breaths. Carlo went at least fifteen miles over the speed limit down Oracle, while I was in charge of cursing at the red lights and hoping if we got pulled over I would know the cop personally. By the time we pulled into the parking lot of the emergency veterinary center I was counting maybe one breath a minute and the dog's body felt boneless, it was so limp.

We ran through automatic sliding doors into a lobby any human hospital would be proud of. The receptionist glanced at the dog, picked up a phone, and shouted, "Triage!" While Carlo signed paperwork, an assistant rushed me into a back room where a vet didn't bother to introduce herself but completed a two-second inspection and said, "Toad. How long ago?"

"I'm not sure."

She had already grabbed the dog and was moving out of the room with me following close behind as she asked, "More than a half hour ago?"

"I don't know."

"How big was it?"

"I didn't see it."

"Did you flush him?"

"I don't understand."

"Activated charcoal probably useless," she muttered, and I felt as if she could as easily have been referring to me. We had entered a small room with a sink next to which she placed the dog. She turned on a faucet with a hose attached and stuck it in the side of the dog's mouth. I almost shouted *no* in horror, but controlled myself and watched the stream pump in one side and out the other. Some no doubt went into his stomach and just a little into his lungs as he coughed and retched and threw up some more.

When she was finished waterboarding my dog she took him into another room and, after shaving a tiny patch on his leg, hooked him up to an IV that the assistant had ready. She got the needle into him without his reacting, watched him for too long as he stabilized, and only then explained what was happening.

"Colorado River toad," she said, as we both finally breathed. "They're deadly, and with all the rain we had over the winter I've seen a few cases, even though it's not quite the season for them yet." The dog was as unresponsive as it had been in the car, the only indication that it was alive a light movement of its rib cage as it took an occasional breath. But it wasn't drooling or seizing anymore. Whatever was in the IV seemed to be working. The vet raised one of the Pug's heavy velvet chops and showed me his gums. "See how pale they are? He's dehydrated from the vomiting."

"Will he be all right?" I said with a wobbly voice that wasn't mine.

"Hopefully between the vomiting and the flushing I gave him we got a lot of the poison out of his system."

"What are his chances?" I whispered, lifting one of his paws and finding no resistance.

The vet put her arm around me and gave me a brief hug like I've never known from a physician. "Excellent chances. Tell you what. Leave him here and we'll continue to give him intravenous fluids to decrease his dehydration."

"There's no antidote?"

"Nothing. If we caught it right after ingestion we could have flushed him with a solution of activated charcoal that absorbs the toxins before they get into the bloodstream. But he'll be okay."

The assistant had shown Carlo into the room while we were talking, and he stood there with the healthy Pug draped over his arm and his other arm draped lightly around my waist.

"He won't die," I told Carlo. I felt like those words made me God and gave me the control that was necessary to do the job I used to do. You can't save everybody, but "This dog won't die."

Gemma-Kate turned on the computer in Brigid's office, keyed in Peter's number. When he answered she didn't ask if he'd been asleep. "Go to your Skype, Peter."

Peter yawned. "Why?"

"I need to see your face while I'm talking to you. It's serious." She waited, then whispered, "Good. I can't sleep. I think I'm in trouble, Peter."

"What happened?"

"Their dog got poisoned."

"Is it dead?"

"I don't think so. They left him at the vet's."

"So why are you in trouble? Did you poison their dog?"

"Not exactly."

"What d'you mean not exactly?"

"It ate a Colorado River toad."

"You fed their dog a Colorado River toad?

Gemma-Kate studied his face. "Okay, yeah. I fucking poisoned their dog. Okay?"

"Because they wouldn't let me come over while they were gone?" He almost looked flattered. "That's extreme."

"It wasn't like that." Gemma-Kate paused, staring at him. She could tell he was trying to tell if she had a bra on underneath her sleep shirt. She was sorry she told him.

"Don't you tell anybody," she said.

Twelve

The next morning when I got up shortly before sunrise I found the other Pug lying with her back pressed up against the door leading to the garage, paws jerking a bit, making little *moofmoof* sounds in her sleep. I woke her from what sounded like a bad dream, and she followed me into the kitchen.

Carlo had left the invoice from the vet on the counter. It specified that the charge of three hundred and twenty-five dollars was for initial treatment and projected costs for three days in the hospital with nursing care. The form listed the Pug's name as Al.

After firing up the first pot of coffee, I grabbed my cell phone off the kitchen counter, and the Pug and I sat together on the back porch watching the sun come up and listening to the coyotes' high-pitched keening in the arroyos behind our property. Two cups later Carlo followed suit. Like any normal teenager, Gemma-Kate slept in. That allowed Carlo and me to have privately a little of the postmortem that only mates can have, a conversation that feels like lazy lobs on a tennis court where no one needs to score points.

"I called the vet," I told Carlo.

"So early?"

"They say they're twenty-four hours, so I took them at their word."

They told me he's stable." I petted the female a bit. "She misses him. I've come to like these guys."

"I like them, too." Carlo gestured at the invoice on the table between us. "At these rates it's a good thing."

"You told them his name is Al?"

"The girl asked, and I was too embarrassed to say we hadn't named him. While you were in having the other guy treated, the girl asked the female's name."

"I can't stand the suspense," I said.

Carlo glanced away with a smile as if he was half embarrassed and half kind of proud of himself. "Peggy."

"Peg the Pug. Al and Peg."

"Well, it's not like they're going to file for Social Security someday. We can always change them. Are you going to call Jacquie Neilsen?"

"I don't want to."

"Why not?"

"Because she's crazy."

"She's not crazy, she's in pain."

"There you go doing that priest-and-the-stray-pup thing."

He made a whining sound.

"Okay, okay, you know I can't stand it when you whimper. I'll call her, I just want to do a little homework before I go over there."

A little while later Gemma-Kate shuffled out in her drawstring pajama bottoms and T-shirt and asked about breakfast.

"What, no crepes?" I asked. If not an apology, seemed like there would be at least that for letting the Pug eat a toad on her watch. Now she just rooted around in the pantry for cereal without speaking, looking more guarded, as if she feared blame would descend without warning.

Thirteen

The Neilsen homework consisted of calling Dr. George Manriquez, a lovely individual first and medical examiner second, who treated the dead as if they were his patients. He told me once that they, or more precisely their flesh, spoke to him more intimately than any of us, the living, are capable of. We were kind of close because we both came from Florida. Florida is a different kind of place.

The eye bank was there removing some corneas for reuse, and it took a while for George to return my call, but when he did he was as helpful as ever. We exchanged a few pleasantries, whether I was okay after a particularly heinous crisis six months before, and what was going on with Laura Coleman. I told him she was staying with her brother in the North Carolina mountains, healing psychologically and physically after working that case with me. She kept in e-mail contact, so I knew she didn't hold me responsible even if that was how I held myself. I asked if he had seen Max Coyote lately, whether he was suffering any residual effects. I didn't ask whether Max had ever submitted that DNA swab he got from me, and Manriquez didn't say. Then I got to the point.

"I'm doing a little work on the death of a fourteen-year-old named

Joseph Neilsen, drowning," I said. I filled him in on a few more of the details to bring him up to speed. "What have you got?"

Computers have made things a lot easier. He didn't have to get up to go to a file cabinet.

"Not much here," he said after a few minutes. "I got a death certificate."

"You sign off?"

"No, it was done before the body arrived at the morgue. Dr. Lari Paunchese."

"Know him?"

"No, but it doesn't take an ME or a coroner to sign off."

"I know, just curious."

"I confirmed cause and manner."

"Death investigator?"

"Sam Humphries. I know him a little. He was green at the time."

"It was only six months ago. He's still green. Why so little information? Didn't you do an autopsy?"

"Not complete. Note here that the father asked me not to do it, would have been too disturbing for the mother, so I did mostly external. But I took some fluid from his lungs to confirm cause of death."

"No bruising, he didn't hit his head on the diving board or something?"

"Mild abrasion on his right zygomatic—"

"English, please."

"Cheekbone. Nothing that would have indicated a blow to the head hard enough to knock him out. I checked that."

"No evidence of autoeroticism?"

"No, why?"

"Rumor going around."

"Nothing but the water in his lungs perimortem confirming drowning."

"What's the blood work show?"

"No tox report here. Could have one, just not posted yet. That's not unusual. They're really backed up, and nobody was pushing."

"You okay that nobody was pushing?"

"You know how it is, Brigid, I'm not the detective, and I'm not Quincy. I call the COD, deliver my report, and advise the investigators whether to pursue the case from there. I know what you're thinking, we should rule it undetermined until all other manners of death have been ruled out. And I think the investigator—I think it was his first case, so he was really thorough, he did a good job. But you have a drowning death in a swimming pool and the chances of it being anything other than an accident are one in three thousand unless you find concrete on the feet. Maybe he took some drugs, but doesn't matter, this has accidental drowning written all over it."

What can I say, I'm a sucker for parents who have lost their children. At least I had something to take to Joseph's mother, to reassure her that a person I trusted had made a good call. After asking George to check on that tox report, I called Jacquie.

A small reedy voice answered, "Tim?" I could tell it was Jacquie. Apparently she either didn't have caller ID or didn't look at the number.

"Mrs. Neilsen, we met briefly last night. I'm Brigid Quinn."

"Yes. Oh. Yes."

"I'm calling to let you know I just talked to the ME. The medical examiner."

"You *talked* to a medical examiner?"

"He's kind of a friend."

"Oh! Can you come over right now?"

Fourteen

On the way over to the Neilsens' I checked in with Mallory via cell to tell her what I'd found out from George Manriquez and thank her for the *lovely* evening. She laughed at me. "Did I tell you I got the call about the Nobel Peace Prize? I'm still licking my wounds. Speaking of licking, what's up with your dog?"

"Vet said he ate a toad."

Immediately veering from quip to sympathy, she gasped. "Oh, that's ghastly. I've heard of animals . . . how did he get it?"

"I'm not sure."

"Didn't Gemma-Kate see him dig it up? They hibernate that way. Or did it jump over your fence and the dog got there before she could stop him? She must be totally heartsick, with her being responsible. Poor child."

I thought of Gemma-Kate that morning, how she looked.

Was there a pause in the conversation just then, another question that came and went without being asked? Or am I misremembering the details again? Did I mention to Mallory that Gemma-Kate did not appear heartsick, or even offer an apology? Or did I just think it?

If there was a pause, I know Mallory heard it. I know we were both thinking the same thing, but she picked up the thread of the conversation again with her usual aplomb, saying all the right things about how it couldn't be helped but that she was sure the Pug would pull through.

"What about Jacquie?" Mallory asked.

"I'm going over there now."

"You realize when I encouraged you last night I was being ironic."

"I got that. But when I talked with the medical examiner there were a few irregularities I'd like to check on. These things happen with equivocal death. Guy pushes his wife down the stairs, kid road-trips her dad who's got dementia and says he must have wandered away . . ."

"Equivocal death. Sounds like Brigid Code for murder. Chilling. I'm chilled."

I laughed. "I'll call you after I talk to her."

I looked at my watch and figured I could delay getting to the Neilsens' long enough to stop by the pet hospital.

The night before I'd been distracted. On arrival today, I noticed the lobby was clean and spare, with those exposed pipes near the ceiling that you find in modern architecture, and current copies of *Your Cat* magazine instead of the usual old issues of *People*.

I had to wait until the receptionist took care of a woman who had come to collect her dog's ashes. The woman reached for the box and held it against her tattered T-shirt formally like a relic in a procession while she walked out, a little dazed.

"May I help you?" the receptionist said with more sympathy than I'd encountered in some intensive care units. She had a long ponytail pulled back severely off her face, like mine, only not white. It was likely she was different from the one the night before. I couldn't remember.

"I'm Brigid DiForenza. I'm here about . . . Al," I said.

Apparently they didn't have a lot of animals staying overnight, because she knew I was talking about the Pug. She called an assistant who took me back to a spacious, well-lit room where my Pug slept. There were other cages, but they were all empty. It didn't appear he minded either being alone or in a cage.

"Do you want me to get him out?" the assistant said, while everything about her body and voice urged me to say no.

"No," I said, "he looks too contented. How is he doing?"

She checked a chart she had brought with her. "He hasn't thrown up since he arrived, and we're continuing to monitor him and keep him hydrated. I would think another twenty-four hours and he should be ready to come home. You just should keep an eye on him in the future. Sometimes they become toad junkies." She pointed to a chair. "Stay as long as you like."

She closed the door behind her. I pulled the plastic chair next to the cage and sat with my Pug a few minutes, reaching my fingers through the mesh of the cage, stroking an unresponsive ear as soft and thick as a wilted rose petal. The pink tip of his tongue stuck out between his black lips.

After trying a faint "Hello, Al," I went quiet. I wasn't used to talking to animals much, so I didn't say anything. When I stood up to leave, the Pug still didn't react. I slipped out of the room, closing the door softly behind me as if that would make a difference, feeling a little dazed, like the woman who left with her pet's ashes.

Over the last couple of years I'd been connecting to the world more than I did when I was with the Bureau, but sometimes I think connecting to the world isn't all it's cracked up to be.

I headed on to the Neilsens', stopping at a drive-through Starbucks on the way.

Fifteen

Tucson is like a stream that runs next to the Catalina Mountains to the north of the city, longer than it is wide. People choose their friends partly based on what part of town they live in. It can take more than an hour to drive from one side of the city to the other. You might see a glimmer of interest in a first conversation sputter out when one person says "east" and the other says "northwest." You're both thinking that driving home after dinner just isn't worth it.

Most of the city flows through the low-lying area, but some of the houses along the stream slosh up onto the sides of the mountains, and this part of town is called the Foothills. It's where the money is.

In my AARP-issue white Toyota Camry, dusty to fit in with the others, designed to make me disappear into the crowd, I wound around a steeply circuitous road that turned out to actually be the Neilsens' driveway.

They had the kind of house where the drive curved under a porte cochere as big as a Holiday Inn, but the more telling thing was the saguaro cacti in the front yard. Saguaro cacti—that's the kind with the arms—grow an inch a year. When you buy them grown, they cost a thousand dollars a foot. The Neilsens had five of them that were twenty feet tall. One of them, that hadn't yet grown arms but jutted rigidly up to the sky, had two big boulders at the base. I wondered if Timothy was a little insecure.

I had to wait a bit for someone to come to the door after I rang the bell that resounded as faintly as a rock dropped into a well. I didn't mind waiting. You may have noticed that I haven't been complaining about the heat. The high that spring day would be under eighty, with twenty percent humidity. Doesn't get any better.

Jacquie opened heavy double doors with low-relief calla lilies carved into them. She smelled like beer. I knew that smell from my own drinking days well enough to tell whether it was old from the night before or new from this morning. This was new beer.

She stood aside to let me in the door and took me through the formal living room without stopping to watch whether I was impressed. After a walk, brief yet something that could definitely be called a walk, we ended up in one of those areas at one with the kitchen. The kind of space that used to be a family room but these days is an entertainment center. She folded into the corner of a couch with her legs tucked under her and gestured at the other end for me.

Her makeup and hair were left over from the night before and hadn't even been reheated. She still hadn't brushed her teeth well. From the way her hair was mashed I could tell she slept on her left side. These are not heartless criticisms. It's just that I've known so many parents who've lost their child, and I note the signs.

"I'm sorry," she said, the first words since she had opened the door. "I was thinking so hard . . . I should . . . have offered . . ."

The pauses in her speech were prolonged in odd places. It was as if, halfway through a sentence, she wanted to talk about something else but lost the nerve.

"Water?" I suggested. People always give each other water in the desert.

"Or coffee?" she said.

I thought of my Starbucks cooling in the car. "That would be even better, actually."

She got up and quickly fixed me one of those single-cup servings that come from a little individual coffee container. She didn't ask if I wanted milk or sugar, but that was fine. In the quiet I detected

72

somewhere the sound of running water, likely a CD with nature sounds, and it made me have to pee. I'm one of those women who has to go to the bathroom on the way to the bathroom. Not wanting to show my age, I did a few Kegels instead of asking for the powder room.

She didn't get anything for herself, which made sense. More beer would have looked bad, and caffeine would have spoiled the effect of the beer. She sat back down on the couch without speaking.

"I'm here to listen," I said. Most people talk. It is the rare person who offers to listen; usually you have to pay someone to do that. So I've found that line is often the best opener to a case.

I was right this time. She was off like the Preakness. Jacquie Neilsen talked for twenty minutes, but she didn't run straight. She had a brain like a rodent, running down one path and then being distracted by a nugget of information that she happened to spot, and running down that path, returning without warning to the topic she'd been on before. I asked questions to try to get her to focus so I could make sense out of what she was saying, but the main gist I could make out was that she loved her son very much and she really really didn't want him to be dead.

That and it had to be someone else's fault besides Joey's. Yes, as Lulu had explained, that was the crux of it. Jacquie would consider accidental homicide from horsing around with a friend who ran away when Joe was in trouble. She'd even take suicide brought about by bullying at school or his stepfather's rejection of his sexual orientation. The only thing she couldn't take was the thought of Joey's senseless death due to drowning while he was masturbating off the side of the pool. Not her son. No, no, and no.

The loops of her conversation got tighter and tighter until all she was left with was that no. Then she got up from the couch and went to a fireplace big enough to spit-roast an elk. A shrine had been set up on the mantel. All of the school photos of a fair-haired Joe, from sweetly smiling first grader through sullen eighth grader with a zit the size of a blueberry on his chin, were lined up. Surrounding them were his crafts: A fruit bowl made of glazed clay with all the little fruits painted to look realistic. A gecko-looking thing made out of seashells. A rock with a cartoon face painted on it. A framed water-color of a house and a family of three. These things looked at odds with the tastefully understated decor of the rest of the house.

Jacquie took a pirate-chest-looking sort of box from the mantel, brought it back to the couch, and opened it before me as if I would see jewels. "He had a happy childhood. See, look at all the cards he made for me," she said. She pulled them out one at a time, a valentine decorated with tissue carnations, a watercolor of a prickly pear cactus with pink blossoms along the ridges. "Joey was always very creative," she said.

The memorabilia continued with handmade cards and little pieces of art and found objects all the way up to the time he died, continuing into the teenage years when you'd expect he would start to detach from Mom. "Do you have any practical effects?" I asked. "Wallet, photographs, calendar, cell phone?"

She was about to answer. The house was so big you couldn't hear the front door open, but we both heard purposeful steps on tile. Jacquie may have jumped a little when she heard it, as if we'd been caught by Dad doing something naughty. I thought of that woman in the shelter again. I made a mental note to watch Jacquie more carefully for other signs of fear. Whatever her feelings, I noticed the too-wide smile from the night before stretching her lips as Timothy strode into the room and offered his hand to me. He didn't look at his wife to appreciate her smile.

Sixteen

"Brigid," he said, without adding anything about what a nice surprise.

"Dr. Neilsen," I said.

"It's still Tim," he smiled, which came across more as a grimace. He glanced at the coffee table in front of the couch, noted my empty cup. "Brigid might like a refill," he said to Jacquie. Now he kissed her on the cheek while she murmured apologies. He had missed her smile because she couldn't hold it that long without looking demented.

"No, I'll do it." He carried my cup into the kitchen-area section of the great room. "I'm having one, too," he said without asking what flavor I wanted, popping another little self-contained package into the brewer and pressing the button.

Jacquie had ducked her head and seemed ill disposed for further conversation at this point, so I turned a bit to observe Tim working in the kitchen. He went into a cabinet, took out a prescription pill container, opened it, and glanced inside without knowing he was watched. Was he counting Jacquie's meds to see what condition she was in? I looked away. It only took a few more moments for him to fix two coffees. He added cream to his, handed me a mug, and went to sit down in a chair close by. He had come in relaxed, but that was already dissipating.

During all this Jacquie had kept her head low, looking over some of Joe's works of art. I got the sense she did that a lot. Now she looked up at Tim. Her mouth went straight and her jaw thrust up and out in a blink of defiance. "How was your golf game?" she asked late, showing how little she cared.

He pretended she did. "Racquetball. Larry whipped my ass," he said.

It didn't take any great intuition to see that Tim guessed my presence had something to do with their troubles, and that he wasn't liking it. I could feel lines being drawn in the marital sand, both of them daring the other to cross. Someone had to speak, so I did. "Mrs. Neilsen wanted to talk to me in my capacity as a private investigator, about your son," I said. "I know some people, and I know how to get answers that you don't have."

A light, not pleased but enlightened, went on in Tim's eyes as he said drily, "You mean, just like on TV."

"Brigid is an FBI agent," Jacquie said.

"Retired," I said.

"I heard," Tim said.

"She wants to find out what really happened to Joey," Jacquie said, though I had said nothing of the kind. She made it sound like I had forced this meeting on her. The defiance had gone as quickly as it had come, pleading now in her eyes.

I watched them lock in silent battle while I sipped my coffee to make it look like I wasn't watching them. Even without having been in a relationship for most of my life, I still couldn't mistake the kind of intimate warfare that only comes with marriage. I would have bet the farm that Tim would win, that Jacquie hadn't enough will to stand up to the force of her husband, but I was wrong.

Tim put his coffee mug on the table next to his chair. He closed his eyes. When he opened them they were glistening. He had given her this round. You just never know with people. I noticed for the first time how blue his eyes were, and how the watery sheen made them look like melting ice. But he didn't touch her now, hardly looked in her direction. I remembered how attentive he had been the evening of the fund-raiser, how he had kissed her hand, had put his over hers, and how he might save that attention for times when it would be seen by more people. Perhaps this would be one of those men not given to private displays of affection.

"Jaq," he said. He turned to me. "We've talked about this before," he said. "Many times."

"Well, since I'm here, and I'm not quite finished with my coffee yet, would you like to talk a little more?"

Jacquie looked to Timothy to begin, but he sat with his mouth in a straight line, resisting. So she started again, telling me everything they must have told the police six months ago, repeating some of what she said when I first arrived and adding some new information. How Joey had seemed to be leading a relatively happy life until he hit his teens. How they had joined St. Martin's in the Fields and were so happy to have found the youth group because Joey didn't make many friends at school. Like Gemma-Kate, I thought, and wondered what else he might have in common with her. Science, I found.

"Joseph talked to me about going into medicine, and we talked about the different fields. He was interested in neurology, maybe research," Tim said, apparently warming to the subject despite himself, or else wanting to show me he knew something about his stepson just like a real father would.

"He wasn't really interested," Jacquie said. "Joey just told you those things hoping you wouldn't hate him because he was gay."

Man the torpedo stations. Stupid Jacquie, that's no way to get what you want.

Tim carefully kept his face turned in my direction, answering Jacquie's accusation without addressing it. I wondered how much or little they actually knew about her son, and how much they really knew about themselves. He smiled before he spoke, but not at Jacquie. The smile wasn't quite in sync with what he said next.

"Has Jacquie told you yet that I found Joe's body? Did she tell you how I dragged him out of the pool and called nine-one-one? Did she tell you yet how I was grilled over and over by a death investigator until I felt like I was being accused of murdering my stepson? I don't suppose you know what it's like to be on the other side of the law, do you, Brigid? To be suspected of killing someone."

"No," I said. Everybody lies.

"Did she tell you they even made me give them the clothes I was wearing when I went into the pool, as if they might be evidence? No, Brigid. We did everything the right way. We followed procedure. We cooperated," Tim said, plaintively, as if life was rational and orderly, as if there was a right and wrong way to process a boy's death if you knew how to plead just right. He seemed to be saying that the universe was now expected to do its part and operate his way. I wanted to respond that I had not yet suggested they did anything inappropriate or illegal. But I stayed quiet for now.

"If you're curious," and his tone suggested that's what I must be and it was distasteful to him, "you can read the official reports. I'm sure that investigator wrote it all down and it's on file somewhere. Somebody like you should be able to get it. Frankly, when you look over the paperwork I think you'll agree there's nothing more to be done," Tim said.

"That's not what she's been saying at all," Jacquie said, crossing her arms over her stomach.

"I don't think we should do this," Tim said. The words were spoken singly, as if he was hoping they would exert sufficient power without communicating why. Was it that he couldn't say it in front of me or couldn't say it at all?

"Why not?" Jacquie asked, and I had to admit I was beginning to ask the same question. "Are you afraid you'll have to give back the life insurance money if Joey committed suicide?"

Blam, another shot fired across Tim's bow. For a mouse, she was very talented at the Who's Afraid of Virginia Woolf zinger, Jacquie was. Tim shot her an angry glance. She had pushed him past politeness. "Honestly, because I said we had done everything." He turned to me. It's interesting how people confuse professional investigators with confessors. Things they wouldn't say to just anyone come out. "We've done the church route, and shrinks. She's been to fortune tellers, for God's sake."

"They're psychics," Jacquie said.

"And talk about hedging your bets. She had me pay for the new air conditioner at the church we're attending now. Like that would bring Joe back. Like God is a heating and air contractor who operates on trade." He turned back in her direction. "Truthfully, that didn't make you feel better either, did it?"

He was losing his cool. I felt uncomfortable in the middle of what was escalating into a domestic. There was a poker by the fireplace but no knives in view.

"But I need to know what happened." Jacquie reached both her hands in my direction as if I she was going under and I was a flotation device. "I was so stupid. Something was going on with Joey and I didn't know and if I knew I could have stopped it, or done something differently. But there's something I don't know. Mothers sense these things. Maybe you can find it." She seemed to hold her breath waiting for my answer.

Tim was holding his, too, and something about that pissed me off a little, so I said, "Here's what I can do. I know people and I know what questions to ask. Sometimes I can get answers that regular people can't. I'll find out if there's anything at all you haven't been told. Maybe there's nothing else to know. Maybe then I can refer you to a support group. Maybe then you can begin to heal."

Jacquie wasn't willing to let it rest. "There was never a blood test done. You know, to see if he was poisoned."

"I spoke with the ME, the medical examiner. He said he took blood and sent it to the lab, but he doesn't have a report back."

"See what I mean? It's been six months! Don't you think there's something suspicious about that?"

"I know this sounds awful, but it happens that way sometimes. There's no conspiracy." I didn't mention that Manriquez told me Tim asked him not to do an autopsy, that it would disturb his wife. It didn't sound right now like that would have been the actual case. Jacquie sounded like she might have demanded one if she'd been given the chance. So I gave her some of the truth now.

"Whether or not there was any controlled substance in your son's blood, the medical examiner would still have ruled it an accidental death. They might have kept the blood samples, but if the tests haven't

79

been done by now, the blood would have metabolized any foreign substance, eaten it, if you will. There wouldn't be anything to find."

Jacquie said, "What about exhuming his body and running more tests?"

I explained a little about how only certain poisons, such as arsenic, gravitated to the tissues, bones, and hair, that in the course of embalming all the blood is removed so for something like prescription, street drugs, or alcohol, there wouldn't be any evidence left even without the metabolism.

"Well, what about arsenic?" Jacquie said, nodding so vigorously she appeared to want to influence my head to do the same.

As she spoke I glanced at Tim to see how he was reacting to all this. He stood up as tall as he could to get the most out of his average height. Jacquie stood up and got between him and me. I never had a child, but I knew that a woman who would never stand up for herself would get between a mountain lion and her kid. Tim took his car keys out of his shorts pocket. "My wife is a huge fan of those *CSI* shows," he said. "But I guess this show's over. Excuse me, I've got some running around to do." Then he left.

He was right about the show. You could tell it was a script they had rehearsed before, probably often. They used to ask me how I could work among the criminal element, encounter evil without being broken by it. Well, the fact is we all get broken by it. We're the walking wounded, dealing with the trauma through drugs, alcohol, sex, or psychiatry. Lucky for me I found Carlo rather than wind up like the Neilsens. I find myself more stunned by this cruel sadness than by the most heinous serial killer. It takes you by surprise no matter how much you know it's the human condition, just under the surface everywhere.

Seventeen

Jacquie turned to me, more spent than triumphant, yet when she spoke her voice was surprisingly steady. "I still don't understand why they didn't do a toxicological test. They can do those in twenty-four hours, can't they?"

"Oh, Jacquie." Seeing her desperation to create information where there was none, seeing how she was all alone in her need, made me want to help her more. "It really isn't like on TV. They don't just press a button marked Poison and the answer comes out. They have to test for all kinds of things."

She protested, "I know that already."

"And they get backed up. There are some larger jurisdictions that have literally thousands of DNA samples waiting for analysis. Even here in Tucson they prioritize. And the medical examiner felt one hundred percent this was an accident."

"I can pay you," she said. "I have my own account that Tim gives me."

I said that wasn't the point, but if she insisted on hiring me I charged one hundred and fifty dollars per hour with a five-hundred-dollar retainer. For that I would do some preliminaries, make sure that the investigation had been thorough, make a list of people who should have been interviewed, and let her know if I discovered anything. I asked her about whether she had found a support group, but she ignored me on that point, too.

Jacquie left the room and came back with a check for a thousand dollars and a more recent picture she had of the three of them, full size rather than portrait. Joe was slight, and in this picture dark like Jacquie, hair nearly the same length and color. No similarity to his stepfather, of course; Tim's contrasting paleness made him look something like a ghost in the background. Joe was toasting the camera with a plastic water bottle, and one of those smiles that people call ironic. His eyes squinted in the bright sun. He stood between his parents with his arm around his mother, a line of light between himself and his stepfather. "A handsome young man," I said.

"It was about five months before he died," she said. "We had just dropped him off for a youth group hike in Sabino Canyon, when the weather was still nice. The pictures were posted on the St. Martin's Facebook page. I printed it."

"Is the lighting different? His hair looks so much darker here than in the younger pictures you showed me. I would have guessed he was a blond, but sometimes that happens as children age."

Jacquie looked at it fondly. "No, he had just done his hair the same color as mine. It was a funny Mother's Day present. So people could see he was proud we were mother and son."

God forbid someone should mistake him for his stepfather's child, I thought, but said, "Is his biological father fair?"

Jacquie nodded, looking a little sadder, but still staring at the photo.

I said, "You don't mind parting with this one?"

She shook her head no.

We spent some more time talking about all the details she knew of Joe Neilsen's life, whether he got good grades, whether he was the sort of kid to get into trouble, again whether he had any friends—male or female—part-time job, credit card accounts, a learner's permit. The answer to everything was a listless no. "We tried to get him involved with different things, like with the youth group at St. Martin's, but he was more of a solitary boy. Wasn't very interested in things outside the house."

"How comfortable were you and he with his sexual orientation?" I asked.

"The Manwarings told you," Jacquie stated with a frown. "I could tell when you didn't react to what I said to Tim. It could have just been a phase, you know? Experimental, right? He could have been wrong."

Noting to myself that she hadn't answered my question, I put an information form on the coffee table for her to fill out when she had a chance to look up some numbers and maybe remember other facts. I could spend a lot of time on this, but there were ways to prioritize the fact-finding, too. "Who did the death investigation?" I said. "Metro?"

"Do you mean the police? I have a card he gave me. But I only saw him once. He really didn't do anything. There was no investigation." Jacquie had it ready, having assumed I would want it. I looked at the card. Sam Humphries.

"I'll talk to him," I said. I would find out if George Manriquez was right about Humphries being thorough. "The ME said there was no autopsy performed."

"Not . . . a whole one. Tim said it wasn't necessary, and he said the medical examiner agreed." Jacquie rubbed her face hard with both hands. "His body was removed, pronounced dead. Funeral at St. Martin's. That was the last time I was there. It all went so fast it's hard to remember what actually happened. It's as if . . ."

"You haven't yet been able to feel that Joe is actually gone," I finished for her, going into my head where there were other times, other parents.

Jacquie opened her mouth and blew out all her air in one rush, my words punching her in the gut. I regretted them, but there was nothing I could do to soften the moment. She nodded. "He's in his room," she whispered, as if he could hear us talking.

"Would you be able to show me?"

Jacquie stood up, and I followed her for another walk, this time up a curving stairway that started in the living room, down a long hallway. It was one of those spaces littered with framed photographs, but I locked in on one of them. It was of all the Neilsens, costumed as the Marx Brothers. They had let Joe be Groucho, a diminutive boy with the glasses, nose, and mustache. He even had a cigar. Tim was Chico, an embarrassed smile, a brown wig under that funny coned cap. And Jacquie as Harpo, in a blond curly wig and openmouthed grin, pretending to blast a bicycle horn in Joey's ear. That was all it took to see why Tim loved, or had once loved, her.

We kept on to a closed door. Jacquie forced herself to open it, revealing a typical boy's bedroom done up in brown and forest green. Lots of electronics; I couldn't tell whether Joe was particularly spoiled or this was just what young people's rooms looked like these days.

From beneath the corduroy bedspread a sheet peeked that had cowboy boots with spurs on it. Either Jacquie was still buying sheets with cowboys for a fourteen-year-old, or she was thrifty and the sheets were so good they'd never worn out. At any rate, it was all nicely masculine. I stepped inside and looked around, trying to notice details that others might have missed. The only detail I could see was that there were none. Someone had cleaned well. I bet I wouldn't even find a candy wrapper under the bed.

I turned around, but Jacquie hadn't followed. She stood at the door of the bedroom and tentatively pointed with a limp index finger at the adjoining bathroom doorway.

"Did the investigator go through this area of the house? Look for missing towels that might have been used to clean up water?"

Jacquie shook her head. "He came up here. I don't remember much. I was sitting on the couch downstairs."

So whatever she told me just now was useless. I walked into the bathroom. It was done in that dark stone tiling that hides the dirt but not the calcium buildup from the hard water. No towels hung on the towel rods, and no half-used soap rested on the sink. The sturdy frame over the door to the shower would have made a fine place for a strangling. I opened the glass door, reached up overhead to grasp the frame with both hands, and let my body sag. That was the only thing I touched. Yes, a fine place for a strangling. If I was going to commit suicide I'd do it here, with some pills, not drown myself.

The quiet was so complete, the shower door closed with what felt like a bang. I came back out of the bathroom to find Jacquie still at the bedroom door, her eyes down and to the left, looking at the carpet.

I asked, "Did you see him? After?"

"In the pool, you mean? No, Tim got home first that night." Jacquie paused, breathed. "I stayed late at my book club."

"Did Tim call you there?"

"He said he thought I was at the movies and had my cell off. He said he was in shock and wasn't thinking straight. By the time I got home Joey was already at the morgue. Tim is very efficient that way. He never misses garbage day, either. He always knows when pickup is off by a day. Due to holidays."

Finally undone by what even she would admit was crazily trivial, she sucked in another huge breath and let it out in a sob. I reached my hand out but, cringing from my touch as if she wasn't worthy of comfort, she sagged against the bedroom doorjamb.

"Joey's father showed up at the funeral, not like he'd been involved much up to that point. He just wanted to come and tell me it was all my fault."

In that moment I could tell that part of her reason for blaming everyone else was that she blamed herself, for staying too late at that fucking book club, sipping that third fucking glass of wine. Oh, those goddamn what-ifs, how they haunt us.

"Did Joseph's father pay child support?"

"Not much. He doesn't make the money that Tim does."

"What does he do?"

"I think he's selling cars." So she traded in a car salesman for a doctor, and ended up with a dead son. Not that I was jumping to the conclusion that Tim had done something, that was just the sum of things. I could tell she was thinking along the same lines when she said, "You know, at first I wanted to keep the peace and went along with everything Tim said. But, you know, talking to you just now makes me realize if I can't have Joey I don't much care about keeping Tim."

Tim probably knew that already, before Jacquie did. You can take

85

a woman like Jacquie Neilsen and assume she's just crazy with grief. It looked like everyone had done that, from her husband to Detective Sam Humphries, who investigated the death.

The fact was, I could understand people losing patience with someone who couldn't accept the answers, but I couldn't blame her for questions she had that were never answered. And if there were no answers, maybe she would be contented with knowing that. Maybe that's all it would take, a lot of time and a little knowledge that something had been done and all the questions asked.

"How long have you been married?"

"Twelve years. Joey's father left us when he was two. Then I developed this muscle pain and went to Tim as a patient. He diagnosed me with fibromyalgia. We started dating, and he seemed to want us both."

"Seemed?"

Jacquie shook her head and went tearier. She looked like she was in danger of beginning to either cry or loop again, and I wasn't sure either of us could take any more of that for the time being.

"How's the fibromyalgia?" I asked to change the subject.

"It went away for a while, now it's back."

Maybe that was the medication Tim had given her. "Are you okay to show me the pool area?"

She nodded, and we went back downstairs, through the family room slash entertainment center, and out some sliding glass doors to the back patio.

The pool was big and curvy with rocks positioned around it to make sort of a grotto effect. A slide curved down between them. "That's amazing what they can do with those fake rocks," I said.

I could feel her bristle. "They're not fake," she said. You never disparage an Arizonan's rocks, even a person preoccupied by her son's death. "Tim had the pool put in when we got married. Said it was for Joey, but I never thought he really liked him."

I thought of that Marx Brothers photograph. I thought if Tim didn't like Joey at least he tried. I scuffed my shoes on the patio surface, nice flagstones that would absorb the water without getting slippery.

There was no cement lip on the pool, more of a tile rim that went straight to water. That you could slip on.

"And you didn't see anything," I said.

"No. Like I told you, he was already at the morgue by the time I got home."

"Jacquie, hard question here, but I have to ask them. Do you know if Joe ever consumed alcohol?"

She looked at me and I was surprised to see a little hatred in the look. "The investigator asked me that, too." But she didn't answer yes or no.

As she was letting me out the front door, though, she said, "Joey didn't masturbate, either."

I thought that was an odd thing to mention at parting; "good-bye" always works so much better. I wondered if she had heard some of the rumors about falling into the pool during autoerotic ecstasy. But I could go with this line. I just had to ask and try to keep the same emphasis on every word so it wouldn't sound sarcastically like *what the hell, lady, everybody masturbates.* "How would you be able to tell?"

Jacquie half-mumbled, "I . . . I would have seen something. His underwear. His sheets. I would have known."

I bet she would. I had the feeling anything touching the son's privates were inspected pretty thoroughly on wash day, and Jacquie didn't have the maid do it. It occurred to me that his pants might have been down because in his parents' absence he was pissing into the pool, but I didn't say that either.

I left the Neilsens' place with the picture of Joe Joey Joseph and a copy of his death certificate, which was the only official record of the event other than the program for the funeral that Jacquie had. Even though there was nothing much here, I felt kind of a buzz, the kind that comes with a new case when everything is questions and there are as yet no answers. A blank slate kind of feeling where there's everywhere to go and every kind of possibility. It would be easy to make the same assumptions as everyone else, but that wouldn't serve Jacquie.

Tim. There were a few too many honestlies and truthfullies and franklies in his conversation. Interrogators will tell you that when suspects sprinkle those words through their dialogue it means they're hiding something. Was Tim lying about something? Did he perhaps know some truth about his son that he was keeping from Jacquie? And what made him come home when I was there? If he knew, who told him?

Coffee drinkers understand that it becomes not so much a matter of how much caffeine you need, but how much you can tolerate. Feeling a little jangly but assuming I could stand even more, I called Mallory and asked if she wanted to meet me at the Einstein's Bagels where I happened to be stopped at a red light. She told me she couldn't leave Owen just then but I should stop by.

"Anything exciting?" she asked.

"I've decided to go ahead and investigate Joe Neilsen's death. I want to know what you know about them."

"What's to investigate?"

"I'm getting creepy vibes about the Neilsens."

"The Neilsens? Oh, come on. Maybe you need to have your vibe meter tuned."

I laughed, headed back up Oracle, and turned right on Hardy.

Eighteen

The single-story Hollinger home was homier than the Neilsens' but even more secluded. The side of Pusch Ridge rose dramatically right behind the house, and there was a public hiking trail next to it that started at the road below and ran practically through her side yard.

It was the two-hundred-foot drive up to the house, though, that got your attention. With a slight curve at, I'm not exaggerating, a forty-five-degree angle, you had to put the car in second gear going down. Once you got to the top you couldn't see neighbors, though there was one off a little to the south of the house, cleverly hidden because it was halfway down the hill that the Hollinger house dominated. The view from the front was a clear shot across the wide valley that only stopped at the Tortolita Mountains fifteen miles away.

Inside, Mallory's elegant style was all over the place. Bay windows with a mountain out back. Ten-foot-tall sliding glass doors off the master bathroom that you could open onto the patio when you were taking a bath. A swimming pool with a small waterfall, though no slide like the Neilsens had. But that sort of thing.

Mallory had told me she was a trust fund baby from someone who made their money with the British tabloids. She went into the art business for the fun and society, she said, and couldn't seem to stop making money. She had a gallery in New York, then one in Boca Raton and one in Shaker Heights in succession. While she had sold her last gallery upon retiring out to Tucson with Owen, she had kept some of the art. There was nothing of the Southwest here, no blond wood furniture or Native American themes. Along with the furniture that could have come from a Park Avenue condo, stark and spare, she was into the modern stuff, Picasso, Rothko, Miró, and that's just what you saw on the way from the front door to the kitchen. I wasn't familiar with all of the artists, but I could read the signatures and they looked like first string.

Mallory Hollinger had wasted no time getting to know Tucson society by joining the symphony and regional theater groups, so she already knew the people who might associate with the Neilsens. I figured gossip was as good a start to my investigation as any, and besides, I could always use some girl talk, which I'd grown to enjoy. Turns out she knew little more than I thought she would.

Annette, Owen's home health care nurse, met me at the front door. With one of those little brunette hair helmets that's good for sports or a busy life, she had a body one describes as taut, like a circus tent, or a barracks bed. Big hands like a man. She had to be that way to toss her patients around the way she did. I liked her because she never acted like Owen or Mallory had cause to feel sorry for themselves.

"Hey, Brigid, how're ya doin?"

"Just fine. How's Owen today?"

"We were just about to turn him and give him some lunch. Come on back."

I followed her into the master bedroom. The distinctive smell of air freshener covering disinfectant covering human sickness grew as we approached what was actually a working hospital room.

It was large, as were all the rooms in the house, with a king-sized platform bed built low to the floor. Shelves of supplies were nearby. A top-of-the-line monitor that constantly read all of Owen's vital signs stood to the left of the bed, against the wall. A small bookcase was crammed with printouts of Internet articles, articles ripped from journals, and weighty medical references, the textured covers stamped with titles like *Neurology, Ninth Edition* that seemed to imply the author knew everything about the topic that could be known, and much of the rest as well. Most of the covers were black, navy blue, or burgundy, with one that stuck out because it was pumpkin orange. Other than that, the collection looked like something you'd see in a doctor's office.

Mallory slept next to Owen every night. The mattress was one of those mechanical things that could be positioned in various ways like a hospital bed. Now his side was up at the back and a little at his knees. Owen stared out at a group of photographs on the wall at the foot of his bed, taken from their happier past. One of Mallory and Owen in a dramatic dance pose with a thinner Mallory showing off an Audrey Hepburn neck, taken during what she had described as a Tango Tour of Argentina. The two of them standing amid a flock of penguins. Another on a vast black lava bed, their figures so tiny you had to guess it was them.

Mallory reclined in the opposite direction from Owen, head to toe, massaging the instep on his foot while she read to him. It wasn't likely that he could feel her touch on his foot. I knew what they were reading, *Moby-Dick*, because they'd been at it for a while. I don't know who picked that book or why. Mallory was somehow aware I was standing behind her, but held up a finger so she could keep reading to the end of the chapter. The only other sound in the room came from the rhythmic *foosh* of his ventilator.

It gave me a moment to watch them together, alone. It was odd how sharing something outside themselves could have such a feeling of intimacy that I felt privileged to witness it. They seemed to me at the time a complex couple, or perhaps it's just that all marriages are a singularity. They had traveled, and danced, before the freak accident on a train track that almost cost Mallory her life and damaged Owen's brain stem so severely that nothing worked but his organs and eyes, looking out of a body that had a fancy medical term but was more easily known as "locked in."

Mallory doted on Owen, yet flirted as well. I could see it the first time I met her, the way she peered at Carlo, whom she had just met, and at the gala the other night, the way she fell into Adrian Franklin and then double-handed his hand when he helped her up. Men, women, children, and animals, those extra pounds she hated seemed to drip off her when she was engaged in her favorite sport.

I brought this up to her once, when we were having one of our brutally honest conversations. "Do you even realize how flirtatious you are?" I once said.

"Ah, that. I'm good at it, aren't I?" She looked a little sad, and I imagined her thinking of a life after Owen when she said, "It's all innocent. Maybe I do it just to stay in practice."

Early on I took her for a saint, before the honest earthiness caught up with the piety. At the time I thought here was someone I could look up to, a woman I could use as a pattern for my own search for myself.

"Look, sweetie, it's Brigid!" Mallory sat up, closed the book, and put it on the table next to the bed. Owen had already spotted me, though, and fluttered his eyelids in greeting.

"Do you want to turn him now or wait?" Annette asked. I jumped a little, surprised that I was so caught up with watching the Hollingers I hadn't noticed Annette come up behind me. That was unlike me. Maybe I was becoming more and more unlike me.

"Brigid doesn't mind." Mallory turned to me. "Make yourself at home."

I had done this enough in the past months to make myself comfortable in an overstuffed armchair a discreet distance from the bed. If Mallory hadn't originally been strong enough to roll Owen over by herself, she had gained the strength over the past year. But when Annette was there she welcomed the help. I knew this had to be done to prevent bedsores and pneumonia. Mallory had refused to let Owen languish in a nursing home, said that was for poor people.

While Annette busied about, replacing Owen's urine bag and giving him lunch through his feeding tube, Mallory sat on the side of the bed, shielding him from my sight out of respect for his dignity. She liked to do it this way, having me in the room so Owen could be a part of the conversation. She reached for a small jar of Vaseline on the table on her side of the bed, took off the lid and reached in with the finger on the same hand, and rubbed it over his lips. Then she rubbed some into his arms that rested on top of the covers.

While the two of them worked on Owen I asked, "What do you know about Joseph Neilsen?"

"As I made painfully clear last evening, the one I know nothing about is Jacquie." Mallory pushed the top onto the Vaseline jar and put it back on the table. "You know, Brigid, my mother always told me if I saw someone crazy coming down the walk I should cross to the other side of the street. Do you need the money that badly?"

"Oh, it isn't the money. It's just that you get tired of investigations that hinge on jealousy and greed. If I can get real answers for all of Jacquie's questions, maybe it will make her not so crazy."

Mallory looked dubious. "So tell me how your dog is."

"I went over to the vet's and visited him this morning. He doesn't look too good."

"What about the toad? Where did he get it?"

"I don't know." I hadn't thought any more about the toad, but now I thought about how these questions, and my answer, echoed those at the vet clinic.

"Were the dogs just in your backyard or did Gemma-Kate take them somewhere?"

"She was supposed to stay at home with them. She didn't say they took a walk or anything."

"You've got those bougainvilleas in the backyard. Things hide under them. Did you see any part of the toad?"

"No."

"Strange."

"Why?"

"Some of those toads are bigger than your dog. You'd think there would have been toad bits in your backyard. You should check. The other dog might lick them. What do you know about Colorado River toads?"

"Hardly anything. Except that they can poison a dog."

"You should google it."

There were TV trays set up in Owen's bedroom, and Annette brought us some lunch, a nice bowl of what Mallory called cassoulet and I called soup, with Parmesan cheese grated over the top. She let me use the master bathroom first, and not a moment too soon, I mentioned.

"You need to do Kegels while you're driving. It helps a lot," she said when I returned.

"It's just the coffee. Sometimes I get the feeling I'm just renting it."

We talked about Joe, and she reiterated how little she knew. Except for one detail. Once or twice before he died he had come over to read to Owen.

Mallory lifted her head and blew a little puff of air to the side like a person does when they're smoking and want to keep it away from you. She had given up smoking some years before but kept this part of the habit. It was the way you could tell she was thinking hard. "It was just a little disagreeable to me, because in one sense I felt like the church youth group was using Owen as a ministry"—she grimaced at the word—"a *project*, and it felt like Joe was dragged over here. But beyond that I didn't mind so much. Everyone benefited. Even Tim Neilsen, who could have Jacquie to himself for a while every Tuesday evening." She turned to Owen. She never talked about Owen as if he wasn't there. "And you liked hearing a different voice, didn't you?"

Owen blinked once. That meant yes. Two meant no.

Annette brought in two cups of coffee without asking, handed one to me and one to Mallory, who gestured to put it on the table next to the bed. Annette looked at the vitals monitor and commented that Owen's blood pressure was up a bit.

"Should I go?" I asked. "Is my being here too much for you?" I spoke directly to Owen the way Mallory and Annette did, and he blinked twice. Slow blinks that I knew meant an emphatic no. Annette put some extra medication into his IV. Then she put some drops into his eyes. She took away our empty soup bowls. Annette was like that, sort of disappearing so you didn't think of her, but appearing when something was needed. She was live-in, there most of the time, with her own room close by.

I noticed one of the photographs on the wall, one that might have been taken by Owen of Mallory in a particularly adventurous pose. I had always wondered and never thought to ask until now. "Is that a real crocodile?"

"Alligator, actually," she said, not bothering to look at the picture. "You've never talked about how one investigates something. Where do you start?"

I got the sense that she was focused on Owen now, and I should leave, so I gave the short answer. "Jacquie is so troubled. If I can just make it look like someone really cares what happened to her son, maybe that will help. It shouldn't be too hard. Seems like everything was slapdash. No autopsy. And she's talking about having the body exhumed. I don't know what that would accomplish, but I think it's best to discourage it."

Mallory turned from watching Owen's chest rise and fall with the machine that pumped air into his lungs. "Exhumed? Didn't I tell you she was crazy?"

"Why?"

"I was at the funeral and interment. Joe's body was cremated. I saw the urn."

There was no body to exhume. Joe's flesh would remain ever silent, would never speak to George Manriquez. No wonder Tim had left the house so abruptly.

I figured I'd be in competition with *CSI*. I'd have to explain you can't analyze ashes.

Nineteen

After talking some more about just how crazy Jacquie Neilsen might be and what I should do about it, I went home, tossed my tote bag by the counter in the kitchen, and planned to settle into a typical evening with a book and dinner. I was in the middle of a Jack Reacher. Carlo was reading Martin Buber's *I and Thou* for about the fourth straight time. When I asked him why he was doing that he said he hadn't gotten everything out of it on the first three go-rounds.

"Where's Gemma-Kate?" I asked him, thinking to offer to help with whatever she had planned for dinner.

"She's in your office. With Peter," Carlo added.

"Peter. In my office."

I walked in on them sitting in front of my computer, their backs to me, hunched.

"Hi," I said.

Peter jumped a little as if he was used to being caught at something, but Gemma-Kate turned to look at me with the chipper smile used exclusively for another generation.

"Remember Peter?" she said.

I smiled back with my own Mrs. Brady chipperness though annoyed by Gemma-Kate treating me like I had a bad memory.

"Why, of course I do! Peter," I purred. "Could I see you a minute, Gemma-Kate? Would you excuse us, Peter?"

He looked baffled by our excessive courtesy, but nodded as if I was actually asking him for permission. Gemma-Kate and I walked out of the office but not so far, and at such an angle, that I couldn't keep my eye on the boy.

"Um, that's my business office. Even outside the locked file cabinets there can be things I don't want strangers to see. Off-limits, okay?"

"Okay. We'll leave."

I stopped her another second, drew her out of his earshot. "What are you guys doing?"

"Looking at stuff on the Internet."

"What kind of stuff?"

"School assignment. I'm just helping him out with a biology class. He's not stupid, but I've got a couple IQ points on him." Gemma-Kate appeared to be amused. "Or do you want to interrogate him yourself?"

I said, "Maybe." I walked into the room, where the kid had stood up. Whether he did so to block the screen with his body I couldn't tell. I pulled aside the chair that Gemma-Kate had been using, one from the dining room set, and sat down, inviting Peter to do the same. "Could we get you something to drink, Peter?" I did my best to get the tone soft enough without it turning oily the way most adults do with teenagers.

He shook his head without thanks. But he wasn't running away. I said, "I met your mom at church."

That not being a question, he apparently felt no need to confess that yes, he had a mother. I said, "What school do you go to?"

"Pima," he said.

"That's the one on La Cholla, right?"

"Yeah."

"Your school is pretty big, isn't it?"

"I guess. I've never been to another one."

"What grade are you in?"

"I'm a senior."

"You know any of the freshmen there?"

"Not really."

"What about St. Martin's? Did you know Joe Neilsen?"

He couldn't stop a suspicious glance, narrowing his eyes like he thought he knew where this was going. "No. Not really." Peter answered that question faster.

"No, or not really?"

"Not really."

I had him now. "I thought you were in the same youth group?"

"Aunt Brigid," Gemma-Kate said, a warning in her tone.

Peter didn't answer, knowing Gemma-Kate had his back. I had a flicker of bad feeling about this kid, thinking about what his own mother had mentioned about getting into scrapes. Maybe cops' kids shouldn't hang out together. Maybe some alchemy could be at work and the chain reactions could come fast. Trouble, in short.

But not today. Peter left without either of them complaining, and Gemma-Kate and I made a meat loaf outside of my usual repertoire, a German-style one with sauerkraut and Swiss cheese. Having only expanded to ten dinners that I cooked in rotation, I encouraged her with praise. Later she helped me clean up, too, scrubbing the pan where the cheese had stuck to it.

I felt good. Hell, I remember feeling absolutely euphoric, a little happy hum inside my head. Hopeful for the Pug and Gemma-Kate alike, I even gave her a small hug when the dishes were dried and put away. We retired to our various chairs, with GK deciding to scope out the offerings on TV. I told her she could do On Demand if she liked. When I heard screams coming from her room I asked her to turn it down some. Apparently she was into horror, but stared at it without appearing horrified. If she'd looked at any of Todd's books while he was studying to be a detective, that was why. Reality is much worse.

Todd. He probably was afraid to call me, in case things were not going well. I gave him a call to let him know things were going well. He answered on the second ring.

"What's wrong?"

Clearly this man had caller ID. I said, "Nothing! Everything is actually very nice. Gemma-Kate is teaching me how to cook, and Carlo has been showing her around. Did she tell you?"

"I haven't heard from her. I was wondering."

I remembered her texting in the backseat of the car when we were coming home from church a few days before, saying it was her dad. "I thought."

"What?"

"Nothing. How're things with you?"

"Fine."

"Okay, fine."

And that was a typical conversation with my brother. I wondered for a moment why Gemma-Kate would have told such an unnecessary lie, but chalked it up to adolescent secrecy and dismissed it.

Though the evening was pleasant enough I had a hard time coming down, even with a glass of wine or two. Didn't want to take a sleeping pill after the wine and instead lay awake for several hours with my heart pounding the way it used to when I was in trouble. I must have fallen asleep at some point, but woke up with an upset stomach.

I pushed aside the covers and made it to the bathroom, thinking I would throw up, but I just had dry heaves.

"What's wrong?" Carlo's voice came from the darkness when I returned.

"Sorry I woke you. Nothing serious, just a little nauseous. Maybe the sauerkraut disagreed with me."

Carlo said, "Could be dehydration. I think you need to cut back on the caffeine."

"The hell you say," I said. I shuffled into the kitchen and fixed an Alka-Seltzer. I watched it fizz in the glow of the night-light plugged near the stove. Then I thought about the Pugs that usually slept on the kitchen floor when it was warm and in our bed when it was cold. We still had the windows open, and this night could have gone either way. I pictured the sick Pug in his hospital room, out cold the way I had seen him last. Do dogs hate the dark? I hoped they left a little light on for him so he wouldn't be scared.

Our remaining Pug wasn't in the kitchen, but I thought I heard a whimper somewhere. My anxiety skipped up a notch. I went into our bedroom to see if the Pug was on the bed.

She wasn't. Anxiety building, and remembering that I felt odd about feeling anxious—this is all recounted well after events unfolded and it's difficult to be precise about how one felt in the past, how strong the feeling was, and why—I roamed through the rest of the house looking for her. I even turned on the back porch light to see if we had accidentally left her outside. Scanned the backyard. No Pug.

There was only one more place to look, behind the closed door of the bedroom where Gemma-Kate slept. I went back to our room and into my closet and gently pulled my robe off the hanger so it wouldn't bang against the closet wall. I slipped on the robe and crept across the living room to the opposite end of the house and quietly as possible—so as not to disturb her, you understand—looked inside. There was enough moonlight coming in through the window to see the silhouettes on the bed. Gemma-Kate on her stomach, hugging her pillow, and the Pug down at the foot of the bed. I tiptoed across the room and placed my index finger on the dog's side. She was breathing. She was asleep, and not whining now.

"Hello, Aunt Brigid," Gemma-Kate's voice came out of the dark.

The nerve on the side of my neck that sparks whenever danger is imminent sparked now. I jumped like I never had when surprised by the man with a knife. You're kind of always expecting the man with a knife.

"Are you having trouble sleeping?" she asked, quite awake.

I coughed lightly to make sure I had my voice. "I had a bit of stomach upset. Just took an Alka-Seltzer and checking to make sure everything is all right. With you."

"I can see that."

"I thought I heard the dog crying," I said.

"No," she said.

"Are you having trouble sleeping?" I asked.

"A little."

"Is something bothering you?"

"No."

"Well then. Good night."

"Good night, Aunt Brigid. I love you."

Her world had done a one-eighty, I thought. I cleared my throat again. "Well. I love you, too, Gemma-Kate."

After that, taking the Pug would have shown a lack of trust, so I left her sleeping on Gemma-Kate's bed, went back into our bedroom, and got into bed.

"Is everything all right?" Carlo's voice came through the dark again.

"Jesus." I jumped. "Doesn't anybody sleep around here? Yeah, it kind of is," I said, feeling pleasantly surprised, and yet. That anxiety. My heart was still pounding and I couldn't think of a reason why I wasn't exhausted after such a busy day. I said so.

"Maybe the wine," he said. "Too much coffee and wine. Drink a big glass of water."

It was a funny thing. After Carlo found out a year into our marriage that I was capable of killing people with my bare hands, and on several occasions had, he had tended to become a little more protective rather than less. He had the notion that my violent past made me more vulnerable. I said, "Stop hovering, honey. Go to sleep."

He had already turned to face the other direction, and I rubbed his back lightly as if he was the one needing comfort. Then I rolled on to my right side and scooched over just enough to feel Carlo's bare bum lightly touching mine, for comfort.

Twenty

Seven in the morning in March: The sky is just lightening up and you get a fine forty-five degrees of dry air. The female Pug was looking downhearted and clung to my side, sitting and staring at me expectantly whenever I sat down. Gemma-Kate left some of the cheddar-and-green-chili omelette she'd made for herself in the pan on the stove, and after eating that and fixing another Alka-Seltzer I felt a little better. Thinking a walk might clear up my lingering stomach upset and general anxiousness, I grabbed my new walking stick that Carlo had made for me, one with a blade in the bottom to fend off critters, saddled up the dog, and headed out to the back of our property.

They say there are five thousand trails running through Tucson and its environs, maybe more, up and over the mountains, and connecting the area like human veins and arteries. Once I had shown Mallory on the map three trails that, if you knew how to go and were willing to walk the four miles, connected our houses. But she would never do the trails with me or even meet me halfway. Like I said, she was much more a shopper than a hiker.

While I'm not much of a shopper myself, I understood how she felt about hiking. When I was working for the Bureau I had no time for nature. It was just something you had to go through to get to the next building. Now I had the time and the peace of mind not only to notice the world but to name the things in it. And springtime in the desert can get your attention like nothing else. You think the color purple does that? Try a purple cactus rimmed with hot pink flowers as big as coffee cups. We'd had plenty of winter rain, not the sudden monsoon kind that makes the otherwise dry riverbeds run and fills the dips in the road so you can't drive through them, but the light cold rain that comes all day, soaking the ground and preparing it for the yellow poppies that coated the ground in certain places now, making it look like someone spread mustard thick over the arroyos.

I was proud of that thought, thinking the poppies looked like mustard rather than some god-awful vision from a memory of a violent past. Where the ice was melting off the higher elevations I could see the sun glinting off small pools. I remembered how Carlo and I, during a walk toward the mountains in the distance, had seen that sparkle, how he thought of a sprinkling of diamonds or some such while I thought of an angry giant breaking a mirror. I was changing, I thought, thinking of poppies as mustard. Just watch, it was only a matter of time before I'd begin to see butterflies and bunnies in the clouds. Everything wouldn't make me think of something hideous.

I was in no hurry, which was just as well since this was the Pug who liked to sniff. Walking is good for thinking, and I put together what I knew so far about Joseph Joe Joey Neilsen.

Son of a helicopter mom and a stepfather who maybe wasn't keen on the thought of having a stepson, gay or straight, living with them forever.

Only hobbies, making handmade gifts for his mother and probably masturbating, maybe in the pool so Mummy wouldn't find any evidence on his bedsheets.

Dragged to church, and the youth group, too, I'd bet. Suitable friends forced on him, what they called "socialization" these days. Come Sunday I'd talk to Elias and Lulu's kid, what was his name, Ken?

Go see Detective Sam Humphries and stop by the medical examiner's lab to see George Manriquez, who was always there during the day unless he was at a death scene, but there weren't that many homicides, suspected or otherwise, in Tucson.

Tell Jacquie Neilsen that you couldn't analyze someone's ashes.

As I thought of each element of my investigation, I found myself tapping my stick on the ground rhythmically and murmuring, "Joe. Joey. Joseph. Joe. Joey. Joseph."

My thoughts were so far away from my surroundings I almost put the dog in danger. She had been sniffing at a pile of rocks—coyote piss, I thought idly, as she started to paw at the ground next to the pile. I watched her, thinking Joe Joey Joseph, until my attention was piqued by a little pronged thing coming out of the earth. Chicken bone, I guessed with more instinct than certainty, and pulled her leash to keep her from chomping down on it.

Wasn't a chicken bone, though. Bird claw? Interested, distracted from my thoughts, I studied it. Then I thought that the pile of rocks didn't look natural. Someone had placed them there. So, still keeping a tight rein on the Pug's leash while she strained at the same spot that fascinated me, I kicked aside the rocks and pushed at the dirt underneath with the toe of my hiking boot. The little pronged thing was the drying foot of a frog.

Bigger than a frog, a dead toad, pretty big. Make that huge, as big around as a saucer. Lying on its back in a shallow grave. I looked more closely, poked at it with my walking stick..

The toad had been slit open from its throat to its butt, too neatly for an animal attack. Only the organs were missing.

I always carry a poop bag with me. Even if the dogs go outside the development, you don't want to encourage any more flies than we already have. I put my hand through the plastic and, still holding the Pug back with a tight leash and my right foot, I bent over and picked up the toad.

Walked back to the house with the Pug frisking around me saying I want it, give it to me. Like she had a death wish.

"No. Bad dog," I said without any real conviction because I was trying hard to get my brain to work with me.

When I got back to the house I got a bigger plastic bag that we save from grocery shopping, put it on the glass-top table on the back porch, and slid the toad from the poop bag onto the larger one. I turned on the hose hooked up at the back faucet and wet down the body, water running just lightly enough to get the dirt off without pushing it off the table. I looked at the toad more carefully. The slit down its abdomen was clearer now. Clean slice, not made with teeth. Its internal organs had been neatly removed. I went inside to the desk in the living room and pulled open the drawer where we stored pens, stamps, and other small tools. The exacto knife we used for opening up that goddamn packaging that coats everything as if the main purpose is to keep you from opening it was in the drawer where it usually was, but it could have been washed.

The Pug was scratching and whining at the back door to go out where the toad was.

"Gemma-Kate," I said, a flare of anger having subsided into a quiet disbelief. She didn't respond. I heard screaming from her room—and went there. She was simultaneously staring at a movie and her iPhone. I think the movie was *Saw* but can't say which one because I haven't watched them. "Gemma-Kate," I said. She looked up at me with blank eyes, but I could swear she knew.

"Outside," I said, then turned and walked away.

Twenty-one

She followed me out to the living room. "What?" she said.

When I turned to look at her, she, to my mind, manufactured a shy smile.

"On the porch. Now," I said, my voice cracking with fresh anger.

I opened the door and, grabbing her by her upper arm none too gently, pushed her outside. I shut the door and directed her attention to the table with the wet dead toad. "You did this, didn't you?"

She looked at the toad, then looked at me. Not denying, not even looking surprised. I looked into her face and saw neither fear nor doubt nor guilt, only the usual combination of full-eyes and half-smile, a lack of affect. For the first time I recognized those eyes from my past, and they frightened me as eyes like that always had. It was what Carlo would call an epiphany.

"You poisoned my dog," I said.

The back door opened behind her. "Don't let the Pug out," I said, but the Pug was out, and Carlo followed. My warning and the momentary focus on the dog seemed to give Gemma-Kate just enough time to assess the situation and resolve it. She slumped into the chair at the table and put her face in her hands.

"What's going on?" Carlo asked, watching Gemma-Kate in the universal pose of dejection before noticing the dead toad.

"She poisoned my dog," I said.

"What happened, Gemma-Kate?" Carlo asked.

Speaking partly through her hands so she didn't have to lift her face, Gemma-Kate said, "The night you were at that party I found this toad out back. I was going to throw it over the fence. But then I thought it could just jump back into the yard so I should kill it. Then I thought, you know, I'm in biology, and I'd dissected a toad before, but never this big. Why shouldn't I dissect it? I didn't have anything else to do. So I did."

"How did you do it?" he asked, off the main track, I thought, but I didn't stop him.

"I got some things out of the house, an exacto knife from the desk, an old pan from under the stove. It was dusty, so I figured you wouldn't be using it. Tweezers from your bathroom."

"My tweezers," I said, temporarily distracted by trying to remember if I'd plucked that one little whisker out of my chin before or after the Humane Society affair.

She went on, her lip trembling a little. "I think your dog must have gotten too close and maybe eaten something I'd pulled out. It wandered back into the house and started throwing up and going into convulsions."

"You didn't tell us when we came home," I said.

"I don't know why not." Gemma-Kate's eyes slid to the side as if she was remembering something that didn't have to do with us. "Everything was happening so fast. I wasn't even sure that it was connected. When you left for the vet's I went onto the Internet and googled 'poison toad' and found out that was what happened. I guess I knew but I didn't want to say. I got scared that you would send me home, so I took the toad out behind the house and buried it while you were at the vet's. Then when you came home you already knew what was wrong, so I figured I didn't need to tell you." It looked like she wanted to cry but couldn't. "Your dog is okay."

Jesus Christ, the girl was as good at lying as I was.

"That wasn't very smart, was it?" Carlo asked. He looked stern, but somehow that wasn't doing it for me.

Gemma-Kate buried her face deeper into her hands and shook her head.

Who was this Gemma-Kate now?

Carlo looked at me as if to speak. I wondered what he would say. We were on the same side, weren't we? I wanted to tell him what I thought, but not with Gemma-Kate present. "I'll throw this in the Dumpster," he said. "They'll be collecting the garbage first thing in the morning, and it's past smelling anyway."

"Wash your hands after," I said.

He gave me a *duh* look, which is unusual for Carlo, wrapped the plastic bag around the toad, and carried it inside. I looked at Gemma-Kate.

"What did you do with the organs you didn't give the dog?" I asked.

"I put them down the garbage disposal," she said like someone who says, *I brought in the mail and left it on the hall credenza.*

I have a very strong stomach. I've watched a car containing a two-week-old corpse get pulled out of the Everglades swamp. Maybe it was because I was kind of sick to begin with that the thought of poison toad guts in my own kitchen sink made the bile rise in my throat. Partly because my anger had turned into a hard block in my gut of something more like apprehension, I put my hand on my stomach and pressed.

"Look," Gemma-Kate said. "Your finger is bleeding. It'll get on your shirt."

Carlo came into the bathroom as I was washing a small dab of blood off my T-shirt and examining fingers I had chewed without being conscious of doing so. With the odd detached feeling that they were someone else's hands, I also noted that they were shaking.

After Carlo washed any residual toad off his hands, I shut the door to the master bedroom area and said, "We need to talk."

He led me to the edge of the bed and sat down with me there. It reminded me of the time Carlo and I had gone to the park at night and talked about what we really thought while sitting in the car not facing each other. This had become our favorite way of talking about serious things, sort of like being in a confessional. Carlo took my hand and put it on his thigh, covering it with his own.

"Tell me," he said.

"Gemma-Kate needs to go home now," I said. "I don't think I'm the right person to look after her."

"That seems like drastic—"

"I've got to make you understand. There are . . . things. Small things but—"

Carlo said, "For your sake I wish she hadn't come. You're clearly upset. Maybe your stomachache last night was nerves. You seem to be making yourself ill over this, and it's not worth it. Even for the sake of your family."

"*Making myself ill?* That's all you think is going on here, that I'm *upset?* Upset is what happens when, when the toilet backs up. Carlo, my instinct is telling me there's something about this girl, something dangerous."

He shook his head harder than a simple no would warrant. "Because she dissected a toad?"

"No, because she poisoned our dog. Somebody poisons your dog and doesn't tell you, that doesn't sound like a person you can trust."

"But her explanation sounds logical, hiding it because she's afraid you'll be angry. And you are."

Carlo put his big hand on the side of my face and drew it to his. "Honey, look at me. I'm on your side. Now think. It's just a few months. Even if you're entirely correct about this situation, what's the worst that could happen?"

"The worst. Hm. There's a so-called triad they talk about that indicates a seriously bad person: hurting animals, bedwetting, and starting fires. So far we've got a Pug in the hospital. You want to wait for worse than that?"

"I have a very difficult time imagining that child purposely poisoning our dog."

"Just for shits and giggles let's say you've got a lousy imagination. What if?"

Carlo gave me the respect of thinking about the what-if. "If she did do it on purpose, she's been put on notice now. It was a good thing, your finding that toad. I don't think she wants to go back to Florida, so she'll be more careful from now on."

"More careful about doing something, or more careful about not getting caught?"

"You can't be thinking your niece would purposely try to harm Peggy."

I looked at him.

"The other Pug," he said.

I paused.

He said, "Brigid . . . You can't be thinking that."

I just said, "You're right, as long as we're very cautious and don't do anything to rile her, we should be safe. If we just let her stay in control."

"Honey. I'll be honest with you. You're sounding paranoid. At this moment I'm more concerned about you than about anything Gemma-Kate might do. It seems to me you're overreacting. And think of Todd. We can't put something like this on him. You'd have to explain why you're sending her back, and it doesn't seem fair, with his dealing with the death of his wife."

Carlo was on my side, I reminded myself, and tamped down a rising huffiness. Maybe I was paranoid. Okay, in retrospect I know I was paranoid in this case. And yet as it turned out I wasn't totally out of the ballpark, either.

"Okay, but you better make sure the batteries are working in the smoke alarms."

"Are you alone?" Gemma-Kate asked.

"Does it look like there's anyone else in the room?" Peter answered.

"At least keep the volume low in case someone can hear. Listen, my aunt found the toad."

"How did she find it?"

"The other dog dug it up where I buried it. Brigid figured out I did it, and lied about it."

"Is your dog still alive?"

"Yeah, but he's still at the vet."

"Why is he still there?"

"The poison made him have seizures and vomit."

"I still can't believe you did that. Some balls you got."

"Everybody's making such a big production out of this."

"Did they do anything to you?"

"Not yet. My aunt is acting very bizarre. I overheard her talking to her husband. She wants to get rid of me."

"Like have you arrested?"

"For attempted murder of a dog? Oh, get real. I think she wants to send me back to Florida. I really don't want to go back to Florida."

"Why not? Beach and stuff."

"Florida sucked. I swear I'm not going to let her send me back to that shithole," Gemma-Kate said.

"What're you going to do about it, slip her a toad?" Peter laughed.

Twenty-two

I let her in my house. I'd been all righteous, keeping my promise to Marylin after she was gone, but I shouldn't have let Gemma-Kate in my house. I remembered a talk I had with a young agent about how we catch serial killers by staying in touch with the killer inside ourselves. Maybe not everyone had an inner serial killer. Maybe it was just the Quinns.

Not for the first time I wondered if my whole family was screwed up that way, if to some varying degree there was a genetic lack of humanity and only a random roll of the cosmic dice put any one of us on the side of good.

After making sure that Annette would be there with Owen and all was well, Mallory agreed to meet me for an emergency lunch. I met her at Blanco, one of the Mexican restaurants that she would go to, not refried beans and enchiladas. At this place you got a salad made with watermelon and mozzarella and they prepared guacamole at the table in a lava mortar bowl.

Typical spring day, the weather was still nice enough to sit outside on the balcony overlooking the valley that was Tucson. They had turned on the misters, a spray that nearly dried in the low humidity before it touched my skin but cooled the air around it.

Mallory was already there and had a bottle of white chilling next to the table, and was nibbling from a plate with roasted elephant garlic, blue cheese crumbles, and bread, which she gestured to me to share. Her glass was nearly empty, but the waiter came and poured one for me, topping her off at the same time. She gave him her flirty smile and gently shooed him away when he asked to take our order. I put some of the blue cheese on a slice of bread, squeezed a garlic clove which the roasting had turned soft on top, and yummed it. Had another. Drank some. Drank some more.

When I looked up I saw Mallory studying me with an uncharacteristic frown. Mallory was not generous with frowns. She said it was a waste of the cosmetic work she had done from time to time, the kind of detail work you can't see.

She said, "Why are you limping?"

"I'm not limping."

"Yes you are. I watched you when you came up to the table. Nothing pronounced, just a little hop-step thing."

"Oh, terrific. That, too?"

She stared at me more intently, changed the subject abruptly. "Brigid, are you all right?"

I realized I couldn't speak because my jaw was clenched and my tongue was jammed against the roof of my mouth. I forced my mouth to relax enough to ask why she was asking.

She said, "You seem agitated. It's not like you."

Her asking that made me suddenly aware I could feel my pulse in my neck. Out of curiosity I pressed a finger against the vein and figured I was doing about one-twenty. "I . . . am . . . very . . . tensssse."

"Funny, I always think of you as almost scary calm. That's why I noticed."

"I know! I feel like the only thing holding me together is my nerves," I said.

"Talk to me," she said, and raised her hand to click an imaginary stopwatch with her thumb. That was the gesture for our acknowledgment that at our age you could talk forever about ailments but we weren't going to allow each other to do that because it was too boring. With me it was insomnia, lower back pain, and allergies. With

Mallory it was constipation, seasonal arthritis, and the eternal quest to lose twenty pounds.

"I'm having a hard time remembering if it just started last night or if it's been going on for a while. I was sick to my stomach last night, and feeling anxious at the same time. Right now I'm kind of befuddled, brain revs without engaging. Maybe that's because I didn't sleep well. Carlo thinks it's stress related. Me, stressed. Tell the truth, my stomach is still a little off."

She clicked the invisible stopwatch as if she was turning it off, as if this was more significant than seasonal postnasal drip or a hemorrhoid flare-up. "Electrolyte imbalance? Too much or too little water."

Having a sick husband must make you a medical expert by necessity. I shook my head. "Nothing different from the way I always do it."

"There's probably some small thing going on, but when did you have a physical last?" she asked.

"I can't remember. Last year, I guess, when I got my flu shot."

She picked up her bag, which had been hooked over the back of her chair. It was the kind of thing you see in a shop and wonder why anyone would pay a thousand dollars for a purse. She took out her cell phone. "I don't know who you're seeing, but it's time for a good internist."

"No, really," I said.

"Yes, really." She pressed a speed-dial number, I guessed because of Owen, and rolled her eyes; the usual if-this-press-that messages must have started. She knew in advance the button to press that would get her to a real person. "This is Mrs. Hollinger," she said when someone answered. "Please have Dr. Neilsen call me as soon as he can."

She paused. "Oh no, Mr. Hollinger is stable. Just have Dr. Neilsen call me." She disconnected without saying good-bye.

"I don't think Tim Neilsen likes me very much right now," I said.

"What's the difference? I'm sure he doesn't like me much right now after I got him and Jacquie to come to that fund-raiser. Don't forget, I was the one who introduced you to them. But he's a doctor, not a date. All he cares about is that we can pay the bill."

I didn't object further. After acknowledging everything that had been bothering me, I was too spent to object to anything. It was easier to let Mallory push me around.

When she put away her cell she took out a pillbox in the shape of a Fabergé egg. I'm certain it wasn't the real thing. "Pill?" she said. She opened it, shook several different-shaped capsules and tablets into her hand.

"What is all that?" I asked.

She pointed them out one by one. "St. John's wort, Valium, diet pill, diet pill, calcium, diet pill, Valium, fish oil. Here, have a Valium."

I looked at it doubtfully, recognizing it from my stash at home but considering my promise to Carlo to be careful about the stuff. "If I relax it could get ugly."

"I'll risk it. You can take it with the wine," she said. "It's only two milligrams. Tim prescribed it for when I get overwrought about Owen."

"I have them at home. If I can't wait till then I'm worse off than I thought. This'll do," I said, picking up my wineglass. But wrapping my fingers around the stem made them cramp, so after I took a decent slug and managed to get the glass back on the table without spilling it, I bent my hands back and forth to make the pain go away. "You should stop worrying about your weight," I said to change the subject. "You look fine."

Mallory raised her arm and grabbed some sagging tricep with a look that said *Gentlemen of the jury, I rest my case.* She said, "This coming from someone who can still wear sleeveless tops. I hate you."

I thought of a short time ago when I had turned the lights out on an army veteran a third of my age. "I hate myself. It's just not me. Can this be hormonal?"

Mallory smirked. "I'm sure you haven't had a hormone for some years now. I'm not sure about the limp, but there must be reason for the anxiety." She had a husband at home who couldn't move and she was asking about my anxiety. "Gemma-Kate?" she asked.

Nice when you get close enough you can communicate so easily. "Gemma-Kate," I answered. "Oh, Gemma-Kate."

"Have you talked to Carlo?"

"Carlo is smitten."

"Does that bother you?"

Not till this moment, actually. Is that what friends are for, to make you think in ways you wish you wouldn't? If so, who ever pays a therapist? "Did you just say you think I'm suspecting Carlo is capable of having an affair?"

Not much shocked Mallory Hollinger, but this did. "With Gemma-Kate?"

"No, no, no. With someone else closer to his age."

I expected her to scoff, but she said, "Women can have platonic friendships, but I've always thought that men's friendships with women have a sexual-attraction component, even if they never follow up. Does he have female friends?"

I thought. "You," I said. I laughed.

"What's so funny?" she said. I could tell she thought that any man having the hots for her was a given. She seemed to consider pursing her lips but decided against encouraging the wrinkles.

Another piece of wisdom Mallory had once shared with me: No matter how people treat you, you can tell their essential goodness by how they treat a waiter. That and always finish the wine. The waiter had appeared to pick up the mysteriously empty blue-cheese-and-garlic plate.

"Please don't go, dear," Mallory said to him, touching his arm lightly with her fingertips. "We've been nattering too long and taking up your table. We should order." She chose the Southwest chopped chicken salad, dressing on the side.

I ordered the same salad because facing the choices in the menu was just more stress and I suddenly couldn't take it. Weird, for a person who had worked undercover in a Mexican drug cartel to be intimidated by a menu. The waiter left, and Mallory said, "Maybe eating a little something will make you feel better. Now what else is bothering you?"

I told Mallory everything, about finding the toad, and the fact that Gemma-Kate had lied about being responsible for the Pug's getting poisoned, and whether it had been done on purpose.

"She said she didn't know the toad was poisonous until she looked it up on the Internet."

Mallory shrugged. "I thought everyone knew."

"I didn't. But it still makes me wonder."

I expected Mallory to kid me out of it, to make a joke about watching too many movies about wicked children, but she just nodded and listened while I talked about all the little things about Gemma-Kate that had brought me to my current state. I was beginning to wish she would make a joke. But all I was hearing was "mm," "ah, yes," and "I *see*." Like Carlo, she was giving me lots of sympathy but no solutions.

"What does Carlo think?"

I told her about my conversation with him, and how, while he was supportive, he didn't see the situation quite the same way I did. "He's way too rational."

"You can't blame him," Mallory said. "You know the classic comment about the man two blocks over in the neighborhood who suddenly shows up as a mass murderer."

I laughed. "He was such a *quiet* man. Never gave nobody trouble. And then they find the bodies in the ice chests."

Mallory said, "Maybe you should get advice from an expert. Is there someone here you could talk to? Maybe have her assessed? I can give all kinds of advice on physical concerns, but I'm out of my depth with psychology. Owen and I are boringly normal."

I had a minor aha moment when the face of an old friend popped into my mind. "There's an old buddy of mine from the Bureau. He hasn't retired yet so I can track him down at the office. He even met Gemma-Kate in the past when I was living in D.C. and she came for a visit. I'll see what he recommends."

"If anything. Breathe, darling. You're holding your breath."

I took another huge lungful and welcomed the waiter, who brought our salads and emptied the bottle into our glasses. Mallory waited for him to leave before asking, "Do you think you could be depressed? Situation you can't control, that sort of thing?"

I scoffed and picked up my fork to start eating, but my fingers cramped again so that I couldn't handle the fork properly. I put it down and, with my hands under the table so it wouldn't be noticed, bent my fingers this way and that until the cramp eased.

We both paused our talk long enough to pick with interest through the salads looking for the good stuff, kalamata olives, poached chicken, red peppers. My hand cramped again, and I eased it out as I had before. If this was stress-induced, the wine didn't seem to be doing much good.

Mallory dipped the tines of her fork into the dressing on the side of her plate and speared a piece of avocado—fewer calories that way. If she noticed the problem I was having with my hands, she chose to ignore it.

"Can I give you one piece of advice?"

"What's that?"

"If you think Gemma-Kate has behavioral problems, you might want to keep her away from Peter. Maybe that wasn't so brilliant on my part after all."

"What have you heard?"

"Nothing terrible. I checked with Lulu after he and Gemma-Kate went out, when you seemed concerned. Not enough to even mention until now. Beer drinking, wrecking the car—you can sort of tell from his mother. She looks as tense as you do. Maybe it has to do with having teenagers around. They induce stress."

I remembered the chipmunk woman. Mallory was right. She looked as if she'd always be on alert.

"They haven't gone out again, but I've overheard her talking to him on her phone. She sounds so different from when she talks to Carlo or me. Almost like another person."

"Well, that's to be expected. Remember that boy in *Leave it to Beaver*? 'My, what a lovely apron that is, Mrs. Cleaver.' She's probably more herself with another young person, whatever 'self' is. I imagine we all do it. But I still would discourage . . . oh . . ." Mallory's fork seemed to have suddenly grown heavy.

"What?"

"Nothing. Crazy thoughts."

"So when did that ever stop you from talking?"

"The way you've . . . no, trust me, lunatic stuff. I've been watching TV too much."

"They call that the *CSI* effect," I said. "I think that's Jacquie Neilsen's problem, too."

My phone rang and, thinking it was the vet, I answered without looking at the caller.

"Brigid? It's Jacquie Neilsen."

"Hello, Jacquie," I said, watching Mallory mouth silently *Speak of the devil.*

"What have you found out?" Jacquie asked.

"Honey, it's only been a day. I don't have any information yet, but I'm going to see the death investigator this afternoon, and I promise to call you back, okay?"

"Okay." She disconnected.

"What were we talking about?" I asked.

"Your husband, your poor health, and your crazy niece. But enough of me. Let's gossip about the Neilsens."

I told her I didn't know any more than I had the day before, but would let her know what I discovered after talking to the death investigator and medical examiner.

"That sounds *so* interesting. Is there anything I can do to help?"

"Like what?"

"Seriously, we could be one of those buddy teams, only women."

Mallory was clearly joking, but I thought about other buddies who had died on me and it didn't seem so funny. I said, "No."

"Okay, maybe we're a little long in the tooth, but still."

"I'll think about it." No.

We finished our salads and split the check. When she watched me sign my credit card bill, I felt self-conscious under her concerted gaze and wondered if she was curious about my tipping. On the way out she watched the way I walked again and invited me over to her place, "so I can give you something that might help."

I drove my own car so I could head straight home afterward. The road to her place was steep and curvy, and as I went around a bend I had to jam on my brakes for a man crossing the road.

It wasn't just a man. He stopped in the road about ten yards from my car and turned to face me. I saw Carlo. I saw him smile his usual bad-boy smile. Then I saw his flesh drop away, turning the smile into the grin of a skull. No matter how capable I had ever been of reacting to unforeseen dangers, I was powerless. I watched, half mesmerized and half horrified, as he continued to become a skeleton from the top of his head to his feet before completely melting into the asphalt, leaving nothing behind.

I have a tendency to imagine terrible things. On occasion those things have been not imaginary. But this time was more real than anything I had ever imagined. Yet I was certain I had not seen something real. Not real, I said to myself. Trick of the light. Mighty fancy trick of the light.

That was small comfort as I found my fingers stiff around the steering wheel, lungs hyperventilating, heart pounding so hard I could almost feel my tongue throb. My underarms felt damp, something particularly notable in ten percent humidity. It took me several minutes to calm down, and then I continued very slowly up the road, telling myself I had not just seen the future.

Twenty-three

When I got to the house the door was open and no one around. No one to ask what took me so long, which was a good thing because I didn't want to make Carlo's skeleton any more real by discussing it. I walked in with the idea of looking for Mallory when I felt a sudden cramp in my gut and veered off to the guest bathroom.

It appeared I was doing more now than vomiting. I hadn't felt this way since I tried mixing Benefiber with my vodka because I found alcohol constipated me. Was it all tied together, another symptom of whatever ailed me? It isn't attractive to mention the runs, I realize, but I'm trying to recount everything that happened even if it didn't seem significant at the time. I washed my hands and opened the door of the cabinet under the sink looking for air freshener. Found something called neutralizer in a fancy bottle you don't buy at Walmart. I looked at the bottom where the price sticker had not been removed and noted that it was $79.95. Thinking that I had bought cologne that cost less than that, I spritzed myself as well as the room.

I put the bottle back where it belonged and took a second to see what else was in there. This time I saw a neat assortment of extra toilet paper rolls, a can of Scrubbing Bubbles, one of those pumice stones that rub away the lime deposits we get from the water, and a small collection of shampoos and conditioners from exclusive hotels. I guess even the rich take them. I wondered how old they were and when the last time was the Hollingers had been able to do any traveling.

I shut the cabinet door and, what the hell, while I was at it I looked inside the medicine cabinet too. There was the same array of over-the-counter antihistamines, aspirin, unused toothpaste, and in the hope-springs-eternal category, an unopened tube of topical estrogen near its expiration date. Note to the premenopausal, that's used for vaginal dryness. For all the talk of our husbands, Mallory and I seldom talked about sex. Most of the time I purposely avoided the subject because I assumed that Owen wasn't having an erection these days and I didn't want to make her feel bad. I doubted Owen would come around before the expiration date, and wondered if Mallory might ever take a lover. I thought of Adrian Franklin.

There was also a bottle of antidepressants, recently prescribed by Tim Neilsen. Looked like she was taking some of that. Antidepressants instead of estrogen, sedatives instead of sex. She must have kept all this in the guest bathroom because Annette was too often in the master bath and Mallory wanted to keep her own medication private. Whatever gets you through the night, my friend.

When I left the bathroom and saw no one in the kitchen, I found my way to the most likely place, Owen's room.

Mallory was leaning over the bed, her hands gripping a bag over Owen's throat. Annette was on the other side of the bed injecting something into Owen's IV port. Mostly I can remember Owen staring at me, all his heart in his eyes, a man panicked but unable to say or do anything about it. A sound like a clogged vacuum issued from his tracheotomy.

I heard the women speaking in urgent tones, no yelling and running, just an intensity that was unmistakable. Annette was clearly in charge and giving direction to Mallory, but the conversation went back and forth as if they had both been here before. They were focused on Owen while Owen was focused on me as if I meant life. With the feeling that my effort was a part of it all, I strained to hear the snippets of the commands and responses that passed between the women.

"—cleaning his trache—"

"—suction him?"

"Nothing—started bucking the vent."

"—fighting the bag, too."

"Keep going. Maybe anxiety, this will help."

"Come on, Owen, calm down."

"Blood pressure."

Mallory glanced at the monitor quickly, as if taking her eyes off Owen's suffering would mean his sure death. "One-eighty-four over one-sixteen."

"Calm down, Owen, you can do this."

"When did you clean—"

Annette started to answer, "I was just," then ignored what she might have felt was a useless question and focused again, finishing up administering whatever she was putting into his IV. "Blood pressure."

Mallory glanced again. "One-ninety-six over one-twenty-one."

The vacuum sound coming from the hole in his throat grew louder.

"Pulse."

"One-twenty-six."

"Come on, Owen. Don't fight it. Gimme that bag."

Mallory stepped away and let Annette take over administering oxygen by hand. After what seemed like a time in which he had to have died, Owen's eyelids fluttered and shut. The sound eased and stopped.

"I'm going to keep bagging him for a few seconds before I put him back."

We stood and watched as Annette did that and then, rather expertly, in my estimation, switched Owen from manual ventilation to the automatic respirator.

Only after that, and a final check of his vitals, did she say, "And we're good." Annette was a pro, but even she sat on the bed and took a deep breath herself. Mallory stumbled into the bathroom, and I followed. I watched her take a pill container out of the medicine cabinet there and try to open the child-resistant cap. "God damn it," she said.

I took it from her shaking hands. With mild detachment I noticed my own hands lacked their usual strength, seemed sluggish, as if my fingers didn't belong to me, but I managed to wrestle open the container and took out a pill. "Water," I said, reaching for a glass.

"Oh, give me that." She took the container and bolted a couple tablets into her mouth, swallowed them dry.

"Shit," Mallory murmured, almost to herself. She sat down on the toilet and put her head in her hands. "Shut the door."

I did. I knelt before her and put my hands on her shoulders. "My dear friend. You could let him go. No one would blame you."

"They wouldn't have to. The night this happened? We'd been drinking at a fund-raiser in Phoenix. Two-hour drive home and Owen was asleep, okay, maybe passed out, while I drove. The car stalled on the train tracks. I jumped out when I saw the light in the distance. Ran around and unbuckled Owen. Pulled on him. He fell out of the car. I tried to wake him up. At the last minute I stepped away," she said, and then openmouthed horror waved over her face. "But not that way. Not that way." Staring at the door as if she could see through it to her husband, she said, "Do you ever pray?"

Whoa. It was my understanding that even in emergencies Episcopalians put prayer and oral sex in the same category: You might do it but you sure don't talk about it. "Why?"

"Just a question I never asked you."

"I'm not even sure I believe in God."

She looked at me a moment as if she was seeing me differently, and I didn't think it was with judgment. She said, "I pray. Oh my God, Brigid, sometimes I'm not sure how long I can take this and I pray that he'll die. But then I know I should be the one." Mallory pressed her hand against her throat as if afraid of what else might come out of her if she wasn't more careful. "I've never said any of this to anyone before. I should lay off the wine at lunch."

Her cell phone went off and she took it out of her pocket. I never thought to ask her why she had chosen "Some Enchanted

Evening" for the melody, what meaning it had for her. This was not the time.

"Excuse me," she said, and wandered out of the bathroom into the living room, leaving me temporarily with Annette, who had come in. I saw that I was still holding the pill container and read the label. Valium, ten milligrams.

I asked, "How is he doing?"

"He's asleep," Annette said, eyeing the pill container as I put it back in the medicine cabinet. She probably could have used one herself about now, but bad idea, working, I guess.

"What happened?"

"Sometimes when they're like this they panic and start fighting the ventilator that does their breathing for them. We call it bucking the vent."

"What caused it?"

"He's on a Q4 regimen. That means I clean his trache every four hours, through the night, too. He can get anxious when I'm doing it, but you never know when it's a ventilator malfunction. That's why we were bagging him by hand, sorry, giving him oxygen manually. He should be in a hospital with full emergency care. I think she keeps him here to punish herself."

I thought how my business had been similar to Annette's, except that when I talked about bagging someone I meant something else. "What about you? It seems like you're here all the time."

"Oh, I get time off. Mallory can watch him for short periods and there's another nurse who comes. I tell you, Brigid, I never let them know I'm thinking that way, but if I was like that I'd want to check out." She nodded in the direction Mallory had taken. "But not them. They both have this incredibly upbeat attitude. You're probably thinking how can I tell, but I just can. You get to know a person by their eyes. Maybe you get to know them even better when they're like this."

I nodded.

Mallory came back, and we stopped talking about her. She had pulled herself together again, and the Mallory I glimpsed gulping Valium in the bathroom was safely under wraps. "You've got an appointment with Neilsen tomorrow at ten. Will that do?"

"That's fast," I said.

"I'm sure he wouldn't do it for anyone but me," Mallory said. "Bit of a pill pusher, but they all are. Brilliant diagnostician. I told the nurse what symptoms I noticed at lunch."

But she wasn't thinking about me. She had turned to Owen, placed her hand on his heart, then on hers. She turned to Annette, and they discussed having a respiratory therapy specialist and a med tech come in to check the ventilator for malfunction, leakage, flow setting, trigger sensitivity, and other things I can't remember. Once again I was impressed by how knowledgeable Mallory had become. That completed, she turned her focus back to me and said to Annette, "Darling, do you know where that lavender wrap is?"

Annette thought she did, and left the room.

Mallory watched her go. "Annette is so efficient." Knowing Mallory as I did, the word didn't sound altogether like praise, more like there was a dash of doubt thrown into the mix. I wondered what else Mallory would share with me about Annette when she was ready. I wondered what else I didn't know.

"She seems to think you're wonderful."

Annette walked in with a boneless white rabbit. "There, I heated it up in the microwave." She draped the rabbit around my shoulders. It was comforting and warm and smelled of lavender. It made me aware of the knots in my muscles as they relaxed. If only it could stop me from seeing things.

Twenty-four

Despite feeling like hell, and jarred by what I had witnessed at the Hollinger house, something I would probably have seen before now if I lived there, I continued downtown to keep my appointment with Detective Sam Humphries.

He had his own small office in the Tucson Police Department. I sat down in the chair next to his desk when he went off to bring me some coffee, and checked out his room. It was neat, without any personal items or clutter, like he hadn't been in it long. A thick manila file folder with a tab that had NEILSEN typed on it was on the desk. When he returned, with the coffee and a little chewy bar he said someone had brought in (nice touch), I found he matched the office.

Sam Humphries: Just out of a cop's uniform and looked like he still felt odd moving about in the dress khakis he now wore as a detective. Sitting with his knees apart so he wouldn't wrinkle the pants. The kind of kid you want to say "Hello, son" to even if you've never had one of your own.

I kept my voice soft with only a dash of suck-up so he wouldn't think I was being sarcastic. The gentle grandmother persona. "Thanks for taking the time to see me, Detective Humphries. I used to be in law enforcement myself, so I know what it's like on both sides. I'd so appreciate anything you'll tell me."

He paused, first savoring the sound of the word "detective," before he said, "Call me Sam."

"Brigid," I said.

So far so good. I was fairly open about my conversation with Jacquie Neilsen. "I met her socially and we got to talking. She's having trouble acquiring any closure on her son's death."

"She called me a few times. I felt bad, but there wasn't anything more I could tell her. We had the same conversation every time, and then I stopped returning her calls. It's a job for a psychologist, you know?"

I gave a deep nod. *You and I are sympatico, my friend.* "Not that you've been anything but professional. Jacquie has just been so addled about what happened that night, and any information she's had she's not satisfied with. Not your fault or anything. I'm just sort of reviewing everything so maybe I can put it in words she'll accept, you know, woman to woman . . ." I let my words dwindle out in a vague way.

He was unpretentious about the case having been his first as a death scene investigator. Joked about having to take a laminated checklist with him that he kept in his pocket. "It was pretty straightforward," he said. "All in here."

I took the folder he handed me and tried to keep it from fluttering in my hands. There were photos taken of the patio area, and all the rooms upstairs and down, but no body. Sometimes you already know the answers, but you ask the questions anyway. Sometimes you're surprised with a different answer the fourth time you ask. "You didn't see the body at the scene?"

Sam shook his head. "They probably should have left it there, but it was taken in the ambulance." He shuffled through the photographs and came up with one. "Here's the body at the morgue. The medical examiner took it. I was just called in after that."

"The same night?"

"Yes."

"Did you go through the house?"

"Sure, here's all the photographs. That was some entertainment center they have. Bigger than my whole house," he said. "And did you see the fireplace?"

"Pretty impressive." I looked impressed.

"I talked to my boss and found out the trouble with drowning incidents is that it's hard to reconstruct what happened. I mean, you have water and no matter how hard the victim struggles, when it's over it's still just water, you know? And no mangled machinery or skid marks like in a traffic fatality. I even looked for blood trails like the manual said to, and didn't find anything. Hell, with the low humidity even the flagstones on the side of the pool where the father tried to resuscitate him were pretty dry by the time I got there."

"The father, Dr. Timothy Neilsen, he said you grilled him good." I added a nod for affirmation.

He took it as a compliment. "Since he was the would-be rescuer I went over the whole thing with him several times, like, you know, 'show me.' We walked in the door together, and he tried to re-create all his moves, into the kitchen, turning on the patio lights because it was all dark except for what he had turned on in advance with his smartphone."

I find that if I jump in with questions that are off track, to prevent an interviewee from delivering a canned message, sometimes I can get interesting information. So I asked, "No paraphernalia, no ligatures indicating some sort of autoeroticism . . ."

"Nothing like that. But if someone does want to do it, all they have to do is hold their breath underwater, right?"

The kid was learning fast. "Right," I said.

Humphries studied the photo of the pool area upside down. "Who knows, maybe he was trying it for the first time and that seemed the best spot."

I turned the photos until I got to a morgue shot. Joe's jeans were unzipped but not pulled down from his hips, and his briefs were in place. What had happened between the time he pulled down the zipper and the time he drowned, that kept him from doing anything more? It seemed odd to me. "Did you ask whether anyone changed the scene? I mean, you know, not to cover anything up, just embarrassed, or wanting to preserve dignity. Say, pulling his pants back up."

Sam looked pleased with the questions so far and his ability to answer them, as if I were administering a test. "The manual . . . I mean, yes, I did ask, and his father said no."

"Stepfather," I corrected.

"That's right." I tried to note in his voice if there was any doubt, any defense, but he seemed very relaxed. I, on the other hand, noticed my knees were bouncing a bit and put my hands on them to steady them without making an excuse for it.

I got back to the story. "I heard from the parents, but I'd really like to know the professional view of what happened that night."

Humphries had to take a minute to review the report, apologizing that he'd forgotten much of it, it being so straightforward and all. Such a polite young man. He partly told me what he remembered and partly read it from the report he had typed up following the investigation. "The father, stepfather, being a physician he knew what to do. He tried CPR. Then he called nine-one-one but confirmed the boy was already deceased when he arrived home around eight thirty in the evening."

"What's the time of the nine-one-one?"

Humphries checked his crib sheet again. "Looks like eight fifty."

"It took him twenty minutes from discovery of the body to placing the nine-one-one." I raised an eyebrow.

"I know, I went over all that, too. He accounted for every minute. He showed me how he walked into the pool—"

"He didn't jump? Like *Oh my God I have to get to the body?*"

"No telling what people are thinking at a time like that, but no, he showed me how he went to the steps, walked into the water. He said he took his sandals off then because they were slowing him down. He pulled the body, it was unresisting at that point, back to the shallow end, dragged it up the steps . . . he knocked the head on the edge of the steps and caused some bruising, but that was the only spot.

Did CPR, but the lips were already turning black and a foam column was coming out of the mouth."

"Sounds like Dr. Neilsen knows his drowning."

"Sounds like."

"So we got maybe ten minutes max so far. What about the other ten?"

"He said he went into the pool with his cell phone, panicked. When he tried to call nine-one-one it wasn't working."

"Did you check it?"

"Yep. They don't have a landline. He went to a computer they keep on the kitchen counter and he texted the friend who had dropped him off at the house. That was the person who called nine-one-one. Emergency services were there in about seven minutes."

"So time of death was . . ."

Sam checked his notes again. "Body temperature at the morgue guesses time of death around seven, seven thirty P.M."

"Given the water temp."

"That's right, that was taken into account."

"So even with the father delaying the nine-one-one call, the kid had been dead at least an hour."

Humphries nodded, and the movement of his head made my focus blur slightly. Then I was aware of him speaking. "Ms. Quinn, are you all right?"

I felt as if I had zoned out for maybe a second. "Of course."

"I'm sorry, but you seemed to have . . . gone away, for a little bit."

I ignored him. "No, I'm fine. What was time of death?"

He looked at me funny. "Around seven, seven thirty P.M."

"What about before that? Was it a school day? A weekend?"

"This was a Monday, September, Labor Day. Joseph had the day off from school. He was in the house from the afternoon on. His parents left around the same time, separately."

"What about friends? Was he with friends that day?"

"He didn't have friends. He wasn't what you'd call liked."

My brain suddenly rebooted. "How do you know that?"

Humphries stuttered. He was covering, and he slipped. This was what I was here for, but I wouldn't get anywhere pressing it now. I let him go and he went on quickly, but repeating himself. "Father at a sports bar with a friend, one of the other doctors in his office. Mother at her book club. Deceased alone at home. Like I said, father gets home first, finds boy's body floating facedown in the pool."

"Did you see the boy's mother that night?"

"The stepfather tried to call her, but her cell wasn't on. The body was removed to the morgue. He was glad she didn't have to see it that way. Kept saying thank God he was the one to come home first. I hung around until she came home, questioned her, but she was a mess. Understandably, I mean," he added, trying to be sensitive. "She kept saying to the stepfather 'What have you done?' but as far as I could see he hadn't done anything wrong. It was just grief talking."

"How long before she came home?"

"I was there till about eleven. She came home around ten."

"Did the father say all the doors were locked when he got home?"

"I asked that, too." Once I hadn't followed up on his slip about Joe not being liked, Sam was back to the guy who was acing his oral exams. He wasn't minding my questioning at all. His whole demeanor seemed to say *Bring it on.* "Except for the patio door they were all bolted from the inside. Father came in through the garage."

I remembered Gemma-Kate asking about other people knowing the garage door passcode. I asked the same thing. "Not that he knew," Sam answered, but his eyes shifted. One point lost.

"And you don't think there's any way it could have been suicide."

"I talked with the paramedics and the medical examiner. If it was going to be suicide he would have done something to keep himself from coming to the surface, some weight around himself, cuff his wrists, something. I can't imagine anyone wanting to commit suicide enough to stay underwater until you stop breathing."

"Or homicide, staged to look like accidental."

A man appeared at the open door of the office, on cue to save Humphries from having to push an answer out of his slightly slack mouth. The man was big in the chest, suited and tied, and looked authoritative. Didn't ask who I was. Didn't look at the folder in my lap as anyone would have done, out of curiosity. Just focused on Humphries. "I need to talk to you," he said. Then he walked away.

"Yes, sir," Humphries said as the man disappeared.

"The sarge?" I asked.

Humphries nodded. He stepped out of the office, which left me to go through the folder and skim the rest of the report. This being his first death investigation, Humphries was indeed as thorough as you could get. Besides taking photographs of all the rooms in the house, and several angles of the pool area, he had also done meticulous sketches showing the path Tim had taken through the house, and where the CPR had been performed. It was so cute I wanted to pin it to a refrigerator.

In a few minutes Humphries came back, apologizing that his boss had some work for him. He held out his hand for the file. Though he didn't say anything, it was impossible for us both to ignore the fact that I had bled on it a little. I looked down to see I'd been worrying my cuticles again without realizing it.

I said, "You should get a new folder. There's blood on this one."

I considered shaking his hand in a heartfelt way and then figured he probably wouldn't want to. So I just stuck my hand in my pocket, where I could wipe the blood from my thumb, and pulled out a business card, which I placed on his desk. Would he please call me if he thought of anything else?

He said he would. I was sure that was the last I'd hear from him if I didn't initiate a meeting myself.

I left the police station and sat in my car a bit, clenching my jaws so my teeth wouldn't chatter. Definitely I was off coffee from now on. For at least a while. The rest of the day, anyway. The brain farts were a bit more problematic, and they were coming more often. But just now the temporary dementia was at bay as my brain clicked on all cylinders.

Stepfather comes home. While processing his stepson's drowning in the swimming pool, attempting resuscitation, and calling emergency services, is careful to note and report all the doors bolted.

Sam could not be certain that no one else had the passcode for the garage door.

Jacquie hadn't mentioned Tim had tried to phone her but her cell phone was off. Did he? Was it?

Had Joe Joseph Joey really been there and alone all evening as the report said? Were any interviews conducted with associates to corroborate that? And where was he the rest of the day?

And how had Humphries arrived at the conclusion that Joe was not well liked? Was it enough to walk away from a kid in distress and let him drown?

Those were just my initial tidbits of interest, little questions that had never been asked by this responsible but rookie investigator who had never processed a death scene before, let alone the more challenging scene that a drowning entails. Sure, it was all probably simple, just what they decided it was, accidental asphyxiation with possible autoeroticism. No known motive or opportunity for anything more dramatic or sinister. But I was beginning to understand Jacquie's suspicions along with her guilt. It was all just a little too simple, the investigation having a few holes. The extreme care taken to preserve her from the horror. I wondered who that really benefited.

I called her. "Jacquie, I just talked with Sam Humphries."

"Who?"

"That's the detective who did the death investigation for Joseph," I reminded her. "There may be a few holes to fill in, but it wasn't bad. He was more thorough than you remembered."

"What holes?"

"Did Joseph have friends? At school? Who were the boys you mentioned that night we met?"

Skipping past the question about school friends, Jacquie went straight to my second question. "They were in his youth group when we attended St. Martin's. Ken was all right, Joey said he was nice to him. Peter used to tease him. Do you think there's something to that?"

"I'm trying not to lock on any suspicions just yet. I'm still fact-finding. How much do you know about those kids?"

She told me not much, that Joey didn't spend a lot of time with the youth group, he was more of a quiet, stay-at-home kind of kid. Daydreamy, imaginative, creative. Maybe a little introverted.

I told her I'd get back to her when I had some news, and she thanked me. In her thanks I felt her isolation, as if I was the only person left in her world. One world, two kinds of crazy women. That was the kind of odds that attracted me.

Twenty-five

Because the police department was close to the medical examiner's office, I stopped in to see if George Manriquez had been able to find any results of a tox test on Joseph Neilsen's blood sample. As I've said, Manriquez was one of my favorite people, sensitive to relatives of victims, and more sensitive to his patients when he really didn't need to be. If I was dead I'd want him to do my autopsy. As it was I'd had to drag myself to get to his office, though I was feeling just a tad more like myself.

"Hello, George," I said. "Thanks for seeing me."

"For a retired gal you sure do show up here a lot." He peered into my face. "You don't look well. Are you doing okay?"

I ignored his question, but it made me realize I was biting the inside of my mouth, which caused my face to look like I'd had a stroke. I released my mouth and said, "It's been a while, hasn't it? Last August."

He had met me in the lobby and taken me to his office rather than the autopsy room, where I had spent more time with him. I remembered the office from another time, when I'd been under more stress but in better health. I explained to him that I wanted to go over his findings about Joseph Neilsen again now that I'd had a chance to talk with the death investigator. "Like I said, it wasn't extra special or strange. I was just asked to take a look at the body of the deceased. A young man in good physical condition."

"And you said there was no internal autopsy."

"That's right."

"Why not?"

"Why are you asking me this again? We went over it, didn't we?"

"Humor me. I'm old and forgetful."

George gave me that dry look. "Don't play the old lady card with me, we both know the truth. A better question than why not do an autopsy would be why. I already do at least one a day, so I'm not exactly looking for work. You know how it is, Brigid. In the movies they do an autopsy for every single death that doesn't occur in a hospital bed with a preexisting condition. You know how many decomposed bodies are brought in every year after lying around in their house for several days? Most of them are heart attacks, and we don't need to open them up to find out."

He sounded a little defensive, but I didn't back down. I said, "I get that, but this one was under twenty-one. You sure his stepfather being a prominent physician didn't have anything to do with it?"

"No. But like I said, the body had been transported to the hospital and I didn't get called to the scene. I looked over the body, questioned the investigator and looked at his photos and description of the house. I called it, Brigid. And I remember the father wanted the whole thing to be over with without some big production. He seemed ashamed, I think."

"That was the stepfather. Shame. Does that seem like an odd response to a death?"

"Shame, guilt, anger, laughter . . . I've seen so many responses nothing seems odd to me anymore."

"What about the mother?"

"I only dealt with Tim Neilsen. The mother wasn't involved. I heard she was hysterical and sedated. I did an external examination and didn't find any defense marks or signs of struggle. So I took a little blood—"

"You told me. You said you'd check with the lab."

"I did call the lab. Let me see if they had anything." He turned to his computer and booted it up. "We're going paperless, which I guess is nice, except the computer they gave me is so old it takes forever . . . here we go." It didn't take him long to find what he was looking for once the Neilsen file was opened. "Here, they entered the report but didn't tell me. Typical."

"So they did test?"

"Yep."

"What was the delay?"

"Same reason as I was saying. They're backed up over there. Plus they've been moving into new facilities. Funded with a government grant. State of the art." He had kept his eyes on the computer screen while he was talking, scanning the report. "Hm," he said.

"Anything interesting?"

"Nothing suspicious, none of the usual toxins, no opiates, stimulants, or antidepressants—they check for those routinely now. Got some ethanol. Is that what you were looking for?"

"Could be. How much?"

"Well over the limit for an adult. Any amount is too much for a fourteen-year-old."

"Why are you only hearing about it now?"

"Like I said, backed up, files moving. I lost track. Besides, alcohol in his system makes the accidental call even more definite. But it says here the report was even given to the parents upon request."

"What? You're shitting me. I've been dealing with a hysterical mother who says she never heard."

"She's lying. It says here the results were given to Dr. Timothy Neilsen about three weeks after the death. The lab didn't send me a copy but the tox test was done. Like I said, alcohol but still nothing that indicated suicide or homicide. It corroborates the finding of accidental death. Kid robbed his parents' liquor cabinet while they were out, took a swim, died. Crying shame."

I knew he wasn't being sarcastic. "Wait a sec. Order to forgo autopsy: Timothy Neilsen. Tox report made and given to . . . Timothy Neilsen. Mother's questions blocked. Are you picking up a pattern here?"

"Interesting, but I don't see anything to prosecute in someone who's looking for information. Want me to print this?" Without waiting for my answer he ran off the reports from the printer on his credenza. They included the death certificate.

"I wonder who this Lari Paunchese is?" I asked, reading the form.

"I don't know. A physician. I remember talking to him the next morning, along with Tim Neilsen. I don't know how he got involved."

"George, I know there's no better ME than you. But are you smelling anything at all sloppy about this case?"

George did not take offense. He'd been pushed around between detectives, families, and attorneys for too long to let my mild doubts ruffle him. "Brigid. You can't look for conspiracies around every corner. It was all pretty plain. And like I said, the investigator and the family—"

"The stepfather—"

"Okay, fine. But all respectable and aboveboard. I would stand by the accidental ruling again if anyone reexamined this case."

Something tickled at the edges of my brain, some memory that I couldn't quite get a grasp on. It was like when you can't remember the name of the actor who played a character with a limp in *Gunsmoke*. I hate when that happens.

Then even the lack of the memory was gone as the room lurched suddenly. I said good-bye, stopped in the ladies' room off the lobby, threw up, and soldiered on.

Throwing up made me think of the Pug, so on the way home I stopped at the veterinary hospital. It had been two days since we first brought the little guy in, and he was still kind of listless, though the vet assistant said he was taking some nourishment. She said she thought I could take him home if I kept an eye on him and brought him back if he started throwing up again and did I want her to go about checking him out? I thought of our situation at home and thought he was safer right where he was until he could fully take care of himself. I asked if they could keep him a few more days, just until I had things figured out.

I sat with him a while, and he licked my fingers as if grateful that

139

I'd taken care of him. He looked sad, but then pugs always look a little depressed.

I told him, "You're important to us, Al. You have to come back and claim the neighborhood bushes back from the coyotes. Your sister doesn't know shit about marking territory."

Twenty-six

The following day I kept my appointment with Timothy Neilsen, partly because I was scared at what was happening to me and partly because I wanted the chance to get him alone, tell him I'd spoken to Detective Humphries, and watch his reaction. I also let slip what I'd found out from George Manriquez about him getting the report about Joseph being drunk. I didn't do it in an accusing kind of way, just soft and wondering. But when I did that, he grew a little cold.

"There must be a mistake. Mallory Hollinger told me you wanted to see me about a health problem," he said.

"I really do. And of course I'll tell Jacquie what I've discovered, too. I just thought you'd be interested and while I was here—"

"Brigid, here's something you probably don't know, unless somehow it's gotten into that gossip mill they call a church. When you saw my wife the other night, that was the first time she had been able to leave the house in months. She has this idea that if she leaves the house something awful will happen because it did the last time. Only she went to that function with the intent of telling off the Manwarings because she hates them. And then she lost her nerve. When she was saying she couldn't do it, that's what she meant."

Rather than me watching Neilsen's reaction to my information, he was sitting there watching mine. Satisfied that I had understood, he said, "There. Now you know what I find interesting. I'm really sorry that my stepson fell in the pool and drowned. I'd like to fill the thing with concrete so I don't have to look at it anymore. Now all I'm interested in is getting back the woman I married, and I don't think what you're doing can make that happen. As a matter of fact, you're about to make it worse by telling her I hid the information from her about Joe being drunk. I'm asking you as a favor, don't tell her that." Neilsen leaned forward a little so he was almost in my space and fixed his eyes on me as if they could pin me to my chair. "Listen to me. You can't do any good here, okay? You can only do harm. Now let's move on to your case, okay?"

If I had been feeling like myself I would have thought of half a dozen comebacks and then chosen the best in the space of a second. But Neilsen mentioning my "case" made me remember why this appointment had actually been set up. My body was going all weird on me and my brain was following suit. So for now I just repeated the symptoms I'd outlined for Mallory, told him how I'd gotten sick in the middle of the night, and that I had these feelings of manic anxiety that didn't seem to have a cause. I didn't tell him about the Carlo skeleton. He asked if I was on any amphetamines and I said no. Alcohol? he asked. Maybe a glass of wine a day. I didn't tell him it was a nine-ounce glass. We all lie, right? Valium to relax. Ambien to sleep. He frowned at that. Not every night, I added. While talking about what was going on with me, I felt a tickle and brushed my hand against my cheek. "Good grief, what's this now," I said, looking at my glistening hand. I thought of the way Todd sweated when he was tense.

"You're crying," Neilsen said.

I went quiet, too embarrassed to acknowledge I didn't know when I was crying. Who let this woman in and what did she do with Brigid Quinn, I wondered.

After taking my vitals and some blood to run through tests as if he doubted my honesty about either the amphetamines or the liquor, he started asking me questions: Have you been feeling very sad lately? I thought of Gemma-Kate and well, yes. Are you sleeping more than usual, or less? Less. Feelings of anxiety, fear? Physically agitated?

Trouble concentrating? Feeling that physical problems such as achiness are symptoms of a serious disease?

I answered truthfully but knew where he was going. I'd been through this routine before when I was evaluated by Bureau shrinks after killing the unarmed suspect in the field, the case that tarnished my reputation and landed me in the Tucson field office. "I'm not depressed," I said. "I don't get depressed."

Tim Neilsen leaned forward from his chair in front of the little desk where he had tapped my answers into his computer, a record for all time. The coldness had been replaced by that compassionate yet firm Dr. Kildare look. "Frankly, all your symptoms are pointing to it. You answered five of the standard questions in the affirmative." I wouldn't have thought it possible, but his look grew even more compassionate and firmer. "Are you sure there are no changes in your life right now? Something you can't control?"

It felt like I was back talking to Mallory. I thought of Gemma-Kate again. That was pretty close to uncontrollable. I didn't like situations I couldn't control. I was thinking about that when he said, "Depression doesn't always manifest itself the way we expect it to. It makes some people manic. It can cause insomnia as often as it makes people crave sleep. It can even give you nausea. Arguably, we can run all kinds of tests, but if you want to see if I'm right I can give you a prescription."

My right hand, which had been resting on the plastic arm of the examination room chair, jumped and shot forward a little. Neilsen noted it.

"How long has that been happening?" he asked.

"It hasn't," I said.

Neilsen looked a little more concerned than before. He took a piece of paper and a pen and asked me to write a sentence. I wrote *My name is Brigid Quinn.*

Neilsen studied the sentence briefly. "Has your writing always been this small and cramped?"

"No," I confessed. I remembered signing the credit card bill at the restaurant. "I've noticed that, too."

"It's called micrographia. Stand up a second."

I started to rise. "No," he said, "don't use your arms to boost your-self from the chair."

I tried to follow instructions, and frankly, it was a little hard.

Neilsen frowned. "Tell you what, walk down the hall for me."

"What? What's wrong?"

"Humor me."

We left the examination room and he watched me walk down the hall toward the front desk. Then he watched me walk back.

"Hm," he said.

"What, hm?" I asked again.

"Your gait is off. Your right foot is slapping a bit. How long has it been like that?"

I wondered if that was what Mallory meant when she said I was limping. I told him I didn't know how long it had been that way.

He said, "Hm."

We were standing in the hallway rather than in a private exami-nation room, but I'd had enough hmmms. "What are you thinking?"

"I'm not sure. I'd like you to see a specialist."

"What kind of specialist? Would you please just tell me what you're thinking? I'm a big girl, I can take it."

Neilsen looked at an assistant passing us in the hallway who had glanced my way, and led me back into the examination room. He in-vited me to sit down. I did not, crossing my arms tightly in a way that, for the first time, I recognized had become a familiar stance.

"So what'll it be," I said, prepared for the worst, thinking about my sister-in-law, about Owen, about anyone I'd known with wast-ing kinds of diseases. "Multiple sclerosis? Lou Gehrig's disease?" That was all I could think of, so I stopped.

"I'm not equipped to make a snap diagnosis. I don't think anyone is. This sort of thing, you have to wait—"

"Would you stop making me play Twenty Questions and just spit it out?"

Neilsen said with studied calm, "This is nothing to be alarmed about yet, but along with some of your other symptoms I think we have to consider the possibility of Parkinson's."

The universe tilted away from me.

My body jolted despite my tough-gal assurance. Then, as when I've been in dangerous circumstances and have to turn into a machine or die, I became someone else. It's the easiest way to put it. My voice felt cold and hard. "What's the prognosis for that?" I asked. "I mean, I don't know much about medicine, but . . ."

Neilsen didn't jump in quickly enough with assurances. He appeared to think that my coldness was me taking things well and just sat there looking sympathetic, as if I had stopped being an annoyance and turned into a patient.

"What can I expect, loss of functioning? How long does it take?"

He shook his head. "This is way premature to be talking this way. Perhaps I shouldn't have said anything, but you insisted on knowing what I was thinking. Look, Brigid, this is all very unlikely. I just would like you to see someone who might be able to rule it out."

He explained that the other doctor might do some tests like a PET scan, which, while not ruling out Parkinson's, would check to see if they could discover some other condition. If anything, Some Other Condition sounded even more ominous. Swell, I thought with a coldness in my gut, let's definitely do some tests. Let's find out if my body is going to fail me just as I was beginning to enjoy my life.

"But don't worry, I'm just covering all the bases, and the antidepressant could even help associated symptoms." Then he tapped a prescription into the computer for twenty milligrams of a generic name I recognized from Mallory's medicine cabinet. He told me to stop taking the Valium because there could be an adverse reaction in combination with the antidepressant. And he said to avoid the Ambien as well because that could be causing my irrational thinking. Irrational thinking, he said. And don't drink. I left thinking he could be right after all. After all, the Valium and the wine, both depressants, hadn't done anything but make me feel worse.

My hand shook while I was signing the charge slip for the insurance co-pay. Me, always so cool under duress, always quick to notice a flaw in another and use it to my advantage, I hated myself for this small weakness. But I left agreeing with Mallory that whatever Neilsen's faults, whatever he was holding back, he was a very kindly and thorough physician.

At least I thought that until, waiting for the receptionist to give me my receipt, I glanced at the little holders containing the business cards of all the physicians in the practice. It was a big practice; there were six physicians with specialties all over the place, sports medicine, orthopedics, rheumatology . . . and that's when I noticed the name of Dr. Lari Paunchese. The doctor who signed Joe's death certificate was part of this practice. He was a dermatologist.

Timothy Neilsen gave the order to forgo the autopsy.

Timothy Neilsen requested the tox report and didn't share the information with Jacquie.

The doctor who signed the death certificate was in the same practice as . . . Timothy Neilsen.

I thought of running back and confronting Tim Neilsen with the fact that I knew, and asking him why he had a buddy sign off. But I doubted they'd let me back into his office. I picked up one of Paunchese's cards, to be played at a later time when I had more chips.

Twenty-seven

I dropped off the prescription at the drugstore and, feeling like I needed to practice before I said anything to Carlo, called Mallory from the parking lot.

"Can I come over?"

"Is it your niece again?"

"No, it's worse."

"How bad is it?"

"It's martini bad. It's dirty martini and extra blue cheese olives bad."

"I'm out of vodka. I can't stay out long, but meet me at Ramone's."

That was off the lobby at the Westin on Ina, what for Mallory amounted to a neighborhood bar. She was already there, her stool swiveled in my direction, while a bartender she probably knew poured our martinis over so many blue cheese olives they looked more like a salad than a drink. He smiled at me as if somehow aware that this was serious. Either that or Mallory had been flirting with him while she waited for me.

"This attractive young man is William," she said. "He's studying for a mechanical engineering degree."

I said hello to William, and he drifted off, likely having been instructed to leave us alone.

Mallory raised her glass, and I clinked obediently if without enthusiasm. She sipped and said, "It's about Neilsen, I figured out that much. What happened?"

I ate an olive. I hedged. "He gave me a prescription for antidepressants."

"That's what they all do these days. Especially women." She cocked her head as if questioning, was this why I sounded the alarm? "Rextal slow release, twenty milligrams?"

"That's the one." We were too honest to pretend. "I looked in your medicine cabinet. He gave it to you, too."

"I tried it. As you know, Valium is my drug of choice. But maybe you *are* a little depressed with having your home so out of your control. I hear it takes a couple of weeks for antidepressants to do any good, so stick with it. And you probably shouldn't drink." She eyed my martini, and I ignored her. "Is that all he did?"

"He was going to run some blood tests. And he gave me a referral to a neurologist. A specialist in movement disorders."

She didn't ask what for, she only blinked. I thought she had read enough about movement disorders to have already come to the same conclusion before Neilsen had.

I gulped, realizing I was telling my friend before my husband, but I had reached the point of no return. "He thinks there's a small chance I have Parkinson's disease."

Even if she already had guessed, that made Mallory gasp. "Oh my God."

"See, that's why I don't want to tell Carlo. I'm afraid he's going to react that way, and it scares me. And while I'm on the subject, would you not talk about this with Carlo? I don't want him to worry until there's something to worry about."

"Of course. But you need to tell him, and you need to make this your priority. You're the one I care about. The Gemma-Kate foolishness, your investigating business, you need to put everything on the back burner and resolve this. You're supposed to be retired, for God's sake. I don't know if anyone has ever told you this before, but you're a little . . . driven."

"This is just who I am," I said.

Mallory laughed. "I can see it on your tombstone now, NEVER TOOK LUNCH."

That made me laugh, too, which I needed. "You're busy," I protested. "All the charities."

"Yes, but I admit that's *my* antidepressant. For me it's a matter of survival."

Even though I still wasn't sure I needed it, I picked up the prescription and some Pepto-Bismol at the same time, taking a swig in the car. I thought about dinner. I wasn't hungry—the olives had filled me up, and I was still feeling a little sick to my stomach—but we had to eat. Well, Carlo had to eat. Still angry about Gemma-Kate hiding the toad, I wasn't caring much what she did. I stopped at a Chinese restaurant and picked up some moo shu pork. The smell of it made me want to vomit, but maybe the other two would find it palatable.

Loss of appetite. Check.

When I walked into the house I heard loud music. Gemma-Kate in her room. Not singing, just staring at the TV, drinking a Coke. She looked up at me, a little blurry around the eyes, and not a happy blurry. She didn't bother to hide a frown. Without turning her gaze from me, she automatically lifted the remote and turned down the volume.

I went into the kitchen and pulled open the door to the cabinet where we keep the liquor we hardly drink. Carlo just has this thing about wanting to keep it stocked in case a guest wants a margarita. The bottles were all opened and the levels down slightly. Gemma-Kate had been at them, and I knew the pattern. A little from this bottle, a little from that, so it wasn't obvious. Now that she had tipped her hand, she wasn't trying as hard to play the sweet innocent.

Neilsen and Mallory had been right about one thing. My very face felt heavy with depression having this load in the house. You'd think someone in my position would be able to figure out the options, take control. But I couldn't see what to do, and whenever I tried to think, my mind hit a wall. I felt powerless. I figured Gemma-Kate might weigh a little more than a hundred pounds, but I was carrying every ounce of her, and pushing against a wall that wouldn't budge.

I took one of the pills.

Gemma-Kate was kind enough to set the table and dish out the Chinese food.

Twenty-eight

The pill didn't make me feel any better, though at bedtime I fell asleep easily enough. But at some point I had a dream I hadn't had for a long time. I'm beating someone up, pulping their face with my fists. I stop and look closely, the face just barely recognizable through the blood. The person I'm beating up is me. I don't like that dream. It woke me up with the sensation of a whishing sound in the ear that was pressed to the pillow. The clock said 3:07.

I had to pee, of course. It was very dark with no moonshine to light the room. As a matter of fact, the room was darker than it usually was. No illumination from the night-light in the bathroom, or the little bulb on the ceiling smoke alarm that says the batteries are good. Even the digital numbers on the clock beside my bed had vanished. I wondered if the power had gone off.

Groggy, not thinking that this was odd, I held my hands out before me to take the few steps to the wall where I could feel my way down the short hall to the bathroom. I took the few steps. I could not feel the wall. I took a few more steps. Still nothing but blackness, no solid surface under my fingertips.

No longer groggy, I carefully stepped out some more. I was aware of the carpet under my bare feet, that much I could be certain of. I curled my toes, taking comfort in the familiar feel of the Berber, remembering how I had had this particular weave installed not long ago. It's beige, I thought. That much is certain. But other than that, I could have been alone in the furthest reaches of outer space.

I turned slightly, in the direction I thought must be back to the bed, and couldn't see anything in that direction either. No light at all coming through the window blinds, if indeed I was looking at the window. I couldn't tell.

I stepped back toward the bed to get my bearings and begin again. Stepped again. As far as I could tell the bed had disappeared.

"Carlo," I whispered, not wanting to wake him up to discover his crazy wife surely standing at the side of the bed sleepwalking in a bad dream. "Carlo." But I couldn't hear my voice. What I am embarrassed to call terror started to settle into my brain and make me afraid to try either moving or speaking, neither of which seemed to work for me this night.

Then I heard something. A whimpering. A dog whimpering, the same sound as I'd heard the other night coming from Gemma-Kate's room. Thinking if I could not find something to see or touch, this at least was something I could hear, I moved in its direction. I hoped I could get there before whatever or whoever was making the dog whimper.

Hearing only the dog and feeling only the carpeting under my feet, I stepped as fast as one can when blind, waving my arms slowly around me so I wouldn't unexpectedly connect with anything hard and hurtful. I kept on this way for . . . I understand it's crazy to say it, but the sensation of the passage of time was in hours. Not walking, but stepping gingerly through the dark, increasingly fearful for the dog, whose whimper kept at the same intensity without ever coming closer.

I must have entered the living room area by now, I thought. I had been walking so long. I kept going.

Then something changed. Instead of the carpet, in the space of a single step the soles of my feet were hurt by the gravel that covers our backyard. I could not remember coming out the door. If I was in the backyard it was still all blackness and no sound. Houses away off across the valley that contained the Cañada del Oro wash always had some lights on somewhere no matter what the time, but tonight they were dark. No lights, and no stars either.

No sound of traffic on Golder Ranch Road, which ran east and west just a few houses down from us. No night birds. No rustle of the paloverde branches in the breeze. Not even my own breath. I opened my mouth and tried to push sound out of it, any sound, felt the air come from my lungs and my throat and tongue strain, but nothing came.

Even the sound of the dog whimpering was gone now.

I stood this way, that same terror ballooning. Yet it was mixed with a share of some detached perplexity. If I could see, I would be staring at myself, wondering what I would do next. It was as if that thing that happens to me in times of danger was terminal. As if I had truly finally drained out of myself for good and would from now on be only a witness to my existence.

I stood there, not wanting to step further and feel the pain of the gravel on the soles of my feet, and not even knowing which was the way to go to get back in the house.

The darkness hit me like a great winged thing from a nightmare. I was knocked over by the nonbeingness of it. With that same feeling of witness I observed myself strain against it. Without success, I struggled, was pinned to the ground, unable to so much as raise my head against this invisible foe. I felt a pressure on my chest, the feeling of being slowly suffocated by the night. I tried to scream, but the night prevented it, filling my mouth with blackness.

The porch light went on.

Night dispelled in that single moment, I turned my head to the right and found myself staring at one of the bare feet of the life-sized statue of St. Francis. Big foot, was my first thought. When I looked up again I saw Gemma-Kate looking down at me. She didn't have a flashlight, nothing but the porch light way off behind her, but my eyes must have been accustomed to the dark and I could easily see her silhouette against a sky filled again with stars. Didn't need to say anything; for now it was enough to process this reality.

Then she said, "I saw the back door open. I heard you yell."

Did I cry out? I couldn't remember. I clutched the hand of my niece when she offered it, not caring if this was my assailant, only glad for the touch of a real human being no matter who it was. I didn't get up at first, just clutched the hand. "What's wrong with me?" I asked her. I felt too weak to ask the real question: What have you done?

"Beats me," she said, and tugged on my hand.

Then I responded, let her pull me up off the gravel into a standing position, leaned on her a bit as I meekly allowed myself to be led inside the house from a night in which, besides all the stars reappearing, all the houses blinked with a hundred lights in the distance. The headlights of a car coming down the hill on Golder Ranch gleamed, disappeared as it went around a turn, then appeared again.

Inside the house it was the same, the clock on the microwave illuminated, the bulb in the living room smoke alarm on, all those half-dozen points of light that I usually took for granted. They didn't light the house but they made it not-black, partly because my eyes had grown accustomed to the dark, but mostly because I was seeing clearly and not caught in whatever nightmare or delusion or hallucination had gripped me. In this dim light I could see the Pug lying on the kitchen tile by her water dish. I went to her and she was fast asleep, her breathing steady and not even a *moof* coming from her. I picked her up. She hardly woke. As if she was drugged.

Gemma-Kate took my arm. "Do you want me to take you to your bed?" she asked. Her words were soft and measured. She sounded like she was talking to a crazy woman.

I said no, and heard myself say it. It sounded feeble. "I'll be okay. It was just a dream," I said, and took the Pug with me into the bedroom, where I closed and locked the door. The little lights in this room and the bath off to the side were on again, too. I easily found and got into the bed. I was grateful that Carlo had not awoken, that it was my niece who found me. I looked at the clock.

The time was 3:19.

I might have remained gripped in the terror I had felt just moments before, felt it drive into me anew with the realization of how little time had passed since I awoke to it, but it had exhausted me and I fell asleep, my hand on the warm Pug, telling myself the dog was real.

Twenty-nine

I must have relaxed enough to doze off again because at five the next morning I slammed awake with the sense that my heart had been pounding for some time. I still felt sick to my stomach, too, though partly because of the thought of what had happened the night before, or not happened at all.

Neilsen had told me the antidepressant could take up to three weeks before I began to feel any real effect, so I shouldn't stop taking it. After three weeks, he had said, we would reassess. And in the meantime if my blood work came back with anything suspicious he would call me. So I took another pill that morning, and an hour later threw up my breakfast.

Looking back, the connections might seem obvious to anyone else, but that morning I could still make no successful link between the way I was feeling and the poisoned Pug. After all, we knew what had happened to the Pug, and I was absolutely certain I hadn't eaten a toad. As for my symptoms, what I was feeling didn't seem in keeping with someone who is poisoned. The vomiting maybe, but not the anxiety. Not what I was slowly coming to admit were hallucinations. A person who has ingested something would feel lethargic. I felt more like a hungover gerbil, nauseous yet still hyper. And Carlo seemed to be just fine. This is to explain why I didn't suspect Gemma-Kate might have slipped something into the Chinese food when she dished it out for us the evening before. I didn't suspect poison at all.

I reached for the cell phone on my nightstand and called Neilsen's office, got the nurse. She said antidepressants can sometimes cause nausea at first and said she'd call in a prescription for an antiemetic. Antiemetic, antidepressant, antibiotic. Someday I wanted a drug that was pro-something. I wanted to ask her about hallucinations but didn't.

What really bumped me over the edge a bit was passing by my office and seeing Gemma-Kate sitting at my desk, the referral to the movement disorder specialist in her hand.

I could have sworn I put it somewhere safer, possibly folded under a book or something. If I hadn't had such a rocky night I might have been more polite. But how do you respond when you see someone reading your private shit and know she's been moving things around?

"Put that down and get out," I said.

Carlo was immediately behind me. "Is everything all right?" he asked. I wondered why he had been following me around. Or had I spoken a little more loudly than I remember and it caused him to run?

I squeezed my eyes shut, trying to shake off a mood made up of equal parts stress and a flare-up of anger that had been in control for some months. "This room is off-limits," I said, and gestured with my thumb out the door.

"I'm sorry," she said, though kind of mechanically. She stood without objection, went into her own room, and shut her door.

That door stood like a judgment till midmorning. We hadn't talked about the events in the middle of the night.

I went back to bed and couldn't bring myself to get out again. This felt more like depression than ever before, but I knew I couldn't count on the pills to bring me out that quickly. My muscles felt immobilized while my brain sort of vibrated, like I was living in two different bodies at once, one that couldn't stop and one that couldn't go. It was maddening. I worried about what Tim Neilsen told me, about the possibility of having Parkinson's, but was too scared to either make the appointment for the tests or look up on the Internet to see exactly what the disease was and what might be in store for me.

When I felt a little better I typed some notes about Joe Neilsen's case in my laptop and made an appointment to see Elias Manwaring on Monday to ask him about who made up the church youth group. That was the most I could do.

I told Carlo I must have some sort of flu and asked would he pick up a prescription. Carlo was attentive as a man could be, though they don't make good nurses at the best of times, and even Gemma-Kate was better, coming into the room carrying the female Pug, which she placed next to me for comfort. I was comforted when I saw her put the dog down. The pills settled my stomach, and when it came time for lunch Gemma-Kate made me a grilled cheese with sliced onions and tomatoes in it, which was quite good and which I kept down.

Gemma-Kate's ministrations made me remember how solicitous she had been with me the night before when she found me in the yard. Is this how she had been with her mother? I wondered. I thought about Mom saying what a good little nurse she was. She's more comfortable with invalids, I thought. More sweet-natured when she's dealing with someone sick.

I didn't want to think about the night before, or about being somehow sick and in need of care.

Thirty

By Sunday morning there had been no more hallucinations except for a few little things, like momentarily thinking my sister, Ariel, had come to stay with us and wondering where she would sleep. The kinds of things you dream, only you're awake. The antinausea meds seemed to have kicked in a bit, so I went to church with Carlo. He talked Gemma-Kate into joining us. She resisted, then put on a dress I'd never seen before, one that showed her ample curves without being out-and-out slutty, and we went.

The service was boring, as usual, but Carlo says it's supposed to bore us into transcendence. So far I don't know what that means. Afterward I stood at the door of the parish hall and looked around the way I always do when entering a place with more than three people.

I smiled at the sight of Adrian Franklin, his ponytail curving down the nape of his neck, conversationally pinning Mallory against a wall, he taking nervous sips of his coffee, she looking guarded. Maybe she preferred doing the coming on herself. I thought about the unused Premarin in her medicine cabinet. What harm could it do anyone for her to take a lover?

Thoughts were preempted by Gemma-Kate offering me a cup of coffee and a powdered sugar doughnut. Maybe I was feeling forgiving after being in church, but I was rethinking the toad episode, whether it might have been an accident and Gemma-Kate, not knowing me well, hid the evidence because she was genuinely afraid of how I might react. Then I thought maybe she was just back in sucking-up mode when she was taking care of me, and I wondered what she wanted.

Lulu came up to where I was musing and pestered me for a bit about the Neilsen case. A couple introduced themselves as the McClays, the wife asking if I'd like to be on the altar guild. Ruth came to chatter. When I thought I couldn't stand any more fellowshipping, Mallory appeared to save me, taking a sip of my coffee without asking because that's how we were, and telling me there was someone she wanted to introduce me to, even though there wasn't.

When we were alone I pounced. "How's Adrian's dog?"

"He said the dog ate his handball glove. I think he's stalking me."

"Don't flatter yourself. There's a small chance he just wants to go to church." But then, "You should encourage him," I said quietly enough so no one would hear. "He's the kind of guy we all had a crush on in high school and thought we'd never have. So what if it's a few decades after the fact?"

"Thanks for your liberality with my sex life, but I have to live it my own way," she said without relish. Then, so as not to display any self-pity, "Besides, I'm more the Clint Eastwood type. How about you?"

I thought about Carlo, and how I've always much preferred an average man with skin on him to a hunk on a flat movie screen. But you have to respond. "That guy who stuttered in *Here Come the Brides*," I said.

Mallory blinked a few times. "I love you, darling, but sometimes you are so weird." Then she pounced. "Did you tell Carlo yet?"

"No, not yet. Doughnut?"

She took a tiny bite, wiped the powdered sugar from her mouth, and then sipped my coffee again. "I didn't think you liked it sweet," she said.

"Gemma-Kate fixed it for me." I started to put the cup down at the end of the serving table, not liking how raising it to my lips showed how much my hand shook these days.

Mallory gestured at it. "Give it here, I'll drink the rest. Did you at least make an appointment with the specialist?"

"Did you know once counts as advice and twice is nagging?"

Mallory gulped some coffee and grinned. "The hell with you, then. I'm going home to Owen who appreciates me." She started to move off, but dropped her paper cup on the floor and swayed.

"Are you all right?" I asked, getting a couple napkins off the table.

"I feel a little woozy," she said. "And sick to my stomach. I think I'll stop in the—"

I said not to worry, I'd clean up the coffee, but she had already gone off without finishing. I got some napkins from the table and bent over to pick up the coffee cup, wiping the spill, which I thought was politely ignored by others in an Episcopal fashion. But when I stood up to throw it all away a high-pitched cry from the other side of the parish hall, near the little table that served as a bookstore, took my attention and that of everyone else present.

Elderly Mrs. Covington had stumbled and slipped from her walker and was lying on the floor with her left leg at an impossible angle. I threw the wet napkin and the cup on the table beside me and rushed to her.

I did not make any connection between Mallory's onset of illness and Mrs. Covington's accident.

After the first cry she was whimpering, and I kneeled beside her to keep her still until help would come. Carlo was beside me and tried to comfort her. She looked up at him and said, "Valerie?" Then her eyes went all jittery. Shock, I thought. Carlo must have thought the same because he was making sure she didn't swallow her tongue. I had put my tote bag down somewhere, and Carlo didn't carry a cell phone, but before I could say *Dial nine-one-one* several people had whipped theirs out.

Focus still on Mrs. Covington, I could hear two voices giving instructions to send an emergency vehicle to the church. The third person fumbled her phone and it hit the tile floor next to me. She didn't bend down to pick it up.

Nervous in a crisis, I thought. I was still not connecting these events.

With Carlo in control of Mrs. Covington, I grabbed the phone and raised my hand and my sight to the woman who had dropped it. She wasn't stunned into immobility. She was swaying and weaving like a drunk.

I looked around the room, and the connections began. No sense of it all yet, but finally linking all these people together.

Have you seen the news reports of the aftermath of a bombing? The rising smoke, the blackened faces, the bloody wounds, the dazed staggering of some and the crying of others? The desperate search for a loved one?

The room looked like a slow motion terrorist attack, only no shouting or smoke or blood. Only the staggering and clutching of heads, the dazed what-the-hell-just-happened look. Some specific activity got through my still-confused cognitive senses. A woman was struggling to get out of her maxi skirt, wet with what might have been hot coffee from the look of the pot tipped over, the coffee flowing across the white tablecloth. A man I didn't know was lying on the floor reaching toward a woman bending over him, drunkenly slurring, "Lulu. Lulu." The woman bending over him was not Lulu. Lulu was in another part of the hall, throwing up in a very unattractive way.

Maybe it was a rush of adrenaline that shook me into crisis mode. Reactions started coming.

First: Make sure Carlo was okay.

I turned back to where he was kneeling beside Mrs. Covington and watched him for a second. He seemed to feel my glance and looked up at me, then turned back to Mrs. Covington when she screamed. He appeared to be unaffected by whatever was assailing the others.

Second: I found a guy who might have placed the nine-one-one call and who still stood with his cell phone in his hand and his mouth open.

"Hey buddy," I said, getting his attention by giving his arm a little shake. "Call again. Tell them we're going to need more buses."

When he turned to look at me with a dazed expression I thought he was succumbing as well, but "Buses?" he said.

"Ambulances. Tell them we got"—I took a quick count, included

162

those who were weaving a bit and might go at any moment—"at least sixteen down."

I kneeled beside an old man, checked his breathing, and looked into his eyes, which were shifting rapidly back and forth like Mrs. Covington's. "What's your name?" I asked. He looked at me like I was the odd one.

Mallory came stumbling out of the bathroom in my direction, holding her head in place. "What the hell?"

"Lie down if you're dizzy."

"No. What should I do?"

"That woman over there, she looks like she's burned. Get ice from the kitchen."

Mallory staggered off.

Third: What should have been first, and might now be too late. Assess the scene to see if anyone knew this was happening, and how, and why.

I scanned the room once more. Except for those on their cell phones who had been calling in the emergency, there were three people neither staggering, lying down, nor helping others. In different parts of the parish hall, not connected to each other except by their stillness, were Gemma-Kate, Peter, and Peter's mother, Ruth.

Ruth looked more tense than when I had met her the Sunday before. On second glance, I realized she was not staring around her. Her eyes were down rather than taking in the train wreck of a room the way any other person would do. She was especially trying not to look at her son. Gemma-Kate watched the activity, the sight of the man on the floor here, the woman holding on to a folding chair there, the elderly woman with a broken leg. Peter only stared at Gemma-Kate. Then my eyes met Gemma-Kate's, and I was convinced I knew.

Multiple buses and flashing lights later, the paramedics came like gangbusters and then stopped short at the door of the parish hall briefly, gazing at the scene, as if they expected an imminent explosion. I told them it wasn't a gas leak and they came in. I helped as I could, pointing out Mrs. Covington of the broken leg, who was the first to be taken away. I walked out with the paramedic who took her.

"I figure about fifteen, sixteen people you'll need to treat," I said. "Not everyone is reacting, but they should all be checked."

"I've never seen such a mess. What is it?"

I guess there was something about me that indicated I was familiar with a situation like this. I said, "We got nausea and vomiting, confusion, dizziness, like extreme intoxication, but they couldn't have gotten that much alcohol that quickly. Mmm, eyes jittering."

"Nystagmus."

"Yeah, that."

"Got any ideas?" he asked.

"I don't know, it's not my line." I handed him a cup. "But you might as well take this coffee with you."

"Thanks, but—"

"Don't drink it. It was the only thing they had in common. I'm guessing it might be the source."

Another gurney passed us like we were having gurney races, bearing Father Elias Manwaring himself. I had missed seeing him in the general panic.

The paramedic repeated, "I've never seen such a mess. I called for more ambulances. You coming to the hospital?"

"I don't think so," I said. If the coffee was the culprit, I was unaffected because I'd only taken a sip. Carlo was fine, probably because he always said what they made at the church was a weak Episcopal version of the real stuff and never drank it. Mallory seemed better after throwing up, but promised to go to the hospital to get checked out. Suspecting what I did, and not prepared to talk to any crime scene investigators until I could talk to Gemma-Kate, I hustled her and Carlo into the car as quickly as I could without looking like we were running. Carlo got behind the wheel and I told him to go.

Didn't waste any time.

"What did you put in the coffee, Gemma-Kate?"

"What d'you mean, what did I put in the coffee? I didn't put anything in the coffee."

"What?" said Carlo.

I said, "Enough bullshit. You wouldn't be stupid enough to use a lethal dose of something. But can the effects get worse?"

"How the fuck should I know?"

I unbuckled my seat belt, reached around to the backseat, and grabbed Gemma-Kate's wrist. "This isn't a good time to get smart-ass with me. I swear I'll turn you in."

She tried to twist away. "Ow! Aunt Brigid, you're hurting me. I didn't do anything!"

Carlo kept driving, but I could feel a glance thrown in my direction. I let go of her and turned back to the front.

"Brigid, what could you possibly be thinking?" Carlo asked.

"Let me think a second, Carlo. On the slim chance she didn't do it—"

"Hey, I'm in the backseat and I can hear you."

"Shut up. On the slim chance she didn't do it, I need to use caution."

"But you will cooperate, right?" Carlo asked. He had every right to ask. I'd hidden some things in the past and will always regret what it almost did to us.

"I swear I will. Right now I'm operating on a strong hunch. Let me just find out a few things first. And line up a criminal defense lawyer just in case."

I didn't add that Gemma-Kate being a Quinn was motivation both for and against turning her over to the cops. On one side there was the family loyalty, and my promise to Marylin. On the other side there was this suspicion of the Quinn thing that came from my father Fergus's side of the family. Not Mom so much. Sure, Ariel and I were bad kids and Mom used to keep a wooden spoon in the car and when we were stopped at a red light she'd flail at us in the backseat while she kept her eye on the light to change. But that wasn't abuse, was it? That was just frustration. The rest of us, the ones who carried the Quinn gene, were different, some undefinable unspecific extra something or lack of something that we never talked about.

When I got home I called Mallory. She told me she'd been treated with an antidote she hadn't asked the name of and released from the hospital. She said she thought Mrs. Covington was going to be okay.

She said it was an awful experience and wasn't it lucky that none of us got dangerously sick. Then she said it was the last time she'd ever drink from my coffee cup.

Most importantly, though, over and over my brain kept repeating *at least no one died at least no one died goddamn lucky no one died.*

"That was craaaazy, dude. Why did you leave so fast? Why didn't any of you go to the hospital?" Peter asked.

"None of us drank the coffee. They think it was the coffee."

"That sounds suspect, that nobody in your family drank coffee. And I saw you by the table."

"Stop playing detective," Gemma-Kate said. "You didn't drink any either."

"I never do. But I went to the hospital anyway. They made me drink whisky."

"No they didn't."

"Yeah, they said there was antifreeze in the coffee, and there were so many people they didn't have enough of the antidote. They said whisky works. I bet you didn't know that."

Gemma-Kate stayed quiet, unwilling to admit ignorance of anything.

"So why did you do it?" Peter asked. "Just for fun?"

"I didn't do it. Maybe you did it."

Peter smirked. Gemma-Kate wished she could disconnect, but something kept her fixed to his face on the screen.

Peter said, "I don't know, Gemma-Kate. First the dog, then a whole church. You even said your aunt wasn't feeling so good."

"I never said that. I said she was acting weird."

"Same thing. You move in and people start puking."

"If you repeat that to anyone I swear I'll get you," Gemma-Kate said.

Peter stopped smirking. Gemma-Kate was going to tell him she wouldn't talk to him anymore, but the screen went dark before she could say it.

Thirty-one

Father Manwaring was in his office alone the next day. When I walked in on him I heard *click click, click, click, click click* from his computer mouse.

He looked up from his laptop. "I'm just writing my sermon," he said.

"No, you're not. You're playing solitaire. I can tell from the clicking."

He leaned back in his chair, the chair barely putting up with it. He looked world-weary, the kind of look I always expect to find on clergy, only more so today. "It eases the stress."

But not much, I thought, watching him. "Mallory told me everyone was treated in emergency and sent home," I said.

"Thanks to your guess that there was something in the coffee. They weren't sure what to test it for, but then the paramedic started reciting the symptoms and they narrowed it down. Whoever was in charge worked really fast, thinking that we all could die. They came up with ethylene glycol."

"Antifreeze." I knew that because of a case I'd heard where a daughter brought her mother a protein smoothie with a shot of antifreeze. The mother died. Dogs love the stuff, too.

Manwaring nodded. I tried to blend concern with indifference. "They suspect anyone?"

"Not from the questions they asked me. They wanted to know the names of everyone in church that day, not just in the parish hall. I mean, it's not that big a church, but how can I remember the names of a hundred or so people? All I could remember is that Vicki Bergesen left during the prayers of the people, but she always seems to have to go to the bathroom right then. Then they looked at the different entrances and exits from the parish hall and quizzed me for who might have come in that back door that leads straight into the kitchen."

"What about that poor old lady who broke her leg?"

"Mrs. Covington." Manwaring sighed. "She's still in the hospital but doing okay. I visited her before I came into the office this morning." He leaned across his desk in a confiding way. "There's crime scene tape on the parish hall. I tell you, Brigid, I got some bad karma going on. We've had too many accidents for one church, and now wholesale poisoning of my congregation. Don't you think that's too much?" He talked about it like the troubles were all his own. "Maybe I should hire you to investigate what's going on."

"One case at a time," I said. "When I made this appointment it was about Joey Neilsen's drowning."

"Ah, that sad story. Sometimes I'm put in mind of what Bertrand Russell said, that the only way to achieve any happiness is to begin by admitting that the world is horrible, horrible, horrible."

His philosophizing got me off track momentarily. "That's what you tell people? You're a priest. What about goodness, and peace on earth, and eternal life?"

Elias shrugged and, reaching for his mouse, exited from the solitaire game without saving it. "Is that what you came here for?"

I thought about my probable disease, but this was one person I wouldn't discuss it with. No benefit to that. "No, I really did want to ask you about Joe Neilsen."

"I don't know how I can help," he said. "It's been a long time since the Neilsens came to St. Martin's. They switched to St. Bede's right after Joseph's funeral. He was put to rest in our columbarium."

"What's a columbarium?" I asked.

"It's where ashes are interred."

"That place out back with the white walls?"

"That's the one." He looked at me more closely, as if picking up on something he hadn't noticed when I arrived, having so much on his own plate. "You look a little under the weather. Very pale and dark rings under your eyes. Do you have allergies?"

I said, "The Neilsens. Tell me again why they left St. Martin's."

"It was her asshole of a husband. I think Jacquie was getting a lot of support here, before Joe's death, you know, when he came out about his homosexuality, and after his death, too. The only thing Tim let her do was to bury Joe here. Then they left for good."

"What about Joe himself? I've been told he wasn't well liked."

"Well liked? I thought he was a spoiled little shit."

"You know, it's admirable that you've been able to get that Tourette's under control enough to become a clergyman."

He looked a little blank.

"Do you talk this way with everyone or is it just me?"

Elias grimaced. "It's something about you. I guess I figure you can take it and it's a relief to speak my mind. Have you ever thought about how difficult it is to be the person everyone expects you to be twenty-four hours a day seven days a week?"

Yeah, I kind of understood that from working undercover. The thought crossed my mind that Elias Manwaring might have some skeletons in his closet from a past as well, though I couldn't imagine his being as bad as mine. After all, mine were real skeletons.

"Back to Joey. What was his problem?"

"This is church. We have to like everyone. People can see that, so they take advantage."

On the whole I thought drug smuggling and prostitution was a whole lot more clear-cut than church work. "How did Joe take advantage?"

"Oh, not only him, but Jacquie. He was a problem for his parents, acting out, getting into trouble, sneaking out at night, some drinking, yadda yadda yadda. Jacquie gave him to us to fix him, though if you were to put it that way to her she'd deny it and say he was perfect."

"You saw him drink?"

"My son told me he bragged about it."

"Did he get along with the other kids?"

"I think they tolerated him as well as I did." Elias looked at me, thinking. "You could get an opinion filtered through my perspective, or you could talk to Ken."

"Ken?"

"My son. He was in the group." Elias picked up a cell phone that was lying next to his computer, pressed a button for speed dial. Waited. "Hi, Lu. I've got Brigid Quinn here and she's asking questions about Joe Neilsen and the youth group. Would you let me know when you get back with Ken?"

He disconnected and turned his attention back to me. "They should be home from school soon. I don't think he had photography club today." There was one of those little pauses where you both wonder who's going to talk next and what it will be about. "You want some coffee?"

"Sure, that would be fine."

Elias frowned. "I just remembered, I drank the last of it." He didn't seem to consider that he could make more. "Water?" he asked.

"Sure, water." Anything to kill time until Lulu called back.

He left his office and came back with a glass of water, no ice. "Sorry, we're trying to be environmentally conscious and not using plastic bottles."

I took the glass from him and drank some. "That's okay. This hits the spot." While he was gone I had thought of something else. "While we're waiting, tell me a little about the youth group. Sounds like Ken is involved in a lot of activities, like most kids today."

"We try, though it's difficult to get him into sports or anything else that gets him off his ass. I tell you, Brigid, I hate kids. And PKs are the worst."

"What's a PK?"

"Sorry. Preacher's Kid. They can be snotty because they don't want people to think they're goody-goody. Ken's not so bad, though."

"Did he get taken to the hospital yesterday? Or isn't he a coffee drinker?"

"No, he didn't go to church. We can't force him. I don't know if he wants more attention from me or what, but it's kind of like the plumber at home, you know? I gave at the office."

I said, "Is there anything about this job you enjoy?"

Elias rubbed his face hard with both hands. The hands looked soft. "Sorry again, getting off track. What did you want to know?"

"Mmmm, how about what kinds of things the youth group does."

"Hiking, movies with a message, writing their own worship services." He rubbed his face again, then pushed the skin back so it only looked like he was smiling. "It's a blast, at least that's what Lulu says. She's the head of the youth group."

"Lulu said the Neilsens threatened to sue the church."

His cell phone rang, interrupting his answer. The tone was the opening bars of "Amazing Grace," no fooling.

"Hey," Elias said. "What's he done now?" Listening. "Okay, we're coming over."

"Was this a bad time?" I asked, picturing some minor family drama.

"Oh, sounds like just another day in paradise. Lulu said they walked in, Ken listened to the message on the machine, and started to cry."

Thirty-two

The rectory was a short walk away from the church, a gravel-coated path down a little hill and across a cactus-studded field. It was quicker that way than driving, Elias said. That was all he said, then buried himself in thought as he trudged toward the place he pointed at. I trailed slightly behind, finding it odd that I was puffing to keep up with this out-of-shape guy, and noticing that my walking was not so good.

Lulu was watching for us at the screen door with a metal coyote on the front and opened it before we got there. A spaniel was beside her, licking the top of her sneaker. You could tell things were serious because she hadn't trotted out a plate of cookies. She said, "Don't be hard on him, Elias."

Elias wasn't listening. He seemed to have built up some steam as we walked from the rectory to the house, and the steam was looking for a way out. We found Ken sitting in the middle of the couch in a neat but carefully shabby living room, with the kind of furnishings that would warm a church mouse's heart. I didn't think you could get plaid Herculon in Early American anymore, and couldn't imagine it was new when the Manwarings bought it. I sat down on it, too, not because they thought to invite me to do so, or because I particularly wanted to comfort Ken. I was feeling a little out of breath and dizzy, and my brain was misfiring again after the walk from the church.

Already saddled with his dad's corpulent body, Ken looked like collateral damage from his father's profession. Too many potluck dinners where the one common ingredient was cream of mushroom soup. He was blowing his nose, pushing up his glasses that slid down with the blow, and blowing his nose again.

Elias didn't waste time with preamble. He was a priest and could smell a confession coming. That soft hand I saw at the church turned into the iron finger of judgment as he jabbed his son in the temple lightly, but definitely. "Start talking," he said.

From that point on I could only listen while Ken talked and Elias asked all the questions. And Elias would have been good at Gitmo. Actually they always say people really want to tell the truth, and interrogation is just a way to help them do it with some dignity. That was how Ken was now. It looked to me like he'd been laboring under this burden ever since Joe's death.

Punctuated by *supsups* and sniffles, Ken described what I had heard about but never dealt with at close hand. The Choking Game.

Lulu gasped at the very name. "What is it?" she asked.

"Kids do it to each other. It makes you pass out. Some kids say there's kind of a rush when it happens but I never—"

"I hope to hell you never—"

"Stop it, Elias," said Lulu. "How does it happen, Ken?"

Ken put the heels of his palms against either side of his neck. "You do this thing where you press here—"

"Don't, Ken," Lulu said.

"He's not," Elias said. "Where did you learn about this?"

"We heard about it at school. Some kids—"

"Who else played the game? Which kids?"

Ken shook his head.

"Which kids?"

Ken said, "He'll beat me up."

"Right now I don't blame him," Elias said, grabbing Ken's shirt and twisting the cloth.

173

"Elias!" Lulu said.

Even I held my breath for a second. Then Elias glanced at me and let go. I couldn't tell if his face was red from embarrassment or anger. Maybe a good thing I was there.

"You don't understand," Ken said. "He'll be in a shitload of trouble—"

"You're in a shitload of trouble right here, my friend." The tone was menacing, but under better control now. After a moment Elias squinted at Ken like he was looking from a different angle. "It's Pete, isn't it?"

Ken's silence confirmed it.

"I know Peter," I said. "Is Peter a problem?"

Elias answered with silence before saying, "He's another kid Ken's age in the youth group. Father's a cop and very strict. When Ken says Pete will be in a shitload of trouble for playing this game he's not exaggerating." He turned back to Ken. "Have you done it since Joe died?"

"No!" Ken said.

"Now tell me, what does this have to do with Joe's death?" Elias asked.

"He talked about how you could do it to yourself, and when your body sagged the cord would give way if you tied it right and you'd fall down and then come to."

"When did you do it last?"

"When we got back to the church from that last hike up to the Romero Pools. Everybody else got picked up and we were waiting for you to take us home. We were hanging out in the library."

"You did it on church property," Elias repeated. "They really could sue us. That's just fucking terrific."

Lulu glared at Elias and said, "Why Joe? You didn't even like Joe."

"He was always, like, being all show-offy with everything. His parents didn't just go on vacation to the White Mountains, they went elephant trekking in Thailand or something weird like that. Everything was, like, oh, I've got a media room. I've got a personal gym. I've got a pool with a slide. Shit like that. He never stopped. Not like he ever invited us over."

"At the church," Elias repeated.

"Pete liked to dare him to do stuff, told him like hey if you can ride an elephant into the jungle you should be able to do this. Then Pete would make fun of Joe without Joe even noticing. So Pete tells us about something his dad showed him, something called carotid control that cops use on bad guys. And we watched some videos. And he asks if Joe would do that and Joe says sure he could do that."

"What videos?" I asked.

Ken sighed. "It's all on YouTube."

"Did you post Joey on YouTube?" Elias asked. His face grew red again.

Ken looked so low he'd have to reach up to tie his shoe.

"Show us," I said.

Ken heaved his body off the couch and led us into the alcove where his computer sat, open to view from most of the house. At least these parents were careful about that, but you couldn't control what happens in other houses. I had worked enough child pornography cases to know that real well.

Still sniffling, Ken booted up his computer while the three of us stood behind him watching. There was a wall nearby for me to lean against, my hands in my pockets to hide their trembling. The spaniel kept working on Lulu's sneaker, creating a dark wet patch on the toe. Lulu remembered herself. "Can I get you something? Water?"

"No thanks. I'm fine." We didn't look at each other during this exchange, like we were afraid we'd miss something if we looked away from the screen.

Ken brought up his search engine and keyed in "youtube choking game." There were over four thousand results. On the first page it was mostly news items and public service announcements warning about the dangers. Ken paused, reluctant to go on.

"Do it," Elias said.

"Dear," Lulu said. I was unsure who she was speaking to.

Ken keyed in a code and pressed ENTER.

"Are you on this video?" Elias asked.

"No!" Ken said as loudly as Elias and then in a quieter voice, "I was filming. My phone."

The video came up and with a tap of Ken's finger started to play. The camera panned over a bookcase. Elias leaned closer to the screen to study the spines of the books. "Tillich. Bonhoeffer. Yep, that's the fucking church library, all right."

"Shut. Up!" Lulu said.

The camera slipped to the left to show the boy I knew from the photograph his mother had given me, standing in front of the books. He was thin and gawky, short, and like most teenagers hiding his insecurity behind bravado. As an adult I could see this, while Ken and Pete would have no idea of the pain behind the face. Joe laughed, a laugh that would have annoyed me even more if he was still alive, then started speaking in what he would imagine was a solemn tone. "Astronaut Joseph M. Neilsen reporting in. First launch for Space Monkey. One small step for man, one—"

A voice, presumably Peter Salazar's, interrupted, "You are such a stupid jerk."

Joe laughed again, either thinking the boys talked to each other this way, or craving the attention so much he didn't care what form it came in. "Commander Peter Salazar, are you ready?"

The boy belonging to that name moved into place in front of Joe. I could only see his back, but it looked enough like Gemma-Kate's buddy. Peter was considerably taller than Joe, but otherwise similar, dressed in the same adolescent uniform, blue jeans and T-shirt.

Ken's voice said, "You gotta move to the side or I don't have him."

Peter moved slightly to the right and reached up his hands to Joe's neck. Paused. "Do I really have to touch him?" he asked.

"Wait," Ken's voice said again. "Better get in front of that chair so when he goes down—"

"Oh man," Peter said, and grabbed Joe by his shirt to move him over by an armchair. "Happy now?"

"I'll be okay," Joe said, though not looking so cocky anymore, maybe a little nervous at the thought of actually falling down. "Go for it."

Peter reached up again.

"Little to the right," Ken said.

Peter moved one step to the right. "This good?"

The camera moved a little more as Ken stepped to the left. Peter brought his hands up again, and with the heels of the palms pressed against the sides of Joe's neck. "This look right?"

"I guess," Ken said.

Joe said nothing. He closed his eyes. I felt the three of us standing before the computer hold our collective breath. It took longer than I would have imagined. Then his knees buckled and he fell into the chair. His head lolled on the cushion.

"Whoo!" Peter yelled and jumped back, and Ken gave a corresponding "Whoo!"

Joe was still.

"Wasn't he supposed to come to right away?" Peter asked, looking straight into the camera, at Ken.

Joe's body started to jerk. Both hands wrenched up and hit his own face like a berserk puppet. His feet bent backward, curling under the bottom of the chair, and his back arched in what could have been a grand mal seizure.

The phone dropped so that all we could see were some cabinets at the bottom of the bookcases.

"Call nine-one-one."

"No! Joe? Hey, Joe."

"Wait, pull him off the chair! Get him flat!"

We heard a tussle, things hitting, maybe Joe's head on the wooden floor. I watched the seconds of the video tick, one, two, three, four, and—

"Aw, fuck man! We thought we lost you! That was so cool!"

"Shh, somebody might hear."

"Man, that was awe-some!" That was Joe's voice. "Let's do it again." The day he didn't die.

Video ended, the rest of us stood frozen in front of the computer. I heard Lulu whisper, "Oh my God."

Ken started sobbing again. "I killed Joe," he said.

"What makes you think you killed Joe?" Lulu asked, putting both her hands on his shoulders.

"If I hadn't agreed to do that with Pete, Joe wouldn't have gotten the idea and tried to do it to himself. Because we wouldn't do it again.

I bet that's what happened, he went underwater and held his breath. Or something."

"Not even Joey Neilsen would do something that stupid." Elias repented of the hasty words and put his arm around the kid, suddenly losing the harsh tone. "Just because you can think of something doesn't make it so."

"Or maybe something happened to his brain and that's why he drowned," Ken said.

Obviously Ken wasn't paying attention to his father's wisdom, and Elias wasn't long on patience. "You didn't kill Joe," he said. "Did he, Brigid?"

"Nah, he didn't kill Joe," I said, as if I was the expert Elias made me out to be. I figured being Father Elias Manwaring's son and all, he had enough on his shoulders. "Do you have Peter Salazar's address?"

"In my office. This office," Elias said, sounding a little shaken. He wandered off and returned shortly with a small stapled booklet that said *St. Martin's Church Directory* on the front. He carried it into the kitchen; I followed and watched him page through to the alphabetized directory and write down the address on a pad for me.

"You flipped past some pictures. Is his family in there?"

"I think they had their picture taken." He flipped to the back of the booklet and paged through photo after photo of full-color families all with Sunday clothes and the same smile. I recognized some people from the times I'd attended services with Carlo, but didn't spot Mallory as he paged past the *H*'s and into the *S*'s, where Peter Salazar appeared with his younger sister, mom, and dad. There was Ruth, and there was Peter, the boy who had made friends with Gemma-Kate. And there was the father, with a bulldog face and barrel chest, puffed out aggressively even at the photographer.

"Son of a gun," I said, cleaning up my language a bit even though it wouldn't be appreciated.

"What?" Lulu asked, coming up behind us.

"I know that guy."

"You've probably seen them at church. Good churchgoers, that family," Elias said. "Decent pledge, too."

But no, I hadn't noticed him at St. Martin's. I was staring at the man who had interrupted me when I was talking to Sam Humphries. The man, identified as Anthony Salazar under the photograph, was Sam's boss, the sergeant. I bet he would shit if he saw this video. Or maybe he already had, and that was why he assigned Sam the Rookie to investigate Joe Neilsen's death. Maybe Ken had a point.

I left the Manwaring family sorting out their issues and walked back to the church, intending to stop off at the columbarium Elias had told me about to see where Joey was laid to rest, as long as I was there. As I walked I called the Tucson Police Department, said I was helping to investigate a case for Anthony Salazar, and asked for his e-mail address at the office. Then I called up YouTube, entered Ken's user name, and sent Salazar the link to the video of his son choking the kid I identified as Joseph Neilsen, now deceased. I wrote that I wanted to see him. Salazar would have my phone number from the message but I added my e-mail address for good measure. This evening at the Salazar house should be interesting, I thought.

I was thinking about this when I reached the columbarium, found the black wrought-iron gate in the middle of the high white adobe wall, and walked through. The first thing I noticed was four crosses made up of individual polished marble tiles, each about seven inches square, many engraved. Presumably urns containing ashes lay under each tile.

The second thing I noticed, sprawled in front of a tiled concrete bench tucked against the wall nearest to the gate, an empty cup next to him, the coffee forming a pool for a number of dead ants, was Adrian Franklin. It seemed the emergency services had forgotten to check the columbarium.

Poor, cute, friendly Adrian. We wouldn't see his blazing, bad-boy smile again. All he wanted to do was find a change of scene where he could mourn his wife and make a few friends who wouldn't constantly remind him of her. Moved all the way to Arizona. Came to St. Martin's for peace. And found the afterlife instead.

Thirty-three

I had made a nine-one-one call, followed by one to Elias, followed by one to Carlo letting him know I'd be home a little late. I was glad Gemma-Kate hadn't picked up the phone. I wasn't ready to hear her voice just yet.

Manriquez was there, joined by the man I had only an hour ago come to know as Tony Salazar, father of Peter, husband of Ruth. Elias was there, too, nearly hysterical, and very distracting.

"Oh my God, it's that man," Elias said.

I had decided to keep my mouth shut unless I was asked a direct question. Elias provided the name of the deceased. Adrian Franklin. "I remember his name because he asked me to make him a name tag."

Salazar had told them to go back home rather than tramp around and possibly spoil some footwear-impression evidence. But he and Lulu stood outside the columbarium, hanging on to the wall surrounding it like they dared not let go.

"What is going on here?" Elias asked no one in particular. "Accidents. Somebody poisons my congregation. Now this." His gesture indicated that *this* was the potential new pledging unit dead on his property. "Is it a hate crime? Who hates Episcopalians? We're one hymn shy of Unitarian, for Christ's sake!"

Tony Salazar must not have received the YouTube link of his son choking Joey Neilsen. He just glanced at me, acknowledging we'd seen each other before. And if he didn't know who I was when he saw me with Humphries a few days ago, he knew now when I told him my name.

"Ah, the mighty Quinn," he said with a wink.

"Heard that one," I said.

He asked me to please calm Elias down while he and Manriquez did a death scene assessment.

"Good thing you can identify him," Salazar said, "because he doesn't have any ID on him."

"You have to find where he's staying," I said. "He told me he has a dog, and it may have been locked inside for more than a day."

We could have all guessed that the body was collateral damage from the poisoning the day before, and it didn't take the ant crawling out of one of the nostrils to confirm that he had been dead nearly twenty-four hours, but it was Manriquez's job and he did it. "I don't see any other signs of violence. We'll take him back to the lab and run the test for ethylene glycol. I wonder why he was the only one to get a fatal dose."

"He comes out here to enjoy his coffee in peace, passes out, gets missed by the paramedics?" Salazar said.

Manriquez nodded. "Not a bad scenario. With half an ounce and no treatment it would have taken just a couple hours to succumb. Maybe I'll find something else."

I still kept my mouth shut through all this. I hadn't even called Manriquez this morning because I didn't want to be asking too many questions given that I suspected my niece might have . . .

What do I do now, Marylin?

Maybe the spirit of Marylin had my back just then, because I thought about the video I had seen at the Manwarings'. Then I thought about the way Peter Salazar had stared at Gemma-Kate in the church the day before. What was that look? Was it *I can do more than poison a dog?* Maybe it was a false hope, or maybe I had locked on to Gemma-Kate too soon. What if?

I took Manriquez aside while Adrian Franklin's body was being zipped into a body bag and loaded into an ambulance. I wanted not only to get some answers but to begin the process of casting suspicion on Peter if it was warranted.

"Do you know about the Choking Game?" I started.

"A.k.a. the Fainting Game? Space Monkey? Sure."

"What do you know?"

"Epidemiology, mechanism, what?"

"Just talk to me. I'll figure out if it's worth it."

"There was a poster session at the NAME conference in Baltimore last year. They figure maybe a thousand kids die every year as a result of the game, but the figures could be higher because if they do it alone it can be mistaken for suicide. I had one case last year that was definitive because there was another kid involved who did the maneuver and confessed."

"I saw how they do it to each other on a video. What exactly happens?"

"Pressing on the carotid artery presses on baroreceptors that cause—"

"You're not speaking English again, George."

"You know how they say when you're exercising you shouldn't take your pulse by pressing your fingers against your neck because you might pass out?"

"Yeah."

"It's like that."

"Can you kill someone that way?"

"Sure."

"Is it obvious?"

"No. It's hard to pin the cause of death on that."

Now for the information plant. I said, "Let me ask you another question. How well do you know this Sergeant Salazar?"

"Some. All-right guy. Why do you want to know?"

"You know that death I've been investigating, Joe Neilsen? I just watched a video of the sergeant's son playing the Choking Game with Neilsen. He said his dad taught him to do it."

Manriquez whistled. "Well, that's awkward."

Thirty-four

My new suspicion of Peter was a long shot, and on the drive home I realized it might be wishful thinking. After all, the poisoning at the church only happened now, after Gemma-Kate arrived. And there was the toad. My spirits dropped again.

When I walked in the house she and Carlo were having a quiet tête-à-tête in the living room. He was sitting in his reading chair, his book turned pages down over the arm. Gemma-Kate sat cross-legged at his feet like a disciple. Carlo smiled at me; Gemma-Kate turned to look and smiled, too, just like Carlo. I felt my face get hot with anger.

"What's wrong?" Carlo asked. I had the feeling the two of them had been talking about what happened at the church the day before; he wanted to glance away, but I was holding his eyes. I forced mine away first and went into my office, where I took a minute to google the name Adrian Franklin. Some hits but none that suggested a restaurant owner in Gainesville, Florida. Didn't mean much, some people really are nobodies.

Carlo had followed me. "Tell me what's wrong," he demanded.

I came back into the living room. They were both watching me now. If I'd been feeling better I might have used more subtle interrogation techniques. "Okay, the situation just got bumped up a couple notches. It's not just a nasty prank where everybody got to drink whisky and was sent home except for the poor woman who broke her leg. Somebody from the church died."

"Who?" Carlo asked, looking simultaneously shocked and relieved that I wasn't the one in imminent danger. "That dear old lady?"

"Adrian Franklin."

"Oh my God."

"I found him in the outdoor area where they stow people's ashes." I was watching Gemma-Kate as I said it. "You and Peter have been out there."

Gemma-Kate hadn't gotten up from the floor. She didn't speak, but she stopped looking bland. Her eyes turned into twin black holes that waited to take in whatever the world gave them. What she wasn't doing was claiming innocence. Like me at the church earlier in the day, she was keeping her mouth shut and waiting.

"Did you do it?" I asked.

"We need to call someone," Carlo said.

"And tell them what?" I said, without taking my gaze away from Gemma-Kate. "Did you do it?"

"No!"

"Stand up."

She did. I grasped the sides of her face between my hands so she couldn't look away, and I hoped for once to see truth in those eyes. I tried to get a grip on myself. "Honey, listen to me. He was a nice man. A man who was grieving for a dead wife, and came here to begin life again. He had just adopted a Labrador retriever. He played handball. This man just lost the rest of his life. Can you hear what I'm saying? I understand this was an accident, and I'll help you deal with it. I don't want to turn you in, but I swear I will if you don't tell me the truth now."

She tried to get her head out from between my hands, but I found myself gripping her harder and I wasn't going to let go now if she broke her jaw.

She sensed this, went still, said quietly, "You don't know anything, and I'm not going down for something I didn't do."

I felt Carlo's hand on my shoulder. It had a tentative feel to it, as if he somehow knew I knew my business in matters like this, but could not force himself to stand by observing uselessly.

My cell phone rang. I let go of Gemma-Kate's face, went to the front hall, and leaned over to retrieve the phone from the tote bag I'd dropped on the floor. When I stood up a wave of dizziness went through me, a black and white checkerboard effect in front of my eyes, and a feeling of being hot and cold at the same time. Must have been moving too fast, because I still got to the call before it went to voice mail.

"Anthony Salazar," the voice said, without a hello. "I need you to come to the office tomorrow at ten."

"About?"

"It's sure not about that bullshit video you sent me, whatever the fuck that's about."

I hung up, regretting that I'd sent that video of Peter choking Joey and gotten on Salazar's bad side at an inopportune time. I told Carlo and Gemma-Kate I'd be going downtown to talk with the police.

"Anything you want me to tell them, Cupkate?"

"Yeah. Go ahead and tell them I buried a fucking toad and that proves I poisoned everyone at a church. Then tell them you're nuts."

Her round full eyes closed into quarter moons and she disappeared into her room. I called after her, loudly enough to get through the closed door, "And with his father being who he is, I better not catch you talking to Peter Salazar anymore."

Gemma-Kate yelled back, "First you think I'm psycho, and now stupid. Fuck you!"

It felt like the run-up to a war and, with Quinn against Quinn, the outcome was unsure.

Thirty-five

Gemma-Kate managed an apology for telling me to fuck myself, and we ate a subdued dinner together, poached salmon with a tahini sauce. I took my pill and wondered when it would make me feel happy. Holding on tight to normal, Carlo and I took our evening walk, me holding the leash for the female Pug and talking about whether she missed her brother.

He was silent for an awfully long time.

"What?" I asked him. And because he was taking what felt like forever to respond I said again, "What?"

"What a mess we've gotten ourselves into," Carlo said.

"We meant well, bringing her here. You meant well defending her. This could have happened in Fort Lauderdale as easily as here."

"I can't see what to do," he said. "Can you?"

I remembered another time when I didn't trust Carlo to be able to deal with hard things. Right now in the midst of this horrible dilemma I felt a rush of love for him, that I could say anything. That I wasn't alone. I'd never had a partner before, in any sense of the word. I told him how strongly I felt about being true to Marylin and how that meant not throwing Gemma-Kate under the bus.

"I can't believe she did this on purpose," he said.

"I can't either. Even accidental it's serious enough we could be look-ing at prison time. At seventeen she'll be tried as an adult. But, like she said, there really is no evidence, just my suspicions. If there is any evidence I want to be the first one to find it.

"Perfessor, the complicated thing is, I want to be wrong. I want Gemma-Kate to be innocent of putting that antifreeze in the coffee-pot. Not only is she family, but I've seen the kind of fallout this causes. One family is going to be ruined forever, and I want it to be Peter Salazar's family."

Carlo didn't know everything I'd been thinking. "Peter?"

I nodded but didn't bother to explain just then. "I want that real bad. But one step at a time. It was good I found the body, because now I can go downtown and see what I can find out tomorrow. I'm glad Salazar has asked to see me, because interviews can go both ways. Then we'll decide," I said, putting a little emphasis on the *we*. I meant it, too; I had learned to be a couple, not just singular, and would de-pend on Carlo for whatever wisdom I lacked. "It's still chilly." I wrapped my sweater more tightly around me, and found it did no good.

"I was just about to say it's a little warmer than it has been at night," Carlo said.

We were nearly back to the house when I stopped walking. Not because of any choice, but simply because I felt as if my body had turned to stone. I wanted to pick up my right foot and take a step, but my foot wasn't having it. The chill I had felt a moment before had increased rapidly to the point that my teeth were chattering. They were the one part of my body that was moving, though without any more control on my part than my walking.

Without realizing I was stopped, Carlo had continued ahead sev-eral paces, turned to me to say something, and noticed I wasn't there. He waited for me to catch up, maybe thinking the Pug was sniffing the gravel, then must have noticed it straining at the leash, its tongue lolling in impatience to go on. He still didn't say anything, just watched me for a few seconds as if I must have a perfectly good reason for stopping.

"Carlo," I said. I was glad that at least my voice was working.

He must have heard that it was not my normal voice. He came back to where I stood but still didn't think to offer aid. He peered into my face, our head lamps making it impossible to see anything that close. He took mine off so he could see better. "Is something wrong?" he said.

Even then, feeling myself shivering from the inside out yet unable to move, I tried to make light of it. "May I take your arm?" I asked. He gallantly offered it, perhaps thinking I was only being playful.

With that physical or psychological advantage, I can't tell which, I was able to get my forward momentum going again until we reached the house. Carlo left me to put the leashes and our head lamps back onto their shelf in the laundry room. I stood in the living room, with the sound of the television coming from what seemed like far, far away. The volume increased, faded, and increased again as if someone was toying with the controls or my hearing was awry.

Gemma-Kate must be watching television, I remember thinking. It vaguely annoyed me that I couldn't figure out what program it was. I wanted to speak to her, but found that when I opened my mouth nothing would come out. I think the last thing I remember is swaying, my legs melting under me. Darkness.

Thirty-six

Oblivion is nice, in its own way. It's what we seek nightly when we go to sleep, it's that desirable feeling that the sodium pentathol is doing its job of putting us "under." It makes me wonder sometimes why we dread it so. Maybe it's the assurance of waking up afterward that makes the difference, for better or for worse.

But what a pleasant thing to think that, along with the nicer aspects of living, there would be a time when none of those regrets, doubts, or fears would slither up from wherever they dwell in our minds. This, I suppose, is the lure of suicide. There was the case of the child who had to go back to the father who had been molesting her, a breach of justice that makes the thought of a second Flood seem like a good idea. My colleague who had been in charge of the case was trying to deal with his failure to save the child. I thought he was talking about her when he said, "God never gives you anything you can't handle."

I was feeling crabby, can't remember about what anymore, and had no spare sympathy that day. "If that was the case, no one would ever commit suicide," I said, lightly.

Three days later my colleague shot himself. I should have been more sensitive that day, and asked, at least, whether he was talking about the child or himself.

When I came back from my own little death, I found myself in the bathtub, still dressed, but soaking. That was not so pleasant. Carlo and Gemma-Kate were kneeling next to each other at the side of the tub, watching me intently. Carlo's intentness was a little worried, while Gemma-Kate's made me feel oddly like a specimen of alien life.

I thought again how she seemed more interested when I was obviously sick. The oblivion might have left, but the paranoia had not. I looked at both of them with some suspicion.

"What happened?" I asked.

"I found you on the floor in the living room, unconscious," Carlo said. "I shouted to Gemma-Kate and she rushed out of her room. I was going to call nine-one-one but then you started to convulse. She said there wasn't time. She felt your forehead and said you had a high temperature and calling the paramedics was fine but we should cool you down. So we brought you in here and turned on the water."

Some of the memories of the past—I couldn't guess how long ago—were coming back. I remembered the chills, and the rigidity of my body when I tried to move. And I remembered hearing the sound of the television swelling and dying in my ears.

Carlo kept talking, seeming a little nervous because of me not responding. "I called an ambulance. It's coming from the Golder Ranch fire station, so it should be here any second. We could get you into some dry clothes."

I hate when people say "we." "How are we today, Mrs. DiForenza?" they would ask in the nursing home. In that moment I didn't want Carlo to know I was sick. One of those nearly undefined fears was slithering up from that spot in my mind where the door was usually kept safely closed and double-locked. Carlo should not know I was sick, and if they started running tests, God only knew what they would find and tell him. One of these days I had to do a little investigating, google "fever" and "Parkinson's" and find out if that was one of the symptoms as well as the difficulty walking.

But for now, Carlo should not know I was sick.

"No hospital," I finally said.

"But," he said. Did he pause a little too soon? Was he glad he didn't have to follow through on that, discover I was another sick wife? That "but" didn't sound very forceful. Okay, so maybe I know at this point it was mostly the paranoia talking, and I've just finished describing all this cozy newfound trust for Carlo, but I'm still trying to recall everything the way it happened and how I felt at the time. I know he glanced at Gemma-Kate before he said, "What if it's a delayed reaction from the coffee at the church? You said you sipped a little."

"That couldn't happen. Maybe that flu I was feeling the other day," I said. "I'm feeling much better."

The doorbell rang.

"You're going to the hospital," he said.

"I'm not," I said.

"You most definitely are."

While we argued, Gemma-Kate went to answer the door. There was a clatter of what I expected was a collapsible gurney in the front hall, and two paramedics crowded into the small guest bathroom behind Carlo. Gemma-Kate peeked around one of them. The four looked at me like they were wondering how to move my body. I stood up from the tub, holding on to the towel bar because I was still a little woozy.

"I don't need to go to the hospital," I said. "If you want to wait a minute while I get some dry clothes on I'll go out to the ambulance and you can check my vitals."

One of the paramedics shrugged. "Up to you."

"You won't insist on taking her to the hospital?" Carlo asked.

"It's up to her," the same paramedic said. "This happens all the time."

I was pronounced stable on-site and promised Carlo I would make an appointment with the doctor.

Thirty-seven

The next morning there was a message on my phone from Jacquie, asking again about what progress I was making. I had started taking aspirin on top of everything else to keep my temperature down and actually was feeling better. That tendency to freeze had stopped for the time being.

I had more pressing issues to contend with, but I couldn't just drop Jacquie. Plus the messages I'd been receiving told me Jacquie was not your back-burner kind of client. When she answered her phone with a "Yes?" I said, "It's Brigid. Can I come over?"

"No," she said.

"Is Tim there?"

"Yes," she said.

"Can you meet me?"

"Yes," she said.

"Beyond Bread, the one on Ina, fifteen minutes." We were beginning to sound a little secret agenty, and it irritated me.

Then she whispered, "Do you have something?"

"Yes," I said. Hey, I can do cryptic, too.

I cut her some slack, though, guessing that was what happened when you spent too much time trying to keep the peace between your son and your husband, covering up for both of them, trying to preserve the denial. I drove to Beyond Bread to find her there waiting for me. I got a coffee and a lemon bar to settle my stomach, and sat down at the table she had chosen.

In answer to her urgent "What have you found?" I reviewed my conversations with Detective Humphries, Dr. Manriquez, and all the Manwarings. I explained that a toxicology test had been found and there was nothing that suggested Joe had been poisoned. I told her very gently about the Choking Game video that was still on YouTube, and how she could watch it. But I recommended she not do so alone. Basically, I treated her like a strong woman.

"Oh oh oh oh oh," she whispered, her lips trembling. Then she dissolved into tears.

I reached into my tote bag and pulled out a couple of tissues, which I handed to her, then waited for her to calm down, which she did quickly. I had chosen to meet her in a restaurant because people don't generally get hysterical in restaurants. That's why they fire you in public.

"Maybe that's why you've been suspicious of Joe's death, why it felt there was something strange about his falling into the swimming pool. Had you noticed anything different about him?"

"Like what?"

I went over part of what I had learned from googling the Choking Game. "Had Joe started to seem disoriented?"

Jacquie tilted her head in a question.

"What about something more specific? Did you ever notice he had bloodshot eyes? Or did he complain of headaches?"

That she could understand, and shook her head no, but she started jumping to more conclusions than a depressed lemming. "Do you think that game hurt his brain? It was those boys, wasn't it? It was Lulu Manwaring. She let them go off alone. I knew it."

I held up a hand to slow down her runaway mind. "Hold on, I'm not done yet. I found a couple of other things about your son's death that are just slightly irregular." For the time being I didn't mention that the kid who choked Joe was the son of the boss of the detective who investigated the death scene. Or how he might be connected to a second death. Seeing how she had reacted to what I'd already said, that was just a trifle too irregular for comment until I could go further into it. But I did ask about Lari Paunchese. "Do you know him?"

Jacquie nodded. "Lari. He's in Tim's practice. They play racquetball. We have Christmas parties and things together."

"Did you notice he signed Joe's death certificate?"

"No. How could that have happened?"

"I don't know. Was he the one out with Tim the night that Joe passed away?"

"He was. I think they might have gone to a sports bar to watch basketball or football or something. Tim once made a comment that it would have been nice if Joe liked football but he figured that would be a no." It hurt her. It still hurt her and probably always would. "Is that legal, for someone Tim knows to sign the death certificate?"

"I'm not sure about ethical, but I know it's legal."

We walked out of the restaurant together, and I helped her into her car. She still seemed a little shaken, and I hesitated asking one last question, but I did anyway.

"Jacquie, were you aware of Joseph . . . drinking?"

She looked shocked. "He was only fourteen years old," she said, then buckled her seat belt and pressed the ignition button to end the conversation. I put my hand out to stop her from closing the car door.

"That toxicology test I told you about? Joey had alcohol in his system the night he drowned."

Without looking at me she shut the door and backed out. Just as well I didn't ask the question that had been on my mind during our whole conversation: *Do you want me to find out that Tim hurt your son?*

Thirty-eight

From Beyond Bread, I was okay driving over to the Tucson Police Department. Only when I got out of the car and started across the parking lot did I have one of what I'd come to call, delicately, my episodes. A police car had pulled in and, seeing me, stopped to let me cross in front of him. I started, and within a couple of paces, I froze. Putting out my right foot to take a step should be easy enough, I thought. My brain was sending messages down to my leg. I was mobile. But nothing anywhere close to forward motion was happening.

I stood, terrified, wondering if the fever was returning and I was going to drop to the pavement at any moment.

The officer got out of the car. He walked around the front and up to me, looking sympathetic. "Can I help you?" he asked.

Damn you, Brigid Quinn, I shrieked inside my head. "I'm sure I'll be all right in a minute," I said. But I still didn't move and, feeling as if he needed to get me out of the middle of the parking lot, he took my arm. "There's a bench right over there by the sidewalk," he said. "Let me just help you to that."

Oh God, he was helping a little old lady across the street. I was not only terrified, I was pissed. But one thing I wasn't was giving up my opportunity to see Salazar. I let him lead me across, somehow more mobile with my arm in the crook of his. I handed him my car keys, pointed out my Camry, and asked him to please get my walking stick out of the trunk. Maybe that would replace the arm when he left me alone.

He did, and whether it was the comfort of the stick or not, I found myself back in motion, the freeze ended, at least for the time being.

They wouldn't let me take my stick past the receptionist, the blade on the bottom making it look a little like a weapon. I was able to leave it up front and trail my fingers along the wall in the hallway leading to Salazar's office, just for added stability.

When I was shown into Anthony Salazar's office, Sam Humphries was already there, appearing more subordinate-like than the last time I saw him. Salazar was behind an official-looking desk, facing me, and Humphries turned around to look at me from one of the two chairs in front of the desk. His boss looked even more like a bulldog than he had in the church directory photo. I sat down in the other without being invited. I tried to put my hands in my pockets so the trembling wouldn't show, and realized these pants didn't have pockets, so I sat on the tips of my fingers instead.

They let me sit there a minute to show that they were in control. I looked at Humphries, who was the lesser opponent in the room. He could have been part of some cover-up to protect Salazar's reputation, but I doubted I would get a chance to find out on this go-round. Humphries was careful to project the same attitude as his boss. Both their mouths were fixed in thin lines as if they had been glued shut.

They started talking, but at first it was over me as if I wasn't in the room. Just a little sign of disrespect.

"Assault," Humphries said. "Accidental homicide."

Like they hadn't already gone over all this immediately after finding the body.

"Attempted mass homicide is what the DA will go for," Salazar countered. "With the fatality counting as murder one."

Good opportunity to screw with them a little and deflect suspicion away from Gemma-Kate. "Dead guy could have been the target," I said, though I didn't believe it. "What happened in the parish hall just a smoke screen for the main act."

Salazar finally acknowledged me, but not to address my comment. "I've heard a lot about you from over to the Tucson Bureau office. You don't play well with others. Why is it everyone on our side of the law dislikes you?"

Maybe it was because I'd spent so much time among criminals I was sometimes mistaken for one? Because nobody could be sure anymore whose side I was really on, not entirely excluding myself? I knew he wasn't talking about that, though, but was just piqued about getting that YouTube video from me. He was going to make me pay.

"You wanted to see me," I said, refusing to automatically act like a suspect, the way a civilian might. "Want to take another spin at starting this conversation?"

"One of the paramedics the other day said a woman was helpful. Father Manwaring said that must be you."

"I did tell one of the guys the symptoms I saw, pointed out an elderly woman who needed immediate help, and told him I thought there was something in the coffee. That's about all."

Humphries passed a notepad over to Salazar when the big guy waved his hand. "And just to check people off the list, you were there with your husband . . ."

"Carlo DiForenza."

"I thought he was your husband."

"He is."

"Different name."

"Sometimes I go by that name and sometimes I don't."

"And your daughter . . ."

"My niece. Gemma-Kate Quinn."

He pretended to consult his notes again. "And none of you were affected by the coffee."

I could have offered a lot more, the way liars do when they're nervous, but even though I was a tad nervous, I knew how to hide it. "That's correct."

"And you left the scene before I got there."

"That would be correct, too."

"Who was in and out of the kitchen?"

"People coming and going. Church ladies bustling all over the place like quail. Then there's that back door into the kitchen. Anyone could have come in, dumped a bottle of antifreeze into the pot, and left."

"Did you see who was serving the coffee?"

"It's self-serve. You must know that."

"My wife is the one who goes to church."

"Maybe she was the one who spiked the coffee." Salazar bloated up good on that one. I said, "I'm sorry, I couldn't resist. But she didn't go to the hospital either."

"Then you found Frank Ganim the very next day, in the columbarium. What a coincidence. What were you doing there?"

"Who's Frank Ganim?"

"That's right. His name wasn't Adrian Franklin. There is no Adrian Franklin that matches this guy's description."

That sweet guy. Assumed name. Why? I couldn't believe it. "So how did you find out his real name? I thought you said there was no ID on him."

"Dr. Manriquez did an autopsy this morning to confirm the ethylene glycol poisoning. But he found out the guy had a pacemaker."

"Is that the reason he died? The antifreeze didn't go well with his heart condition?"

"Manriquez doesn't think so. But the important thing about the pacemaker is that it has a serial number traceable to a Francis Ganim, and it was implanted in Cleveland."

I could tell he was enjoying himself a bit now, watching me seize on the information.

This is Tony Salazar giving Brigid Quinn a little information to make her think he sees her as a colleague, that he trusts her. Watch out.

"What about the dog?" I asked.

"What dog?"

"A black Lab. He adopted a black Lab."

Salazar turned to Humphries. "Any sign of a dog at the motel?"

"No sign. Motel doesn't allow pets," Humphries said.

"He was staying at a motel?" I asked.

"That cheap motel down by the airport. We found a receipt in his rental car in the parking lot next to the church's," Salazar continued.

"So we're following up on the Cleveland connection. Maybe he has something he didn't want strangers to know about. But it could also be that he was in the wrong place at the wrong time. If that's the case, can you think of anyone who might have something against the church as a whole?"

I thought of Jacquie and Tim Neilsen, but didn't say. It wouldn't be fair, even if it did blow a bit of smoke that might be useful if Gemma-Kate was innocent. And Gemma-Kate did not know Frank Ganim. Could not have known him. Could she? I still thought it was accidental, a prank, a nasty prank though it might be, gone horribly bad. I was mightily pissed at the fraud that had been Adrian Franklin, and the dog he used as a distraction, but right now all I wanted to do was get out of this office before I unintentionally incriminated my niece.

Salazar wasn't finished with me, or thought I wasn't finished with him. "Now let's talk about that video you sent me. I had a talk with my son last night. He says Joe Neilsen was a bad kid. Used alcohol. Played around in his parents' medicine cabinet. And I reviewed the case file. I'm not bringing my son into this foolishness, and I stand by Detective Humphries's finding. Accidental death. Go ahead. Now you go. Have you got any questions about my son?"

His barrel chest got bigger and bigger until I felt a little claustrophobic in the small office. I said no, though not because he intimidated me. In light of the dead guy we found, and the possibility that Gemma-Kate made him that way, I wasn't in the mood to follow this tiny lead into the cause of Joey's drowning. But I did see that my intuition was right, and that this guy would defend his son to the death.

Salazar said, "Good, that you don't have any questions, because we're usually the ones who ask them."

Sam offered to show me out, but I said never mind, I knew the way. That way I could step outside the office and stand for a bit to clear my head and listen for anything that might be said.

Sam, with sympathy: "I don't think she's a problem, boss."

Salazar: "Shh." Small pause, then, "What I've heard, put you both in the ring and it's even money."

Thirty-nine

Come cheer me up. Bring Carlo, Mallory had e-mailed. I was still feeling shitty but had discovered this was the price of friendship. When someone needs you, you go. So we left Gemma-Kate in the house, loaded the Pug in the Camry, and drove over there for brunch.

I told her the latest about Frank Ganim, the real name of the guy who had come on to her at the Humane Society do and at the church. I told her how I had found that out.

She was shocked, less by the fact that he'd lied about his name than by narrowly escaping his fate. "That could have been any of us," she said, touching the kitchen counter as if needing reassurance that she would not fall. "We could have died."

I had decided Carlo was the only person who should know about my suspicions of Gemma-Kate's involvement in the poisoning.

"I'm here because of you," I said, diverting the subject.

"But."

"What's for lunch?"

Mallory shook her head and busied herself taking an artichoke, morel, and Swiss quiche out of the fridge. "Annette made it this morning," she said.

"Do you ever cook?"

"Not if I can help it. I open dessert, though," she said, and showed me a bit of sponge cake with raisins that was molded in the shape of a large tuna fish can. "It's called spotted dick, I kid you not," she said. "I got it at World Market, hadn't seen it since I was a child." As if hypnotized by her memories she reached out and started to break off a piece.

"Freeze. Step, away, from, the cake," I said in my best cop imitation.

She jumped when I said "freeze," and I felt a little cruel pleasure in still being able to pull that off.

"My saddlebags thank you," she said, with mild regret. "You and Carlo can eat it. I have some lemon curd to go with it." She poured three glasses of an incredibly dry rosé, carried one into the bedroom, where Carlo was visiting with Owen in a way only Carlo could do, and we took ours out to the patio along with a plate of roasted garlic and blue cheese because I had liked it so much at Blanco's.

She was thoughtful not to notice my right foot slapping on the patio paving stones, something that had gotten more pronounced after my freezing episodes. "How's Owen doing?" I asked to get her started talking, when we were settled in the chaise longues next to the pool.

Mallory said, "No change." Then, minding her manners, she said, "And how are *you*?"

"Still on edge. Confused thinking. I had a high temperature the other night. I'm less sick to my stomach, but I still have the runs, which might be stress related." I clicked the imaginary stopwatch. "Your turn."

"Here," she said, fixing me a bit of French bread, with a healthy glop of cheese and a little of the softened garlic squeezed over the top. "Maybe this will help bind you."

Good Lord, is that what it comes to? Talking so casually about our bowels? But I took the concoction without protesting, and then, after Mallory had fixed a smaller one for herself, helped myself to seconds.

We sat in silence for a few minutes, me waiting for her to talk, with the sun high up over the mountain to our right, enjoying that pleasant sensation you find only in the desert, where your arm facing the sun is hot and your arm in the shade is cold. When I turned to the little patio table to get some more bread and cheese, I noticed Mallory was crying so quietly I hadn't been able to hear her.

"Hey, kiddo," I said. "Why did you want us here?"

"Life is so fucking difficult sometimes," she said. "Sometimes I'm afraid. I can't see . . ."

Mallory didn't say what it was she couldn't see. The future, I thought.

She said, "I'm sorry I get overwhelmed with this self-pity. Sorry to be a wet blanket."

"Wet blanket? Hell, you're my hero."

"What's important is that you're my friend, right?"

"You have to ask?"

"What I wanted to ask is, if something ever happens to me, would you look after Owen?"

"Why? What's going to happen?"

"It's not like some premonition. I'm not talking that kind of hooey. It's just that sometimes I can't sleep at night thinking about what if I get sick or killed in a car crash." Her face twisted, and I guessed she was thinking about the train that destroyed her life. "There's a fund set up and all that, but both of us are fairly alone in the world. I'd like to think there's someone looking out for him besides a money manager and a home health care nurse, even if Annette is wonderful."

I was touched. I agreed with the solemnity the occasion required, but then as always was embarrassed by the feelings and needed to lighten the mood. "And would you agree to take care of the Pugs if something happens to me?"

She smiled. "Of course. And Carlo."

"Oh no," I said. "Even if I'm dead you can't have Carlo. I'll give you the Pugs, but not Carlo."

Mallory laughed. "Agreed. But you realize, if you're gone, within twenty-four hours he'll get a half-dozen casseroles from church ladies."

Seeing that she seemed grateful to get past the seriousness, I added, "This doesn't mean we have to watch *Beaches* together, does it?"

203

She reached over and patted my arm. "Hell no. Neither of us is the wind beneath anyone's wings. We're either the eagle or we're nothing. Let's eat something."

Conversation over lunch swung in the direction of Joe Neilsen. I told her what I had discovered about the Choking Game. Mallory listened, then put down her fork and listened some more, then sat back in her chair and paled to an extent beyond her usual empathy.

"He didn't," she said.

"Didn't what?" I asked.

"The couple of times he had come over to read to Owen we had a Coke and talked. Well, he had a Coke and I had a glass of wine. You know how I am, Brigid, you've said it yourself. I flirt with men, women, children, and animals. And they respond. Joe told me about the game."

"You knew?"

"Uh-huh. He told me how he played it with the young men in the youth group. The way he described it he said everyone was doing it and it was perfectly safe, even the police did it to get control over violent criminals. I supposed I was flattered that he was telling me something that he might not tell most adults. I'm afraid I went what you call 'all Auntie Mame' and told him we should try to experience as much of life as possible. So he probably tried it on himself and it's my fault. I should have gone straight to Lulu about it, but I thought it might be like that game we used to play at slumber parties where you press your arms against the floor and lift someone up . . . Oh God, I can't believe how stupid I am."

I thought about how Lulu had said she felt responsible for Joe's death because she had encouraged him to come out to his parents. And how Ken said he thought he had killed Joe because there was a connection between the Choking Game and drowning. Now Mallory was taking responsibility. I felt like Hercule Poirot in *Murder on the Orient Express*, where everyone on the train stabs the victim (sorry for the spoiler). Only for me there was a twist. Everyone was *taking responsibility* but no one was *being responsible*.

Carlo and I both reassured Mallory as best we could, but ultimately failed at the purpose of our visit, which was to cheer her up. She seemed undone by what I had told her. She was able to serve us a bit of dessert, the spotted dick with a healthy dollop of lemon curd on top, trying to hide that she was ready for us to go.

I stopped in the bathroom before we left, while Carlo attempted to comfort her more at the table. I came back to that sudden silence that makes you know people are either talking about you or talking about something they don't want you to hear.

Mallory drew her hand away from where it had been resting on Carlo's forearm. Who was counseling who? She got up from the table, went to the kitchen counter, and picked up a copy of some pages she had printed from the Internet. She'd been reading about toads and I might be interested, she said.

Whatever it was that she had been talking about with Carlo, though, I didn't think it was about either Joe, Owen, or Pugs eating toads. Then I suspected I knew.

Forty

I'm a better driver than Carlo. He tends to think while he's driving, and when he thinks he slows down until people behind us get angry and honk and shake their fist. So I was driving when we left Mallory's. My driving us does not, however, prevent him from giving advice like "Whoa, honey, you cut off that fellow."

"Did not," I said, despite the fact that said fellow had rolled down his window to yell at us because his horn wasn't satisfying enough.

We were heading north on La Cañada, a straight road that dips into and back out of an area called Oro Valley. It wasn't the most direct route home, but Oracle can get really boring after a while. Despite the fact I'd only had one glass of wine (glass and a half) (maybe twelve ounces tops) I felt uncustomarily tipsy. "Would you please read me that thing Mallory gave us? It's in my tote bag."

Carlo reached around to the backseat, petted the Pug because she thought that's why he was reaching back there, and pulled my bag into the front, then fished around till he found the paper folded in half.

"Bufotenine," he said. "Not sure I'm pronouncing that right. 'Toxic compounds found in the parotid gland, venom, and skin of a variety of toads.'"

"Can you skim down to a more interesting part?" I asked.

He did, and picked up again with "1994 a California wildlife instructor was arrested for possession . . . dried skin . . . huh, toad smoking. Drooling, seizure activity, arrhythmias, here we go, toxic to dogs."

"Now you're getting too sketchy. Why would a person want to have those symptoms?"

He read further. "It's a hallucinogen. Euphoria. Visions. Changes in perception of time. How do you tell if a dog is hallucinating?"

Brain seriously fuzzed, I didn't yet make the connection. "Mallory is good to take an interest in the Pug," I said.

"Mallory was asking about you," Carlo confessed. I knew it was only a matter of time. Besides being an indifferent driver, Carlo is not well equipped for keeping a secret or telling a lie.

"I figured that's what you were talking about when I left the room." I smacked the steering wheel with my hand. "I told her I was going to tell you myself."

"I have every right to know this, and I'm going to insist you make an appointment with the doctor that Neilsen referred you to."

"Wow, you know everything. Maybe you know more than I do. What else did Mallory say?"

Carlo and I usually don't argue. I'm tired of it, and he doesn't know how. He switched from demanding to more of a wheedle. "Honey, we're just concerned."

"We? I don't see anybody else here and I'm getting really tired of this 'we' business. You got a mouse in your pocket?"

"Keep both your hands on the wheel," he said, as I waved them about for emphasis.

"I've got it with my knee."

"Don't be annoyed."

"I just don't like people talking about my personal health behind my back," I said. "I don't like people telling me not to be annoyed when they've done something annoying."

"Now you're over the line," Carlo said, sounding a little harsh.

I started to flare up, not understanding what line he meant, then I saw that I was crossing into the oncoming lane and wrenched the wheel to the right. What I took for harshness in Carlo's voice was alarm. At the same time I thought I saw some rust-colored things whip across the road. I yelled, *"Snakes!"* and swerved to miss them.

I spun into a doughnut, an oncoming car missing me by a quarter inch. Another one behind it might not be as lucky.

Instinct kicked in. I stepped on the gas rather than trying to brake. That worked; the car came out of the spin and headed straight. Unfortunately it headed straight into a saguaro cactus, a nice old one with six arms raised to the sky. The cactus stopped the car. The air bags stopped us.

Now, maybe multiple snakes was another hallucination, but there must have been at least one. Carlo to this day doesn't remember the snake, but he probably would have if the air bag hadn't broken his nose. The bags deflated like punctured bladders but we still sat there, stunned and groaning. The Pug ended up straddling the console between the seats, having been propelled from the back to the front. She appeared shaken by hitting the gear shift, but seemed generally unharmed. When the Oro Valley cops showed up, I explained what had happened, trying to avoid the snakes. Snake, I amended. Just one snake. It seemed more sensible. Maybe I was slurring a bit because of my general befuddlement and having just taken it in the face with nearly two thousand pounds of pressure of ballooning plastic traveling at two hundred miles an hour.

The cop peered into my eyes. "Are you okay, ma'am?" he asked. I know what they usually mean when they ask that question. I assured him I hadn't had anything to drink. He looked doubtful, perhaps because he could smell the bit of rosé on my breath, and told me to stay put, which was fine with me. When he came back from his car he informed us he had ordered an ambulance.

He asked if I could get out of the car and I did, though stumbling a bit. He asked where the snake was.

I looked at him with what I'm sure was a you're-an-idiot expression, swerved my hand in a slithering gesture, and said, "Gone."

He pointed to a bit of tire tread in the road, asking if I had mistaken that for a snake.

I said, "Does that look like a snake to you? It doesn't look like a snake to me."

"Ma'am, you seem angry at me. I was just asking."

He went to his car, came back with one of those Breathalyzer tubes, and asked me to breathe into it. I told him what he could do with his Breathalyzer. That seemed to make him suspicious and a little angry in turn. When the ambulance arrived I heard him talking with the driver about the snake I'd seen. Maybe it was a little green snake, he said. Or maybe it was a little elephant. A pink elephant.

As Carlo and I got into the ambulance I glanced at my Camry and the cactus it had hit. The front of the car was buckled, and the cactus leaned at a forty-degree angle, stopped by a concrete block privacy wall in front of a housing development. I heard somebody say they'd have the car towed to the nearest dealership.

They took us to Oro Valley Hospital on Tangerine and checked us into the emergency room. Carlo and I were put in separate areas. The receptionist held the Pug in her lap. They took blood. From both of us, they said. Routine. Apparently we had both suffered abrasions from the air bags, Carlo had a slight nose fracture, and we needed to be checked out to make sure the impact hadn't broken any other bones in our faces. We were released with the warning that we were likely to feel sore the next day and that our faces would be black and blue.

Apparently the blood test didn't show high enough levels of alcohol, but with more than usual pleasure the cop gave me a ticket for killing the saguaro. I asked him how he knew the cactus was dead. He just smiled.

I called Gemma-Kate to come get us in the other car. She asked where we kept the keys, and got directions. All very responsible. She didn't ask how we were.

"What was that about a snake?" asked Carlo while we sat in the emergency room waiting for Gemma-Kate. They had given him some pain meds, and he had a large bandage across his nose. Later I might joke that the air bags were never engineered for a nose that size, but now was not a good time.

"You didn't see the snakes?" I asked.

"No, I didn't. The policeman asked me about it."

Certainly there had been one snake. It was red. No, that sounds too much like a hallucination. It was reddish brown. But I remembered Carlo turning into a skeleton on the road to Mallory's, and losing my way in my own house the other night, and didn't push the issue of the snake.

Sitting there, waiting for Gemma-Kate to arrive, I started to free associate.

Pug, I thought, stroking the dog that draped over my lap. One of the nurses had brought her some water, and she was sleeping off the trauma of bouncing around the inside of the car.

Then, I thought, snakes in the road.

Must have been a hallucination.

Why am I having hallucinations?

Visions. Changes in perception of time.

Then, toad. Hallucinations from smoking toad skin.

Then, poison. Pug poisoned by toad.

Then, Gemma-Kate.

By the time she arrived at the ER waiting room, one can understand my state: agitated, confused, and ready to pick a fight.

Forty-one

There's a phrase that investigators use: Lock in, lock on, lock out. You develop a likely suspect, lock in. Then you search until you've found the evidence to prove your case, lock on. Everything links together and whatever doesn't link gets eliminated—lock out. It might not be the smartest way to approach an investigation, but it works surprisingly often.

Maybe I could buy that the Pug had been poisoned by accident. Maybe I could even buy that Frank Ganim's death was a prank gone horribly wrong. But if I was being poisoned, it was no accident. And if Gemma-Kate was purposely poisoning me, then it was difficult to think of any other person spiking the coffee and killing Ganim.

The dominoes fell straight toward Gemma-Kate.

I would be looking for something that looked like powder or dried skin, and I knew where to find it. I kept this to myself on the drive home, simmering in an anger stew. But while Carlo went to lie down for a few minutes, I went into the spare room, where Gemma-Kate had been staying. I hadn't been there since I'd gone in looking for the Pug.

Gemma-Kate might not have been your typical teenager, but over the days this had morphed into a typical teenager's dump. Underwear nested in jeans on the floor where she had stepped out of them. A half-empty bag of tortilla chips on a plate where the salsa had dried. A pile of books thrown haphazardly against a wall, including a couple of Carlo's that I remembered seeing on a bookshelf; that was the only thing that made the room different. I didn't think kids read actual books anymore. Unmade bed.

"What are you doing in my stuff?" she protested, as I opened drawers in her dresser and scrabbled through T-shirts, underwear, a little makeup. I opened up a container that looked like it should contain blush, and that's apparently all it contained. I slammed it on the dresser upside down to see if she had hidden something underneath. I knew how to find drugs. But nothing.

I ignored her question, and she followed me into the bathroom she was using, where I looked under the sink and into the medicine cabinet without finding anything. I took off the lid of the water tank in back of the toilet, but there was no plastic bag taped to the inside. Where else might she go where she wouldn't worry about me finding something?

The kitchen. That took a little more time because I had to go through a dozen or so cabinets. Maybe it was hidden there because as Gemma-Kate cooked more, I went less and less into the pantry and the cabinet where we kept the spices.

Gemma-Kate followed me, watching, but not asking any more questions once I failed to answer her first one.

Spices. I took the little containers out, opened them one at a time, and sniffed. Coriander, oregano, cayenne pepper that made me sneeze. Everything looked and smelled like what I would imagine.

"Where is it?" I finally asked. "Did you mix it in with this stuff? Did you powder it?"

"I don't know what you're talking about," Gemma-Kate said, doing what I took to be a good impression of bewilderment. "I swear I don't know what the fuck you're talking about."

I was holding a large plastic jar of dried parsley, and I slammed it on the counter. As I did my hand knocked a ceramic dinner plate onto the tile floor, where it broke into a half-dozen pieces. That made me madder. I picked up one of the larger pieces and turned to Gemma-

Kate, who looked at it as if it was a weapon, and looked at me as if I was the one who was crazy.

And that kind of pissed me off.

Apparently the noise of my searching in the kitchen had roused Carlo, who was looking at the ceramic shard in my hand along with Gemma-Kate. Poor Carlo, he had never witnessed my uncontrollable fury before. He came over to calm me down but he didn't have a chance. I sum this up because it's too embarrassing to recount what I really said when I let it all out: By the time I was finished, I had accused Gemma-Kate of purposely poisoning my dog. Then I accused her of purposely killing Frank Ganim as some kind of deadly game. Then I accused her of trying to kill me though I hadn't figured out how or why.

Boy, nothing quiets a room quite like blaming someone for murder. Carlo gasped, not having had the benefit of all my suspicions to this point. Gemma-Kate gasped, too, a very convincing gasp after she saw how well Carlo's worked. More realistically, the blood drained from her face. I finally had her on the ropes.

Do I sound like I was acting nutso? Dish of crazy with a sprinkle of paranoia? Well, here's the scoop—at some point in the days preceding that one I had crossed over the edge and had gone, as Mallory might put it, not so quietly mad.

Gemma-Kate regained some composure, left the room, and came back with her cell phone so we would see she was calling—

"Don't you dare bother your father about this," I said, instantly wondering what repercussions my outburst might have. Gemma-Kate was totally aware of those repercussions and was counting on them.

When Todd answered she spoke calmly, with no hysterics, but with the little-girl voice that she used to great effect when she needed it.

"Daddy, Aunt Brigid's tweaking. I think she's on meth."

I was powerless to do anything except stand there and listen to her side of the conversation. The only alternative I could see was to grab the phone away from her, and that would only support her accusations that I'd gone bonkers. I put the broken piece of ceramic on the counter without making a sound, in case Todd asked if I was holding something that could be used as a weapon.

"Her dog ate a poison toad and got sick . . . No . . . Yes . . . She says I did it." She listened, and when she wasn't listening spoke mechanically. "Uh-huh . . . Not so much . . . Daddy . . . No . . . Okay, the dog licked it a little. It was an accident." She listened. "The dog's in the hospital . . . No . . . He's not going to die. He's fine." She listened. "I hid it because I knew Aunt Brigid would go all berserk and blame me for poisoning her dog. And she is . . . That's why . . . She's even accusing me of poisoning her." She had the presence of mind to not mention Frank Ganim. Then she listened. "I didn't do anything and I'm in the middle of a shitstorm here . . . Sorry. Can you talk to her?"

Gemma-Kate put the phone down faceup on the counter in front of me. From this point Todd would be able to hear anything I said. Then she took her upper lip between her front teeth and smiled. In retrospect it could have been one of those nervous smiles, but I still wanted to connect that smile to my knee.

I'm not the only one in my family who does anger. Except for Gemma-Kate and my mother, all of us do anger pretty good. We learned it from watching Dad. Dad was the sort of father who, when he heard you scraped your knee, yelled at you. "Were you running?" he would yell, as if running was a third-degree felony. If we confessed to running, he would nod, satisfied with another successful interrogation. The greatest challenge in our childhood wasn't avoiding bloody knees but hiding the scabs from him.

Not realizing that the phone had been resting on the counter for a moment, when I picked it up and pressed it to my ear Todd was already into his harangue. Plus with a three-hour time difference there was little doubt that he was fueled by at least the second of his Johnnie Walkers. In one fairly continuous scream it went something like this:

"—unt, I ask you for a simple favor like when was the last time I ever asked you to do anything for me but no I'm the one who's left to deal with our fuckin' parents and a dying wife God rest her soul and a teenager who never had a real childhood while trying to hold down my fuckin' job and do you have any thought for anybody but yourself there you are living the retired life with a new husband out in Arizona you've both probably got great pensions but me no I just got word that the state has cut our fuckin' pensions in half because of the economy and there's no fuckin' way they're going to give it back now that they took it from me even if the economy improves I had enough put away to send GK to school out there as long as she could use you to establish Arizona residency and now this what's this about GK poisoning you I never heard such fuckin' bullshit you should get some help you're the one who needs help you crazy bitch we always said Dad Ariel everybody that you were the craziest one in the family you crazy bitch."

At that he seemed to have spent himself.

I'm the person who fights the bad guys. I'm the superhero on the side of Truth, Justice, and the American Way. And here I'm being screamed at by my little brother in a family squabble the likes of which I hadn't seen since I was sixteen and Mom found my birth control pills. How did I get into this position? And why wasn't I reacting in kind?

I should have been riled. I should have gone berserk, too, and destroyed something else breakable. And yet I found Todd's anger had an interesting effect. Without responding to him I looked at Gemma-Kate with her icy demeanor. I looked at Carlo with his the-world-should-be-reasonable attitude. And it felt kind of good, strangely calming actually, when I felt Todd's anger match or surpass mine. Plus getting beat up by an air bag a couple hours before might have had a lulling effect.

Now, you might not be able to tell from all this that Todd and I are actually close. He's come to my defense on many occasions, and once even stood between me and Dad. And nobody knew what it was like working in law enforcement better than I, the taut nerves. Added to that the fact that the wife he had nursed for more than seventeen years had just died, and maybe a little guilt over not being the best father, I could understand where he was coming from. So while I didn't apologize to Todd for what I had said to Gemma-Kate, or everything I suspected, I defused him as best I could, assured him I wasn't going to renege on our deal to allow her to claim Arizona residency. I didn't add *unless she went to prison.* With a final parting shot about how crazy I was, he hung up on me without saying good-bye.

I was spent, sucked into a blackness of depression with Gemma-Kate at the source. I felt my face go hot in a way it hadn't in years, but that was happening more and more often since Gemma-Kate had come to live with us.

Carlo recovered first and took the phone from my hand. Until he did that I didn't realize I was still holding it. He said to Gemma-Kate, "Please give me a moment alone with my wife." She obediently went outside (she always seemed to do what Carlo asked) and sat next to the St. Francis statue.

Carlo watched Gemma-Kate from the window for a moment and then turned to me. Now he'd heard for himself the kind of person Gemma-Kate actually was, I thought. So I didn't expect his tone of voice when he said, "What is *wrong* with you?"

"Didn't you hear what she said? Did you hear her admit to poisoning our dog? And, and, I've been seeing and hearing things and I think she caused it."

"I was here, I heard what I heard. And the person I'm concerned about right now is you. I just had to hear from your friend that you might be seriously ill. Now I'm hearing that you think you've been poisoned. What's this about seeing and hearing things?"

"She cooks," I said, and heard how lame an accusation it sounded.

"You think she's poisoning our food?" He held up his hands palms outward like he was trying to keep a mountain lion at bay. "Honey, I'm not saying I know better than you, but wouldn't there be an easier way? We both eat, we all eat what she cooks," Carlo said. "Gemma-Kate and I appear to be fine. And it's beginning to occur to me that you're probably wise not to go to the police with your suspicions about her involvement at the church."

I glanced at the broken plate on the kitchen counter and thought about breaking more, but that would have only solidified my status as a crazy woman in Carlo's eyes. I reminded myself he hadn't put in for this gig, having two shrieking harpies in his home. Actually, amend that, I was the only harpy shrieking. I backed off, wondering if maybe it wasn't poison after all that was causing all my symptoms, the anxiety and the stomach upset. Maybe that was Parkinson's along with the cramped handwriting and odd walk. Hallucinations? Could it be that?

So instead of breaking plates I bent over at the waist with my arms wrapped over myself, trying to press the anxiety out of my gut. I could even hear the slur in my own voice when I said, "I admit I don't know what's wrong with me. All I know is that it feels like my bones are crawling around inside my body and it's all I can do to keep them from jumping out of my own skin. I can't sleep at night."

Without a beat Carlo relented. He wrapped his arms around me wrapping my arms around myself as if he wanted to help hold me in. I felt soft and weak and hated myself for feeling it but couldn't help accepting his comfort. When I had stopped trembling so much, he disengaged and held me at arm's length to take a look at me. He repeated, "Honey, I'd do anything for you, pack Gemma-Kate back to Fort Lauderdale tomorrow and damn her father. But I always consider myself a reasonable man, so I think it through before I take any action that might hurt people or cause you regret. Anxiety doesn't seem like any kind of poison. You didn't call a specialist yet, did you?"

I was still feeling a little tense, and I got defensive when he said "specialist," as if he meant "psychiatrist." "Do you think I'm paranoid?"

"No, more of a neurologist," Carlo said. "So far I don't know what I think." He let go of me, opened the back door, and stepped into the yard. He called out, "Gemma-Kate, put on some shoes with socks, not those sandals. We're going out."

"Where?" she called back.

"To look at some petroglyphs. You and I."

"Where are petroglyphs?" I asked.

He pointed to the Catalinas. "Right about there. It's probably a half-hour walk from here."

"Why are you doing that?"

"To get her out of the way so you can get yourself together." He kissed me gently but without sentiment on my bruised mouth. "Or am I one of your suspects now?"

Of course not. It occurred to me that there was still so much I didn't know about Carlo. He knew the worst about me. Did I know the worst about him? I shook off that thought, the paranoia again.

Gemma-Kate came back into the house and went off to her room to get her shoes while Carlo explained. "Maybe she'll talk to me. It's

217

the best thing I can think of and I'm going with it," he said. "Then you're next."

While Carlo went off to get his own hiking boots on, Gemma-Kate came back and stood in front of me. I saw a different person from the one who like a child had skipped along the sidewalk when she first arrived. This was Gemma-Kate when she felt attacked, and when the charming little girl didn't serve her purpose anymore. Now her voice was as flat as her eyes.

"Have you ever read Nietzsche? No, probably not." As if she felt more in control, knowing something I did not, Gemma-Kate's voice got stronger. "There's something called the death drive. That's what they call the nihilistic inclination to destroy. It's that feeling when you're holding a kitchen knife and for a second you wonder what it would feel like to stick it into someone. Do you know that feeling? Or when you're standing on a high place and you get the urge to jump. These urges are not extraordinary, though some people have them more than others. They want to die. Or they want someone else to die. Maybe right now you wish I were dead."

Still amazed that this person could have eluded me while living in my house, "What the hell are you talking about?" was all I could say.

"You think I don't know what you're thinking. I do. You're thinking I'm one of those psychopathic kids like in the movies. I'm not. I've got an IQ of one hundred and forty-five and I've been listening to Dad and Grandpa talk about you since I was four. I'm no sicker than you are. You really think you and I are that different?"

In no hurry to press me for an answer, if indeed she wanted one, Gemma-Kate licked her finger and bent to pick up a small shard of pottery from the plate I broke. She tossed it into the trash and turned back to me. "I know, Aunt Brigid. Let's talk about the number of people we've killed in cold blood. You go first."

"Okay, you, let's get going," Carlo said to her, having come into the room without hearing what she had just said to me. "And Brigid, we've got to pull ourselves together here. We're supposed to be the grown-ups." He turned to go, then turned back. "You look quite pale. We won't be gone long. Are you sure you'll be all right here for a while?"

I nodded, still too stunned to speak, and that was a good thing because no matter what ever happened with Gemma-Kate I couldn't tell Carlo what she just said because I feared it was a little too true.

They left. I watched the Pug position herself at the door in the hopes they had gone to fetch her mate. It was only then that I realized I was rooted to the same spot I had been standing in while Todd reamed me a new asshole. I felt a muscle at the surface of my abdomen spasm like a bad running stitch. I rubbed at the spot until the cramp eased. It took some will and deliberation, but I finally managed to take a step, and then another, until I ended up in our bedroom, sitting on the bed, opening the drawer of my nightstand where I kept something that could kill.

Forty-two

I got out my FBI special and the box I kept it in, a wooden hinged job with a foam insert carved out for the gun. When I first married Carlo I had hidden the weapon in back of some broken computer equipment in a cabinet attached to my desk. Once we got to know each other a bit better he understood why I felt better having it beside me at night, and was not adverse to its presence in my nightstand next to the lubrication gel.

The box of shells was in a Victoria's Secret gift box that had contained perfume from a Christmas present. I pocketed the shells with hands that didn't used to tremble so.

The gun itself was already loaded. I wondered for a moment whether that was wise with Gemma-Kate around, the image of using it to frighten her out of her controlled smugness was so vivid, but I wouldn't decide just now.

I took Carlo's Volvo.

The Pima Pistol Club is a convenient three miles south of our house, but a torturous three miles it is. Like a mini mountain road it snakes between carved-out chunks of hill, and rattles your teeth over a washboard surface more rutted than not. I wanted to speed but would have been thrown against the roof of the car, so I kept it below thirty miles an hour, still jouncing.

The owner, a lean cowboy who I only knew by the name of Roger and the sticker ONE DAY AT A TIME that was stuck onto his service counter, greeted me at the window when I gave him my membership card.

"Hey, Brigid. Your husband tune you up?" he said, with what some guys still thought was humor. Just because he's sober doesn't mean he's not an asshole.

I wondered what the nameless woman at the shelter was doing today. Whether she'd gone home. "Had a run in with an air bag, air bag won," I muttered, not having the inclination just now to deliver my "Battered Women Jokes Aren't Really Funny" lecture.

"I bet you could have taken it in the second round," Roger said.

I indulged in one small glare as I signed the check-in sheet, then walked down the concrete pavement to one of the narrow cages, wood and chicken wire, with a small wooden shelf where I put the gun, and beside it, the box of shells. The cold range light was flashing, so there was no shooting from the several other members, all male. In front of my station there was already a target set up, a metal plate hanging loosely from a frame, that someone had neglected to bring back when they were done. Far in the distance was a dirt embankment that surrounded the range on three sides in case you missed the target.

A buzzard circled over the range. I tracked it with my weapon but didn't fire. It's a felony to shoot a bird of prey. I was in enough trouble with killing the saguaro.

I hadn't brought my earphones to muffle the fire for a reason. I wanted to blast the sound of Gemma-Kate's voice out of my head.

The cold range light stopped flashing as I sighted the target. "Hot range," the loudspeaker said. I clenched my jaw and loosened my grip that fought against the trembling. I fired at the target, and fired again and again. I was hitting it pretty good but didn't really care. Mostly what I was going for was the feel of the angry power in my hands and the shout of the rounds as they exited the muzzle. The ping of the bullet as it hit the metal plate was an added satisfaction. I imagined the plate was Gemma-Kate.

You want death drive? *Blam.*

I'll give you fuckin' death drive. *Blam.*

I did no one harm thinking that way.

I kept reloading, and shooting, and used up all the shells in the box. When they were gone, along with my hearing, which I trusted was a temporary condition, I waited for the cold range light, pulled in the target for the next person, loaded my gun into its wooden case, and left, calmer than when I'd arrived.

Along with the calm, the shooting also provided a little clarity of mind that I had been lacking. I went over my options apart from killing Gemma-Kate. Shipping her back home wasn't one of them; Todd was stubborn and would probably just ship her back. And what would I tell him, you spawned an evil child? Given the Quinn reluctance to accept constructive criticism I knew he wouldn't take well to that.

I could put her in a motel until it was time to move into the dorm. That was it, I could put her in a motel close to a McDonald's and give her a little money every day so she wouldn't starve. It would be expensive, but worth it to bring the peace back into our home. Then I could bring the other Pug home without worrying. Wait a second, I'd left the Pug in the house. No, that was okay, Gemma-Kate was off hiking with Carlo, so the Pug was safe at home. Carlo. Putting Gemma-Kate in a motel. Carlo would back me on that, wouldn't he? Would he?

Then, what would happen when she moved into the dorm?

My cell phone rang. Thinking it might be Carlo worried about me, wondering too late what kind of spin Gemma-Kate might put on things, I pulled over and rooted around in my tote. It was too late to catch it, but I noticed it was Mallory's number. I decided to drive home first and call her from there, partly because I was still feeling kind of pissed that she'd told Carlo my secret when I told her not to. That made me think of Mallory, and her unhappy situation.

I kept trying to get her to come out to the firing range with me, thought it would be good for her, but she always said she hated guns. Hated guns. How do I get mixed up with people who are so not me?

When I got home I put the gun back into my nightstand without cleaning it immediately as I usually did, and though it was empty and there were no more shells in the house, I still covered the box with some provocative underwear.

I washed my hands. Rather than pick up messages I figured it would be faster if I just called Mallory back, so I went into my office to call her. I started to, but then I saw the prescription for the movement disorder specialist on the desk next to my computer. Funny, the things you never dream will take more courage that you ever needed in the past.

Trying to avoid thinking about it turned all the calmness I'd achieved at the gun range into full-on gerbil brain. I thought about everything that had happened since Gemma-Kate arrived, how she had single-handedly fucked up my contented life in Arizona.

Then I thought again that maybe that was the whole Quinn family, that all of us had more than our share of evil inside. There was that time when I watched a man slowly die and was happy except that it went too fast. Okay, he was bad, he was very bad, but in extremis shouldn't the impending oblivion of even a bad man make you feel regret? Maybe I, too, lacked that gene or whatever it was that created empathy, that discouraged what Gemma-Kate had called the death drive. Maybe Gemma-Kate was only the culmination of generations of bad-seed evolution. Did it come through Mom's or Dad's side? Dad's probably. You could sort of see it in him.

Then I thought about something Mom had said once, Mom whose whole philosophy of life was based on other people's platitudes, a stitch in time saves nine, you work as fast as you eat. Better the devil known than the devil unknown. She knew things about our family.

Aside from Gemma-Kate, one unknown I had been trying to avoid was Parkinson's disease. But this was something that was in my power to know. The words of the guy we called Black Ops Baxter, who had trained me to fight, flashed through my skull. It was in the early days when I was afraid of being hurt.

Don't be a pussy, Quinn.

I googled Parkinson's disease and chose Wikipedia because that was the easiest. I took a deep breath and started to read, feeling ice crawl up my legs as my hands trembled over the keyboard.

I read through symptoms, prognosis, treatment. Jerky hands, odd gait, cramped handwriting, sensation of freezing, and on through memory loss, anxiety, depression.

So instead of incontinence, as I sometimes joked, this was what was going to carry me off.

I'd almost gotten kind of soft about God, thinking he was going to leave me alone for a few years, maybe shitting on easier targets for a while. I thought going to church would placate him. No such luck, Quinn, you're in the divine crosshairs now. Life with Carlo was just a way of showing you everything you're going to miss.

And to hell with my self-pity. What about Carlo? Carlo married a woman who could best him at arm wrestling. Now he was going to find himself married to a woman with a disease so debilitating he would have to push her around in a wheelchair. I thought of Owen with poor Mallory. Poor Carlo, people would say. Seven years ago he lost his first wife to cancer. Now he'd lose his second wife to some slow wasting neurological disease. He hadn't signed up for this gig.

Would Carlo take care of me the way Mallory took care of Owen? Would I want him to?

I thought about how only a few hours ago I had been angry with Mallory for telling Carlo that I was afraid I had Parkinson's. She had her own problems, and she had done what she did out of love. So get over it, Quinn.

It's funny how I now had both a husband and a friend, and yet until now I had never felt quite so lonely. I wanted Carlo and Gemma-Kate to come home. At the same time I was cheered by imagining her fallen off a cliff, her skull crushed against the rocks below. Maybe there was something to it, that death drive.

I thought about the fury that she had inspired in me, the chaos she had brought into my world, with seeming purpose. I thought about looking into those eyes and seeing nothing, or worse.

But I had no evidence. I needed evidence. Evidence. I sat there repeating the word again and again, my fingers still resting on the keyboard. And then I almost laughed because it was right there in front of me. Looking through her room and all the cupboards in the kitchen was a waste of time. Gemma-Kate had been using my computer. All

I had to do was look at the browsing history to find the evidence. When I did, I saw all the words she had searched on.

Bufotenine. The toad poison. Of course.

Some random selections, sibutramine, chloral hydrate, sodium disulfide. Ketamine.

Neurotoxins.

Ah, ethylene glycol. Antifreeze.

I thought again about the pile of books I'd seen in Gemma-Kate's room. Now I exited from the browsing history I'd found and went back in there, knelt before the pile that she hadn't bothered to hide. Sure, there was Carlo's *Man and Superman*. I'd never read it, but I could see from the author's name that Gemma-Kate had quoted it. Yeah, Gemma-Kate would think she's superman, all right, and the rest of us were some inferior race. I brushed that book and a couple other philosophy titles aside, and hit the good stuff.

Karch, *Pathology of Drug Abuse*
Dean and Powers, *Forensic Toxicology*
Jain, *Drug-Induced Neurological Disorders*
Caligiuri and Mohammed, *The Neuroscience of Handwriting*

What was I, another home experiment like the Pug? Or had I inadvertently done something to make her angry? Was I on my way to becoming another victim? She might have slowed me down, but she hadn't stopped me yet. It was time to call Sigmund.

Forty-three

Sigmund isn't his real name. It's David, David Weiss. But like all of us in law enforcement he had a nickname that said something about him. In his case, he was a psychologist, a behavioral profiler who helped start the FBI's Behavioral Science Unit in the eighties. We had been chums for as long as I could remember, part of the same training class. I think once or twice we had had sex, which tells you something about how memorable it was, and what was the true nature of our relationship. I loved him, and I love him still. Feelings are not all neat and compartmentalized that way. I wouldn't like to think about Carlo having the feelings for another woman that I have for this man.

I was always called Stinger. Some may surmise it's because I'm small but hurt like hell, but it's less clever than that. When we graduated from the academy we all got drunk, I on that drink popular at the time, made of crème de menthe and brandy. The thought of them still makes me queasy. They were called Stingers, and Stinger stuck.

So that's how the conversation always started.

"Sig."

"Stinger."

No *how are you;* Sigmund is practically one hundred percent cerebral, like talking to Mr. Spock on a boring day.

Sigmund said, "Skype me."

"Why?"

"There's something in your voice I can't quite read. I want to see what you look like."

And all I had said was his name. The guy knows me. I touched my face and felt the roughness of the scabs peppering the bridge of my nose and forehead. "I can just tell you, I'm not looking too good," I said.

There was stubborn silence on his end of the line, so with a "You asked for it," I clicked on the icon and then the little green phone to call him. As I did so, I noted that Peter Salazar's number was already on the contact list, but I didn't think much on it because Sig's face popped onto my screen.

He was a heavy, bearded man whose aging face had shocked me when last year I saw him for the first time in a while. I had grown accustomed to this older version then, and saw that the smaller inset of my own face on the screen was faring much worse than his if you took into account the black and blue patches and scabs.

He said, "That's better. I've never liked phones. There's always a piece of the other person missing." He took a few moments to examine my face. "You're right, you look like hell."

I felt the first smile of the day tug at the corners of my bruised lips and didn't mind that it reopened a little cut on the bottom one. Sig could do that to me at the worst of times, and if you told him he was funny he would deny it. I gave him a brief description of the accident so he wouldn't worry.

"Why did you call?" he asked.

"To hear the voice of sanity," I admitted.

He stared at me without response, looking like a cross between Freud and Winnie-the-Pooh, waiting until I was ready to talk.

"I need to talk to you about psychopathy," I said.

"Have you been worried again about where you fall on the empathy scale? I told you if you stopped working you'd start to brood."

"It's my niece, Gemma-Kate. Todd and Marylin's girl. She's come to stay with us."

"And how is the bad seed?" Sig knew all about my family from many talks over the years.

"I don't think we were joking. I think she's really a psychopath," I said.

"They're calling it Antisocial Personality Disorder now."

"When are they going to get the name right and call it Piece of Shit Syndrome?"

"I admit the term takes away all the mustache-twirling sadism. You have to excuse the psychologists who write the diagnostic manual. They make up these terms because 'crazy' lacks elegance. Why, have you been reading again?"

"Don't fuckin' patronize me, Sig."

"It's just that this business comes in and out of fashion. A couple of years ago every novel had a psychopathic character."

"Look, I haven't forgiven you for not trusting my instincts when I told you that agent was abducted. And I was right, wasn't I? I'm making connections here, Sig, so when I tell you this kid creeps me, pay attention."

"What has she done?" he asked.

I wasn't ready to share my suspicions about the dead guy at church, but I told him about my symptoms, and about finding the browsing history on my computer for all kinds of substances I myself hadn't searched for.

"And you're certain there's a link between the browsing and your symptoms?"

"Yes. Because she definitely poisoned one of the Pugs. And the poisons she searched? The substance she used on the Pug was one of them."

He hitched around in his chair some, a huge reaction for Sigmund. "Well, that is significant. Give me the details."

"That's much better, thanks." I told him how it happened, how I discovered where she had buried the toad, and how she denied it.

"Unmotivated cruelty." He nodded. "How old is she now?"

"Going on eighteen."

"It may have taken a longer time than one would assume, but of course this may only be the incident we know of."

"And then when she was forced to admit it she tried to turn it so that all the trouble was my fault, for what she called overreacting."

"Fascinating," Sigmund said.

"I'm glad you think so."

"The idea of your overreacting, I mean," he said with a straight face. When I didn't laugh he went on. "I remember your talking about Gemma-Kate from time to time. Her father was detached from her rearing, her mother too sick to give her much attention. Her grandparents would have been in denial or as a result of their own pathologies wouldn't see anything wrong with her. And there's nothing you nor I can do about it. It can be frightening. You say she's functioning well?"

"Apparently she got her GED early and was getting good enough grades at the community college in Florida so she didn't have any trouble getting into the university here."

He nodded again. "Elevated IQ, but lacking empathy. As children, they slip under the radar because we aren't born empathetic. You don't expect a small child to feel from another's point of view. We're born thinking the whole universe revolves around us. One big lump of egocentricity in the crib. Then, hopefully, we grow and learn to realize it's not so."

He went off into his own head again. I tapped on the screen as if it would get his attention back. "Gemma-Kate," I reminded him.

He was half back with me. "Ah yes. If Gemma-Kate has Antisocial Personality Disorder, and that is a very hesitant if—a psychologist doesn't make this sort of judgment without even seeing the person suspected, let alone delivering a battery of tests—"

"Just say it, Sigmund, we're losing daylight."

"If Gemma-Kate is what you say, you have no more importance than a wet Kleenex. To her you are one of three things: an amusement, useful, or in the way."

"What are the stats on likely outcomes? Is there any hope for her?"

"Chances are, you're completely wrong. Or she's so far on one end of the scale she'll never go any further than putting back her seat in coach. Maybe she'll just be annoying in a hundred different little ways that show she thinks the world is hers. You already know that it is the rare confluence of nature, nurture, intelligence, and opportunity that turns Jeffrey Dahmer into a cannibalistic serial killer. More often you get a Bernie Madoff. Or a politician."

"What should I do?"

"If you're convinced you're being harmed, you already know. You do whatever it takes to get her out of the house as quickly as possible."

"What, thrust her on an unsuspecting world? Hasn't anyone developed programs for treatment? Carlo would say we should help her, that we're responsible."

"The lions count on that from us."

"What lions?"

Sig sighed with the heaviness of the life we both had known. "Someone once said if a lion could talk we still could not understand him. There would be no words in our language he could use to express his lion-ness. Understanding a psychopath is like talking to a lion. They are untreatable because they're unable to understand that they are different.

"Stinger, there are creatures that not even your priest can redeem."

I agreed and made my decision.

Forty-four

Immediately after I disconnected from Sig, Jacquie called, as if she had been waiting in line. Cell phones have made confidential conversations so much easier. She was out of the house, wandering around Sears at the Tucson Mall, which sounded like a depressing thing for a rich woman to do. I told her I knew little more, only that Joe had apparently bragged to Mallory about playing the Choking Game.

"When?" she demanded. It was definitely a demanding kind of "when." "When did he tell Mallory?"

"I don't know. One day when he was over reading to Owen."

"I can't believe Joe would have told Mallory something and not me."

"Oh, you know how Mallory is."

"No. I don't. How is she?"

"She has a way of eliciting information. I'm sure Joe couldn't help himself. Besides," and here I tried to say it so Jacquie wouldn't get upset, "at a certain age, children tend to start keeping secrets from their parents."

"Not Joey. Not from me." Her voice trembled like a woman who'd been cheated on, one part enraged and one part stricken. "I've been thinking. You said Joey had alcohol in his system when he died. Who do you think gave it to him?"

"There's no way to tell that."

"Do you think it was Mallory Hollinger?"

"No," I said. "I'm certain she did not."

"I'm going to go over there and ask her myself." Something in her voice, something vengeful as that of a woman scorned, made me regret sharing the information with her.

"Just stay out of this and let me keep working." I wanted to placate her. "I think you've been right all along. I think there's more to discover." I hoped the affirmation of her suspicions would ease her for the time being until I was able to find out everything.

I had just hung up the phone when the back door opened and Carlo and Gemma-Kate came in, both looking a little flushed from being out in the afternoon heat. The remaining Pug frisked around Carlo, sniffing for her mate but settling for the aroma of the great outdoors. After my sanity check with Weiss, I found myself able to appear relatively calm. "How did it go?" I asked.

"The petroglyphs were still there," he said. "I think Gemma-Kate was not impressed by ancient graffiti."

Gemma-Kate didn't comment. "Can I borrow your computer?" she asked me.

"Sure," I said, pretending to offer the olive branch when what I really thought was that this was one way I could find out what she was up to. The little biologist wasn't as smart as she thought she was, I thought.

She went into my office.

"How did it go?" I asked again, this time expecting a real answer.

"More importantly, how are you?" Carlo asked.

"So so. I worked a little, and that makes me feel better. Did you have a nice hike and talk? Did you find out how crazy I am? How crazy my family is?"

"We talked some, yes."

"Are you going to tell me or do you want me to keep asking you questions?"

"We talked about you, actually. She was worried about your thinking you've been poisoned, and she asked me what I knew. She said she's noticed some odd things lately about your behavior, that she

232

found you wandering in the yard in the middle of the night, disoriented. You didn't tell me about that."

It felt like an accusation. "It was just a nightmare," I said.

"Are you thinking that your temperature the other night might be related to all this?"

I handed him one of the books I found in Gemma-Kate's room, the one about forensic toxicology. "So you won't admit the kid is just plain bad."

Carlo read the title and handed it back to me. "I think it's dangerous to associate a book with actions or even ideas. After all, I read Christopher Hitchens, and I'm not an atheist, I just respect his thought. My love, I don't want to sound disloyal to you, but I have a hard time admitting I can't answer your questions without asking others. Such as, if Gemma-Kate means you harm, why did she have me put you in the bathtub the other night to bring down your fever?"

If there was a logical answer to that, I couldn't see it. But did there need to be any logic in what Gemma-Kate was doing?

I had never been afraid of anyone, not really, until now. What to do with this person? Used to joke about her being a bad seed. Not laughing now. I'd spent time among psychopaths, serial murderers and killers for profit, men and women who never flinched when they pressed the trigger, and never thought about it after.

But I'd never entertained someone like that in my home. Gemma-Kate had all the basic equipment. And it looked like for the first time in her life (or maybe not the first) she was using it.

I got Subways for dinner so I knew they hadn't been tampered with. And while I was cleaning up I threw away all the spices, anything that had been opened. Took my pill with the sub so I wouldn't be so sick. Felt sick anyway and took some more antinausea drugs. I was starting to feel the effects of the accident, too.

When Carlo turned off the lights for the night I brought the Pug and her water dish into our room and locked the bedroom door. We both took something the hospital had given us for the pain that was sure to feel worse in the morning.

Suppressing a grunt, Carlo rolled over onto his side facing me and kissed my hairline above my ear, then studied me in the half-dark.

233

When he spoke he sounded like he had a cold, maybe from swelling in his nose. "How's it going, O'Hari?"

I shook my head, not wanting, or rather not able, to describe what was going on inside and outside my head. I imagined my face looked as sad as his. The cuts and darkening bruises were bad enough. He opened his mouth again, maybe to say something that would fix the problem, ease the pain, but then he shut it again. Our love was still there, but it felt like we were caught in a huge icy bowl with the sides too steep and slippery for either of us to crawl up and over the edge and help the other one out.

I didn't tell him that, after my talk with Sig, certain that I could no longer deal with her myself, I had decided to turn Gemma-Kate over to the cops.

Forty-five

I slept soundly for the first time in many nights. Next morning I got up to find Carlo and Gemma-Kate already up and about. Stiff and sore from yesterday's accident, tight in muscles that I hadn't realized had been punished, I shuffled like a zombie into the kitchen, poured out the coffee in the pot, and made some myself. I stood by the pot watching until there was enough, and filled a cup. The cup felt heavy. Funny how in movies people get flung around on helicopter blades and don't feel like this the next day.

Too out of it to recognize the irony of doing a threat assessment in my own house, I looked out back and was relieved to see Carlo standing at the fence, staring at the mountains and meditating or something, from the back looking as droopy as I felt. The female Pug, was it Peg? That shouldn't be hard to remember; she was lying on the back porch.

I could hear an aggressive tapping from my office and took a couple steps in that direction to see Gemma-Kate at my office computer. The heavy-heartedness I felt at letting Marylin down sucked out the will to scream at her. It was too early to call Tony Salazar and tell him I was bringing my niece downtown. I nuked the lavender bunny Mallory had given to me, draped it around my neck, dropped an

Alka-Seltzer in my coffee, and took it out on the back porch along with the toxicology book I'd taken from Gemma-Kate's stash. It was hard going, lots of formulae and chemical structures. I wondered what normal looked like anymore, wondered how I could bring it back without putting Marylin's child in prison.

Gemma-Kate came out and sat in the other porch chair across the table from me. If she noticed I had her book she didn't say. She acted as if our blowup the day before had never happened. She had several pages she said she'd printed off of WebMD. "I keyed in all your symptoms I knew about and got from Carlo," she said, dispensing with any cutesy name she had for him. "They're pretty strange. Nausea with vomiting, anxiety, insomnia, paranoia, hallucinations, bizarre behavior. Are you constipated?"

I made a mental note to get a recommendation for a good criminal defense lawyer who handled insanity pleas. I might turn Gemma-Kate in, but for Marylin's sake I wouldn't just walk away.

I said, "Oh, leave me alone, for God's sake. I'm too sick and tired to deal with you. And I'm hurt. Please," I added, remembering that we were supposed to treat her with kid gloves lest she murder us in our beds or set the house on fire. Carlo turned from the fence and saw us, gave a gentle wave, crossed his arms, and kept watching.

"I'm sorry I implied you were a psychopath," Gemma-Kate said, her eye now on the book in my lap. "You shouldn't have come at me that way, Aunt Brigid. We got angry. We said things. Maybe we even meant them. But you started it."

Oh, she was good. I put the book on the table, the title toward her. "What's with this?" I asked.

Gemma-Kate turned the book around so the title was facing me. "All that weirdness lately, you were pretty scary that night I found you in the backyard, muttering 'all dark, all dark,' and then the referral to the movement disorder specialist, and the sudden high fever the other night. You weren't doing anything about it. I got curious. So I started researching. But it wasn't till yesterday when you brought up intentional poisoning that things started to fall into place. Maybe you're right."

"Why didn't you say something yesterday?"

"You're hardly listening to me now when you're calm. Do you think you would have listened to anything I had to say yesterday when you went berserk?" She paused to write "irritability" on the page in front at her, then said, "Almost everything is neurological."

"Just like what happened at the church. Small doses of antifreeze, maybe?"

Would they arrest Gemma-Kate on my accusation? And if not, what would I do with her? Get her out of the house, a room in that motel down the street, I remembered. *I'm sorry I failed you, Marylin.*

And in the meantime, don't take any chances. I had thrown out the spices. Today I'd get rid of everything else in the cupboards and the refrigerator and restock them again.

Gemma-Kate said, "What about a combination of nutritional supplements? You can have some weird-ass symptoms by overdosing on certain vitamins and things like melatonin or St. John's wort."

Until you can get her out of the house, just play along. "I don't take anything but a multivitamin," I said.

"That's not true, Aunt Brigid. I looked in your medicine cabinet. You've got enough controlled substances in there to make a living on them. By the way, your doctor's office called the other day when you were out."

"Neilsen?"

"I suppose so. Some assistant. They just said your blood work was normal. Cholesterol a little high."

"You're trying to tell me I'm not being poisoned," I slurred. My lips hurt.

"Not necessarily. But it could be some environmental toxin. Even mold. Ergot causes hallucinations. What you're complaining about is just weird, and if you're ingesting something it doesn't seem to have instant effects. But on the chance you're right, I checked out some of the typical poisons that wouldn't kill you immediately. Not strychnine or cyanide. Or a good dose of sodium chloride."

I'd need evidence. You just don't drop someone off at the police station. They wouldn't incarcerate her on my say-so. They might question her, and then I'd have to bring her back home. Boy, if I thought she was pissed at something now . . . "If it was any of those poisons, I'd be dead, right?"

Get her out of the house and then make an appointment with a toxicologist. Was there such a thing? I'd check the yellow pages. Could go to Neilsen, but I didn't trust him either. There was something too coincidental about my getting sick just at the time I started asking questions about Joey. But then what about Gemma-Kate's connection?

Maybe I could pay George Manriquez to draw some blood and send it to the lab.

Come on, brain, work with me.

"Right," Gemma-Kate said.

I looked at her. She was a little blurry. "What?"

"If someone is poisoning you—and we're not certain about that—they're either inefficient or they don't want to kill you. Or not immediately."

"Arsenic."

Gemma-Kate nodded. "Obvious. Arsenic is a good slow poison. I read about a guy who went blind in one eye before they found out his wife was giving him small doses of arsenic." She looked away from me, toward Carlo and the mountains, seeming to have forgotten about me. But then she turned back. "The initial symptoms are good skin and bright eyes, and that's not your case. Even if you weren't all scabby, your skin is bad and your eyes are bloodshot. Even that tells me it's organic rather than psychosomatic."

"Thanks, Cupkate."

If she noticed my sarcastic use of the family term of endearment she didn't acknowledge it. "Plus, as time went on with arsenic you'd get a black edge on your gums. Let me see your teeth."

I lifted my upper lip in something like a sneer. A painful prick told me I had again cracked open that spot on my lip where the air bag hit it.

"No," she said, after a glance. "I don't think it's arsenic."

The caffeine was slowly making me more alert. I looked over at her again. "Why are you toying with me like this?" I asked.

"I don't want you to die," she said, purposely ignoring my implication.

238

Gemma-Kate smiled as much as she ever did. It struck me again how the sicker I was the kinder she was.

"Why not?" I asked.

She stared at me without comment. If eyes are windows to the soul, I would have sworn she didn't have one.

"Why don't you want me to die?" I asked again.

"You really need me to answer that?"

"Sure, give it a shot," I said, wondering how good this lie would be.

She seemed to consider various responses while actual undefinable emotions traveled across her face so quickly they could have been my imagination. When she spoke it wasn't to hand me some bullshit about loving her Aunt Brigid. "Okay, I've got two reasons. The first is that you've accused me of multiple poisonings, including one that resulted in homicide. You've locked out all other possibilities, and if I don't clear myself, I'm fucked. You're going to turn me in, aren't you?"

I didn't answer her question. "Good reason. What about the second?"

"Even if you couldn't successfully build a case against me, if you think I'm trying to kill you you're going to get rid of me. I'm too young to live on my own and I'm not eligible for in-state tuition. I'm not going back to Fort Lauderdale. I hated it there."

It was, I thought, the first honest exchange we had had since Gemma-Kate arrived. Not so kind after all. But while her words were harsh, the logic of them wedged the first little doubt in my mind that I could be wrong about her. The rest of my mind considered that she was really smart and playing me big-time.

Consider having a psych evaluation done. Maybe she was certifiably insane and we could head off a murder charge that way. A side benefit of putting her away would be others might be saved.

Carlo had walked from the back of the yard to where we sat on the porch. Now he was close enough I could see the white bandage stuck over the top of his nose.

"Elias is picking me up to go get a rental car," he said. He still sounded stopped up.

"Do we need it?"

239

"Might as well, the insurance covers it. How are you feeling today?"

"Like I ran into a saguaro cactus," I said. "My face hurts."

"Mine, too. Will you be all right here?" he asked, glancing inadvertently at Gemma-Kate.

"Sure. Go."

By this time Gemma-Kate seemed to have totally shed her childlike perkiness, an unnecessary disguise. Without acknowledging Carlo she had gotten up and taken the forensic toxicology book with her into the house.

Questions I knew it would do no good to ask aloud:

What would Gemma-Kate do to prevent my sending her home?

Was this an elaborate ruse to make me think I was crazier than I actually was?

A ploy to convince me of her innocence?

Was thinking these things proof that I was crazy?

Or was Gemma-Kate not poisoning me?

And if she was not, what the hell was wrong with me?

Could she actually help me find out?

But I couldn't ask her these questions. What I could ask when I followed her into her room and indicated the pile of books was "Where did you get all these?"

"Online."

"How?"

"I used your credit card."

Either Gemma-Kate was truly bad, or for the first time we were, if not on the same page, at least in the same library. Whatever the case, I used it as an excuse to delay calling Salazar. Just as I was about to make a second pass through my questions, my cell phone interrupted my gerbil-in-a-wheel mind. Thinking it might be Mallory finally calling me back I muttered, "Do not move from this place," and stepped into the living room, where I trusted the phone to be in the bottom of my tote by my reading chair where I left it. Oh for the days when you could be certain where to answer your phone. When the phone rang again I noticed it was actually the landline on the kitchen counter. It started to go to voice mail but I interrupted in time.

It was Mallory. "What the hell are you doing to me, Brigid?"

I used the kitchen counter to prop myself up. "Can you be a little more vague?"

"Jacquie Neilsen just called. She's threatening me."

"What for?"

"She says when Joe came over to read to Owen I gave him alcohol. She says I made Joe an alcoholic. That I got Joe drunk the night he died and that's how he fell into the pool."

"Did you?"

"No!"

"You said yourself you told Joe about the bucket list. You sure you didn't pull one of your Auntie Mames, 'Here, Joey, you might as well learn to live life to the fullest' crap?"

"You sound angry."

"Damn straight. I'm losing my patience with people who won't tell me the whole truth."

"Look, all I'm saying is that you've really opened a can of worms here. Do you hear how absurd this is? Jacquie says I turned Joey into an alcoholic."

"Christ."

"Can you talk to her?"

"How did she threaten you?"

"She was all over the place. She was going to get me for murder, then she was going to sue me, I didn't understand half of what she was saying. Then she said, 'I may look weak, but I can hurt you.' It really frightened me, Brigid. No one has ever blamed me, and for purposely . . . purposely . . ."

"Contributing to the delinquency of a minor?"

"Hurting a child. I'm sick about it."

"I don't have to ask if you keep a gun in the house, do I?"

"Of course not." But she sounded shaken at my even asking.

"I always said you should have one. Yesterday when you said you were worried about something happening to you. Maybe it was a premonition."

"You're scaring me."

"You should get a gun," I said. I disconnected and called Jacquie back immediately, closing my eyes to concentrate on the words forming in my mouth.

"Did you just tell Mallory Hollinger you were going to have her arrested on a murder charge?"

Silence. Then she said, "You told me Joey had alcohol in his system. Joey was over there that day. She'd been giving him alcohol. That's the kind of thing she would do."

"Jacquie, how many times altogether did Joey go over to the Hollingers'?"

"Maybe three, four times."

"You don't turn someone into an alcoholic that quickly."

"I didn't say she did. I just said she encouraged him to drink."

"She also said you threatened her. What about that? Did you threaten her?"

There was a pause. "I don't remember exactly what I said."

"How about, 'I might look weak but I can hurt you'?"

She murmured something about maybe saying something like that.

I said, "Listen to me. I'm not going to deal with you if you do things that are nuts. This qualifies as nuts. Do not do these things. Are we clear?"

"Yes."

"Let me repeat just to make sure I'm communicating. Don't tell anyone what we discuss between us. Not even Tim. Don't call anyone."

"Okay."

"Do I have to worry about you doing something crazy, Jacquie?"

"No." She sounded appropriately meek.

I had seen her in a confrontation and didn't trust the meekness, but I said, "That's good. Now I want to hear one more time that you're going to keep our conversations confidential for the time being and not take any action on your own."

"Okay."

"Okay what?"

"I won't call anyone."

Forty-six

I disconnected one more time, belched, and took a deep breath. Having to get tough with Mallory and Jacquie appeared to clear up my brain fog some, and it felt like I was finally able to open my eyes all the way. Figuring I had that situation safely taken care of for the time being, I got more coffee (I was quite certain Gemma-Kate hadn't been near the pot) and went back into her room, where she sat on the bed engrossed in *Drug-Induced Neurological Disorders.* Something about the book seemed familiar, and I wondered if I had run across it in my previous life.

I sat down next to her and absent-mindedly picked up *The Pill Book* from the stack. I thought of her question about what I was taking, vitamin, occasional sleeping pill, and antianxiety meds. Just occasionally. Except for the antidepressant Neilsen had prescribed. I turned to antidepressants. There were pictures of everything. It's funny how with thousands of different pills they manage to make them all look different so you can pick them out in pictures. I found the one I started taking shortly after I started investigating the death of Tim Neilsen's stepson. Maybe it was a long shot, but. I shoved the book at Gemma-Kate. "Find out what happens when you take this stuff. Find out how much is usually prescribed and what happens if you take too much. Find out about interactions between this and other drugs."

Gemma-Kate looked up. I could tell for a moment her mind was still in the book, and then she slowly focused on me. What she saw she didn't like. "You started taking those after you had the blood test at the doctor's office, didn't you?"

"That's right, so it couldn't—"

"I know, but that makes me think of the hospital you went to after your accident. Did they take blood there?"

"They did. They were looking for alcohol."

"Did they find it?"

"Didn't say. I don't think we were there long enough to get the results, and the cop never showed up again, so I guess not."

"Couldn't hurt to follow up on that report. They probably tested for several kinds of drugs. Go to the hospital."

I had been following Gemma-Kate along her line of reasoning until, at this second, an old television show came to my mind, about a boy and his family being marooned on another planet. His robot buddy would say, "Danger. Danger, Will Robinson." I could hear that robot buddy inside my head, and he was saying, "Sucker."

"It's not just the books," I said.

"Now what?"

"It's poisons. You were specifically looking up poisons on my computer. Before you said you started to research my condition. It's in the browsing history."

"Because of the dog. What do you think I'm going to get a biology degree for? Is it suddenly suspicious that I want to go into forensic lab work? What do you think I should be, a cop?"

"Awful lot of sudden interest in poison. And then people get poisoned. Don't play me for a fool, Gemma-Kate."

"Don't play me for one. If I was looking up ways to poison you, do you think I'd leave the browsing history for you to see?" she said, looking like I'd grown a second head and the head was talking nonsense.

"You would if you thought I wasn't smart enough to look at it. I can't believe I was just about to let you manipulate me again," I said, standing up from the bed. I think I may have thrown the book at her. She ducked. It hit the window behind her. Strong pane. She looked over my shoulder.

"What the hell is going on here?"

I turned to see Carlo. He hadn't left yet. I don't know if he saw me throw the book. If I threw the book.

I think he saw me throw it. "Is that how we're solving problems now?" he asked. "Let me help." He grabbed the books that were piled on the bed and threw them, one at a time, against the wall. One hit the lamp and it crashed to the floor. He picked up one that Gemma-Kate had open. "Maybe this'll help, too," and he ripped out a wad of pages and threw them into the air. They floated down to the floor. "There, have you reached a resolution yet?"

He stopped to catch his breath and maybe get a grip. Gemma-Kate let out a brief nervous giggle. I kind of felt the same way. We'd seen this kind of action throughout our lives. No matter what Carlo did he simply couldn't match a Quinn when it came to losing your temper.

"Both of you. Sit down right now," he said.

We obeyed. Sat down next to each other on the bed. It seemed the best course of action. I must also reiterate here, in Carlo's defense, that he didn't know, couldn't know, that everything that was happening to me, all my reactions, were a result of drugs affecting my neurochemistry. I didn't even know this.

"Now that I have your attention, let's get started. You," he said, pointing at Gemma-Kate. "You may or may not be a homicidal maniac. You may or may not have poisoned a person or persons. All we can be certain of is that before you came into this home it was a very peaceful kind of place, but now I've got a wife who throws things. *I* throw things. You're creating chaos.

"And you," he said, jabbing his finger in my direction. "What the hell are you doing with these books?"

I explained, keeping my tone as reasonable as possible, that Gemma-Kate had been trying to get me out of the house, why I didn't know. Gemma-Kate countered that all she wanted me to do was check the results of the blood test at the hospital, taken after the accident, to see if there was anything suspicious in my system.

Carlo looked back at me. "So go to the *hospital*," he said. "Maybe you'll find out something to incriminate this kid and we can get rid of her. You want me to take you there? I'll take you there."

"I don't want to leave her here alone," I said, beginning to feel that everything I said was a little lame.

"Fine," Carlo said. "I'll tell Elias to hold off till I call him. I'll watch her like a hawk so she doesn't kill me while you're gone."

I went into the kitchen, picked up the landline, and asked directory assistance to patch me through to Oro Valley Hospital, where Carlo and I had been taken after the accident. It felt like it took me half the morning to talk to the right person in the lab, and more than that to arrange to go there. In the meantime, Gemma-Kate gathered all the tossed books, shoved the torn pages back into the right one, and carried them to the dining room table for further study where Carlo could keep an eye on her.

I still didn't trust that she wasn't pulling some kind of scam, but at least I knew the house was safe. I drove myself to the hospital, found the lab, and presented some identification.

A guy the color of milk—you can always tell someone born and raised in Arizona, like vampires they never go into direct sunlight—came to the waiting room and handed me my report, a column of names and numbers, which of course was unintelligible to me. I could tell from his polite smile he knew I was clueless and felt superior for it.

"Help me out here," I asked, not having the time to play his game. "Is there anything on this list that looked abnormal to you?"

"Oh yeah, we got a real high level of MAOI," the lab tech reported, warming to the topic he must know and love. "That's this number here," he added, pointing to a spot on the report.

"What's MAOI?"

"A form of antidepressant."

"Real high. Is it in keeping with twenty milligrams once a day?"

"Oh no, this is more than four times that."

"Don't you think it would have been wise to notify me?"

He huffed a bit, withdrawing his magnanimity at my sarcasm. "I guess not. They would assume you were smart enough to know what you'd taken. It says here they sent the report to your doctor's office. Is your doctor Timothy Neilsen?"

I called the house. Gemma-Kate answered. "Put Carlo on," I said.

"Did you find something?" he asked.

"Possibly. Listen, I'm myself right now, not crazed. Would you please go into my bathroom and look at the pill bottle with Rextal on the label?"

He did, carrying the phone with him. "Got it."

"How many milligrams is prescribed?"

"Twenty milligrams once a day."

"This is going to sound crazy, but I swear I have a good reason. Please count the number of pills."

He did, and told me.

I thought back on how long I'd been taking them. It calculated. Gemma-Kate had not been giving me extra doses. Unless she ordered some from an offshore pharmacy. I asked to speak to her again.

"Please look up antidepressant overdose and tell me what symptoms you find. I'll wait."

It didn't take long. Gemma-Kate said, "Nausea, diarrhea, palpitations, anxiety, cramping, irritability, hallucinations. Serotonin syndrome."

"What's that?"

"This says it occurs when there's too much stimulation of the biochemical that makes us feel good."

"What happens then?"

"It starts with a feeling of euphoria that rapidly deteriorates into cramps, nausea, diarrhea, anxiety. Rapid pulse."

"Paranoia and hallucinations?"

"Yes, at the extreme. And toward the end, when the body's control mechanisms start failing, fever."

Fever. Toward the end. "How can a person find out if they have this syndrome?"

"I'm not a doctor, but I think you just did."

Doctor. "Tell Carlo I'll be home in a little while."

Forty-seven

It was Saturday. If they were both at home I didn't care. I didn't care who knew what because I was really pissed and wanted answers.

No one answered the front doorbell, so I walked around the side of the house to the pool area, where I slammed the palm of my hand on the large plate glass window. Before too long Timothy whipped open the back door. "You don't demand to be let into someone's house. Get off my property before I call the police."

"You know what the police are like. A suspicious lot. Do you want to know why I'm here before you call them?"

He blanched. It was a shot in the dark but it made him look guilty.

"Where's Jacquie?" I asked.

"I don't know. Either talking to her priest or her psychic."

"So she does leave the house? You told me she doesn't go out."

He looked genuinely sad. "She doesn't tell me anymore. Those are the only two places she'll go. She has groceries delivered."

"I'm glad she's out. Whatever you're about to tell me I suspect she doesn't know, and it's probably better for her that way."

Timothy laughed, but there was nothing funny in it. "I told you before. What's better for her is if you just leave us both alone."

"How do you figure that?"

"She shouldn't have agreed to let you get information. If only she'd left well enough alone."

"You know what happened. And you tried to stop me from finding out."

"Oh no. Just because I'm not having the police haul you away doesn't mean I have anything different to say to you."

"Jacquie doesn't know anything, does she? You know something about the night her son died and you didn't tell her. That's pretty disgusting." I looked over at the fireplace and saw Joe's shrine. I went to the mantel and with my index finger moved the little ceramic fruit bowl to the edge and a little further. "Talk to me," I said.

"You won't," Timothy said.

I moved my finger a millimeter and the fruit bowl crashed to the flagstone floor, where it broke into an ungluable number of pieces. Timothy jumped off the couch and came for me but had no real concept of what going for someone would accomplish. I swept his leg out and he went down on his ass.

It subdued him a little. "I haven't done anything illegal." He didn't bother to get up off the floor, just spoke from where he was sitting. He put his face into his hands and rubbed hard before looking up at me. "There's no more truth than that. What else do you want from me? I've got nothing else to give."

I moved on to a shell gecko while he heaved himself to his feet, blustery but afraid to approach me again. "Where did Joe collect these shells?" I asked. "Not around here, I guess."

"Vacation in Bali," Timothy said with a quaver in his voice, seeing as how I wasn't impressed by the bluster.

I stroked the shell gecko. "One of these things broken looks like a dusting accident. Two and it makes you look bad."

Timothy started to cry and dropped back to the floor, kneeling by my feet.

"Please stop," Timothy whined. "Can't we just get control and talk like civilized people?"

"All right, let's talk. Why didn't you tell me the hospital gave you the results of my blood test? And that it looked like I had an antidepressant overdose?"

"What does that have to do with Joe's death?"

"That's what I'm here to find out. I start nosing around, you prescribe antidepressants. I mysteriously overdose on them. I get tested and the hospital sends you a report. Why didn't you tell me about an antidepressant overdose?"

"What overdose? I didn't get any message," he said.

"Bullshit. Your own lab called me. All they said was that my cholesterol was up." I started to finger the shell gecko again.

"We didn't run a drug test. That's a different lab!" Timothy dropped to the couch and buried his face in his hands again. It looked like dejection, but he was actually thinking.

"Besides, we took your blood before I ever prescribed antidepressants," he said, still thinking. "My usual assistant is on vacation, I've got someone filling in. Do you want me to call her right now? I could call her right now."

I could kind of tell that my accusation of intentional overdose wasn't as great a threat to him as whether his malpractice insurance was paid up, and it defused my suspicion. "Let's get back to Joey," I said.

Tim took a deep breath. He needed it. "I was glad he wasn't in my life anymore. I hated the little weasel."

"So far you're not the only one. You had trouble accepting his sexual orientation?"

"Oh, bullshit. It wasn't always that way. At first I loved the kid. I thought we'd be a family and he'd be the son I'd never had because I loved Jacquie so much. I still do. But over a couple of years Jacquie got jealous that he might like me more than her. After that it got weird, it always seemed like it was the Joe and Jacquie show, and no room for me. I took them everywhere, I tried to be a good father. But I could tell that he saw how things were and he had the upper hand. It got worse and worse. Did you find out he dyed his hair to match his mother's because he didn't want people to mistake him for my son? Did the medical examiner tell you that?"

I shook my head no. "Jacquie told me."

"She thought that was so cute. Oh, he knew exactly how to play Jacquie. I saw through it, but if I didn't give him his way he'd do something to get back. They used to watch *CSI* together, sitting on our bed, and telling me to go away because I wouldn't like the show. One night I told them to watch it in the entertainment room so I could go to bed. Next morning I went into the garage and saw my Lexus had been keyed, all along the driver's side. I came back into the house, accused Joe. Jacquie got on his side. Joe got into my face and I pushed him against the wall. I didn't hurt him, just pushed him. But he called the cops on me.

"The cops came and arrested me, said they had to, for child abuse, and I spent a night in jail before they let me out. Oh, you should have seen it, I got the full treatment. Fingerprints, mug shot, orange jumpsuit, baloney sandwich, and a cot in a room with thirty men who screamed at each other all night. In Tucson money works for some things but not assaulting a child. Jacquie didn't do a thing. She didn't even come pick me up. I took a taxi home. But you have to understand, I still didn't do anything to hurt Joe. That night I went out with my associate, and he dropped me off."

"Lari Paunchese?"

"That's right. I found Joe's body in the pool. I pulled him out and tried to resuscitate him, but he'd been gone a while. I looked all over the place for a suicide note, but I couldn't find one. I was afraid Jacquie would blame me for his death, and I was right, wasn't I? She's telling you Joe killed himself because of me. Or worse. Which is it?"

"And you called Paunchese back to the house. He was happy to help you out."

"I said I didn't want an autopsy, that it was unnecessary because it was clearly an accident and I didn't want to put Jacquie through more pain. I meant it. Oh God, we're prominent members of this community. I thought it would keep everything low-key. And then, probably because I was arrested for assaulting him, they suspected me of drowning him. Oh God, it's all such a complicated mess. Oh God."

"No it's not, Timothy. It's death. There's nothing more simple than death. The real question is whether you had the balls or whatever it would take to kill your stepson and try to kill me so I wouldn't find out."

He was crying now, and denying knowing anything at all.

"Timothy, look at me."

He looked at me.

"I know you got the report. You got the tox report from the medical examiner and you didn't bother sharing it with Jacquie. I have to ask why. Why would you not tell Jacquie you got the report and that Joe had alcohol in his system? Why wouldn't you want her to know that? Because you gave it to him?"

He took a deep breath, looked away, and when his eyes came back to my face they were washed of hope.

"I'll tell you why. Because she already knew. Jacquie was the one who got him started drinking. A couple beers when he turned thirteen, and then whenever they watched movies together. She thought he was so cute when he was a little drunk. The kid is dead."

"I have to tell you I already told her this."

"About the tox report? Oh shit, what did she say?"

"She doesn't know you got the report. But she called Mallory and accused her of getting Joe drunk when he was there reading to Owen."

Timothy shook his head in disbelief even though he had to know it was the truth and now there was no stopping it. "Denial, right? She was turning her son into an alcoholic and there wasn't anything I could do to stop them. She used alcohol to bind him to her. When I spoke up they banded together closer and I felt even more on the outside. But even then, I loved Jacquie enough to keep from her that she was at least partly responsible for Joe's death. The kid was already dead and nothing was going to bring him back. There was no good reason for her to know he'd been drinking. I wanted to protect her from blaming herself. I never thought she would blame his death on me.

"You're right, it *is* simple." He held up his thumb. "See, I loved Jacquie." He held out his index finger so it looked like a gun. "She loves Joe." He held the finger to his head in the classic pantomime of a shot to the temple. "Even dead, the little mother fucker wins."

Why did he love her? Maybe the better question was, who did he used to love? The her before Joey died? Before her first husband left her? Maybe that's the woman Tim could see, someone vibrant and full of life. Somebody who would go to a party dressed like Harpo

Marx. Someone who was a good mother—until she became only a mother and when the motherhood was taken away had nothing left to live for.

I said, "This is what you didn't want me to find out."

"That's right. But I wouldn't hurt you. I wouldn't hurt anyone."

I thought about my appointment with him, and the ease with which he jumped to the possibility of depression, and from there to Parkinson's. Doctors always think of depression, especially in women. "What made you think of Parkinson's?" I asked.

"Mallory—when she called to make the appointment and they asked her what it was for, she said she didn't know what was wrong, but something about you walking strangely, and your handwriting being off when you signed the check at a restaurant. She didn't know what she was seeing, but those are both signs. Then I saw the way your hand jumped, and I put it together."

There was one other thing to check. I walked into the kitchen and pulled open the refrigerator. There were three bottles of Sam Adams spring ale chilling on the shelf in the door. I remembered visiting Jacquie around midmorning and smelling the beer on her. I quickly went through the cabinets and found the one with bottles of Tanqueray, Johnnie Walker Red Label, Jose Cuervo, Grey Goose. They were all at least three-quarters gone. Then I believed Tim. He had the sound of truth in him this time.

When I turned back to the couch where Tim sat, his head was hanging over clasped hands, and he talked more to himself than to me now. "She was always so funny, so much fun. I could never match her, what she wanted. So she was molding Joe to be that."

I looked at the ceramic fruit busted on the tile in front of the fireplace. Tim had lied by not coming clean with me right at the start, and I wasn't sorry for what I had done, but I still gestured at the mess. "Can I help you clean up?"

"No," he said.

"What will you tell Jacquie about the broken ceramic?"

He gave a humorless snort. "I'll make up something. We both know I'm good at that, right?"

I stared at him and he shouted at me. "Just get out of here. Don't ever come back. Leave us in peace."

"Do you keep a gun in the house?" I asked.

"No."

"Good."

Forty-eight

I sat down at the table where I had left Gemma-Kate. She was still reading *Forensic Toxicology*. *Neuroscience of Handwriting* draped over another chair, and *Pathology of Drug Abuse* served as a paper-weight for some printer paper. She didn't look up when she said, "Carlo left with Elias to get the car. I promised I wouldn't do anything bad until you got home."

"I still don't know if Timothy Neilsen is telling the whole truth. He's trying to protect himself and his marriage," I said.

"I read up more on antidepressant overdoses."

I said, "I wonder what Sam Humphries will say if I ask him about Neilsen getting arrested for child abuse. Nobody mentioned that until now, not even Jacquie. Maybe she was hoping I'd discover it on my own."

Gemma-Kate said, "This stuff is so interesting. I've been reading about Caravaggio. Ever hear of him?"

I decided to pay attention to her since she wasn't paying attention to me. "No."

"Renaissance. Master of chiaroscuro but I guess also something of a dick. It says someone tried to poison him with mercury but they got the dose wrong and it ended up curing his syphilis instead. Good example of why they say the dose makes the poison."

"Could we get back to me for just a second? Can't you look up antidotes?"

"I tried, nothing. It just has to work itself out. How bad are you feeling?"

I took a moment to assess my state. I thought I heard the male Pug snocking by the refrigerator, but it couldn't be because he was still at the vet's and the female was sleeping on my lap at the dining room table. I didn't mention that I heard it. "It comes and goes. I'm not feeling like I want to kill you right now."

Gemma-Kate went on. "It says here if you take a solution of activated charcoal it can help keep poisons from being metabolized. I read another thing about a professor who drank activated charcoal followed by a dose of strychnine in front of his class to show how it works. It only works if you drink it in solution immediately before or immediately after ingesting the poison. But forget that for a second. It might be useful if you can focus on this instead."

She pulled the papers out from under the book and displayed a kind of flow chart that she had hand-drawn and -lettered. Her lettering was unnaturally neat. She took a moment to gather her thoughts and words, then lectured me like I was a rookie.

"I remember when Dad was studying to become a detective he would tell me what he was learning. I couldn't forget the three words, motive, means, opportunity. I was thinking what if we were right, that someone is trying to hurt you, or at least slow you down, and they were using drugs as the means. There's no way to know the motive at this point so I figured I'd concentrate on opportunity next. I've tried mapping your activities since the time you first started to feel sick. The funny thing is, in order to get enough of the drug into you, I couldn't think of anyone except me or Uncle Carlo who could do it. Here's what I came up with." She held the paper so I could see it. The lines and words seem to float and make sudden little lurches across the page, but I was able to follow pretty well as she took me over my recent life. There were gaps, and she had a pen ready to fill them in.

"See, here's where I arrive. You're feeling perfectly fine then, we have dinner with Carlo and your friend Mallory. Same over the next several days. You go to that fund-raiser—"

"That's the day you poisoned my dog," I added. I was interested to see where she was going, but wary just the same.

"—I asked Carlo, and at the fund-raiser you were with your priest from the church and his wife, and the doctor and his wife."

"Right, the Manwarings and Neilsens."

"We should probably differentiate between husband and wife in case you saw either of them apart from the other."

"Elias and Lulu Manwaring. Timothy and Jacquie Neilsen."

Gemma-Kate wrote down the names. "You eat and drink there."

"Maybe a piece of rumaki or two. And wine."

"Are you sick yet?"

"No. I'm fine. The dog is sick."

"Day two."

"That's when I went over to the Neilsens."

"No."

"No?"

"First you had coffee. I made the coffee that morning. You have to remember everything, Aunt Brigid. Even if it incriminates me."

"But Carlo drank it, too."

"The thing is, maybe we're not talking something that could take effect with one dose. Antidepressants have a cumulative effect, and Carlo might have had some without having any reaction. Now. You visit the Neilsens and agree to investigate the death of their son, Joe. Do you have anything to eat or drink there?"

I was sort of fascinated watching her mind work and played along. "Yes, I had a cup of coffee. One of those Keurig single serves."

"Who fixed it?"

"Tim Neilsen, I think. Yes, Tim Neilsen. Wait, Jacquie fixed me the first one, then Tim Neilsen gave me another one." I closed my eyes, imagining the scene. "I turned around at one point and he was opening a pill container on the counter. I thought it was to see if Jacquie had taken her drugs, and I turned back, not wanting to seem nosy."

She made a note of that. "Something could have been added to the coffee either after it came through the machine, or injected into the little plastic container with a syringe beforehand. After the Neilsens' what do you do?"

"I call . . . called Mallory and stopped by her house. I complained about you."

"Do you eat there?"

"Gemma-Kate, this is absurd."

"Humor me."

"I did. The health care aide brought us both some soup."

"What's the aide's name?"

"Annette."

She wrote that down. "What kind of soup?"

"Something with beef broth and kale and beans and Parmesan cheese grated on top. We both ate it on TV trays in Owen's room. And coffee."

"Are you sick yet?"

"No. It wasn't until the middle of the night I started to get nauseated. I might have thrown up. That was after your meat loaf with the sauerkraut and Swiss cheese."

"I lose the thread here. Next day?"

"I was with a lot of people that day. I visited the detective who had investigated Joe Neilsen's death, such as it was, went to the vet to visit the Pug, maybe I went to the gym to work out and talked to my trainer . . . maybe not." I struggled to remember, feeling some for all the people I'd interviewed this same way.

"What do you eat and drink that day?"

"Coffee at Starbucks and a plain bagel. That's about it. I was feeling sick to my stomach, so I didn't eat much except a few crackers here."

"All right, next day."

"I forced myself to take a walk, thinking the fresh air and activity might help. That was when I found the toad you used to poison my dog."

"But you weren't with anyone else that morning."

"I tried to talk to Carlo about you, but he wasn't listening. Men are nice, but they don't always see things the way we do. So I met

Mallory for lunch." I filled in before Gemma-Kate could ask, "I had a salad, and some wine." I paused. "And some blue cheese with garlic. We both ate the same thing. I was anxious at that point and she offered me a Valium but I turned it down. Then I went over to her place, and they gave me a lavender drape."

"You mean that rabbit thing you had on?"

"That's the one."

"Who's 'they' specifically?"

"Annette. Annette got it for me and nuked it in the microwave."

Gemma-Kate carefully noted Annette's name on her timeline for that day and wrote the number two next to her name. "Where is it now?"

"What?"

"The rabbit thing."

"I threw it over a chair in the bedroom."

Gemma-Kate disappeared for a moment and came back with the boneless rabbit. She sniffed it suspiciously, shook her head, and draped it over the edge of the table like Exhibit A.

Seeing it made me shudder. "I was on the road that day and had my first hallucination. But I can't remember when it happened."

"What happened when you were driving?"

"Carlo turned into a skeleton," I whispered. It was real, dammit, it was real.

"Carlo," Gemma-Kate said.

"He walked in front of my car. Then his flesh fell off. I jammed on my brake and watched him melt into the pavement."

"Did you have anything there?"

"No. Owen had a crisis, they stabilized him, gave me the lavender drape, and told me I should take it home. Then I came back here. You cooked dinner again. You've been cooking every night except last."

"Incorrect. You brought takeout Chinese one night . . ." She scanned the chart, thinking.

"See, it's not so easy."

"Still sick then?" she asked.

"I can't remember. I think so. It's all sort of running together, and my brain isn't helping. I was sick enough to keep an appointment next day with Timothy Neilsen. He gave me a prescription for an antidepressant."

Gemma-Kate wrote down that information. "How much?"

"Twenty milligrams of Rextal. Before that I was on two milligrams of antianxiety meds up to twice a day and ten-milligram sleeping pills for when I had trouble sleeping. The doctor told me to stop taking those."

Gemma-Kate nodded. "It's called polypharmacy. Combinations of drugs that are fine by themselves but taken together can really mess you up." She rifled through the pages of the book on the table while I got up and got a refill of coffee, carrying the Pug gently so I wouldn't disturb her. The coffee was cold, but at least I was beginning to think Gemma-Kate might not have added anything to it.

When I came back I said, "I forgot to say I went down to the police station to talk to the death investigator on the Neilsen case. He gave me a cup of coffee."

She wrote that down and then tapped on one of the books opened on the table. "The drugs you had been taking are really low doses. But I couldn't find what if all three were taken in combination, so maybe your doctor is correct."

"I didn't take them in combination," I said.

She wrote that down. "Do you remember how you were feeling at the police department?"

I remembered the blood on the folder, that I was so nervous I'd been biting my cuticles without noticing. "Anxious. Real anxious. Like my esophagus was rigid as wood and my heart was trying to crawl out of it. And I was having these brain farts where I'd zone out."

Gemma-Kate wrote that down. "What next?"

"I can't remember. Oh wait. The appointment with Neilsen was the day *after* I met with the detective." I pointed at the date on her chart and she erased what she had and wrote that in correctly. "And right after Neilsen I met Mallory at Ramone's bar, it's in the Westin on Ina, and had a vodka martini. Olives. Blue cheese olives. The bartender's name was William."

"What night did you have that episode?"

"Episode?" I was being coy, I know, but I still hated to even think about that night.

"When you wandered into the backyard like a crazy woman. That was when I started getting curious and noting your symptoms. That was when I ordered the books."

"You were observing me all that time?"

"Uh-huh. So back to your first major hallucination."

"I . . . I think it was the very night I started taking what Neilsen prescribed. Maybe I let Neilsen off the hook too soon. Maybe it's a conspiracy with the pharmacist."

"Whoa, not so fast. We're not done. Keep going."

"What are you thinking?"

"You stayed home until we all went to church."

"The antifreeze," I said.

"That's right, but not you."

"Not for lack of trying. You gave me a cup of coffee. And a dough-nut."

Gemma-Kate looked at me sharply.

"What?" I said.

"Nothing." She wrote down the coffee and the doughnut. "What next?"

"Next day I went to see Elias Manwaring. At the church. Did I have coffee?"

"You really need to back off the caffeine, but that's beside the point."

"Nothing at the church. Wait, he gave me a glass of water and I drank half of it. No, I didn't see where he got the water. We talked for a while, then we went over to the rectory and I saw Lulu and their son, Ken. I was dizzy and had to sit down or lean against the wall. That was when I found out about the Choking Game."

"Off point. Did you have anything at the house?"

"Lulu offered, water I think, but no. I didn't eat or drink anything there. Found Frank Ganim's body."

"That's okay. What about the next day?"

"It's amazing how you lose chunks of your life when you have to spell it out. Shows you how mundane it all is. I went to see the

sergeant in charge of detectives, Tony Salazar. My initial plan was
to find out if Peter was responsible for Joey's death—"

"Peter! You think he had something to do with Joseph Neilsen's
drowning?"

I said, "But the meeting turned into a cat-and-mouse thing about
Frank Ganim, and I think I was the mouse. They questioned me about
finding his body, gave me a little information but wanted more. You
fixed dinner. I had toast in the morning. Nothing more until brunch
at Mallory's the next day."

"Was this Annette there?"

"No, Mallory gave her some time off."

"What did you have?"

"Quiche."

"What kind?"

I thought I detected a more culinary curiosity. "Artichokes, mush-
rooms . . . Swiss cheese."

"Who made it?"

"Annette did. Wine. More of that blue cheese and garlic like at
the restaurant. We all had the wine, and quiche, and the cheese. Mallory didn't have any dessert, but Carlo did. Something called spotted dick with lemon curd."

"You're shitting me."

"Seriously. It wasn't bad."

"Are you sick?"

"On the way home I'm so off-kilter I maybe start to hallucinate
about red snakes in the road, although I could swear right now there
was at least one. That's when I ran into a cactus and the cop thought
I was drunk. We went to the hospital in an ambulance, and they
x-rayed both of us for anything broken besides Carlo's nose and treated
the abrasions on our faces. If they'd found elevated levels of blood
alcohol I would have been arrested."

"Then you came home, and we both know what happened then.
You went off on me like a meth addict."

"I did not go off on you like a meth addict. And if I did I had good
cause."

Gemma-Kate didn't argue with me. She was too busy filling out her flow chart of the days since I started to get sick. "That brings us to today. Still sick?"

"No. Yes. I'm so befuddled I can't tell anymore how I'm feeling."

Gemma-Kate stretched her neck muscles as if she had been a little tense herself. "I'm going to have some lunch. Do you want anything?"

"I'll get something for myself."

She wandered off studying the flow chart. When I followed her into the kitchen she was microwaving a can of chicken soup she had dumped into a bowl. While it heated she scribbled on her pages. She looked at the chart and began circling certain areas and frowned at them. I thought I heard her murmur "cheese" but couldn't be sure. The microwave timer went off, and she got the bowl out, arranged it with a spoon, napkin, and her papers at the sit-down counter, and studied her notes while she slurped the noodles.

She had pulled me in despite myself and I couldn't help my curiosity. "What do you think?" I asked, getting my own can of lentil soup that couldn't possibly have been doctored, but pretended not to care about her answer as I popped the metal lid off the can, and dumped it in a bowl. I didn't bother to heat it.

Gemma-Kate sat back in her chair, apparently satisfied that she had finished the soup and found a plausible theory at the same time.

"Here are the facts I have so far," she said to my back. "A doctor didn't find a clinical cause for the way you were immediately feeling. He fell back on a diagnosis of depression like a lot of doctors do, especially with women. If you have been poisoned it seems to be with an overdose of that same antidepressant, one which has a cumulative effect, and that you can't detect immediately after dosing."

"So far you're not giving me anything new."

"I'm reviewing for my own sake. An interesting sidelight is that the drug is one that other people can take a single small dose of now and then without it affecting them. You're the only one who would react because you'd already ingested so much. Also, I tasted one of your pills and it's flavorless so it could be ground up and even, say, brushed onto the powdered sugar of the doughnut at church. Either someone is doing a very poor job of poisoning you, or they don't want you dead. Maybe they want to incapacitate you without killing you, someone who fears that it would be too easy to trace back to them. If you knew why they wanted to weaken you, it might lead you to them."

I got a tablespoon out of the drawer and started in on the cold lentils. "Still no surprises," I said.

Gemma-Kate did not seem cowed by my remarks. She tapped the pages in front of her with her spoon, not realizing there was still a little chicken soup on it. "If you can trust Carlo, there are two other people who were in contact with you more often than any others, which means often enough to deliver doses of the substance.

"I'd say at this point it's either me or your BFF, and I know it's not me."

Forty-nine

Gemma-Kate stared at me as if there was dramatic organ music playing. But there was only the silence of my utter amazement.

"That's what all this has been leading up to? All this paper and charts and shit? You're trying to pin this on Mallory Hollinger?" I didn't know whether to laugh or smack the kid.

"Why not?" she said.

"Because Mallory is the only person in the world I could trust not to poison me. Okay, Carlo, too. I wouldn't even put it past my own mother if she thought she had a good reason."

"What if you found out a good reason?"

"Exactly. The question is, why believe you? I'm going back to the assumption you've poisoned a dog, me, and were at least an accessory to Frank Ganim's death. What are we, home science experiments?"

"That would be really stupid, wouldn't it? Just like looking up poisons on your computer. Also buying toxicology books with your credit card and leaving them lying about. Likewise stupid. Do you think I'm that stupid?"

"No. Maybe you just underestimate the rest of us. I saw bufotenine in the history. You knew that toad was poison."

"PS, any digital investigation would show I accessed that page after you took the Pug to the vet, not before. Think differently. Maybe the dog isn't connected to you and Frank Ganim. Think about that."

"Maybe Ganim and I aren't connected."

"Go back to Mallory, just give me that, for God's sake."

We were firing ideas back and forth pretty good now. It would have been exhilarating if my life wasn't at stake. "Okay. Maybe you've figured out a means and the opportunity. What could the motive possibly be for Mallory Hollinger to poison me?"

"Not poison you, but give you something to weaken you enough so you'd give up. The question really is, give up what?"

"You're trying to get me to say asking questions about Joe Neilsen, because that's the only variable in my life other than you. And that's absurd."

"Is it? No disrespect, Aunt Brigid, but have you been in any condition to judge absurdity? If you weren't so strung out from the overdose of drugs you'd probably see it yourself."

I shook my head, partly to reject what Gemma-Kate was saying but also to clear some remaining fuzz from my brain. "But that still doesn't give us a motive. What would she want to keep me from discovering?"

"Maybe if you stopped investigating Joe Neilsen and started investigating Mallory Hollinger, you'd find out."

Not so long ago I had accused Carlo of a lack of imagination when it came to suspecting Gemma-Kate. Now I paused a moment to consider whether she was right, and I was doing that locking-out thing that investigators do sometimes. I thought.

Apparently I wasn't thinking fast enough for Gemma-Kate. In a rare show of emotion, this one impatience, she grabbed me by the hand and pulled me over to the microwave over the stove. She set the timer. "There," she said. "I'll make a bet with you. You take thirty minutes to do a quick background check on Mallory Hollinger. If you don't find anything that you don't already know in that amount of time, I'll go back to Fort Lauderdale."

"It's just—"

"Otherwise you'll never get rid of me. Unless they get me for murdering that man. Then you'll have to come visit me in prison." She glanced at the time. "Twenty-nine minutes forty-eight seconds."

I thought I knew what there was to know about Mallory, and even more. But what secrets had Mallory and I really shared? We had both kept the truth to ourselves. I thought I was so circumspect, not talking much about my own past and the role I'd had with the Bureau, while having no idea how much she wasn't talking about hers. When did she find out about me exactly? Was it when she had been in the house by herself when she brought over the Pugs and the chicken tikka? She had plenty of time to look through my office files, see the awards on the wall, even find my weapon in the nightstand.

The dilemma was, I wanted to prove Mallory was innocent. But for Marylin's sake, for the sake of the screwed-up family I loved, I also wanted Gemma-Kate to be innocent. And I couldn't have both.

Gemma-Kate interrupted my thoughts. "Twenty-eight minutes nineteen seconds. But even with that I think you're good enough. Do we have a bet?"

"No. I'm not playing your game."

Gemma-Kate glanced at the timer. "Remember when you said I brought you the cup of coffee at church the other day?"

I sighed, tiring of her pressure. "Yes, I remember."

"I didn't pour that coffee. Mallory handed it to me. There was already cream in it. I thought that was strange because I know you like it black, and I told her. She said, 'I know, but if it's coffee she'll drink it.' That's why I remember so clearly, because she said that with a kind of *I'm-her-friend-you're-not* attitude and I wanted to smack the smirk off her face. And she gave me the doughnut, too, with the powdered sugar on it."

"But if there was antifreeze in the coffee, why would she drink it?"

"Are you sure she drank any?"

I put the bowl of lentil soup on the counter, appetite gone. Noting twenty-seven minutes four seconds on the timer, I went into my office and got on the computer. Starting with the latest event that had been corroborated, I pulled up past issues of the *Arizona Daily Star* and found the article about the Hollingers' car totaled in a train wreck. Nice that you can now do this on a computer rather than going to the library and fiddling with microfiche. At least the train wreck story was factual. There was even a photo of her looking stricken, and without lipstick. Her blouse was torn, and the blood on the sleeve was likely hers. A cut down the side of her face reminded me of the thin scar she still carried. And the car. Made you wonder how Owen got out of that thing with even the life that had been given him. Score one for Mallory. Maybe.

The Internet had made background checks much easier than they used to be, and Mallory hadn't tried to cover her trail. Covering your trail means there's a trail that needs to be covered. It was shrewder this way. Unless you suspected she was poisoning you to prevent your investigating someone's increasingly suspicious death, her past would have appeared to be sad, somewhat fraught with fortune both good and ill, but not incriminating. What was suspicious was that, in all the talking we did, she never really told me about that past.

I called a contact in D.C. to get her Social Security number. Yes, my dears, there really is a Big Brother, and I am him. Getting the Social Security number took some doing because it turned out Mallory had lied to me about her date of birth. I had to get a list of Mallory Hollingers and match her up to the most likely birth date. One I found would have made her eighty-three, while another only forty. The one that was the closest was still suspicious, not because she lied about her age, something a woman like Mallory would likely do, but because she lied in the wrong direction. She always said we were the same age and shared the same birth month, July. Leo. But turned out she was four years younger than me. And a Pisces. Why would she do that?

Lock in.

As I mulled, I realized Gemma-Kate was standing at my side. "Time's up," she said. "You've been at this for nearly an hour. You found something, didn't you?"

"Go away," I said.

She did.

The rest was just remembering what Mallory had told me and finding out if it was true.

In the early days of our friendship she had too casually let drop facts about herself in a way that she might not have if she knew who I really was, that I was a criminal justice professional.

I had art galleries in Boca Raton, New York, and Shaker Heights.

I checked that now. Nothing. And I mean nothing. No Mallory Hollinger with any tax identification number for the galleries she said she'd owned. Nor any other business listed with her as the owner. If she lied about that, what else did she lie about?

The marriage license between her and Owen Hollinger listed the date of their union as six years ago. That was what she had told me. The two of them must have had a whirlwind life for all those travel photos to be taken in such a short time, a little over five years before his "accident." When they had traveled, was it on his dime?

Not all, as it turned out. She had money, and she got it from a former marriage. Her name on the marriage license was Pope. But that wasn't her maiden name. She had been married once before to Geoffrey Pope, in Cleveland, Ohio.

Frank Ganim's pacemaker had placed him in Cleveland, Ohio. Granted, it's a big city, but the coincidence was too enticing.

Google Earth showed the last known address for Geoffrey Pope, and a fine mansion it was. Made his money off some patent in the seventies. And what had happened to dissolve the marriage between herself and Geoffrey Pope? Death.

More money, less Pope. She was so convinced she was smarter than anyone, she could indulge in private jokes like that. Lock on.

The information kept building. Cause of death: pneumonia. Obituary: Deceased is survived by nurse and loving wife of three years, Mallory, and one child by a previous marriage, Geoffrey Pope II.

Long marriage? Not hardly. The obituary said nurse and loving wife of three years, the subtext oozing from the words, which must have been composed by someone other than herself, probably the son; otherwise the duration of the marriage wouldn't have been mentioned, nor the fact that she had been his nurse. When she married him she would have been, what, forty-six? Something like that. Just past middle age and not wanting to spend the rest of her life changing catheters.

Nurse. Then I found out she hadn't been schooled *abroad*, and the precise enunciation and phrases that she used sometimes, that sounded vaguely British, were faked. She'd gotten her degree at Oklahoma State.

One more document I found online: a lawsuit brought against Mallory Pope by Geoffrey Pope II, contesting the last will and testament of Geoffrey Pope.

Phone numbers are easy to find. I called Mr. Geoffrey Pope II at Pope Engineering. When I told the receptionist I was looking for information on Mallory Pope he came on the line immediately.

"Who is this?" he asked without introducing himself.

"Is this Geoffrey Pope?"

"Yes it is. Who are you?"

"My name is Brigid Quinn. I'm a private investigator."

"What has she done?"

I said, "I'm the investigator. You tell me."

He barely chuckled but stopped, because this was after all about his father. "Please, after you."

I said, "Okay, I don't mean to be vague, because the fact is I don't know much. I only suspect that there is a second husband who is in danger. Plus I'm not feeling so good myself, so I'd appreciate it if you just laid it out for me."

I could hear his deep breath over the phone. "My father had Lou Gehrig's disease. Mallory was his nurse. She got him to marry her. I always supposed she figured he'd just die naturally within a short enough time. But I don't think he was going fast enough for her taste. He hung on for three years. I always thought she did something with pool chemicals to bring on the pneumonia, but I couldn't prove it. I contested the will, though. She ended up settling for half the estate, which was still considerable. She probably knew I wouldn't be able to prove anything but opted for the safest route. Is that enough information to hang the bitch?"

If I hadn't already been looking for the dark side I might not have trusted this man. But he could provide some facts that would tell me the extent of her lies. "Did she ever own an art gallery?"

"Not that I know of. As far as I know she was always a nurse. What did you say your name was?"

"Brigid Quinn."

"Well, whatever you are, and whatever you're doing, I hope you get her, Ms. Quinn. Because now you know."

"One thing I still don't know. You ever hear of a guy named Frank Ganim? Balding with a ponytail?"

"Nope, can't help you there."

I thanked him, hung up the phone, and thought about what I had shared with this woman I knew as Mallory Hollinger. Feelings of betrayal, rage, were still mixing with a steady infusion of nah, couldn't be. Everything I had told her. About Gemma-Kate, about my most personal fears. About Carlo's and my sex life, for Christ's sake. And what had she told me? About her fears for what might happen to Owen if she died.

Please tell me you'll look after Owen if anything happens to me.

About her dreams and wishes and everything she had done in her life, and that meant everything. She had certainly shared, but was any of that true, was there anything about her that was real? I thought of the photographs I'd seen, Mallory on exotic trips and Mallory and Owen in tango poses. How fucking heartbreaking.

I flirt with everyone, just to stay in practice.

I could picture how it might have been with Joe, gay or straight, how she flattered him into trusting her. He was used to getting that attention from his mother, so it felt right with Mallory. *Have a beer, Joe. Ever done a tequila shot? I'll show you how, only promise me you won't tell your parents. Oh, your parents already let you have it.* It made me remember the first time I had seen Carlo talking to Mallory in the parish hall at St. Martin's. How I thought she could have any man in the room. Even Joey.

We're either the eagle or we're nothing.

She even got me. I, who had lived undercover among the criminal element most of my life; who thought I was so smart no one would ever be able to scam *Me*. I was royally pissed because she'd used my pride and my need, and played me for a sucker. A gun or a knife I might have been prepared for. But not a friend.

You had to admire her. I've always bragged about how cops are *so naturally* suspicious. I've said I did a background check on Carlo, if not the first time we had sex then certainly before we married. But you don't do a background check on someone you go out to lunch with. That's where a healthy cynicism crosses the line into paranoia. So I had had lunch with Mallory Hollinger once or twice, and then we got to be as close as two unrelated people can be, and there was no reason that I could ever see for investigating who my friend was.

All those parts I'd played while I was working undercover, and here I was, bested by someone who could play a part better than I ever could. She might have befriended me originally because I amused her, but after I started investigating Joe Neilsen's drowning I had become her prey. She had encouraged my suspicions about Gemma-Kate, who was convenient to her plans.

What a schlemiel I was. What a dupe. What a, and this is worse than any part I'd played before, *victim*.

I'd never been the victim before. I was always the victor, the righter of wrongs, Joan of Arc, goddammit. I was the one who got on her horse and rode off to save the kingdom. I was never the patsy.

Goddammit.

I remembered she had tried to discourage me from attending that function where I met the Neilsens. Maybe it was because by that time she found out who I was, that I had been a very special federal agent, and it was too late to cut me off without raising suspicion. So she had used our friendship to hold me close, keep her sights on me. But once I started discovering details about Joe Neilsen's death, the stakes were raised and she took action rather than risk I might discover she had . . . had what? The stakes had to be pretty high to slip me those drugs.

It was easy to call Lulu and find out Joe got dropped off to read to Owen the night before he drowned. And to call the home health care company to check records and find out the night Joe went to read to Owen was Annette's night off.

Motive: Joe saw something at Mallory's house.

Mallory Hollinger killed Joe.

Lock out. It had taken just a couple of hours.

Fifty

And Frank Ganim, arriving from Cleveland with an assumed name and fake story. Hanging around where we are. I went back over the antifreeze incident, not reconstructing exactly, because there was too much I didn't know, but rather imagining how it might have played out.

It's not attempted mass homicide. Though I don't yet know why, it's Frank Ganim she wants that day at the church.

If it's Mallory who slips the antifreeze into the coffeepot, how does she do it? What do I see? What can I be sure of? Run it backwards. Mallory at the scene, helping out. Mallory coming out of the bathroom. No, I don't see that. Where is she between the time she leaves me to go to the bathroom and the time she starts helping the victims? Unknown.

Before that.

Mallory with me inside the parish hall. Mallory shaky, saying she's going to the bathroom. Mallory taking my coffee from me and drinking it. No, I can't be sure she actually sips from the cup. Unknown.

Mallory in church. Doesn't sit with me that day, so I don't know when she arrived. Was she late? Where is she between the time she arrives and the end of the service? Can she have gone into the parish hall after the coffee has been turned on? Unknown.

Does Mallory agree to talk to Ganim in the columbarium, a place that's public enough for his satisfaction and private enough for hers? Does he go out there with his coffee so he doesn't see what happens to other people who drink it, and she goes to him during the confusion in the parish hall to finish him off? Does he simply succumb after a couple hours without treatment like George said? Or could Mallory have ensured his death by pressing gently on his carotid artery while he was passed out, like with the Choking Game? Unknown.

Back up. Even before I tell Mallory about the toad poisoning, she has her plan for me. Coupled with her dosing me with the antidepressants, she has everything she needs to make me suspicious of Gemma-Kate.

And if the whole plan at the church falls apart, there will be no suspicion of Mallory and she'll come up with some other way to get rid of Ganim.

Back up. The day of the Humane Society fund-raiser, when Mallory meets Frank Ganim and appears to stumble toward him. Is she flirting? Or is he telling her why he's there and she nearly collapses in shock? Unknown.

There was only one person who could answer these unknowns, because Mallory probably told him everything that she was doing, knowing he had no choice but to keep her secrets.

Owen.

Indeed, whether Geoffrey Pope II wanted me to get Mallory Hollinger for the sake of his dead father or the sake of half the inheritance, I couldn't know. But I still didn't have anything to go to the cops with except all my conjectures and unknowns. What would I say, my best friend gave me prescription drugs and I took them? She killed her first husband and then she tried to kill her second? You don't believe me? Just ask the man in the bed. All you have to do is ask questions that require a yes or no. He'll blink the truth.

And if the cops did believe me, and went to the Hollinger house, if Mallory suspected I knew what to ask Owen, Owen would be gone with his next heartbeat. She would know how to make it happen.

Hanging on to life with nothing but his eyes and that still-beating heart, Owen held the answers to what had happened to Joseph Neilsen. And beyond getting to the truth, I was duty bound to save him. You might retire from the business, but that "serve and protect" thing doesn't die.

Owen was the slim scrap of humanity I was bound to protect.

I thought about Owen lying in that bed, probably knowing that his killer was ministering to him with such care that no one suspected. I thought about the equipment, and the private nurse, and Mallory's insistence that Owen be cared for at home. I thought about the bookshelves with all the books that Mallory said she had read, just a bunch of stage props to make her look good.

I happened to be walking around the house while I thought this, taking a break from the computer and stretching my back a bit. That was why my eye happened to light on one of the books Gemma-Kate had ordered. It was lying closed on the dining room table. I took another look at the book. It was an odd color. Pumpkin orange. You don't see many medical references with pumpkin orange covers. Now I remembered why it had been tickling in the back of my head. I had seen this book on the shelf in Owen's room.

I read the title again, something about drugs that induce neurological disorders. With a husband who had locked-in syndrome due to trauma, why would a person have a book on drugs that cause brain damage? What use would a person have for a book that showed how prescription drugs could be used to weaken or even kill someone?

And what about Frank Ganim? Other than the fact they both came from Cleveland, and he was clearly a fraud, I didn't have anything to tie him, and his death, to Mallory. I asked Gemma-Kate about it.

"Easy," she said. "Everybody your age is on Facebook. Look him up there."

Sure enough, he was on it, and a social guy he was. Pictures at tailgate parties and in bars, arms thrown around shoulders. I downloaded all the pictures, and e-mailed them to Geoffrey Pope II. He e-mailed back that he recognized one of the men Frank was cozied up to, his father's accountant. "I never was sure, but always thought the accountant and Mallory were having an affair before Dad died. It was one of the things that pissed me off, like what if she gave him a cut of the inheritance."

Easy jump to Frank Ganim knowing something through Mallory's lover, at least enough to blackmail her. I didn't have to ask Gemma-Kate in order to make this connection. It doesn't take genius; more importantly, it takes having part of the dark side of the world inside you. I was a Quinn, too, and we all knew that.

The evidence was enough to lock out any other possibilities. But still not enough to take to the cops, nail Mallory, and save Owen. If anyone was going to ask him what happened the night the train hit their car, it would have to be me. I remembered the day that Owen had panicked and fought against his ventilator as his blood pressure soared. I'd have to talk to him without frightening him, without a bunch of strangers, so he could confirm my suspicions without panicking. I'd be going back undercover for the first time since my retirement, this time into the web of my best friend the black widow.

Oh, and before I move on, do I need to remind anyone that if my brain hadn't been fried by the drugs, I could have figured all this out without Gemma-Kate's help?

Fifty-one

A salesman who thought I was fourteen years old talked about being undercover after I arrested him. He said that sales is a lot like being undercover. You have to pretend a lot and not let on. For example, he said, if you go into some jerk's office and he's got a stupid stuffed marlin on the wall behind his desk, you have to be very careful not to look at it and think *stupid fish*. Because he might not be aware you're thinking it, but he'll pick up on some vibe you're sending, and he'll reject what you came to sell. People aren't as stupid as you'd like to believe.

The initial tactic when you're going undercover is to convince the suspect you don't suspect them. So I would drop by Mallory's house the way I always did. The plan was to make sure I talked to Owen alone while Annette was on the premises. Annette could be used as a distraction and also would prevent Mallory from doing anything stupid in the event she discovered my purpose.

To know everything, yet behave as if you know nothing—that's the art of undercover.

When I got back from the drugstore Carlo still wasn't back with the rental car.

"He called," Gemma-Kate said. "He stopped for lunch with Elias, and after they're going over to Home Depot, must be a male bonding thing. He said he was sorry for blowing up and did we need anything from the grocery store."

"I have to tell him what I'm doing," I said. "I promised him I wouldn't do things behind his back."

"I figured there would be something like that," she said. "You haven't lied to him. I gave him a list of things I need for dinner."

"Like what?"

"Panang curry, cellophane noodles, and sriracha hot sauce."

"Oh, no, that sucks, GK."

"Look, Aunt Brigid, you tell Carlo about this and he'll try to stop you. And if something goes wrong and he knows, he's in danger. He's not a good liar. Mallory would be able to see through it."

Anybody could. It's the price of being honest.

Gemma-Kate had told Carlo she'd been an idiot and wanted to make it up to him by cooking a great dinner. "You'll be back before him," she said.

"I'll be back before him," I agreed. I still felt guilty. And a little manipulated by this girl I still half-suspected. But the mission was waiting. I threw the bag on the kitchen counter. "There you are, three bottles of activated charcoal, forty grams."

"Did you remember the phone?"

"*Yes*, I remembered the phone. It's in the bag."

While we broke open the hundred or so capsules and mixed it into a to-go container with apple juice, I reviewed with Gemma-Kate the part she was to play in the operation.

I had a hard time believing Gemma-Kate and I would be working together on anything, but there you are. While she mixed the concoction I loaded my weapon and put it into my tote, a little regretful that I couldn't wear a big blouse that would cover its bulge in the back of my jeans. I'd taken to wearing the form-fitting T-shirts. Mallory might notice.

When I walked into the kitchen Gemma-Kate was finishing up. She fastened a top on the container and handed it to me.

"Are you sure this will work?" I had asked.

"I hope so."

"*You* hope so."

"I just read about it. Do you want to try it before you go? I read about some professor showing his class how strychnine had no effect after he drank this."

She was repeating herself. She must have been nervous. Or excited. I had the fleeting thought that Gemma-Kate was manipulating me just for grins.

I had the fleeting thought that she was somehow in league with Mallory.

Paranoia, right? How can a person tell what's paranoia and what's a healthy suspicion? But there was no turning back now. I said, "So what do you want me to do, chug some drain cleaner? Just give it here."

I took the to-go cup, stainless steel so you couldn't see what was in it, and picked up my tote bag. Gemma-Kate handed me another bottle, plain water. I asked her what that was for.

"Before you get there, swish this around your mouth just in case. The charcoal might turn your teeth and gums black."

"That's what you said arsenic does."

Gemma-Kate shrugged, not bothering to differentiate between the two. "Are you sure you're feeling well enough to do this?"

"If what you say is correct, I haven't had a dose in a while, and I'm feeling a difference. Now I can see how I would have been up and down."

I had already called Mallory and told her, whispering into the phone, that Gemma-Kate was driving me nuts and I had to get out of the house, could I come over? Murmuring her concern, Mallory said of course. I felt good about my deception, like I hadn't lost the knack.

I was about to walk out to the car when I thought of something I wanted to get straight just in case I didn't come back. After all, I would be leaving Gemma-Kate with Carlo, with the Pugs, with what had been my life. I told her this, hoping that, even if she was a lion with a different frame of reference from me, at some level she could understand how I felt.

"I need to know that you won't do anything."

Understandably, Gemma-Kate looked puzzled.

"To hurt anyone here," I added.

Gemma-Kate shook off my words like a disagreeable chill. "I'm thinking you don't have to do this," she said. "You'll be okay now that we know it was the drugs. You won't bring that boy back."

"I have to get Owen to corroborate what I think. Otherwise I've got nothing to take to the cops."

"But why?"

"Because I can't bear the thought of Owen enduring every minute, unable to scream when Mallory finally decides to end him. I can't imagine anything more horrible than that."

I could see that she was thinking that over, maybe weighing my life against Owen's and not finding him worth the risk. "You can't see yourself the way I can, Aunt Brigid. I don't think you're as strong as you think you are. Not right now."

I said, "Hey, it's what I do. Look, sweetheart, it's just another undercover gig. Besides, Annette will be there. Mallory isn't going to slip me strychnine with witnesses around."

It should have all gone very easy, very quick, and Mallory Hollinger should be in jail today.

Fifty-two

I was dealing with a murderer whose method of choice was poisoning, so the activated charcoal was my sole protection. I sipped the concoction slowly on the short ride over. It had no taste, but only a thick, oily feel to it, like thin sludge. Gemma-Kate had warned me the effect only lasted a half hour or so, and even that wasn't precise, so I was going to have to time it right, to eat or drink something at Mallory's within that time frame so she wouldn't think I suspected her. I never turned down a cup of coffee or a glass of wine. To do so now would tip her off, because I knew, better than I ever had before, this woman was smart. She was so smart, and by this time she knew me so well, I was going to have to go deeper undercover, be more convincing as the character of Brigid Quinn, than I ever was before. The thing with really smart people, though, is they often underestimate the rest of us.

Sitting at the bottom of her hill just before pulling into her driveway, I glanced at my watch for the last time as I drank the remaining solution. 1:35 P.M. If I was going to eat or drink anything it would have to be by two to stay on the safe side. I looked in the rearview mirror, and sure enough, my teeth were a little dark. I uncapped the bottle of water, filled my mouth enough to swish it around, and spit.

Better. I drove up the steep drive, got out of the car, and rang the doorbell.

"Look at your poor face!" she exclaimed when she opened the door. She put a comforting hand against the side of my face, and I fought against cringing away from her touch. Did she notice? I needed to get more convincing if I wanted to get Owen alone.

I remembered the quip I had made to Roger at the Pima Pistol Club about having a run-in with an air bag. I repeated it just to get into character, and started to feel like Brigid Quinn. "Do I smell coffee?" I asked, as I put my tote bag on the hall credenza as I always did, hoping the sag from the weight of my FBI special wouldn't show, taking just a little extra care to put it down gently so the clunk of metal against wood wouldn't give it away.

"You sure do. I'll get some for you. Come on in the kitchen."

"I can go say hello to Owen and join you in a minute."

Her back had been turned to me as I followed her through the living room, but now she faced me as she continued moving backwards, as gracefully as a dancer would, into the kitchen. Maybe she did the Tango Tour after all. She said, "Owen's fine, he's not going anywhere. I want to hear about Gemma-Kate."

"Is Annette with him?" I asked, trying to make it sound like idle curiosity.

"No, she's out for a while. Birthday card for her daughter or something."

Mallory turned back, and I followed her into the kitchen, where we had sat so many times before in chummy fashion at the table in the nook by the bay window that overlooked the back patio. I sat down where I could see the digital time on the microwave. 1:25, it said, ten minutes earlier than my watch in the car, which might have been, how much, four minutes ago? Longer? I made a decision and did a quick calculation that according to this clock I had until 1:50 before the activated charcoal might fail to work.

"Would you rather have wine?" Mallory asked. "I have a nice Cab blend I've been saving. Only got an eighty-five, but I've heard good things."

I gave what I hoped was a convincingly regretful shake of my head, then watched Mallory pour us both coffee from the same pot and bring the cups over to the table without adding anything to mine. She could have always done it this way, knowing that a bit of prescription drug couldn't hurt her if she took it in small doses. Now that I knew who, what, Mallory really was, every gesture, every affect about her struck me differently. For example, I considered for the first time how lately she sipped her coffee or wine so delicately, and often did not finish it. I thought it was about avoiding calories, but when we were friends she always finished the wine.

Mallory had introduced the topic of Gemma-Kate, and Gemma-Kate was an easy topic. Part of me hated myself for dissing her after what I had just found out, but I swore I'd make it up to her. So I laid it on thick.

Mallory shook her head back and forth three times, each shift marked by a "mm." She took another deliberate sip of coffee, choosing her words in advance. If I didn't know her now, I wouldn't have noticed how careful she was. "So you think Gemma-Kate was slipping you antidepressants and that's what caused all your symptoms? What about the Parkinson's?"

"Well, not that, I guess. But the rest, the anxiety, insomnia, even hallucinations and fever."

"But how did she get them? They're prescription."

"You can get anything shipped in from India." The phone should be ringing about two minutes ago, I thought, steeling myself against letting my eyes shift to look at the clock on the microwave oven.

"How did you find this out?" Mallory asked, unable to keep from smiling, at what I couldn't know.

"Find out . . ."

"That she ordered the drugs from India." My thoughts did some tap dancing of their own. I started to say, "She used my credit card," but I stopped, heart pounding with the near mistake. Mallory would know I couldn't have found a charge for the drugs because she knew Gemma-Kate didn't do it. Instead I said, "Where else?"

"I wonder how long it would take. Doesn't seem like there would have been enough time," Mallory said. Was she looking just a little more alert, even though her body was draped comfortably in the kitchen chair? Maybe I'd lost the knack for this, or maybe I'd never gone undercover with someone who knew me as well as Mallory did. I just knew I wanted the phone to ring before there were many more questions and I dug myself into a hole before I got what I came for.

"But not Carlo," Mallory said, leaving the drug shipment question behind and going to another one. Her eyes narrowed ever so slightly as she studied me. Did she suspect me because I was accepting Gemma-Kate's guilt so easily? Or was it because she had given me something that should have taken effect by this time? If so, why did she need something to happen now? It was never imperative in the past that I have an immediate reaction; better if it was delayed, after I was away from her for a while, so as not to create suspicion. Could she have found out what I had discovered? Could she read it on my face, that I wasn't her best friend anymore? Maybe Mallory was hypersensitive to others' liking or disliking her. Or was I suddenly reading meaning into a conversation, a look, that had always been there and meant nothing at all?

If only I could be certain whether something was supposed to be happening to me. I wanted again to look at the clock, but Mallory was fixing me so steadily in her gaze I didn't dare. She'd know I was looking at the clock and ask why. She'd had the past six months to observe me to an extent I hadn't matched, and she knew me that well.

"No, not Carlo," I finally said. Come on, Plan B.

She must have run out of questions for the time being, or knew that much more probing might sound suspicious. "So what else have you been doing lately?" Mallory asked. "Anything interesting going on at church?"

"I don't spend a lot of time there. I get uncomfortable around people who feel guilty because they want to use their organs for a while before they donate them."

Mallory laughed to hear me joke again the way I always did, and then switched to serious. "What's wrong?" she asked, her face bland but her eyes like sparks.

All I could think of was my conversation with Sig Weiss and how we weren't talking about Gemma-Kate at all, like I had thought at the time. The superficial charm, the overriding motivation to satisfy your every desire, the chameleon-like behavior that comes from years of observing normal people . . . Sig and I had been talking about Mallory. "Nothing," I said.

"Yes there is. Remember when we were having that little bonding moment out by the pool and you asked whether we had to watch *Beaches* together? You always make jokes when you're uncomfortable. Or nervous. What's making you nervous, sweetie? Is it really Gemma-Kate or is it something else? Come on, I already know."

The nerve in my neck that comes as a warning of danger sparked. "What do you know?"

She stared at me for a couple beats before she said, "That plain coffee just isn't the thing for right now. Hold on a minute." She got up and went into the living room, out of my sight. I took the opportunity to glance at the clock. 1:45. Five more minutes and I wouldn't be able to count on that stuff working. That was, five more minutes if I had calculated right to begin with.

Mallory came back to the table gaily rubbing the dust off a bottle of Talisker. "There's some would say using a twenty-five-year-old whisky for Irish coffee is a sacrilege. But I say liquor is made for man, not man for liquor."

"I shouldn't. I promised Carlo I wouldn't drink in the middle of the day."

"You made that promise before the bad seed moved in with you. It doesn't count." Mallory twisted out the cork from the bottle. The seal had already been broken before she came into the room. She poured a generous amount into my mug, and a somewhat less generous amount into her own. I wondered if the same stuff in the coffee was in the whisky. Or maybe she knew alcohol would increase the effect of whatever she had given me. I sipped the mixture. So did she, so I didn't think it contained anything more toxic than what she had put in the coffee. I have to admit even at that moment I thought it was good and hoped the charcoal was still working, if it ever had.

Mallory's cell phone rang with the melody of "Some Enchanted Evening." She glanced over to where it sat in its little charging station. "I'll let it go to voice."

Da da DA da da da . . .

"Good Lord, no. Could be a Humane Society emergency or a Symphony Guild catastrophe. Besides, I have to go to the bathroom," I said, and just in case I needed to show some effect, "I'm still not feeling too well."

Da da da da da DA

She stopped me from getting up. "You haven't mentioned how you've been feeling lately. You know"—she paused, trying to appear sensitive—"those other symptoms you were having. Did you make that appointment with the neurologist like Tim told you to do?"

The phone stopped ringing; she must have waited too long to answer it, and it went to voice mail.

"I'll be back," I said, recognizing I couldn't suddenly not have to pee or whatever it was I was hinting at. I, too, had to work a little harder at being myself. "And then I want you to remind me to rake you over the coals for telling Carlo what I told you the other day. I asked you not to."

Mallory looked appropriately contrite. It was only now occurring to me how talented she was at behaving like a human being.

Da da DA da da . . .

I pointed toward the phone as I got up. "Sounds important."

While Mallory went to answer the phone I walked out of the kitchen, making sure the angle of the walls was such that she wouldn't catch me going into the master bedroom instead of in the other direction to the guest bathroom. On the way I grabbed my tote off the hall credenza. I could hear her talking to someone, Gemma-Kate preferably, but anyone would do. Mallory said, "No, I didn't know I had an appointment with the conductor. For a photo shoot? . . . When did you say it was? . . . I'm so sorry. Does he want to reschedule?"

Yup, that would be Gemma-Kate. Plan B. She was good enough, and Mallory was egotistical enough about having her picture in the paper, that they could be on the phone for a while. If this wasn't such a deadly game I was playing I would have chuckled.

I don't know what I would have done if Owen was asleep. I wonder if he ever was. He was watching the door when I came through it. It also struck me for the first time that he always kept his eyes on the door. I wondered briefly if he lived his whole life in fear, wondering when Mallory was going to finish the job. It was as if I was seeing everything for the first time in a different light. But think of that later.

I put my tote bag on the side of the bed, reached in for the weapon I'd brought with me, and pulled it free. I pushed both the tote and the gun just under the bed, easy for access but unable to be seen by anyone entering the room.

I leaned over the bed, glancing at the heart monitor to see his pulse rise slightly at the sight of me. I said a quick prayer to Who Knows that my questions wouldn't send him into one of those episodes where he bucked his vent. "I'm sorry I don't have time to prepare you for this, Owen, but I'm in a hurry and need to know quick. Did Mallory do this to you?"

Owen's eyes widened until I could see all the terror that had been stored in his soul while he had been kept a captive here, held down by nothing but his own body and these silken sheets. That terror poured out from his eyes, but it didn't look like there was any less inside him. His answer wasn't necessary, but I still watched for the blink. He hesitated. Then blinked once.

No.

"Come on, Owen, this may be your only chance. Don't be scared. She can't hurt you anymore."

One. Two. *Yes.*

I could still hear Mallory talking to Gemma-Kate across the house. I said, "Did Joe find out? Joe Neilsen."

Owen started to blink erratically, and I thought he might be having a seizure. But it didn't take long before I picked up a pattern as his eyelids fluttered, squeezed shut, and fluttered again. Short short short long long long short short short. For anyone who's ever been in trouble it was simple.

SOS.

"Fuck," the word formed silently between my lips, not daring to so much as allow that *k* to click in my throat.

Then his blood pressure monitor started to beep loudly. Other than that, I noticed for the first time, there was silence in the house. Still hoping I had retained my cover, I didn't let on that I was aware of

Owen's warning, and said, "Would you like me to read a little to you, Owen?"

"Owen's right, Joe didn't know," I heard Mallory say behind me. "Or at least didn't know what he was seeing when he came over too soon and caught me putting No Salt in Owen's feeding tube." I heard her suck air between her teeth the way she did when she was testing a new wine, as if saying the words out loud tasted good in her mouth. My left hand went down for the gun I had placed underneath the bed but within reach.

"Uh-uh," Mallory said. "I noticed your tote bag wasn't on the credenza where you left it."

I stopped and turned around to see her with a .32 in her hand instead of her cell phone. It looked quite natural, like she knew how to use it. A little nervous movement around the muzzle, not quite cold-blooded, but steady enough to shoot straight, and a large enough caliber to do sufficient damage at this range.

"I thought you hated guns," I said, stupidly.

Her words were stone cold but her lips twitched nervously. "You must have me confused with a different Mallory Hollinger," she said.

Fifty-three

"So you figured it out," Mallory said.

"Mostly. A few gaps, like was Frank Ganim blackmailing you, and did you finish him off with that choke thing to make sure it looked like he died from the antifreeze? And if that hadn't worked, what was your follow-up plan?"

While I talked I stepped a little to the left, instinctively coming between Owen and the gun. Mallory didn't seem in a hurry to take the next step, or act like she was even sure what the next step was. I took advantage of that assumption, poking at her pride. It was certainly useless to try to pretend I didn't understand what was happening.

"But it doesn't sound like you, Mallory, trying to off Owen with Joe around. Did you have a short window, between Annette leaving and Joe arriving? Get the timing wrong?"

She was very careful to shake her head only slightly so as not to throw off her aim. It wasn't an admission as much as it was letting me know she wasn't going to be sucked into answering my questions no matter how much she wanted to. But she couldn't keep her mouth shut altogether.

"I tried, Brigid," Mallory said. "Remember I tried to talk you out of going to that dog thing so you wouldn't even meet the Neilsens. Right after I saw your office. Remember? But noooo, you had to come and meet the Neilsens. Whatever happens next is your own damn fault."

The tone of her voice sounded just like the Mallory who had been my friend instead of my killer. Even knowing what I did about her, this moment felt strange, like we were playacting at being enemies, like she would fire blanks and I would pretend to die.

I tried stalling for some time until I could figure out how to get my own weapon. "So how did you get Joe drunk and into his own pool?"

Mallory swallowed before she spoke, and in the hollow way her words came out I could tell she was nervous, that the casual tone seconds ago had been put on, like everything else about her. "You know I always love our chats, but I think we need to move the agenda a bit, darling."

I did a quick calculation of Mallory's distance from me, where the gun was pointed, how quickly I could move, and whether she could hit a vital organ before I got to her. I figured the chances were against it.

"Well, go ahead. Shoot me," I said, feeling my muscles galvanized to dive across the bed, taking Owen's body with me.

Mallory's eyebrows raised as she appeared to consider that option. Almost as if leaving it up to me she said, "If I shoot you here I'll make sure I kill you. Then I've got nothing left to lose. So then I call Annette and tell her I won't be needing her for a week. I cut out of town. Owen slowly starves to death."

We both looked at the man on the bed. Owen's eyes had moved to the right, in my direction. He was begging me. The beeping of his heart monitor told me his pulse had climbed over the safe point. This was his life and he wanted to keep it.

One more idea: Remembering that Mallory had likely put something in my coffee, and something stronger in the whisky, I brushed the back of my hand against my cheek. I swayed. I swooned. I dropped to the white carpet next to the bed. Knocked my head on the frame as I went down, but that only made the fall seem more realistic. Let's see what she would do now.

If she had put something in my drink, though, Mallory had more sense than to get close to my body to see if I was actually gone. I felt her giving me a wide berth as she walked to the other side of the room.

Next I knew a book landed on my head. One of the big neurology textbooks, I thought, from the weight of it. When I opened my eyes to look I noticed it was the same pumpkin orange book Gemma-Kate had ordered to learn about serotonin syndrome. I wondered if they would think to look for fingerprints on the pages in question after I was gone. There was still Gemma-Kate, after all, and she was a cop's daughter.

I heard Mallory say, "You idiot, it was only supposed to make you disoriented. You're faking. Get up."

I started to, but the knock to my head in combination with the activated charcoal and whisky triggered a wave of nausea and I threw up on the white bedroom carpet. The vomit was frighteningly thick and black, likely from the charcoal. Gemma-Kate didn't say anything about throwing up. That must have just been me and the way I'd been feeling lately anyway.

"Oh, gross," Mallory said. "What is that?"

"Activated charcoal," I said, pulling my face away from the sludge. I wiped my mouth with the back of my hand and studied the residue there. Right now, Mallory with a gun. But I wasn't all that worried yet. I'd been in worse fixes. I knew I was more fit than she was—at least I used to be before I'd been poisoned. All I needed was an opportunity. Plus I remembered my own gun was only ten inches or so from my fingertips.

Mallory nodded, impressed at my attempt to beat her at her own game. "How did you know about the charcoal?"

I almost mentioned then that Gemma-Kate and I were in cahoots, but it was important that Mallory think that no one else knew about her. In case I didn't make it out of this alive, Gemma-Kate would be the next at risk. And maybe Carlo, too. "Old undercover trick," I said.

"I tried to warn you," Mallory said. "So many times I told you to stop the investigation." She looked a little sad. I wondered even then if she might actually feel that way or if the show was a habit. Then she frowned, and I knew it was a show when she said, "I don't know if I'll ever get that out of the carpet. I'll stop and get a throw rug to cover it so Annette doesn't notice."

I felt my fingers creep toward the gun under the bed, but I had to hand it to her, she was on top of things. "I said uh-uh," she said. "Roll away from the bed. About halfway to the bookcase. On your back."

I obeyed, and stopped in the middle of the big area between the bed and the window where there was nothing to use as a weapon. I stayed there on my back. Amazing how after you've thrown up not even a gun pointing at you is more troublesome. "What was supposed to happen?" I asked.

"Just the usual. I dissolved some of the antidepressant in the coffee. The whisky was to increase the effect. Let's go."

"Where are we going?" I asked.

"On a hike. You like hikes, don't you? I'm sorry I always preferred shopping."

"What about Owen?"

Mallory rolled her eyes. "Oh good Lord, how that man hangs on. He should have been gone months ago. People his age don't survive this long with locked-in syndrome. Unless I want to keep killing people I'm going to have to take care of him soon, before the next person starts nosing around in my business."

"How did you kill Joe?"

"The kid bragged about drinking, but he couldn't hold his liquor to save his life. He came up a few times, but it was easy to hold him under with the pool strainer."

"Jacquie was right."

Mallory shrugged and tilted her head toward Owen. "For now he's not going anywhere."

She might have been doing her best to be all tough gal, but I knew her well enough to know she was nervous. The roll of her eyes was to cover up the fact that they were jumping. Her whole body was kind of jerky, not the usual fluid moves I had been accustomed to. I didn't think she was nervous at the thought of killing, just nervous about the possibility of making a mistake that would get her caught at it. Afraid the killing might fail somehow.

Still, for all her nervous twitches she had enough wits about her to stay far enough away so I couldn't grab the gun, but close enough so that I could tell she could hit a vital organ. She'd been a nurse; I figured she knew anatomy well enough.

She told me to stay where I was, and she stepped close to the bed and kicked the gun further under the bed. She pulled the tote out with her toe and reached down for it, still keeping her own gun trained on me. Good balance; she was a dancer, after all. She sat on the edge of the bed and reached around inside the bag while I kept my eyes on her. I could feel Owen's eyes on her as well, while I think both of us willed to be able to move just a little, and fast enough, to knock the arm that held the gun. She was a rightie, and made sure she kept her gun in that hand while she felt around inside the bag with her left. The first thing she found was my cell phone. Keeping both her eyes and gun trained on me, she was able to turn it off. Then she found the car keys and tossed them to me. I caught them neatly.

"Okay, let's go for a drive," she said. She gestured with the gun for me to finally stand, and I did so. I looked over at Owen. His eyes had moved as far to the right as he could manage, trying to see me.

"Sit tight, Owen. I'll be back for you," I said.

Mallory didn't bother to laugh. "Owen will be too busy. We have a date to play the Choking Game now that I know how well it works," she said. "Out the door. Keep your arms by your sides." With a sense born of long experience I could feel the gun trained on my back, so one well-aimed bullet would sever my spinal column, and if not that, at least hit something important on either side of it so a second shot would finish the job.

We walked through the living room and out the front door. When we got into the front yard I glanced around, but everything was customarily quiet. No one passing by on the street way down the steep drive could see us from where we stood in front of her house. When we got out to the car she made me go around to the back and open the trunk.

"Get in," Mallory said.

"I still don't know why you don't just shoot me," I said again.

"I could. Enough guns go off in this part of the world that nobody pays attention. And I will if I have to. But I really don't want to hurt you. I just want to take you somewhere where you can't do any harm."

Whatever she said, I didn't think getting in a trunk was a real good idea.

I turned to run. It's always better to run because it's really hard to hit a moving target.

Mallory fired. I heard the sizzle and smelled that combination of what seems like burnt hair and sulphur before I felt the pain. Lucky shot—it barely grazed my left thigh, but the impact made me stumble, and I rolled to a stop just before the driveway descended.

"God damn it, Brigid. Why did you make me do that? If you're not screwing up one thing you're screwing up another. Get off the ground."

"I think I need my stick. It's in the backseat."

"That one with the little blade at the bottom? Forget it. Crawl to the car and use the fender to get yourself up."

I did that.

"Now show me your leg. Does it hurt much?" Mallory took off her Eileen Fisher overblouse and threw it to me. Awfully solicitous, that blouse. Her words reinforced her action. "Tie that around your leg to help the bleeding, and we'll get it taken care of when we get where we're going."

Once I did that, she said, "Now face away from me and throw the keys on the ground behind you. Then get in the trunk."

Understandably, I hesitated.

"Look, Brigid. I don't want to hurt you. I just want to take you somewhere so I'll have a head start on whatever you do next. But you know now I'll kill you if I have to."

She wasn't tying me up, and that gave me all kinds of options. Safety latch. Fold-down backseat. Surprise when she opened the trunk. I tossed the keys and got in.

"Thank you," she said. "You got me into this mess, the least you can do is die quickly."

She shut the trunk. I immediately felt around. No safety latch in this older model.

Though the breeze outside wasn't Africa hot, the trunk was. It was also not terribly well soundproofed. She must have picked up the keys where I threw them. I could hear her getting into the driver's side and turning on the ignition. She spoke, but not to me, practicing her words in what must have been her way long before I met her.

"Yes, she was here, Carlo. She asked me if I wanted to go for a hike, but I didn't have anyone to look after Owen. She must have left, oh, about three hours ago. I can understand your concern. Would you let me know when she gets home?" She paused as if listening to her own words and then started again. "Uh-huh, she was here, but she left hours ago! I don't know, maybe three? She wanted me to go hiking, but I couldn't leave Owen. That idiot, she should have known not to go by herself at her age." She repeated this second version with a different tone, this one frantic. Then once more, hitting a tone between the first and the second. Only this time, she added the phrase "No, she didn't say where. She seemed troubled." Apparently pleased with that, she did what I felt was a neat three-point turn and pulled out of her driveway.

Die quickly, she had said. Tucked safely in the darkness, in the heat, I figured out her plan. She wasn't going to road-trip me. She was going to drive around until I succumbed to heatstroke, and dump my body on a hiking trail.

Fifty-four

Cause of death, hyperthermia.

This was what George Manriquez would dictate into his drop-down microphone while doing the external examination of my body during autopsy, if there was one. If I was found before the coyotes had fought over me with the buzzards. Or if I was found still locked in the trunk, the car dumped out in the desert where no one would find it for days. You could do that in the desert and you didn't have to go far. I imagined my still-unscavenged body lying naked on a gurney under George's gaze, neither of us finding the situation absurd.

Two possible causes of hyperthermia are excessive heat, causing stroke, and adverse effects of drugs. In the case of Brigid Quinn, a puzzling combination of the two, heat and high levels of tetracycline antidepressants, proved deadly.

Manriquez would have taken blood, and this time would have had a faster analysis done than when Joe Neilsen died. He would mark how I had elevated levels of antidepressants in my system. If they did an investigation, Mallory might helpfully provide information, suggesting that the detectives do a search of my house, that I had been concerned about my niece poisoning me. Carlo would reluctantly corroborate this. The evidence would mount against Gemma-Kate. Anything she said in her own defense, any accusation of Mallory, would just look like more of her lies. Carlo would see this, too. He would be convinced that I had been right all along, and that Gemma-Kate had finally succeeded in killing me.

But I wasn't dead yet. For now I was wedged more comfortably than a tall woman would be inside the spacious trunk of Carlo's Volvo. The atmosphere was close, but not enough to suffocate. Mallory would have thought through that in advance and known that if she was going to drop my body in the wild, heatstroke would be a more plausible cause of death than suffocation. Trunks have some ventilation, and if I could figure out where this one's was coming from, I might find a way out. I wondered how she would account for the wound that had started throbbing in my leg.

The wound reminded me that Mallory had seemed concerned about it. Why? Because if I got blood in the trunk my death wouldn't look like simple hyperthermia? Before figuring out what could save my life, I needed to be sure I saved Gemma-Kate's. I took off the blouse that had been tied snugly around my thigh and, though it hurt like hell, I dug at the wound with my fingers until I could feel the slick blood. If I died, and Mallory dragged my body out of the trunk, she would see it on the pad and clean it off. I slipped my fingers underneath the pad and left a blood mark there instead. Then I dug into my leg for more, trying not to grunt so loudly Mallory might hear, and marked the inside of the trunk lid, where you couldn't see it immediately upon opening. I wiped my fingers on the blouse as thoroughly as I could in the dark, hoping Mallory wouldn't spot the blood under my fingernails. I retied the blouse around my leg.

Now there was evidence, for anyone who was clever enough to find it, that I had been in this trunk, been driven somewhere, and hadn't died from poisoning or heatstroke on a hike. Even if the investigators missed the blood, Gemma-Kate wouldn't. Plus Mallory would still have to do something about that hole in my leg.

That taken care of, I took a moment to let the pain subside, and started assessing what was at hand.

There's an urban myth about getting imprisoned in a trunk where the victim kicks out the rear light from its frame, sticks his hand out of the hole, and waves down the car following it. That doesn't work, at least not in the particularly well engineered Volvo.

Signs and symptoms of hyperthermia vary. We can see in this woman the remains of dry skin, and swollen lips. Some traces of vomitus around the mouth indicate nausea prior to death.

Too bad I had thrown up the activated-charcoal solution. I could have used those fluids about now. I wished I knew how long I had to live.

This was followed by organ failure as the blood pressure dropped and the heart was unable to sustain adequate circulation. Besides insufficient water consumption and exposure to high temperatures, the heatstroke may or may not have been exertional as in the case of strenuous hiking. Non-exertional heatstroke is more prominent in the elderly.

That's right, George. Death likely occurred from non-exertional heatstroke, caused by being locked in the goddamn trunk of a car with internal temperatures exceeding two hundred degrees.

Take high doses of antidepressants, get locked in the trunk of a car, and it doesn't matter how much activated charcoal you've had or how young you are; you're fucked.

At first I tried to figure out where we were going, but the car turned so many times I gave up and concentrated on what might be in the trunk that would help me get out. Like Black Ops Baxter had said, use whatever you've got. Except that, unlike my trunk that often served as a second office, with lots of clutter that might prove useful, Carlo kept his pristine. There wasn't any tool I could use to pry myself out in any direction. Then I thought about the spare tire. I pushed against the backseat with my back by curling up in a fetal position and pushing on the outer part of the trunk with my feet. The seats wouldn't give. I curled around in another direction, this time to make it easier to reach under the covering over the tire well. In the blackness I could only feel around, identifying the spare tire, jumper cables, the jack. A short bungee cord that Carlo used to tie the trunk down when he transported things that wouldn't fit with the trunk closed.

Like our last Christmas tree, for instance. I nearly sobbed with self-pity, then stopped being a pussy and returned to the tools at hand. Any of these things would make a good weapon if I could only get out and use them. I pulled out the jumper cables, the bungee cord, and the jack, and rolled the covering back over the tire well. Then I hid the materials behind my back and settled in to survive.

Mallory was probably hoping I would die while en route so she wouldn't have to wait around wherever she was going to stage my heatstroke death. She was also probably hoping that whatever I had ingested over the past week or two would speed the process. Except for the fact that high levels of antidepressants would be found in my system, it would look like a most natural death.

The spring weather had been leaning toward summer during the days. High eighties outside meant two hundred in the trunk, with the midday sun heating the metal of the car. Running the engine helped raise the temperature, too. Hot enough to cook a turkey.

Mallory pulled to a stop. Maybe a parking lot, or maybe a light. Half in desperation and half in sheer rage, I yelled and banged against the side and roof of the trunk with my feet and fists. But no one came to help before the car started into motion again. Just as well; the exertion only raised my respiration and heart rate, and I noticed it failed to come down quickly the way it usually did when I exercised. If I had any hope of surviving, it was important to be aware of these changes in my condition.

My condition: Let's say you've accidentally spent too much time in a dry sauna. Aware of your heart beating, and more than a little woozy, you get up and go to the door. The door is locked. How do *you* feel?

We must have been on a good road; the drive felt smooth, except for small plunges into those dips where the road crossed a small wash or arroyo. I lost track of time then, or may have slipped into unconsciousness momentarily, but came back when the car started to bump. A dirt road, probably approaching what would be the dump site for my body. If Mallory was smart, and I wasn't quite dead yet, she should leave me somewhere off the road but drive the car a good distance away so I'd have no chance of getting back to it. That's what I would do.

The car finally slowed and then stopped. My mind was beginning to go along with my body. The best I could figure was that it was still daytime. Once the sun started on its downslope at this time of year the temperatures cooled very quickly, and the trunk would follow. But I could tell it was still hot. If I had the will to reach my hand up to feel the surface of the lid, I thought, it would be very hot. I thought about the horrible experiment where the frog was put into a pot of water and the temperature slowly, slowly raised to see how long the frog would survive. I thought about the toad. I thought about the Pug. I thought about Carlo.

The Volvo's backseat folds down in two parts to allow a larger space for transporting things. Rather than being equal size, one side is narrower than the other. This side folded out a bit, now, letting some light into the trunk. I had been curled with my back to it, but I managed to turn enough so I could face the opening, and at the same time moved my tools to the other side of my body so Mallory couldn't see them.

I discovered how blurred my vision was. I saw Mallory's face, two of them. She had crawled into the backseat. That would mean we were in a place far enough away from traffic and hikers where she didn't have to worry, at least for a time, about being interrupted. I thought she might be holding the gun on me. I had a hard time caring about such a thing.

"Brigid, dammit," she said, sounding exasperated. "This is awful. You should have been dead by now."

I opened my mouth, feeling my lips pull apart. My mouth was too dry to speak, and my tongue felt swollen. I tried to swallow, but that wasn't working so good either, so I just lay there looking at her with eyes that wouldn't open all the way. I wondered if she could see the jack and other stuff, or if my body was hiding them from her.

"I didn't need you dead before, I just needed you distracted. You don't distract easily, do you?"

Just to test my strength I tried to grip the jack. I didn't think I had enough swinging room to hit her with it, even if she obligingly stayed still long enough. If she came around the back of the car and opened the trunk she would see it. I remembered times when all I had to worry about was a bad back. In some little part of my brain that was still functional and watching what was happening to the rest of me, I chuckled. I was caring less and less what happened.

"Well, I'll keep you company for a while," Mallory said. She pushed the seat back just far enough to leave a crack without letting much of the air-conditioning get back to me. I heard her get one of the bottles of water that Carlo kept on the floor of the backseat, open it, and make herself comfortable lying across the backseat with her back against the door so she was only twenty inches away from me, though we were divided by life and death.

"Sorry I have to do it this way, but it needs to look natural. I even figured out what to do about that hole in your leg." She sounded so normal; it was as if Mallory had spent so much of her life cultivating the picture of perfection, the picture was all she had left. "You must feel terrible," she said, not without sympathy. I had the sense that even in the course of murdering me she would want me to like her.

It didn't matter to her that I wasn't responsive, and I thought it was probably better for her this way, not having to worry about paying attention to another person. She kept on, talking as she had in countless friendly conversations over a glass of wine. Only now she was taking gulps of water I would have killed her for. And she was talking about the future in ways she never had before. "Santa Fe seems like a nice place. Everybody from someplace else, like Tucson. Lots of arts and crafts. Money. I'm planning to sell the house once Owen dies. Boy, what a mess I made of that. It's true, all the rest of this is your fault, but I take the blame for botching Owen." A sigh, and another gulp of water. Some silence, maybe thought. She said, "Maybe Carlo would like Santa Fe. Did you really mean what you said about not wanting me to look after Carlo if you died? I even sort of like Gemma-Kate. She's a girl after my own heart."

I stayed silent because I was too far gone to protest that Gemma-Kate wasn't anything like her. Or at least not much. But Mallory mentioning Carlo sparked my mind and my muscles into whatever life was still left in me. Carlo would not be the next.

As she felt me weakening, she grew less tense. "It's too bad you can't talk right now. I'd like to know more about how exactly the drugs affected you. In case I want to try it again sometime. I was experimenting with you, but you're tougher than you look. I'm not sure of the optimum dose."

Mallory pushed the seat back into place. More time went by, but the car didn't start up again. She must have still been in the backseat, because I was able to hear her cell go off.

Some enchanted evening. She waited a few beats without answering it, to make it appear relaxed and normal.

"Hi, Carlo!" she said brightly, and even I would have sworn she didn't have someone dying in her trunk. "Oh, Gemma-Kate." I tried to yell loudly enough to be heard through the backseat upholstery, but the most I could summon in my state was something like the sound of a newborn seal. Mallory couldn't have possibly heard me, but I could hear her. "Uh-huh, she came over a while ago . . . I think she said she was going hiking. I was busy with my husband Owen and not paying too much attention . . . Maybe up the Linda Vista trail? . . . I'm sorry . . . You know, now that I'm thinking about it, she wasn't looking so good . . ."

I gathered all my remaining strength and battered against the back of the seat with my fists.

Mallory said, still brightly, "Oh, you know, I think I hear the UPS guy at the door. When Brigid gets home, would you have her call me so I know she's all right? Thanks. Bye." Swallowing that last word with the seductively breathy swallow she always used for her good-byes. Picture perfect.

I heard the back door of the car open and shut again, and shortly the car started up, started to move. I listened for the sound of other cars, but heard nothing. Wherever we were it was on a road well away from any traffic so Mallory wouldn't have to worry about being seen. Maybe we weren't even on a road at all.

I may have lost consciousness. As it is I can't say how much time elapsed before I was brought back by a pounding on the lid of the trunk, maybe with the butt of the gun.

"Are you still with us?' Mallory asked through the lid.

The lid of the trunk opened, letting in much more light than cracking the backseat had. I still couldn't be sure how much time had gone by; the sun was in my eyes, and I struggled to remember whether it was afternoon or morning so I could tell where in the sky the sun was, what direction I was facing. Mallory floated in front of me, or maybe it was the two Mallorys. They were both blurry.

I tried to grip the jack, but she took it out of my hand easily. "Do you think you have enough strength to get out of the car or do I have to pull you?"

I think I might have moved my mouth, but no sound came out. Mallory made a little perturbed sound. "I don't want you to think I'm enjoying this, Brigid. You've been a good friend. It just seems like one thing follows another and options get limited. I hope on some level you understand. I'd hate to think of you thinking badly of me. Here, this cord should help."

Mallory balanced her gun on the fender and then, first cautiously feeling the side of my neck to make sure my pulse was as weak as it ought to be, jerked the bungee cord out from where I was half lying on it. She checked my pulse again, seemed satisfied. Wound the cord around my shoulders, bracing her hip against the back of the car, and tugged. "Come on, help me out just a little. I need to get back to the house. You'll feel better outside the car. Better than both of us sitting around here forever waiting for you to go."

I tried to lift my hands to leverage against the back rim. They fell away. With a sigh Mallory pulled some more until I was sitting up, then with one hand wound around my hair that had at some point fallen out of its ponytail, she pulled my still-unresponsive body with a final heave out of the trunk. I bumped against the fender on the way down to the ground, where I lay on my side.

"Okay, nearly there," Mallory said. Apparently this stretch of road was so flat she could see far off in both directions. She took a careful look and, seeing no cars coming or going, leaned down to roll my body off the road into a small ditch dug out by seasons of rain.

I heard a sound, either a bird or a cell phone. It must have been the cell phone, because I heard Mallory say somewhere above me, "Hello?" Then, "Hello, Carlo! Didn't you talk to Gemma-Kate? I told her Brigid was over here asking if I wanted to go hiking, but I couldn't leave Owen . . . Oh, I don't know, maybe two hours ago? Does that seem long to you? . . . I know, I know, I told her she probably shouldn't go by herself with her condition and all, but you know our Brigid. She didn't look so good, just not her usual self. Would you call me when you hear from her? . . . That's just me, I'm a worrywart. Bye."

Still unresponsive, I lay there at the bottom of the drainage ditch, my mouth and eyes grainy with the sand through which I'd been rolled. Mallory's face floated across my field of vision, out, then back. When the face came into focus it looked like a different Mallory I'd never seen before. It looked scared. Not nervous, like before, but scared. "They're concerned, Brigid," she said. "It makes me wonder if you've been telling me the whole truth. Who else knows, Brigid?"

I moved my lips but couldn't get any sound out. She got down on her knees to try to hear better what I was saying, but was careful not to come too close even now. She said, more loudly this time, "Who else knows, Brigid?"

"No. One," I managed.

"I want to be very clear on this. Did you tell Gemma-Kate?" When I didn't answer, Mallory reached down to where the bullet had hit my thigh. She pushed her thumb into the wound, and I managed to get out a scream that sounded like "no."

She pushed again as she said, "Carlo?"

I tried to speak but couldn't, though I needed desperately to save them. "Wa," I blew the air through dry lips.

Mallory sighed impatiently. "Maybe just a little so we get this straight." She left me in the ditch and went back to the car, returned a moment later with the water. She poured a few drops onto my lips but pulled away when I tried to get my mouth around the bottle. I pulled the drops into my mouth to wet my tongue and felt the bit of liquid ease down the back of my throat.

I rasped, "If they suspected they wouldn't call you."

She considered that. "Because I swear I'll kill them both if you did."

Hearing her say that made me aware of the tremble in her voice. Her extravagant threat and the tremble meant bravado. It had just occurred to her that maybe she didn't have everything as neatly planned as she thought. That things were unraveling and she was unraveling with them. But it was too late to change course. "I've gotta get out of here," she said, mostly to herself.

She left me for a moment, and when I next saw her standing above me she had the jack in one hand and the gun in the other. She knelt down at the edge of the ditch and raised the jack over my leg. I groaned at her not to. Surprisingly, she stopped, and sat back on her heels.

"You're right, they might be able to tell," she said. She glanced around, left the jack on the ground, got up, and used the barrel of the gun to knock off an arm from a teddy-bear cholla cactus nearby. She knocked the arm across the ground with the gun until it fell into the ditch beside me. Kneeling again, she put the gun down beside her, placed the spiny appendage over my leg wound, and used the jack to tamp it down. I cried out again, still more of a grunt than a scream.

"Did you ever notice how these things have little hooks at the end of the spines? Once they go into you it's really hard to get them out."

She went back to the car and returned with my stick. It was made of light wood, so she could break it in two under her shoe. "You broke the stick, and tried to dig the cholla out with the blade."

She dug around in my leg, busily disguising anything that might have looked like a gunshot wound. I heard someone making high-pitched barks of agony. "But poor Brigid, you succumbed and only succeeded in making your leg a mess."

Mallory stopped to admire her handiwork. She had put the gun down on the ground close to her side. I suppose she had stopped worrying about my fighting back, having seen that I had trouble holding on to anything, and now I was further weakened by the pain.

But maybe the pain helped. I thought about the girls at the women's shelter, the one who preferred to be a victim.

Even if she never knew, I'd show her now what it meant to not be a victim.

I reached up more slowly than I would have liked but had the element of surprise on my side. Sightlessly I grabbed for the gun but found my hand on the barrel rather than the grip. Mallory saw what I was doing and dropped the stick, grabbing for the gun herself.

I was weak and wounded, and she was strong and well hydrated. What do I do now, Baxter? Got any good ideas about what to use when there's nothing to use?

My body, I thought. The weight of my body was all I had left.

I rolled over onto my side, which helped pull my arm underneath me and the gun closer. That meant it was in danger of hitting me in a vital organ if it went off again, but it also put Mallory off balance. She slipped down the side of the ditch on top of me. I had the gun and her right arm under me. With her left hand she was slapping my head. At any other time it would have made me laugh.

We thrashed about in that narrow space with as much benefit as a couple of fish on deck. I might have been almost useless given the effects of the drugs and the advanced hyperthermia. But Mallory, while a murderess, was not experienced at hand-to-hand combat and by her own admission wasn't in the best condition. I had maybe this much of an edge. While she continued to punch me, now in my lower back, which she knew was a vulnerable area, I succeeded in moving her arm closer to my face. I bit down on whatever flesh was available and hung on. She did what I hoped she'd do. Her fingers opened reflexively. She wrenched out her arm but left the gun behind.

I could tell she knew that the balance had tipped in my favor. Mallory scrambled backwards on her butt, trying to get up the side of the shallow arroyo without turning her back on me, as if that would protect her. There were lots of rocks lying around. If she got to one of them it would only take one good hit to finish me off, I was that gone. She was about ten feet away from me when I rolled back over on my side and aimed the gun at her. There was still more than one Mallory scrambling up the dirt. I chose one of them and fired.

I don't know if a round hit her, or if it did, where. She kept moving. With a small-caliber pistol it's like that; no one shot brings them down like in the movies. I fired again, and hit the car's right rear tire. It sank. The practice range was nothing like this.

I got her in my sights once more. She was crawling across the top of the arroyo. Maybe I had gotten her once, maybe not. I pulled myself up the side of the arroyo after her and balanced the gun on the lip. She had managed to get up and was stumbling toward the car. Even with a flat tire she might be able to get far enough to get help, say I was crazy and had tried to kill her. I couldn't let her leave me here. I was near death and needed her cell phone to call for help. I was ready to kill for a cell phone.

I squeezed my eyes to control the blur and fired once more. She had gotten close to her car and sagged against it, the front of her face hitting the rear fender and dragging over the tire as she went down. Chances are that meant I had her. Mallory was far too vain to let anything happen to her face.

I kept my hold on the gun, though, as I crawled over the dirt up to her body. I felt through her pockets for the cell phone, but she didn't have it on her. Maybe she had dropped it. I hoped to God she hadn't left it in the car, because I wasn't sure I had the strength to climb into the front seat. Instead I crawled over Mallory's legs and felt blindly around the car.

My fingers finally touched it in the dirt not far from the trunk. I could hardly see the little icons but managed to choose one and dial nine-one-one. A woman answered.

"Shot . . ." My hand dropped to the ground and I watched it lie there, still grasping the phone. I was never going to be able to speak loudly enough to be heard at that distance, so I focused everything I had on raising my hand again, trying to speak into the phone. "Track m . . . dy . . ."

It was the best I could do. I left the signal on and slumped against the side of the car next to Mallory's still body, listening to the now urgent voice of the emergency operator asking what were probably nonessential questions like was I hurt. Mallory's eyes were open and staring at the mountains in the distance, so I knew she was dead. I watched the blood seeping through the dirt on my jeans and thought I should get that bungee cord that had been dropped behind the car and make a tourniquet. I also knew it would be a smart thing to get a bottle of water out of the front seat where I kept it. And if I could get myself into the front seat, I imagined I could start the car and drive somewhere. If I could find the keys. I imagine I was still thinking about how I should do all that when I passed out.

Fifty-five

I woke up in an ambulance, still not knowing where I was. It didn't help my confusion when I saw Carlo's face hovering over mine, with the expression of a man looking into a coffin. There was dirt streaking his face, and a little smudge of what was probably my blood, though I couldn't think how it got there.

He turned to one of the paramedics, who was sitting on the other side of me. "How are we doing?" he asked.

We feel like hell, I thought.

"Temperature is coming down. We've got her on fluids. She's stable," he said.

"Good," Carlo said. Then he looked back at me. "I'm not saying it's a huge problem, but are you going to keep pulling shit like this?" Carlo can be salty enough, but he usually doesn't talk that way unless he's really upset. He was really upset.

I shook my head no, not sure my voice would work. I felt bad but figured I had an excellent chance at survival and needed to ask a few questions. I reached down to my thigh and felt about. My fingers encountered flaps of denim where they must have slit the fabric while I was out.

"Leg," I asked.

Carlo gripped my hand more tightly—I noticed now he was gripping my hand—and shushed me.

But the paramedic nodded, possibly knowing a pro when he met one. "You've got a bad wound in your left thigh, but it doesn't look like a lot of blood loss. They'll get the cholla out at the hospital."

I didn't have to ask if Mallory was dead. I lifted my right hand and with my thumb stopped an imaginary stopwatch. My private joke. "Whe—?" I whispered.

"On your way to Oro Valley Hospital," he said.

I shook my head, impatient even in that state. Tried to talk again. Couldn't. "Wa," I managed.

The paramedic grabbed a bottle of water and put a straw in it for me. After I wet my mouth and throat, licked my lips, and gave an extra experimental swallow, I said, "I mean . . . where did you find me?"

He looked puzzled, but he answered anyway. "On the road that runs up Calle Concordia to the hiking trails on Pusch Ridge. You didn't know?"

Mallory had driven me around and then ended up right behind her property. That's how she could easily walk back from the car. And she could say I'd gone hiking from her house. And I could disappear and even be found later without putting any suspicion on her.

"Owen," I said. "Hollinger."

"That's the woman's husband . . . the woman who was shot," Carlo said to the paramedics. I noticed he was careful to put things in a passive voice, not to phrase things in a way that implicated me in wrongdoing. He said to me, "I went to the house first, and found Owen alone. I found Annette's number and she's with him."

My voice started to come back a little, and I licked my lips to get them moving. "What were you going to do at Mallory's house?"

Carlo grinned. "I don't know, I wasn't thinking clearly, but imagined things. Kicking down the door, clubbing Mallory to death with a bottle of Asti Spumante. The thought was strangely satisfying."

That meant he wasn't going to stay angry at me. I held up a thumb, but when I remembered how she had a gun I put the thumb down and gripped his hand a little harder. They must have given me something, because then I think I passed out again.

Fifty-six

I got discharged the following day after spending the night for treatment of the wound in my leg, observation, and more rehydration. Carlo helped me into the front seat of the rental car, and he drove.

"Good thing I had that cell phone so they could track me," I said.

"Oh, they were already looking for you before you called," he said.

"Why?"

"When I got home Gemma-Kate was upset that she hadn't heard from you in a while. She told me everything, Mallory poisoning you. Mallory poisoning you! It sounded so outlandish I got angry with her and with myself for not taking you more seriously when you told me Gemma-Kate was dangerous. But then when I called Mallory there were three things—"

"What, Perfesser?"

"First, before I could say anything, she said you were hiking. You always tell me what trail you're going on when you're alone."

"And second?"

"Mallory said you weren't looking so good. Now, if Gemma-Kate hadn't told me what was going on I might not have been suspicious, but Mallory didn't say anything about your bruised face. Mallory would have said something specific about that, not just use the general phrase 'not looking so good.' "

"What else?"

"A linguistic anomaly. Mallory said you weren't 'looking so good.' She would never have said it that way. She would have said 'well,' that you weren't 'looking well.' Everything about the conversation—again, given the assumptions that Gemma-Kate had provided—was just wrong. Finally, when I checked your nightstand where you keep your gun, and saw that it was missing, I knew you had taken it with you, and that meant serious business."

"I didn't lie to you. Gemma-Kate delayed you coming home."

"She told me," he said.

"So you called the cops?"

"I tried that first, but it wasn't that easy. They said not enough time had gone by to start a search. They wouldn't listen to my crazy story about Mallory, and I have to admit I probably wasn't making much sense. So I called Elias, who called a parishioner, someone who's a detective on the police force."

"Tony Salazar."

"That's him. He took me, or Elias, that is, seriously, and they had already gone to the Hollinger house and were searching for the car by helicopter by the time your call came in. I drove over there like a bat out of hell and made sure Owen was okay. So when they found you I was within running distance."

"You saved my life," I said. I didn't have to say thank you because I could tell by the look on his face that he was satisfied this was the case.

I stared out the car window at Catalina Ridge on our right. Much of the time the mountains looked painted flat against the sky, but the late afternoon sun cast shadows so you could better see the depth of canyons running through them. They're more interesting that way.

We were on our way to the Hollingers' house straight from the hospital. I had spoken with Tony Salazar and Sam Humphries from my bed. Privately I told Tony that I would make an even trade with him. He would have Owen corroborate my story so I could get off on self-defense for shooting Mallory in the back, and I wouldn't spread the truth about his department screwing up the death investigation on Joe Neilsen. But I figured that would get around anyway. Lulu Manwaring would see to it.

Annette was at the house, to take care of Owen if anything happened during the interview, and also to act as another witness to his testimony.

Owen was awake, and his eyes lit with recognition, then questions, when he saw Carlo, Tony Salazar, and Sam Humphries come into the room behind me. I sat down next to him on the bed, where I had seen Mallory sitting so many times, and laid my hand on his arm. Remembering what I had read about his condition on the Internet, I asked if he could feel my hand, and he blinked once, yes. At first the only other sound in the room was the airy suck of the ventilator. If the others noticed the smell I'd gotten used to, they didn't show it.

"Hello, Owen," Carlo said. Couldn't hurt that we had both a priest and a nurse in attendance. It was hard to know what would happen.

Owen blinked twice in greeting.

I said, "Owen, this man is Anthony Salazar. He's the head of detectives for the Tucson Police Department, and this is Detective Sam Humphries. They want to corroborate with you some information concerning you, Mallory, Joseph Neilsen, and a man named Frank Ganim. Will you help?"

Owen blinked for yes, and I could swear he did it with a relieved sigh.

Salazar stood at the foot of the bed with his hands clasped before him, chin tucked down slightly so that he looked like he was bowing even though his eyes stared intently at Owen. His whole posture was reverential, and I liked him for it.

I began. "Owen, do you know what happened to Mallory?"

He blinked once. *Yes.*

"I think I have a good part of the story now, and maybe you can fill in the blanks for me. Would you do that? All you have to do is guide me with yes and no."

Clearly this was leading a witness, but under the circumstances Salazar didn't object.

Yes.

"Sometime after you were married, you found out that Mallory had killed her first husband."

Annette was trying to be professional but couldn't help gasping at this information. I turned to her and said, "I might need you. You can take it, right?"

She nodded. I glanced at Carlo and understood he would be there for whoever needed him.

I said again that Owen must have found out Mallory had killed her first husband, but,

No.

"You had no suspicion."

No.

"You felt you were happily married."

Yes.

"But you told me yesterday that Mallory had done this to you."

Yes.

"She stopped the car on the tracks, left you in it. Did your seat belt jam?"

His eyelids fluttered. I'm not sure he even knew all the details of that night.

"Where did you learn the SOS, navy?"

Yes.

"Mallory told me she tried to kill you but that Joe saw her putting No Salt in your feeding tube. So she killed Joe."

Yes. Such a sad blink. I hadn't noticed before how expressive Owen's eyes were. I might have been able to communicate more with him if Mallory hadn't always been a distraction.

We went on that way for a while, me guessing and Owen putting me straight when my guesses were wrong. He had been awake and witnessed with terror as Mallory set about pouring No Salt into his feeding tube. Joe had arrived and walked in on her, intent as she was on doing the deed. He innocently asked what she was doing, and seemed fascinated when she said it was for constipation. He said he would tell his stepfather about it. It appeared that Joey wanted his father's love and respect more than either Tim or Jacquie assumed. Annette filled in blanks, too, explaining how potassium chloride in

314

sufficient quantity, unlike sodium, would lower his blood pressure until death occurred. How because of Owen's condition and a living will there wouldn't be a death investigation.

"I couldn't be sure that Mallory killed Frank Ganim with a combination of the antifreeze to make him pass out and pressing on his carotid artery to finish him off. Did Mallory talk to you about Ganim?"

Owen's blood pressure spiked again as he remembered. *Yes.*

"Why didn't she use it on you? It would have been so easy."

SOS, he blinked.

"You want to tell me in code? Go ahead."

Frnk frst.

"She was testing it on Ganim to see if it would work without the ME picking up on it. Annette, could you help us out here?"

Annette gave him something to slow his pulse and when he was recovered enough he blinked *Yes.*

We took a long time, with stopping for breaks, but it went faster than it might have because I had guessed so much of the story already and knew what questions to ask. Mallory killed Frank Ganim because he found out what she had done, tracked her down to Tucson, and was going to blackmail her. When no one was around, Mallory would talk to Owen, tell him everything that was happening, and what she was doing to deal with it. She had told him she was slipping me antidepressants to slow me down. Finally she told Owen she was going to have to kill me, and then him.

When Owen started looking exhausted and we thought we had enough facts, he gave me the SOS sign again.

"What else?" I asked.

Long blink. "*T,*" I said.

Short short short short. "*H,*" I said.

Long short. "*N,*" I said.

Long short short long. *X.*

"You're welcome," I said, saddened by such gratitude for saving such a life.

Outside the house I talked to Tony and Sam for a while. Overnight in the hospital I'd had some more time to think it all through, how Joe's drowning might be reconstructed, all conjecture, of course.

How Mallory could walk the back trail over to the Neilsen house when Joe was alone. Joe wouldn't know she'd done that, only that she showed up at the house with a six-pack. Did the job, carried home any remaining beer before either of the grown-ups could return home.

Carlo made another stop with me, this time at the Neilsens' house, where I was expected. Tim looked nervous when we sat down on the couch opposite him and Jacquie. I let Jacquie know that her instincts were right, that Joe hadn't died because of a senseless prank or getting himself off. I let her know her son had not committed suicide because his stepfather rejected him, nor because he was bullied by the boys in the youth group. I told her he was murdered because he had been in the unfortunate position of doing something good, reading to Owen, and that was as much truth as she needed to know. I didn't tell Jacquie what I knew about Tim concealing the tox report from her. When he saw I wasn't going to do that, he took a deep breath that Jacquie mistook for sympathy. Carlo and I left the two of them consoling one another.

I never did meet Dr. Lari Paunchese.

Owen died shortly after I finished writing all this down, but at least he spent his last days without terror. Elias Manwaring didn't know everything. The Hollinger fortune went half to St. Martin's, which greatly eased Elias's stresses about church finances, and half to Interfaith Community Services, a Tucson food bank. What would it have been like if Owen had died six months before from cardiac arrest due to the No Salt in his feeding tube, or a year before in that train wreck? Joe Neilsen would be alive. Mallory Hollinger would be alive. We would still be best buds. And maybe she would have already set her sights on husband number three.

Fifty-seven

When the mail came the next day, I found out the fine for killing a cactus is ten thousand dollars.

Late that afternoon we went to pick up Al, who trotted into the house and casually humped his sister to reestablish his alpha standing.

Over dinner, the three of us talked like we were a family. Only we didn't talk about how was your day at school and how is the book coming Carlo and gee, isn't this homemade pizza good. We talked like Quinns.

"Why did Mallory kill Joe, but not you or Owen?" Carlo asked.

"She's dead, so there's no telling for sure," I said. "But my guess is that it was easy to kill someone who had no real connection to her except occasionally reading to her husband. That way, not so much risk of suspicion. Second husband dies on her watch and somebody might discover there was a first one. That's why she wanted Joe to be a witness to Owen's cardiac arrest, only Joe got there too early and Mallory was afraid he'd tell his doctor stepfather about the salt in the feeding tube. She panicked, probably. Me, she figured she could make me sick enough to stop investigating."

"Oh, that reminds me," Gemma-Kate said. "I was reading some

more about antidepressants. There was this thing about aged cheese. Remember how you've been eating a lot of cheese?"

"What about cheese?"

"That book I was reading says that coupled with antidepressants, besides serotonin syndrome, it can kick you into Parkinsonism."

I remembered the Parmesan cheese on the soup, yes, the blue cheese at Blanco's, the bartender at Ramone's smiling at me as he poured the chilled vodka over the stuffed olives (was it because Mallory supplied those olives?), and more at Mallory's house . . . even the cheese that Gemma-Kate had used, quite innocently, in her cooking.

"How?"

"I don't know the mechanism yet. Just that it creates Parkinson-like symptoms. Odd gait, muscle spasms, shakiness, loss of strength, instability, even cramped handwriting."

"So you're saying that all those symptoms—"

"Were brought on by the high doses of drugs and cheese. Aged cheese in particular. Isn't biology fascinating?"

"Holy Mary Mother of God," said Carlo.

"That bitch," I said to the goat cheese on my slice of pizza, my appetite greatly diminished. And to Gemma-Kate, "How long were you going to wait to tell me this?"

"Of course, you're still limping, but maybe it's from that wound in your leg," Gemma-Kate said and got up. "I'm eating the rest of this pizza."

Mallory had broken my stick, but Carlo bought me a cane at the drugstore before I left the hospital. With the help of that, I insisted on walking the Pugs. Slow going, but nicer than it had been recently.

"What would you do if I was seriously incapacitated?" I asked as I limped down the sidewalk.

"Give me specifics."

"Let's say paraplegic."

"That's easy. I'd put you in your wheelchair and take you on a one-way walk into Sabino Canyon."

I laughed as I was meant to. "What a romantic."

Then it was night. Seems like everyone turned in before me. Maybe I was still a little revved from the adrenaline surge of recent events. The house was quiet and mostly dark. One pug sat hopefully by the back door, and I let it out, hoping there were no toads hiding under the bougainvillea. The light of the full moon had washed most of the stars out of the sky, but you can't have the moon and the stars, too. The Pug wandered over to the statue of St. Francis, lifted its leg (I knew then it must be Al), and peed on his foot. Then he trotted back to the house and sat expectantly as if he considered my sole purpose for existence was to open doors for him. I did.

I went into Gemma-Kate's room. She was in bed but not asleep and still had the light on.

"Do you ever sleep?" I asked.

"Not so much. I like it that way."

"How are you feeling?"

"I feel . . ." She paused, searching her mind for something like feeling to communicate. And if it was there, she didn't know how to say it. The only thing she could find was "I want." Then she stopped.

"What do you want?"

"I want . . . to be touched. Mom used to touch me before she couldn't anymore."

I sat down at the end of the bed and put my hand on her foot where it poked up the covers. She seemed contented with that, didn't sit up or come close to me for anything like a hug.

"Did you mean to poison the Pug?" I asked, intentionally out of the blue.

"No. It was an accident. He chomped down on the head where the poison glands are before I could stop him."

It sounded specific enough to be true. And while we were on a roll, "Gemma-Kate, did you love your mother?"

That one took a couple seconds while she thought. "I don't think so, no." She moved her foot away, having had enough of human contact, or at least of the assurance she could get what she wanted. "But I'm not like Mallory."

"No. You're nothing like that," I said.

There was something about that halfway honest exchange that

made me feel Gemma-Kate and I were communicating like normal humans. Either that, or the lion in me spoke to the lion in her. It made me think about what made us different from Mallory, from any other cold-blooded killer. It was the Quinn thing.

I said, "Using the toad to raise suspicion, through Frank Ganim's death, and my poisoning, Mallory was framing you. You're not a psychopath, you're just a Quinn."

Her sneer was at odds with the innocent roundness of her face. "What's the difference?"

"I don't know. I'm guessing it's why we make good cops, because we have more equal measures of dark and light than most people. Or some of us have a little more dark and we're not smart enough to fear it. But emotion is highly overrated. Even if you don't feel good about doing right, or bad about doing wrong, I think it's the doing that counts."

Did I say that, or did Carlo? I've begun to get confused about where his thoughts end and mine begin. I did feel something just now, a surge of gladness that Gemma-Kate had come away from the rest of the Quinns to Arizona. Now that I knew who Gemma-Kate was and who she might have become, I understood better my promise to Marylin. It wasn't just about letting Gemma-Kate stay with us for three months. The promise was to watch over her and make sure her journey continued on a righteous path.

"Well I'm not going to be a cop," she said.

"You're going to be a biochemical researcher. Get holed up safely in a lab somewhere."

"No, I was thinking I might become a veterinarian."

I felt my viscera recoil in horror at the thought of Gemma-Kate hurting small animals. "Terrific. You think some more about that." I pulled up her covers because it felt like the house got chilly, which often happens in the spring after the sun goes down.

But before I turned off the light, or maybe because of the reflection of it in her eyes, I caught something in her look, like the North Star in an otherwise black sky. She knew what she was saying and what effect it would have on me. With that crack about being a veterinarian, she was making a joke about herself. And I realized that wherever there was real humanity there was the capability of not taking yourself too seriously. Wherever there was humor there was hope.

I said good night, and went about turning off the lights and securing the house. I wouldn't lock Al and Peg in our bedroom tonight.

Feeling my way through the dark, I remembered what Elias Manwaring had told me about the guy who said the only way to achieve any happiness at all is to start by admitting that the world is horrible, horrible, horrible. The guy was right about that. Children died before their parents. People you thought were friends betrayed your trust. Wives let their husbands beat them up and sometimes there was nothing I could do to stop it. There was too much haze over which of us was good and which was evil.

Shit, if you allow yourself to think of all that, sometimes you think it's better not even to love anymore because all love ultimately ends in abandonment, betrayal, or death. And that is truly horrible.

Well, shit.

But what if you think beyond that? If the world was so clearly and completely horrible, then every moment of life that wasn't horrible must be a bloody miracle. A gift, more valuable for being rare. Like the fact that, for today, I was well, mostly. Like the discovery that Gemma-Kate's humanity might be limited, but that there was hope she might be made whole enough to live. That she was more like me than she was like Mallory.

Either way it made no sense to worry about anything else tonight. We were safe right now. Empathy is nice, but sometimes you have to put the death, the mistakes, the suffering, and the betrayals aside. Allow yourself moments of not-feeling rather than get dragged under by the drowning victim you're trying to save. The way I felt about the nameless woman at the shelter. Not feeling is a way of protecting ourselves to fight another day.

Because if you can't stop to appreciate those moments when nothing bad happens, it's like kicking aside a gift someone left in your path. Everyone was safe in the DiForenza house this night. So while I couldn't go as far as saying the world was wonderful, wonderful, wonderful, I could say that in this particular moment, in this small space, it wasn't half bad.

Welcome to the human race, Quinn.